FIRE & FROST

A Bluestocking Belles Collection

BLUESTOCKING BELLES   RUE ALLYN

SHERRY EWING   JUDE KNIGHT

AMY QUINTON   CAROLINE WARFIELD

Kingsburg Pres
P.O. Box 475146
San Francisco, CA 94147
www.kingsburgpress.com

Cover Design by Jude Knight

ePub ISBN: 9780463922217
Mobi ISBN: 978-1946177-53-7
Print ISBN: 978-1-946177-54-4

MELTING MATILDA

JUDE KNIGHT

Melting Matilda
By Jude Knight

Her scandalous birth prevents Matilda Grenford from being fully acceptable to Society, even though she has been a ward of the Duchess of Haverford since she was a few weeks old. Matilda does not expect to be wooed by a worthy gentleman. The only man to attract her interest gave her an outrageous kiss a year ago and has avoided her ever since.

Charles, the Earl of Hamner is honor bound to ignore his attraction to Matilda Grenford. She is an innocent and a lady, and in every way worthy of his respect—but she is base-born. His ancestors would rise screaming from their graves if he made her his countess. But he cannot forget the kiss they once shared.

CHAPTER 1

I f the two of them made it out of the near-invisible city streets alive, Matilda Grenford was going to kill her sister Jessica, and even their guardian and mentor, the Duchess of Haverford, wouldn't blame her. Angry as Matilda was—and panicked, too, as she tried to find a known landmark in the enveloping fog—she couldn't resist a wry smile at the thought. Aunt Eleanor was the kindest person in the world, and expected everyone else to be as forgiving and generous as she was herself. Matilda could just imagine the conversation.

"Now, my dear, I want you to think about what other choices you might have made." The duchess had said precisely those words uncounted times in the more than twenty years Matilda had been her ward.

When she was younger, she would burst out in an impassioned defense of whatever action had brought her before Her Grace for a reprimand. "Jessica is not just destroying her own reputation, Aunt Eleanor. Meeting men in the garden at balls, going out riding without her groom, dancing too close. Her behavior reflects on us all."

Was that the lamppost that marked the corner of the square before Haverford House? No; a few steps more showed yet another paved street with houses looming in the fog on both sides. Matilda stopped while she tried to decide if any of them were in any way familiar.

Meanwhile, she continued her imaginary rant to the duchess. "Even in company, she takes flirtation to the edge of what is proper. This latest start—sneaking out of the house without a chaperone or even her maid—if it becomes known, she'll go down in ruin, and take me and Frances with her."

Matilda had gone after her, of course, taking a footman, but she'd lost the poor man several mistaken turns back. Matilda had been hurrying ahead, ignoring the footman's complaints, thinking only about bringing Jessica back before she got into worse trouble than ever before. Now Matilda was just as much at risk, and she'd settle for managing to bring her own self home, or even to the house of a friend, if she could find one.

Home, for preference. Turning up anywhere else, unaccompanied, would start the very scandal Matilda had followed her sister to avoid. If Jessica managed to make it home unscathed, Matilda would strangle her.

In her imagination, she could hear Aunt Eleanor, calm as ever. "Murder is so final, Matilda. Surely it would have been better to try something else, first. What could you have done?"

Matilda startled herself with a bark of laughter that echoed oddly in the fog.

"Why did you not tell me, or your nurse?" Aunt Eleanor had asked a thousand times, when Matilda had found herself in hot water because she'd tried to pull Jessica from trouble of the girl's own making. She could never explain; not without hurting Aunt Eleanor's feelings.

Jessica had been her best friend since they were babies in the nursery, nearly as close as twins though they had different mothers. She and Jessica—part of the Grenford family, but only by Her

Grace's charity—belonged to one another and didn't quite fit anywhere else. They were a family of two. They finished one another's sentences, dried one another's tears, and kept one another's secrets. Their half-sister Frances, the youngest of Her Grace's wards, was separated by a gap of years from their magic circle.

Matilda began walking again, alone in the fog. Surely, if she kept to streets of the houses of the wealthy, she might at last come to a place she knew? She crept along the paved footway, seeing the houses loom one by one out of the gloom into sharper detail then sink away behind her into oblivion again. The sun was somewhere above the fog. At least, she supposed it was still shining, and strongly enough to illuminate a small space around her, as if the fog grew thinner wherever she moved.

Perhaps it was the same with her and Jessica. They had been separated by the fog of Society's expectations, and could no longer clearly see the love that had shone between them for their entire lives, since Jessica was a few days old and Matilda not quite six months.

From the time they came out in the Season of 1812, they had grown apart, as those around them accepted suitors, married, and started families of their own. No one wanted wives of dubious origins, even if they had been wards of the Duchess of Haverford since infancy and would be well dowered by the marquis, her son. Matilda tried harder and harder to be a pattern-card of ladylike behavior, while Jessica took more and more risks.

Now, they each moved in their own little circle of fog, but they still kept one another's secrets, and that was why Matilda had not confided her worries to the Duchess of Haverford, or even to her guardian's son, the Marquis of Aldridge.

Today's escapade was beyond enough. She must tell Aldridge. If she made it home safely, she would unburden herself to him.

She swallowed a little—not from fear, exactly. She was not afraid of the marquis: source of presents, occasional donor of curricle rides, and stern protector against gentlemen who could not be trusted to behave with respect. Awe was a better word than fear. Aldridge might be the Merry Marquis to the rest of the world, but to the sisters, he was more proper than the most rigid maiden aunt.

She thought of the power of his raised eyebrow, which had more than once warned her and her sisters from stepping outside the boundaries of acceptable behavior. Aldridge could save Jessica from herself. Matilda should have talked to him before.

Having dealt with the future to her satisfaction, she stopped on another anonymous street corner to face the present. Was that the sound of someone walking towards her? Yes, surely. Smothered by the fog, but coming closer. Should she call out? Hide?

She longed for rescue. She feared attack, or even discovery, which would be a longer drawn out agony but quite bad enough. Torn with indecision, she stood as if her boots had become frozen to the paving slabs.

❧

Charles Stapleton, Earl of Hamner, could have been alone in London. Fog muffled sound as well as sight, so that his boots and his walking stick rang out their cadence in a little bubble of clarity bounded by half-seen shapes and half-heard noises.

Every sixty or seventy paces, he came to another oil lamp, left alight long after dawn since even the lamplighters might get lost in the gloom. He counted doorsteps and corners to find his way, and welcomed each new lamp that confirmed his position, though its dim light failed to do more than illuminate the moisture in the air so he moved from halo to darkness and back to halo again.

On the very edge of visibility, a formless shape resolved into the silhouette of a person, standing just within the penumbra of a lamp. As he drew closer, it became clear she was a lady, or at least dressed like one. What was a lady doing alone in the streets on a day like this? On any day, of course, but especially in such gloom.

Charles lifted his hat in greeting, and sensed rather than saw her shoulders ease. Did she think an assailant unable to ape good manners? Stride by stride he approached, and stride by stride she came into better focus.

His heart sank as he recognized her. Of all the females to need his help, it had to be the Haverford Ice Princess. Nonetheless, manners demanded that he lift his hat again, bowing. A slight bow, peer to commoner, but still a bow. He fiercely resented the necessity, telling himself that a female with her breeding—or lack thereof—should not expect such recognition from a gentleman, but the ward of the Duchess of Haverford had every right to be treated with respect.

Miss Grenford returned a small curtsey, though a quick darting look at the fog hinted that she no more wanted to be rescued by him than he wanted to play knight errant to her.

Matilda Grenford had been bedeviling Charles since she first made her entry to Society, side by side with her equally problematic sister. No. Matilda was more problematic.

"Lord Hamner." Just that, and in freezing tones. No explanation of her presence alone in the street. No pleas to see to her safety. No smile.

"Miss Grenford." How he wished Miss Grenford were more like her sister so he could blame her, instead of himself, for the insult that had sunk him so low in her regard. He'd fought an unwelcome and inappropriate lust in her presence since he asked her to dance at her debut ball two years ago. It was, of course, only lust. He would have recovered long ago, he was certain, if she had been in his keeping, but that would never happen.

Besides, for all that he told himself he would tire of her, he could not imagine it. He would not take a mistress he could not give up. He had sworn on his father's grave that he would have no other women when he married. He would never do to his wife and children what his father had done; marrying a proper lady when his heart was with his irregular family.

To marry Miss Grenford was unthinkable. When he wed, it

would be to a maiden of pure bloodlines, both maternal and paternal. He owed it to his name. He owed it to the heir he and his wife would raise to the dignities of his title, and to any other offspring.

To offer protection to a ward of the Duchess of Haverford was impossible. She behaved like a proper lady, whatever her appearance. If he compromised her, he would be honor bound to offer for her, and would do so even without the incentive of an angry brother. The Marquis of Aldridge would avenge insult to any of the Grenford sisters, and Aldridge was deadly with both sword and pistol, but Charles's own sense of what was due a lady would propel him to the altar, no threats required.

Sometimes, he struggled to remember that would be a bad outcome. If only she were more like her sister.

Miss Jessica Grenford appeared a proper Society maiden, but she skirted the edge of propriety and would soon fall over it, just as one might expect from someone with her family history. Miss Matilda, on the other hand, looked like every man's dream of the perfect courtesan, from the dark curls that framed her lovely face to the lush form that the most demure gowns ever made for a Season could not disguise.

The most optimistic of rakes could find nothing of the *demi-monde* in her speech or behavior. One wag had suggested that the 'ice' of her nickname was the sweet confection for which Gunthers was famous, but it was a lie. She was cold, and all the efforts of the cleverest flirts, the most lyrical poets, and the most ardent charmers could not strike a spark to heat her above freezing.

Only Charles had seen a glimpse of the vibrant passionate woman within, on one occasion that remained memorable no matter how hard he tried to forget it.

His lust—and it must be lust, for he would not allow it to be anything more—was doomed to remain unrequited. Even if some less honorable cur compromised her and failed to give her the protection of his name, the duchess was unlikely to cast her off. The woman had an unaccountable habit of offering refuge to fallen women, and would surely extend such help to her own ward.

"May I escort you home, Miss Grenford?" Charles asked. "To Haverford House," he added, lest she mistook his intentions.

Stiffly, she accepted his offered arm. They took a pace or two into the fog before she spoke.

"I must thank you, my lord," she said, her voice redolent with barely subdued resentment. "My footman and I were separated in the fog, and then I lost my way. I despaired of finding my home again."

Sympathy with her predicament warred with irritation at her tone, however much he might deserve her contempt. It was not his place to scold her, but he could not resist. "You should not have been walking in this at all. The fog hasn't lifted in days, so you cannot have thought it safe to be wandering around the streets, without so much as a footman to protect you from nuisance."

He could barely see the beautiful face turned up to his, but the wave of anger at his presumption was palpable. Her voice was chillier than ever. "I am obliged to you for correcting my faults, Lord Hamner."

She attempted to withdraw the hand that clutched his arm, but he refused to allow it, covering hers with his own. "Tolerate my arm for a short while longer, Miss Grenford, lest we become separated in the fog."

Her reluctant hand was a brand on his arm, setting fire to his whole body. He should have let her leave his side and would have, had not the danger of the fog been very real.

Their silent march brought them to the gates of Haverford House. "This way," Miss Grenford said, stopping by a little side gate that let onto the side of the large entry courtyard.

She released his arm. "Thank you, Lord Hamner," she said again. "I do not know what..."

They were interrupted as the gate opened, and a woman darted out, her mouth already moving. "Oh, miss. You're safely home. I was that worried, miss." She danced around her mistress, patting one arm, brushing off the back of the cloak, poking a finger at the reticule.

Behind her came a footman, who also ignored Charles as if he did not exist. "My lady, I'm that sorry. I thought you'd be here ahead of me, and then you weren't, and I was going to go back out and look for you. But my lord said I'd only get lost again, and then…"

They were interrupted by a firm, "Enough, Beckham." The marquis had followed the two servants through the gateway. "Your lady is here, Marsh, and she is safe," he told the maid. Now off you go and make sure she has water to wash and a nice cup of hot chocolate to warm her."

Aldridge smiled at Matilda before turning to Charles with his hand extended. "Thank you for seeing my sister safely home. As you can see, she lost her footman in the fog."

"She should not have been out in the fog," Charles grumbled. He had more to say, but a look from Aldridge stopped him.

The marquis's response was quiet, almost contemplative. "I do not permit others to rebuke my sister, Hamner, however grateful I might be for her rescue."

Charles could do nothing but accept the set down. However much Miss Grenford needed to be reined in, he had no right to argue about it with Aldridge, who was ten years his senior. He was acting head of the ducal family, besides, with the old duke suffering the final consequences of decades of dissipation.

"I will take my leave, then," he said, his bow just a shade on the correct side of perfunctory.

"Will you not come in for a drink before you brave the fog again?" Aldridge asked.

"Thank you, but no. Navigating in this weather means every trip takes twice as long as it should, and I am already late."

"I am sorry to have taken you out of your way," Miss Grenford said, polite if reluctant.

Charles bowed again. "I shall hope to see you in more clement weather, Miss Grenford, Aldridge."

He was nearly out of sight in the fog, but not out of earshot, when he heard the lady say, "Aldridge, Jessica is out..."

The marquis interrupted her. "Shush, Tilda. Not out here. Everyone is safely inside. Let's get you in, too."

So, it was as Charles thought. Miss Grenford was once again putting herself at risk to save her reckless sister.

CHAPTER 2

Matilda couldn't bring herself to betray Jessica. She had to admit she'd gone out after her sister, for which she received a gentle scold, but she didn't tell Aldridge about the other occasions and about her fears.

She would make one more attempt to reason with Jessie, she told herself, to justify assuring Aldridge that everything was fine; that he needn't worry. If Jessie wouldn't promise to stop taking such terrible risks, then Matilda would tell Aldridge.

He frowned down at her. When did he develop those fine networks of worry lines in the corners of his eyes? She put up a thumb and tried to flatten them out. "Truly, Aldridge. You have enough to concern you."

"I will always have time to be concerned about my sisters, sweet Tilda," he assured her, the pet name making her feel even guiltier about her deceit. He changed the subject. "Did Hamner bother you?"

"No more than usual," Matilda said. Aldridge's face hardened, and she realized what he meant.

"He is always such a prig," she added. "He dared scold me as if I were a thoughtless child. He has no right."

Aldridge offered his arm and escorted her to the door of the family wing, where he left her to return to his own quarters. She hurried upstairs. She expected Jessica to be waiting for her in their private sitting room. She did not expect to be attacked as soon as she walked in the door.

"How could you set Aldridge onto me?"

"I did nothing of the sort. I will though, if you won't promise me to be more careful, to stay home, and to stay safe. Jessie, anything could have happened to you out there."

"I was perfectly safe. You should just trust me. Instead, you take off after me, and then you let your footman come back first and tell Aldridge that we are both missing."

"I didn't *let* the footman come back," Matilda protested. "I lost him in the fog. I thought you were lost too. I certainly was. If Lord Hamner had not been the one to find me... Please, Jessie, won't you tell me what is going on?"

Jessica turned to look out the window, hiding her face. "I can't, Tilda, and you mustn't ask me. Just trust me."

It was other people Matilda didn't trust, and the physical yearnings that Jess, too, must surely have inherited from her own mother. Matilda had kept the secret of her own reaction to Lord Hamner and his devastating kiss; could she really insist on knowing Jessica's secret? "I do. I just worry. Jessie, if people find out..."

Jessica spun back around, her eyes widening in alarm. "People mustn't find out. Tilda, it is not my secret, and I am doing nothing wrong. Don't ask me questions. Don't follow me. I promise I will be careful, and when I can, I will tell you all about it." She flopped down into one of their fireside chairs, somehow making the unladylike drop look graceful. "Now, tell me about the Granite Earl. Did he really rescue you?"

"I suppose he did." Matilda giggled as she remembered Lord

Hamner's face. "He was very unhappy about it too. Dear gracious, the man deserves his moniker. He does not unbend even a little."

His arm felt like granite, too, under her gloved hand. It wasn't just that he had once kissed her. Something in her—and what could it be but her mother's blood—had thrilled to the touch of him since the day they first met two years ago, in the early days of her first Season. Why it should be Hamner and none other, she had no idea, but it was so.

Perhaps it was fortunate he had treated her from the first with a distant courtesy edged around by disapproval. On the one occasion he did not—if he had not backed away stammering, she might not have stopped him. Heaven alone knew how far her low appetites might have led her astray.

Instead, she avoided him. When she couldn't, she met his strained politeness with her own frosted civility.

Jessica rose to her feet. "We had best change for the meeting, Tilda. The Society for Brats is coming."

Oh, yes. One of the duchess's charities was meeting here today, rather than in the Oxford Street bookshop and tearooms that was their usual meeting place. *The Ladies' Society for the Care of the Widows and Orphans of Fallen Heroes and the Children of Wounded Veterans* intended to hold a fundraising event in a few weeks, when most of the *ton* had arrived in London. Even the dreadful fog could not be allowed to interfere with deciding what that event was to be.

The maid they shared brought them warm water to wash, and they helped one another into afternoon gowns suitable for receiving company.

"This is my third change today," Jessica commented. "Yours too, I take it."

Matilda knew what was coming. She and Jessica had been deputed to the duchess's causes since they were old enough to help, but for some reason this one had got right under Jessica's skin, and just last week, she had all but accused their benefactor of hypocrisy.

Jessica ignored her silence, repeating the essence of what she had said to the duchess. "The cost of the gowns we have already worn today alone would have provided a year's care for one of the indigent families for whom we were fundraising."

Matilda gave her the answer that Her Grace had given last week. "If we both dressed in sackcloth, Jessie, it would still be not enough. Aunt Eleanor says that we need to draw money out of those who would not otherwise give. To do that, we need to be seen as part of the *ton*, and that means we need to dress accordingly."

Jessica was not convinced. "If Aldridge would give me my dress allowance, instead of paying my bills, I could get by with half the clothes I have. I know I could."

They dropped the conversation as they entered one of the less formal parlors, where the duchess waited for them, her current companion at her side, and Cedrica Fournier, her previous companion, already seated before a table, pen and paper ready to take notes.

Madame Fournier had left her position to marry, but she had volunteered to be secretary for this committee. Jessica and Matilda took turns in greeting her with a kiss in the vicinity of her cheek, and as they did, the other ladies began to arrive.

The first part of the meeting was given over to reports. The work of the Society was organized by small groups, sometimes as few as two or three ladies. Lady Felicity Belvoir, through her connections to half the families of the *ton*, kept them aware of social events at which they could canvas for votes in Parliament. Lady Georgiana Hayden was in charge of writing pamphlets to sway opinion, and Lady Constance Whittles marshaled a miniature army of letter writers for the same purpose.

Many of the Society's members also volunteered at hospitals where injured veterans were nursed and orphanages that cared for veterans' children. They visited widows where they lived, some in very insalubrious areas. The duchess agreed with the necessity; how else were they to meet real needs if they did not first talk to those who were suffering? She insisted on the volunteers and visitors travelling in groups and being escorted by stout footmen.

Once all the groups had reported back, they discussed their next fundraising event. The ladies offered one idea after another. The duchess would hold a charity ball, of course, as she did every year, but none of them felt that would be enough to really draw attention to the cause. Something special was called for. Something unusual.

Matilda was not sure who suggested a Venetian Breakfast, but the star suggestion of the day came from a shy girl who was new to the Society. Miss Fairley rose to her feet and waited for Mrs. Berrisford, the meeting's chair, to notice her.

"I wondered if we might hold a basket auction," she said, flushing pink at being the center of attention. "We have done them at home as fundraisers for the church, and they are very popular."

Two of the ladies objected that parish fundraisers were hardly a model for high society, but Mrs. Berrisford called for silence. "Go on, Miss Fairley," she encouraged. "How does it work?"

"The ladies provide a basket of food," Miss Fairley explained, "and the gentlemen bid for the right to share the basket with the provider. It is usually the single ladies, of course." Her voice faded almost to nothing as her blush deepened to scarlet.

Mrs. Berrisford called for order again, as the Society's members all tried to express an opinion at once.

The duchess rose, and those who had not already stopped talking fell silent to see what she thought. "The Venetian Breakfast becomes a picnic meal, in fact, with each lady bringing her own contribution. If we can ensure propriety, ladies, such an auction would be just the thing to bring in donations from the younger gentlemen, who are far more likely to spend their funds on less helpful activities."

That settled it, of course. Discussion turned to ways and means, and before the meeting was over, several more groups had been established, to cover the various aspects of three events: Venetian Breakfast, auction, and ball, all on the same day.

"Could the auction prize include a dance at the ball later?" Jessica made the suggestion. "That way, gentlemen who have bought a basket will also be obliged to buy a ball ticket."

The suggestion was met with a hum of approval.

"We will need to enlist the ladies of the ton," Mrs Berrisford said. "I suggest each of us talks to as many as possible; older ladies to the mothers, younger to the girls. The men, too, of course; but ladies first."

"We can start at Lady Parkinson's in two days' time," one of the other ladies proposed.

That seemed to be the end of the decision making, though many of the members lingered for another cup of tea and one of the delicious little cakes Monsieur Fournier supplied to the duchess for her meetings.

Matilda and Jessica, in their role as daughters of the house, moved from group to excited group, knowing Her Grace would wish to know what was being said in these more casual conversations.

Everyone was excited by the plans, and more than one person was hoping that the fog would lift so that Lady Parkinson's soiree would proceed and they could begin their campaign.

❧

Charles had promised to escort his mother to the evening event with which Lady Parkinson intended to start the Season, some two weeks ahead of anyone else. They would only go, he insisted, if the weather allowed.

To his private dismay, the morning of the event dawned clear, with no fog. Charles pointed out that the heavy clouds presaged snow, but his mother declared she was starving for a sight of her friends and a little bit of company, and she would not be staying in tonight unless the snow was actually falling.

"We will leave Lady Parkinson's if the snow starts," Charles insisted. He would rather not go at all. Two Seasons ago he had set his sights on a bride, and around this time last year, his courtship had been roundly rejected. He'd managed to avoid most of last year's Season, but meeting Lady Felicity Belvoir had not become less awkward on the few occasions they met. She was in town again; he knew that. Would she be there tonight?

He consoled himself that Lady Parkinson had called it a "small evening gathering of close friends, with perhaps a little dancing for the young people", but she had misrepresented the event. Over two hundred people were jammed into the lady's string of reception rooms. It seemed that everyone who had come early to London was of the same mind as Lady Hamner, desperate to leave their own homes.

Charles escorted his mother through the rooms until they found her friends.

"Now run along, dear, and find someone to dance with."

Did he ever enjoy this kind of event? It wasn't fashionable for men to admit to any kind of pleasure in a ballroom, but two years ago, this would have been a treat. He would not have sat out a dance; nor would he have danced twice with the same female.

He loved the company of women, from the innocent pleasures of dancing and conversation with Society's maidens to the more robust and earthly delights to be savored with discreet widows.

A wealthy earl needed to be cautious. But if he went nowhere alone, and paid attention to them all and not to anyone in particular, he raised no expectations and could simply enjoy himself. He had. Until he met Miss Grenford. No! It wasn't that. His downfall was setting his sights on Lady Felicity.

There she was now, in conversation with the duchess's two wards. For the last two seasons, Miss Grenford, Miss Jessica, and Lady Felicity had been close friends. After the duchess's house party last Christmas, the lady's older sister had married and almost immediately gone into mourning for her husband's grandfather. Rather than miss the Season, Lady Felicity had been taken under the duchess's wing. The three young ladies clearly intended to spend this Season together, as they had the last.

It was intolerable that he wanted to yearn after Lady Felicity, who would have made him a perfectly unobjectionable wife: an ornament to the Hamner name. Instead, he could barely look at her. Not when she stood next to Miss Grenford.

As he continued around the room, he fought to control his reaction to the pernicious female's presence. He was not the only one. He heard her name, and slowed to listen.

"Miss Grenford is the living image of Angel," sighed Lord Amhurst. The elderly earl, recently elevated to the peerage in his brother's shoes, was leering at Miss Grenford and her sister. The old lecher was talking to his new young wife's brother, Basil Driscoll, and two of his other drinking companions

"What a woman Angel was," said one of the others. "Do you remember back when Winshire's cub George nearly got shot by Haverford for singing love songs outside her bed chamber window, accompanied by a small orchestra?"

"Should have chosen another night," Lord Amhurst chuckled. "Haverford did not appreciate being disturbed while swiving."

Charles had heard such stories before. Angel Kelly had brightened their disreputable youths like a shooting star. Warm-hearted and merry, she traded one lover for another till she reached the zenith of the courtesan's profession with a duke for a protector, and not just any duke, but the Duke of Haverford. Angel then disappeared, and a short while later, Matilda, the first of the Grenford wards, turned up in the keeping of the duchess.

Lord Amhurst sighed. "If ever a girl was born to follow in her mother's footsteps… I mean, just look at her."

What a disgusting comment. Miss Grenford was not her mother. She was a walking incitement to lust, but that was hardly her fault. She was also a properly behaved lady, who had never—to his knowledge—by word or act given the rakehells cause to hope for her fall. Even that kiss—it was the innocence in her response that had finally penetrated his mad desire enough to allow him to wrench himself away.

One of the other old lechers shook his head. "Want my opinion, the Duchess has ruined her. Born to be a mistress; raised to be a wife. She will never find a place to fit in."

"It's disgusting," Amhurst agreed. "Foisting the spawn of a woman like that on decent people."

"It's the sister we should be watching, Amhurst," remarked Basil Driscoll. "That one is ripe for the picking. It's only a matter of time until she falls into some lucky bastard's hands. So to speak." He smirked. "If she hasn't already. What else was she doing in Berkley Street in Clerkenwell a few days ago, all on her own, coming out of one of the houses?"

"Did you ask her?" The man who asked the question was leering, and signaling his opinion of the encounter with both eyebrows.

"I lost her in the fog, but I think we can all guess what she was up to. Exactly what I want to do with her when I get her alone."

Charles was sorely tempted to smear Driscoll's lascivious grin from one side of his smug countenance to the other, but the Grenford sisters did not need the scandal of having men fight over them. Instead, he went hunting for Miss Grenford. He needed to grit his teeth and petition her for a dance, despite how the lady's touch stoked his inappropriate response to her. It was the only safe way to find the privacy to warn her about the rumors.

CHAPTER 3

Matilda stared in shock at the elegant figure before her. If the Granite Earl was imposing in his daytime wear, he was enthralling when dressed for the evening, all in black but for his white cravat and gloves, and his embroidered silver waistcoat.

"Miss Grenford?" He was too polite ever to sound impatient, but his imperious hand hinted that he expected an answer, and assumed it would be affirmative.

Jessica gave her a nudge. If Matilda did not accept Lord Hamner's invitation to dance, she would be unable to accept any others this evening, and then Aunt Eleanor would wish to know why. She managed to smile and curtsey.

"Thank you, my lord." She placed her hand in his, and even though they were both gloved, his touch set her quaking. Heaven's mercy! It was a waltz: an entire set dancing with him alone, holding his hand, his arm around her, staring into his eyes. Why had he asked her to dance?

No one she had danced with since she came out—whether bored, charming, slyly lecherous, condescending, pompous, or openly eager to court the favor of Her Grace or Aldridge through her—no one affected her like Lord Hamner.

She had felt it the first time they danced, a week or so into her first Season, nearly two years ago. A tingle when they touched. An awareness of his physical presence even when they were separated by the patterns of the dance. An aching response in her own body, as if she were suddenly hollowed out and yearning for something unknown.

He did not ask her again that Season, though they frequently attended the same events.

The next time was at the Masquerade Ball held at the duchess's Christmas house party at Christmas that same year. When she accepted his invitation, she hoped that her previous response reflected her inexperience. But all the dances in between, all the partners in between, made no difference. If anything, the sensations were worse.

He felt something, too, she was sure, because he became stiffer than ever, and would barely look at her. When the music ended, he held his arm away from his body and escorted her to the nearest side of the floor. Noticing how flushed she was, he suggested some fresh air, but as soon as they were alone, the proper distance between them vanished. He kissed her. She kissed him back, her heart singing, only to drop through her dancing slippers when he walked away. She repulsed him with her wanton response: she just knew it.

He left the party the next day, but that was nothing to do with Matilda. Lady Felicity— her friends called her Fliss—told those closest to her that he had proposed and Fliss had refused him. The proposal had come the very next morning after that magic kiss, the rat. If Matilda hadn't known he thought her only fit for dalliance, that news would have confirmed it.

He'd been missing for the first months of last Season, and transformed into the Granite Earl by the time he put in an appearance.

Now, he seldom graced a Society ballroom, and even less frequently a dance floor.

They took their positions, with their nearest arms along one another's shoulders, their other arms clasped in front of them. Four march steps, and they changed, Hamner grasping Matilda's right hand with his behind her back, as she put her left hand in his. She could feel the warmth of his arm against her back.

Dear Merciful Goodness. How would she ever bear an entire waltz? If last time's occasional touches had been bad, the amplified response this time threatened to destroy her. What had been a tingle was now sharp enough to be almost painful, except it was somehow pleasurable, too, coursing through her body from the points at which they touched to the lower parts of her torso one would never speak of or even think about.

Barely aware of her actions, following the cue of the music, she faced him and offered him her right hand. He lifted it for the pirouette and they turned slowly, their hands resting on one another's waists.

Her insides ached until she feared she would lose the contents of her stomach. She was so hot, she thought she might melt, and wouldn't that cause a sensation? Matilda Grenford, smeared across the dance floor in a puddle of desire.

She was nearly two years wiser than when she first met Hamner. Still an innocent, in every sense that mattered to Society, but not so naive as to be unable to name the feelings he aroused in her so easily, while he—unspeakably annoying man—showed nothing but his granite mask.

"Miss Grenford?" He had been speaking, and she hadn't heard a word.

"I beg your pardon, Lord Hamner." How very rude she was being.

He was polite enough not to roll his eyes, but both expression and tone were so bland as to hint at his irritation. "I asked for this dance, Miss Grenford, so I could warn you."

Her eyes opened wide, and —for the first time since the waltz began—she fully met his gaze. "Warn me of what?" she asked.

"You must be very careful. Your sister, too. Especially your sister. I don't like to repeat what I've heard, Miss Grenford, but you must be careful to go nowhere alone or with a gentleman."

What did he mean to imply? "Are you performing this public service for all the young women here tonight, Lord Hamner? Lady Felicity, for example?"

That cracked the stone façade. He lifted his chin, and a light flush stained his cheeks. "I am not concerned about Lady Felicity, Miss Grenford."

Of course not. Fliss was legitimate and a Belvoir, of impeccable lineage on both sides. "I see," she replied, turning her head deliberately so she was not looking at him.

"Miss Grenford, you misunderstand." Lord Hamner didn't miss a beat in the dance, gliding to one side so that her right arm pressed against his chest, and his crossed her torso under her breasts. The effort not to melt into his arms made her snappy.

"Do I misunderstand, Lord Hamner? Do you not intend to imply that women of our scandalous heritage cannot survive the smallest and most innocent misdemeanor?"

"Just listen to what I say," he growled, his voice strained.

That, and the superior scorching look, set a match to her temper. "I do not answer to you for my behavior; nor does my sister. I will thank you to keep your opinions to yourself. You are not my keeper."

He had been reaching for her hands again, having dropped them as he moved to take her back into the first waltz position. She drew out of reach as her words brought him to a halt.

"Someone needs to be your keeper," he snapped. "Your brother has no control over you, it seems."

Had she really used the word 'keeper' with all that it implied? Burning, she turned her embarrassment into outrage. "You pompous prig. How dare you."

"Devil take it! Keep your voice down. Come. I'll escort you back to Her Grace." Lord Hamner offered her an arm.

Conscious of their fascinated audience, Matilda forced her mask of unconcern back into place. She put two fingers on Lord Hamner's arm and allowed him to escort her from the dance floor, being careful to stay as far from his side as she could.

The duchess hurried to meet them, her eyebrows raised in question. "Aunt Eleanor–" Matilda took a deep shuddering breath, determined not to further entertain the assembly by releasing the tears that threatened.

Aunt Eleanor, her eyes sharp as she examined first Matilda and then Lord Hamner, took both Matilda's hands in hers. "My poor dear. Is it one of your dreadful headaches again? My thanks, Hamner, for bringing her to me. She needs a darkened room, and no noise. I will take her home."

With her arm around Matilda's shoulders, the duchess began shifting towards the door, sending those around her on errands: one to make her apologies to Lady Parkinson, another to fetch Jessie, a third to send for the Haverford carriage.

Hamner was given his own misson. "Find Aldridge, Hamner, if you would be so good, and explain to him exactly what has happened."

Matilda was swept along, with nothing to do but retain what dignity remained to her by refusing to succumb to her tears. Consumed in her own struggle, perhaps she was only imagined the hint of a scold in Aunt Eleanor's voice when she dismissed Hamner with his own errand.

❧

Charles obediently set off to look for the duchess's son. Thank all the powers that be for the great lady's social skills. She had taken the disaster he had made of his attempt to warn Miss Grenford, and defused any possible scandal from their altercation on the floor, provided no one heard the lady insult him. No. Her tone might have been clear to those dancing nearby, but not the actual words.

The supposed headache was a convincing excuse for Miss Grenford's pallor, the strain around her eyes that hinted at incipient tears, the way she wilted against the duchess. Charles had done that, with his ill-chosen words. If Aldridge called him out for it, it would be no more than he deserved.

Aldridge met him before he'd completed his circuit of the first room.

"Hamner, a word," the marquis said. He was in full ducal mode; no hint of the charm with which he usually masked his formidable nature. Charles followed him out into the entry hall, which was as crowded as the reception rooms. After one glance at the mob, Aldridge led the way up the stairs, and then past the card room and the withdrawing room where more party goers clustered. With an autocratic wave, he passed a footman stationed to protect the private parts of the house, and opened the first door beyond, into a private sitting room clearly furnished for the lady of the house.

"I'll have an explanation for that scene on the dance floor," he said, his voice arid.

Charles swallowed. "First, I have a message from Her Grace." Best carry out that commission while he was still in one piece. "She has taken Miss Grenford and Miss Jessica home. Miss Grenford was unwell. A severe headache."

"Taken unwell suddenly while waltzing with you, Hamner. What occurred to bring on this 'severe headache'?"

"I meant—" Charles swallowed again. "I meant only to warn her to be careful, my lord. I overheard a conversation..." How to put this? Already, he had insulted Miss Grenford without meaning to do so. Insulting her and Miss Jessica again, and this time to the dangerous man who called them his sisters, would be foolish in the extreme.

Aldridge narrowed his eyes, perusing Charles's face, then his own face relaxed, the familiar hints of humor lighting his eyes. He crossed to a row of decanters on the other side of the room, and filled a couple of glasses. "Brandy," he explained as he handed one to Hamner. "Lady Parkinson has an affection for it, though she would prefer that fact not be widely known."

He waved to a chair and sat down himself, completely at ease with appropriating the lady's private room and her decanters. "I have always thought you a decent sort, Hamner, even when you were on His Grace's leash. Indeed, your good character is the reason you no longer bark to his command." Charles made no comment, merely nodding in acknowledgement of the restrained compliment. He had, indeed, been the Duke of Haverford's disciple until he was forced to realize that the man was completely without honor.

"That being the case, I shall give you five minutes to explain the reasons you felt urged to 'warn' my sister. You have a tendency to be pompous, but I have seen no evidence that you are crude or immoral. Or, at least, not more immoral than the rest of us."

The term 'pompous' hurt, especially since Miss Grenford had used the same words. Still, Aldridge was in the right. Charles laid out exactly what had happened, from the overheard conversation to what was said during the waltz.

A couple of judicious questions later, he found himself recalling as much as he could of the walk in the fog, and even what he'd heard of Miss Jessica venturing where she shouldn't, and his own observations of Miss Grenford putting herself at risk to keep her sister safe.

The five minutes was long gone when Aldridge allowed him to fall silent. He sat and sipped his brandy while the marquis stared into nothing. Finally, the man gave a single nod.

"I will have your word you will say nothing of what I am about to tell you to either of my sisters, Hamner. You have shown an admirable concern for them, and you have earned the right to know. Besides, I have no wish for your uninformed concern to drive Jess, in particular, to defy me by practicing the very behavior we are trying to avoid."

Charles inclined his head in agreement, saying, "You have my word, Aldridge."

"I have men following both of my sisters at all times. I am aware that their invidious position makes them vulnerable, and my own commitments mean I cannot always be in place to warn off those unwise enough to think I would not protect my own." His lips curved in a smile that looked more like a threat.

"Had you been anything less than a gentleman that day in the fog, my friend, you would have met one or more of those guardians."

The smile vanished. "I am pleased to be alerted to young Driscoll's interest. I shall deal with it, I assure you. Next time you hear anything of the sort, bring the information to me or—in my absence—to my secretary, Edmund Markinson, who is fully in my confidence."

He stood, and Charles put down his empty glass as he got to his own feet.

"Shall we?" Aldridge waved towards the door. "Oh. And Hamner? Two more things. First, you should know that one of my first duties once I am Duke of Haverford will be to publicly acknowledge all three of my sisters as daughters of the previous Duke of Haverford."

Charles blinked at that. The recognition would make a difference with many, if not with the highest sticklers. In one stroke, the duchess's orphaned wards would become acknowledged connections to the might and power of the House of Haverford; accepted sisters of its head.

Aldridge had followed his thoughts. "Yes, precisely. Given the state of His Grace's health, my sisters' days on the fringes of the marriage mart are certainly numbered, though in my eyes, their actual status will not change. They are very dear to me."

Charles knew that to be true. While the Duke of Haverford

ignored the existence of his wife's wards, and would certainly have denied being their father had anyone had the temerity to make the accusation in his presence, the duchess and her sons treated them as if they were legitimately the daughters of the house. Nor was their paternity in any serious doubt. The youngest, still in the schoolroom, was a female version of her father. The eldest was clearly the daughter of a woman the duke had in his keeping at the time the child was conceived. The whole world assumed the middle one was from the same stable.

"The second thing?" Charles prompted.

Aldridge wrinkled his brow in question.

"You said 'two more things'."

Aldridge regarded him steadily until Charles had to fight not to shift as uncomfortably as a truant schoolboy under the eyes of his tutor. "I think that one thing is enough for today, Hamner," he said at last. "Shall we return downstairs?"

Charles followed him from the room. He'd survived the encounter with nothing more than a mild scold. Further, Aldridge had favored him with a couple of confidences. He could avoid Miss Grenford and her sister with an easy conscience. Why, then, did the thought of doing so fill him with dismay?

CHAPTER 4

M atilda came down to breakfast, heavy headed after a night of confounding a dream version of Hamner with one witty and devastating retort after another. Between each victory, she slipped into an uneasy sleep, only to wake restless and aching with the fleeting remnants of a dream in which she and Hamner waltzed again, sometimes in a crowd and sometimes alone, but always with his touch opening yearning possibilities within her.

Aldridge was before her at the table. Since he lived in the heir's wing, on the other side of the mansion's massive public rooms from this, the family wing, his presence was unusual. Matilda wished she had taken a tray in her room, or waited for Jessica, or perhaps run away to Spain, now nearly free of the French, to join a convent.

Anything to avoid an inquisition on her early departure from the soiree.

The marquis stood to greet her. "Good morning."

Matilda dipped a curtsy, and took the chair he held for her. One of the footmen poured her coffee, and another fetched her a soft bread roll, all that she felt she could eat this morning.

"That will be all for the present," Aldridge told the servants. "Wait in the hall, if you please."

Matilda put down the piece of roll she had been about to eat, her mouth dry. "I'm sorry I made a fuss. Was it very bad?"

Aldridge put his hand over hers and smiled. "Everyone accepted you were taken ill with a sudden headache, Tilda sweetheart. I am not here to scold you. Hamner took complete responsibility for the whole incident."

Even as she breathed a sigh of relief, Matilda fought the urge to deny Hamner the right to full responsibility. How dare he explain things to her brother? Pompous, arrogant, self-righteous man.

"Is that what you came over to tell me?" she asked.

"That, and to assure you that I am looking after our Jessie. You and Hamner don't need to worry. I will handle it. Trust me, Tilda?"

"Hamner? Worried?" Unladylike though it was, she snorted at the thought. "Hamner is worried about his own consequence."

From the twist of his lips, Aldridge was amused. "He is accounted charming by some. You might ask yourself why he is so stiff with you."

Matilda was well aware of the reason for that. "He disapproves of my entire existence."

Aldridge's smile broadened.

"He does, Aldridge, and it is not funny."

Aldridge shook his head. "He is certainly different in your presence than he is in the company of anyone else, including Jessica." He said nothing more, addressing himself to the last few items on his plate.

Matilda knew this trick of his. She was not going to be the one to speak first. She took a sip of her coffee, followed by a piece of bread roll. Aldridge seemed to be implying that Hamner had an interest in her. It was ridiculous. Hamner would never court the daughter of an Irish harlot, and he was far too righteous to insult the sister of a peer with the other kind of offer.

Aldridge had followed his breakfast with a tankard of light ale, and Matilda had finished her own repast before the silence was broken by Jessica. She entered the breakfast room followed by the servants who had been waiting in the hall.

"Am I interrupting anything?" she asked.

Aldridge held the chair on the other side of Matilda, and pushed it in as Jessica sat. He leaned over and gave each of the sisters a kiss on the cheek. "Have a pleasant day," he said. "It's snowing quite heavily, so take that into account when you're making your plans."

He left without saying anything more.

Jessica finished giving her breakfast order to a footman. "What did Aldridge want?" she asked Matilda.

Matilda had to tell her something. For Aldridge to join them for breakfast and then to send the footmen out of the room required explanation. "I will tell you later," she promised.

When they got back up to their sitting room, Matilda was able to content Jessica by saying Aldridge wanted to discuss the incident at Lady Parkinson's. Of course, Jessica also wanted to know why Matilda had been so upset but 'Hamner was rude' was enough to stop her questions, and they settled down to make a joint list of names of the ladies they had spoken to the previous evening about the coming fundraising event.

Over the next few days, the snow proved to exceed Aldridge's worst prophecies, making evening engagements impossible, and daytime outings perilous. The two sisters were deputed to one of their least favorite activities: writing endless letters to men and women of influence, alerting them to the conditions facing the families of those injured or killed while protecting Britain against the aspirations of the Corsican.

A slight thaw came as a relief—one compounded for Jess when her friend Miss Cummins came to stay. A scandal had driven Miss Cummins into hiding, but Aunt Eleanor intended to see her reestablished in Society.

Matilda was pleased. Being even more determined than Aunt

Eleanor to promote Miss Cummins' restoration, Jessica was being a pattern-card of demure behavior. She was encouraging her friend to join them at as many social engagements as she could, and Matilda could simply relax and enjoy them.

⚜

The snow continued on and off for days, beginning to pile up in high banks, made even higher when servants hurried out from all the houses between snowfalls to clear sufficient room for their employers' carriages.

Charles had heard that the poorer parts of town were almost impassable to wheeled traffic, and reports circulated of people found frozen to death. The workhouses were overwhelmed with people seeking shelter. Even those who could show evidence of their connection to the relevant parish, and who therefore must be supported, were three or more to a bed. Those who couldn't prove their right to relief soon filled all available casual spaces, so that others had to be turned from the gates.

Charles joined several of his friends in asking around the clubs for otherwise empty properties that could provide some shelter for those who otherwise would freeze in an alley. Aldridge was organizing the campaign with the Marquess of Glenaire, the Earl of Chadbourn and others, but Charles had no doubt that the Duchess of Haverford was behind it. Certainly, Charles's mother was behind his involvement. She had joined the Society for the Care of Widows and who knew what else was in the ridiculously long name. The Society had a list of ex-soldiers and ex-sailors and their families, and a separate list of widows with children, and would not rest until all were comfortably housed somewhere warm.

Charles dutifully escorted his mother to several meetings of the Society. He'd given up trying to convince himself that seeing the elder Miss Grenford played no part in his willingness to oblige his mother, though his stated excuse was true, too, of course. "The ways are so treacherous, Mother. I will not leave it to a hireling to make sure you are safe."

Today, they'd come once again to Miss Clemens' Book Palace and Tea Rooms. Charles browsed for a book while he waited, then found his way to the tea rooms. Quite a number of men he knew were sitting at the tables, presumably here with the same purpose as his. His friend the Earl of Hythe, brother to Lady Felicity Belvoir, was reading a newspaper while drinking coffee.

He pulled out a chair at the same table. "Hythe," he said, in greeting. "I heard you were out of town."

Hythe looked up and folded the newspaper. "Hamner. I suppose you brought your mother to this interminable charity meeting. I arrived yesterday, and was roped into escort duty imme-diately." He added, with a shade of embarrassment, "Felicity is in there."

For the past year, Charles and Hythe had not discussed Charles's unsuccessful courtship of Hythe's sister, nor had the subject come up, since Charles had avoided any event Lady Felicity might attend. Charles, cautiously prodding his feelings about greeting the lady, realized that somewhere in the past year any attachment to her had faded into a friendly interest.

If it had ever been anything more, said the inner devils that insisted he felt more for Miss Grenford than was comfortable.

"I haven't seen her for some time," he replied to Hythe. "I trust she and your other sister are well?" He ordered another cup and poured himself a coffee as they chattered about Felicity and Hythe's older sister, Sophia Lady Sutton, who had just been deliv-ered of a daughter. Charles had made an ass of himself when he assumed Lady Sophia's suitor was courting Lady Felicity. He was, on the whole, pleased that the Suttons were in the country for Lady Sutton's confinement.

As if he'd heard the thought, Hythe said, "They'll be in town by the end of the month." He fiddled with his cup before adding, somewhat wistfully, "They are so happy. They married for love.

Have you ever thought of such a thing, Hamner? Not that they weren't perfectly matched. He's heir to a duke and Belvoirs can look as high as they like. But love... It seems a risky business."

Charles's shake of the head was more wonderment than negation. "There is almost a fashion. The Suttons are lucky. There was nothing against their marriage except that ancient feud between Haverford and Winshire. To have love on top of it..." A man didn't expect to be in love with his wife—he wanted good breeding, a pristine reputation, sufficient intelligence that he need not fear for the wits of his heir. He owed his wife respect, yes, and a familial affection. But romantic love?

Hythe was nodding. "And then you look at the Chirburys—all those children and still they raise the temperature of the room just by looking at one another across it."

"Hence all the children." Charles's remark got the laugh he was looking for, but it did not lighten Hythe's mood.

"The meeting must be almost over," the other peer said. "Shall we go and wait outside the door?"

They took up station outside the meeting room, nodding to the other men who were also waiting.

"The Thames is the worst I've seen it for ice," one of the others said.

"They can't get barges or boats past London Bridge at all," another commented.

"The weather has to clear, surely?" said a third. "It's just two and half weeks until the Society's big event. I'm looking forward to the auction!"

Hythe made a low-voiced remark under cover of the laughter. "I hope she is somewhere safe out of the cold."

He was talking to himself but Charles felt compelled to comment. "Someone important to you? Can I help?"

Hythe flashed him a smile that reached no further than a quirk of the lips. "The widow of a friend. I arrived back yesterday to a letter telling me she had arrived back in England and planned to stay at his family home, but they have not seen her, and neither have her own family. According to the Horse Guard, she reached England, but they have no further information. Nothing anyone can do except wait for her to write again, I suppose." This woman meant more to Hythe than he was admitting. Charles thought of asking another question and then let it go. It was not his business.

The other men were debating which picnic baskets to buy, some leaning towards the lady with the best cook, and others to the one with whom they wished to spend time. "I'm told the Society has taken measures to ensure the ladies will be well chaperoned," said one gentleman.

His sigh fetched another laugh, interrupted when the meeting room door opened, and the ladies began to stream out, all talking with great excitement. Charles heard mention of the Thames, and a marquee, and the need to transport large carpets. Then his mother reached him, arm in arm with the elder Grenford sister. With his focus on the female who bedeviled his dreams, he hardly noticed Hythe as the man nodded a farewell and went to meet his sister.

"It is decided then," Lady Hamner said, just before she noticed Charles. "There you are, dear. You know my son, do you not, Miss Grenford? Charles, Miss Grenford and I have been charged with making lists of all the things we will need to have ready in case the Thames freezes hard enough to walk on. I have offered room in your warehouse down by Blackfriars Bridge, subject to your approval, so we may be ready at a moment's notice to put up everything we will need. This is very exciting!"

Her enthusiasm was such that Charles had to smile. "You may have room in the warehouse, of course, Mother. But for what, may a mere male ask?"

"An alternative venue, dear," Lady Hamner said. She was looking around with the vague expression that signaled she had just remembered something. "Excuse me, Miss Grenford, would you? I had one more matter I wished to discuss with Her Grace. Charles, you don't mind waiting with Miss Grenford, do you?"

Without pausing for an answer, she headed back into the meeting room. Charles smiled at Miss Grenford. "For what do you need an alternative venue?" he asked.

She returned his smile, her eyes dancing, and his breath caught. She was unbelievably lovely. "For the Venetian Breakfast and Auction, Lord Hamner. If the Thames is frozen on the third of February, we plan to hold it on the ice."

He was silent a moment, picturing it. If anyone could put such an audacious plan into spectacularly successful action, it would be this particular group of ladies. "The ball, too?" he asked. That might be harder to implement. But no, Miss Grenford was shaking her head.

"The ball will be at Haverford House, as planned. If the freeze continues, though, we will erect a large marquee on the Thames and hold the auction there, with small tents around it just large enough for groups to eat whatever they win in their picnic baskets."

She gave a little jump of excitement, and blushed at her lapse of decorum. "I do hope it freezes," she said.

CHAPTER 5

Heavy snowfalls in the next few days kept the Grenford sisters and their guest indoors. On the first fine day, Matilda, Jessica and Lord Hamner set off for Hyde Park where they would meet Miss Cummins and her childhood friend, Lord Trehallow. Hamner's carriage had some difficulty negotiating the streets, heaped with snow on either side where it had been pushed off the roofs to protect them from collapsing.

They were meeting friends to skate on the iced-over Serpentine, and the going got easier the closer they came to the open spaces of the park. In small groups of three or four, they set out on the ice. Deep in conversation, Matilda suddenly realized that Jessica had left her friends. Her deep wine redingote was unmistakable as the wearer steadily skated alone on the ice, almost out of sight around a curve.

On the path, two men were running in and out of the people who thronged the park, enjoying the fine weather after so many days inside. Aldridge's men, presumably, but on foot, they had not been able to keep up with the skater.

Matilda excused herself to follow her sister. She had not cleared the cluster of skaters she knew before she realized another person was keeping pace with her on her left. The frisson of awareness warned her of his identity before a glance to her side confirmed it.

"You are following your sister?" Lord Hamner asked.

She was about to snap that it was none of his concern, but Aldridge's insinuation gave her pause. Instead, her voice was mild when she answered. "I am. She is outpacing her footmen, and she may not realize." Let Hamner understand that the Grenford sisters had protectors close at hand.

She expected the arrogant man to rebuke her, but his response was polite, and almost tentative. "May I escort you, Miss Grenford? I promise not to interfere, unless she is in danger."

"Very well," she found herself saying. The thought of possible danger had her increasing her speed, but Lord Hamner kept up with her. "Thank you," she added.

When the next stretch of the Serpentine came into view, Jessica was nowhere in sight. No. Wait—there, on the bank, she was walking with a gentleman. As Matilda and Lord Hamner drew closer, he hissed, "Driscoll!"

"You know the gentleman?" she asked.

"He is no gentlemen," Lord Hamner said, as he skidded to a halt at the bank and stopped to untie his skates. "We must hurry."

Matilda was delayed by trying to keep sight of her sister while undoing her skates, and was several yards behind Lord Hamner as he hurried across the snowy path in pursuit of the couple.

He had not reached them when Jessica drew away from Mr. Driscoll, saying words that did not reach Matilda, though the sharp tone did. Mr. Driscoll did not accept his dismissal. He grabbed Jessica's arm before she could escape, and tugged her towards him, so that she lost her balance on the snow and fell towards him, clutching at him to stay upright.

Before the man could take advantage of Jessica's forced embrace, Lord Hamner was upon them. Mr. Driscoll found himself dragged backwards. Jessica, released so suddenly she almost fell again, caught her balance, saw Matilda, and threw herself into Matilda's arms.

Lord Hamner interrupted his low-voiced argument with Mr. Driscoll to say to Matilda, "Get her away, Miss Grenford. You should not be part of the scene."

Matilda looked around to see that the altercation had drawn the attention of others in the park. Just then, the two Haverford footmen she had seen earlier arrived, breathing heavily from their exertion. Two more were approaching. She had not realized that Aldridge had watchers on her, too.

"Come, Jess," she said. "Let us return to our friends."

Followed by the four footmen, they collected their skates from the water's edge, and headed along the path toward their starting point. Matilda turned back at the corner, and was just in time to see Lord Hamner fetch Mr. Driscoll a mighty punch.

☙❧

"Leave Miss Grenford alone, or I'll rearrange your face for you, and then leave you to Lord Aldridge's mercies," Charles warned Driscoll.

"What business is it of yours," Driscoll snarled. "The bitch was just playing coy, but she wanted me. Why else would she come to meet me?"

Charles glared. "Good question. How did you inveigle her? She was not welcoming your attentions, that is certain." He had seen blind panic on Miss Jessica's face at the moment she realized Driscoll was not taking 'no' for an answer.

"She wanted it," Driscoll insisted, but his eyes shifted away from Charles's. "She was pretending to protest. Women do that."

"Leave her alone," Charles repeated.

"Come on!" Driscoll pasted on a smile. "All this fuss over a woman like her?" The smile slipped to a leer. "This is what they're born to, Charles, and everyone knows it. Even the duchess will have to face facts in time. Aldridge is a man of the world. He indulges his mother, but he certainly doesn't expect men to leave two such honey-pots alone."

"You are mistaken, Driscoll. He expects it, and so do I." Charles grabbed the stupid man by the capes that adorned the shoulders of his heavy overcoat and pulled him closer, so he could hiss his final warning straight into the man's face. "Leave. The. Grenford. Ladies. Alone."

Driscoll struggled ineffectually, his face reddening in his anger. Still, he continued to sneer. "Want both of them, do you? What's it like, tupping the Ice Princess? Does she freeze your d—"

Charles dropped the man's coat and stopped his foul mouth with a punch that sent him reeling backwards. Driscoll landed splayed in a snow bank, flecks of blood spattering the white beside his head. He opened his eyes and glared at Charles, but made no effort to do more.

Itching to haul the villain to his feet and repeat the blow, Charles forced himself to remember the Grenford sisters. He should make sure they were unharmed. He should escort them home. "Remember what I said," he ordered, and turned away, allowing himself a wince and a certain satisfaction. The bruising his gloved hand had suffered was a rather nice indication of the damage to Driscoll's face.

When he looked back before rounding the corner of the path, Driscoll was gone.

Miss Grenford and Miss Jessica had not rejoined their group. Instead, they had found a bench and were talking earnestly while the footmen hovered. Those watchful guardians didn't prevent Charles from approaching. Instead, his rescue of Miss Jessica won him nods of greeting.

"I thought the note was from someone who could help Lady—my friend," Miss Jessica was saying. Charles glanced at the piece of paper she handed to her sister.

'I have what you were seeking in Berkley Street. Skate north.

You will find me around the corner wearing a red cockade in my hat. Red for love.'

"I don't understand it," Miss Jessica said to Miss Grenford. "I asked him what information he had about… What information he had, and he would not say. He wanted me to go with him somewhere warm, where we could…" She shook her head as if to dispel Driscoll's words, and Charles wished he had punched the bounder harder.

"He kept saying whatever I got at Berkley Street, he could give me better, but I did not get anything there. I take them food and clothing, and money when I have some. I do not expect anything from them." Miss Jessica took the note back from Miss Grenford's hand and stared at it in confusion.

"Driscoll knows nothing of your real purpose, Miss Jessica," Charles told her. "Nor do I, come to that, but I do not share his assumptions." Or, at least, not any more. Whatever took her to a scruffy middle-class street in Clerkenwell, it was not a tryst with a lover.

"His assumptions?" Miss Jessica looked from Charles to Miss Grenford, her brows drawn together in confusion. As his meaning dawned on her, her eyes widened and she flushed. "How dare he! I have never even met the man! Why would he think…? O-o-o-h!" She stamped her foot in her anger.

"He saw you coming out of the house you have been visiting in Berkley Street," Charles explained.

Miss Grenford's eyes narrowed. "How do you know this, Lord Hamner? Is he a friend of yours?"

Charles threw up a hand in rejection of the accusation. "Indeed not! He is a careless rakehell whose dissolute lifestyle has so far not crossed the line enough to have him banned from Polite Society. Enough, though, that no hostess would dare Her Grace's anger to introduce him to you. No, I overheard him boasting at Lady Parkinson's soiree. He said he had tried to catch you, Miss Jessica, but you escaped him in the fog."

Miss Jessica paled as her eyes widened. "That was him? Mercy! I very nearly stopped to ask him to help me find the way home!"

Miss Grenford spoke at the same time, lifting both brows and nodding her head. "That is what you were trying to tell me when we were dancing! Why on earth did you not say so?"

The last thing Charles wanted was to tell her the truth, that his wits went begging as soon as he touched her. Instead, he chose to answer her sister. "Just as well you did not, Miss Jessica. He is not to be trusted."

"So I just found. Oh no!" Miss Jessica turned to Miss Grenford, gripping her arm with both hands. "Tilda, he is Amhurst's brother-in-law! What if he goes to Berkley Street?" She spun on her heel, saying over her shoulder, "I have to go there now. I have to warn L —my friend."

Miss Grenford took three swift steps and stopped her with a hand on her shoulder. "Jessie, you cannot go to Clerkenwell."

"You do not understand." Miss Jessica put her hand over Miss Grenford's, though she did not go as far as to try to pry up the fingers. "Even if he does not attack her as he did me... You have no idea what is at stake."

"Indeed, I do not, for you refuse to tell me anything." She cast a quick glance sideways at Charles, and said, "Tell us how we can help. You know you can trust me, and Lord Hamner has shown himself to be a true friend."

Charles warmed as the words struck home and felt a burning desire to prove himself worthy of the accolade. He nodded to Miss Jessica, doing his best to look both reliable and unthreatening. "Why not write your friend a letter, Miss Jessica, and I will carry it to her? The streets in Clerkenwell will be even harder to negotiate than here, outside of town, so going by carriage will not be an option."

Matilda added her persuasion. "You know Aldridge will not permit you to go back to Clerkenwell."

Miss Jessica paused in thought, and Charles and Miss Grenford waited. At last, the younger sister nodded as she came to some kind of decision. "It will be sunset in less than an hour," she noted. "Lord Hamner, if you are really willing to help, will you come to Haverford House early tomorrow and escort my friend Miss Cummins to deliver that letter? She has to go in that direction, because she is almoner at The Benevolent Pauper's Hospital of the Apostles, and you will be there to keep her safe."

⚜

Charles not only escorted Miss Cummins to Clerkenwell the following morning, he waited outside in the sleigh his coachman had unearthed from the back of the carriage house so he could take her on to the hospital.

Despite the blankets and furs he'd ordered piled up in the sleigh, it was a cold wait. Colder still for the coachman up on his perch in front, though he was swaddled in an enormous coat, with a hat pulled down over his ears and the lower part of his face hidden in layers of scarf. Even the footman Charles had brought for extra security was possibly warmer than Charles, who had his face mostly exposed as he watched the narrow terrace house into which Miss Cummins had disappeared.

It seemed much longer than the actual twenty minutes that elapsed before she emerged, clambering over a bank of snow to where they waited in the narrow cleared path in the center of the street. Charles managed to struggle out of his covers and was waiting beside the sleigh to hand her in by the time she reached him.

"Success?" he asked. He had agreed to return after taking Miss Cummins to the hospital, and provide transport back to Haverford House for Miss Jessica's friend and a child, if the lady agreed. But Miss Cummins shook her head. "She has written a letter to Jess, my lord. She says you are not to come back."

Charles instructed the coachman to return to Haverford House by way of the hospital. The sleigh made the trip possible, but not comfortable, and the snow was starting again, just lazy swirls of insubstantial crystals that seemed far too ephemeral to be so close to shutting down the city, not to mention the countryside.

Back at Haverford House, he gave Miss Jessica her letter. She opened it eagerly and read it, but from the look of her face, the news was not what she hoped for. Matilda laid a consoling hand on her arm.

"She is leaving Berkley Street. She says she has another place in mind, out of London. She asks me to keep my silence for two more days." Miss Jessica took a deep breath and heaved a sigh as she threw up her hands, the letter in one hand rustling as it flapped.

"She cannot have thought… The snow, the roads. And what if I find someone who knows…? Lord Hamner, would you be kind enough to take me back there? Now? Tilda, will you tell the duchess I am with Lord Hamner and safe?"

Nothing Miss Grenford said soothed Miss Jessica's agitation, and before long, Charles had retrieved his poor coachman and several stout footmen from the Haverford kitchens and was once again traversing the near silent streets. Aldridge would have his head on a platter for helping his sister to disobey a direct prohibition.

In any case, it was to no avail. When they finally arrived at Berkley Street, the landlady reported that Miss Jessica's friend had packed up all her things and left.

CHAPTER 6

"The snow makes everything much harder, Miss Grenford," complained the carrier, as he lugged another heavy packing case of bunting—swathe after swathe of fabric in the colors of the Union Flag. Some of the crates held actual flags to be hung, along with the bunting, in the great public rooms of Haverford House, including the ballroom. Not just the British flag, but the more ancient flags that made it up: those of Scotland, England, and Wales.

"It does," Matilda agreed. "Thank you again for agreeing to deliver everything early, so we can be sure of its arrival."

The carrier, blushing at praise from one of the gentry, touched his cap in deference, and went back to shouting at his laborers with renewed vigor.

Matilda hesitated. Someone needed to supervise the delivery, but she had many other things to do. With just over a week until the event, the uncertainty about whether the Venetian Breakfast and auction would be here or on the frozen Thames and the disruptions caused by the on-again off-again snow, meant all of the ladies of the committee were filling every possible moment with preparations.

"Lady Hamner is coming early for today's Society for Brat's meeting," Jessica reminded her, "so that you and she can talk about the things you have ready for the Frost Fair."

"Yes!" Matilda agreed. "I need to bring my lists down and make sure the Unicorn Parlor is ready."

"Go, then," Jessica said. "I can manage here."

Matilda stopped with one foot on the stairs. "I have not forgotten you promised me your explanation for the lady in Clerkenwell today."

"After the Society meeting," Jessica promised. "If Aldridge is here, I can tell him at the same time."

"And Lord Hamner," Matilda suggested. "He will be escorting his mother to the meeting." He had been assiduous in his attendance on his mother since she and Matilda began working together. Matilda thought nothing of it until Lady Hamner commented. Apparently, he had always before been content to send her on her errands and calls around town with a groom and a footman as escort.

"I can guess," Lady Hamner had laughed, "the reason for his sudden devotion." Did she mean that Lord Hamner came to see Matilda? If so, she certainly did not seem to disapprove.

Matilda shook off her preoccupation with the earl and made a speedy trip back up to her chambers for the notes she had made ready for her talk with Lady Hamner and the meeting to follow.

With slightly more than a week to go, it seemed more and more likely they would need the marquees, tents, carpets, and other equipment that they had been collecting in Hamner's warehouse. Vast quantities of ice clogged all the waterways of London, and the weather-wise predicted that the cold would continue.

Heavy drapes had been drawn in the Unicorn Parlor—so called for the unicorns carved into the fire surround, molded on the ceiling plaster, and pictured in tapestries around the room. A water urn and tea pot stood ready on a side table, and Matilda measured tea from the waiting canister and made the tea so it would have time to steep before Lady Hamner arrived.

The curtains meant the fire in the hearth had a better chance of keeping the room warm, but the corners were still chilly. Matilda maneuvered a pair of chairs closer to the hearth. She was busy positioning the second chair when someone spoke from behind her.

"Whom do we have here?" It was the Duke of Haverford. Matilda straightened, turned around, and curtsied. The duke squinted at her. One of his eyes was almost closed by a loathsome growth, under which an open ulcer seeped—outward signs of the disease that was killing him by inches. "Angel?"

"No, Your Grace. It is Matilda."

The duke took no notice, lumbering toward her with his arms out. "Angel! Come here and give me a kiss."

Matilda did her best to evade him, arguing all the time that she was not Angel, but Matilda. "Matilda," she repeated. Desperate, she said the words he refused to allow spoken. "I am your daughter, Your Grace."

His Grace roared, a wordless prolonged bellow of rage, as he grabbed her by both arms and shook her. He pushed her backward as she struggled, shouting for help, until he had her crowded against the wall, his weight pinning her in place so that, when he let go of her hands, she still could not free herself.

With one hand on her throat, he cut off her breath, and with it her screams. The other hand must be scrabbling at her gown. She felt the chill air first on her calves and then on one knee as he lifted it higher and higher. She flailed with her arms, striking impotently at his head and shoulders as her eyesight blurred and darkness began to close in.

All the while, he muttered obscenities about what he planned, and the frequent endearments to Angel only added to the horror.

Then, of a sudden, she was free, and gasping for breath. As her eyes refocused, and her air-starved brain began to make sense of the scene before her, she saw His Grace send his duchess reeling across the room to fall in a heap against the wall. Behind him, a footman stood indecisive, hesitating to wrestle with his master but reluctant to leave his mistress to the man's non-existent mercies.

"Get Lord Aldridge," Matilda hissed, trying to keep her voice low enough to avoid attracting the duke's attention, but he turned his head towards her, and growled, the sound coming from low in his chest. He began to stalk towards her. She slid along the wall, trying to get further away, though she had little hope she could evade him and reach the door.

Behind him, Aunt Eleanor stirred. Thank God. Matilda had feared the duke had killed her.

"What the devil?" The expostulation came from the doorway. "What's going on here?"

The duke swung his head to glare at Lord Hamner, who was crossing the room in long strides. "Get out!" he commanded. "This is none of your business. The girl is mine."

"He thinks I'm his mistress," Matilda explained. "He struck the duchess."

Lord Hamner's eyes fell to her neck and his eyes blazed. "You have hurt them both, you monster," he told the duke, his voice low and furious.

"Get out, puppy. You have no right to interfere between a man and his pleasure," the duke snarled, and he struck out at Lord Hamner. Matilda winced, but Hamner somehow swayed just far enough that the blow did not land. Instead, His Grace's arm shot past Hamner, who grabbed it and pulled, so the duke stumbled after his own blow, crashing over a low sofa and falling to the floor beyond.

"Quick. Go to Mother," Hamner told Matilda. Lady Hamner was crouching over Aunt Eleanor, and Matilda hurried around the edges of the room to join them as Hamner vaulted over the sofa to thump the duke on the back of his head as he began to get up.

Matilda kept one eye on their fight while assisting Lady

Hamner with the duchess, who was trying to sit up, declaring she was perfectly fine while half swooning in their supporting arms.

Then, suddenly, it was over.

Aldridge entered the room, took in the scene with a single glance, and ordered the three hefty men who crowded after him into action. Matilda didn't recognize them. Their sober clothing suggested they were upper servants, but their burly physiques spoke of some more vigorous profession. In moments, the duke was struggling under a pile of all three.

"Laudanum," Aldridge instructed. Matilda couldn't see details through the melee, but he must have been obeyed, because the duke suddenly went limp. Aldridge ignored the men who were now untangling themselves and standing, and reached out a hand to help Lord Hamner to his feet. "My thanks." Several swift strides brought him to his mother's side. He crouched, reaching out a hand to gently skim the bruise that was rapidly purpling the side of her face.

"I beg your pardon, Mama. He should never have been able to evade his watchers." He narrowed his eyes at the men, who were now lifting the duke between them and carrying him towards the door. "I shall find out what happened and it shan't happen again." One of the men met his gaze. "My lord—"

"Later, Stebbings," Aldridge growled, and the men left, shutting the door behind them.

The duchess patted his shoulder, soothing him as she would a frightened child. "I am a little bruised, my son, and nothing worse." She met Matilda's eyes, a question in them.

"I am well, Aunt Eleanor." Her voice was a little husky. She cleared her throat, hiding a wince at the pain from her bruising. "You intervened before any harm was done."

The duchess made to get up, and, with Aldridge on one side of her and Lord Hamner on the other, she managed to rise. They supported her to the nearest sofa, and Matilda and Lady Hamner followed. The duchess was insisting she was perfectly well.

"I will just rest for a few minutes, and I will be perfectly ready for the meeting of the Society."

Matilda murmured to Aldridge, "She was knocked out for a moment, Aldridge."

"Mama, I want a doctor to examine you," Aldridge told the duchess. "That was quite a bang on your head."

"I want no fuss," Aunt Eleanor insisted. She looked thoughtfully at Lord Hamner, and then at Lady Hamner, who had made her a cup of tea and was bringing it to her.

"I had a fall," she declared. "Most clumsy of me."

"Yes, Eleanor," Lady Hamner agreed. "Hamner and I will say nothing to the contrary, you can be sure. I assume your servants will keep silent?"

Aunt Eleanor put out a hand to draw the other lady down beside her. "Aldridge's men will not speak of this, Clara, and I know I can trust you and your son. Lord Hamner, we owe you a debt for your intervention."

The edge to Aldridge's voice, and the restless flexing of one hand, were the only indications of his distress. "The men will explain how His Grace came to be here, alone, and in a condition to attack my mother and my sister. But yes, they will be silent, though it won't be necessary for much longer. I have also spoken to the footman you sent for me, Matilda. He will not betray us."

Hamner was as tense as Aldridge. "And how will you make sure that your father is not again enabled to attack Miss— to attack the ladies? The man was trying to—"

Aldridge interrupted; his tone arctic. "Thank you, Hamner. I am aware, but we do not need to further distress the ladies."

"Do not be concerned, Hamner," Aunt Eleanor said. "As soon as the hearing is over, His Grace will be confined at Haverford Castle."

"Mama!" Aldridge protested.

"Calm yourself, my dear." The duchess was back to her usual dignified self. "Clara is my friend, and Hamner is... a fine gentleman, and has been friend to us all, especially today. After what they have witnessed, and what poor Matilda has been through, they deserve to know we are taking measures to have His Grace declared incompetent. We do not want the matter discussed until the result is decided, Clara."

Aldridge sighed. "I had the duke brought from Haverford Castle to be present at the hearing. The deterioration in his mind is obvious to anyone who speaks with him, so it can only help. Today was the last day of presenting evidence, and he will return to the castle as soon as the roads are passable. Nor do I expect them to linger over the decision."

"If it helps," Hamner offered, "I would be willing to testify about what I observed."

The duchess sipped her tea, as if discussions of competence hearings were perfectly normally drawing room conversations. Aldridge answered Hamner, but his voice seemed to come from a long way away. Matilda's heart raced as if she were still under attack, her skin felt clammy and there seemed too little air in the room. She did not realize she was swaying until Hamner was there, his solid presence anchoring her to the room. He helped her to a chair.

"You are safe," he assured her. "Just sit here and take a deep breath. Here. My mother has made you a cup of tea: a little bit of cream and one teaspoon of sugar, just how you like it."

Hamner knew how she took her tea. Wasn't that nice?

"He thought I was my mother," she told him. Tears filled her eyes. "I have tried so hard to be a lady, but people only ever see my mother."

"Not I," Hamner assured her, crouching at her side and taking her free hand. "I see a lady to admire; one who reminds me very much of the fine lady who raised her. I see a lady with excellent manners, high moral standards, and a kind, generous heart. You have the beauty of the woman who birthed you, Miss Matilda Grenford, but you are far more than the offspring of that man and his mistress. In every way that counts, you are the daughter of Her Grace, the Duchess of Haverford."

"Hear, hear," said Lady Hamner and Aunt Eleanor, in chorus. Their support frayed the last of Matilda's self-control, and she found herself crying, in great wrenching gulps. On the granite earl's shoulder, too. Who would have thought it?

CHAPTER 7

"Will you give your testimony now, while it is fresh in your mind?" Aldridge asked, and when Charles agreed, Aldridge asked him to wait a moment while he made arrangements.

First, the marquis insisted on his mother and sister retiring to their chambers while he sent for a doctor. Matilda, after she'd spent her tears, went without complaint, though she assured Charles's mother she would call on her tomorrow for the conversation they had missed today.

The duchess made more difficulty, but Lady Hamner countered every one of her arguments for carrying on, pointing out that Her Grace needed to consider the lacerated feelings of her son, that the other ladies of the Society were well equipped to meet without her, that Lady Hamner herself would report after the meeting so the duchess knew what had taken place, and that the duchess was not showing much confidence in the abilities of those she herself had appointed.

Defeated, she agreed to see the doctor and to follow his advice.

Charles waited, helping his mother to restore the room to rights before the ladies arrived for the meeting. A footman came to conduct him to Aldridge's study just in time for him to avoid the first arrivals. He felt far from ready to speak social nothings.

In the study he found the marquis had already produced a lawyer to take Charles's testimony. Aldridge was not there, but he returned as the lawyer packed up the signed and witnessed statement.

Aldridge showed the lawyer to the door, then crossed to a well-stocked shelf of decanters.

"You'll be ready for a brandy, Charles. The doctor suggests Mama and Matilda both rest, and he will return to see how they are tomorrow. Bruising, he assures us, and some shock, of course." His lip twisted in a quick smile. "Mama told him that she has not survived to this age by allowing small inconveniences to overset her."

"I am sorry," Charles said. "That business the year before last when His Grace tried to kill Winshire's sons... It was beginning then?"

Aldridge shook his head. "He has been having... spells of madness on and off for several years. Rarely, and then more often. He used to recover after a few hours, then days, then weeks. This time... It has been three months, and the duchy cannot continue with him at its helm. I have his proxy to do most things, but he can countermand my orders at any time, and I cannot trust that my control will continue to prevail."

Aldridge sounded almost apologetic. "You are doing the right thing," Charles assured him. "Today... I was never more shocked. He was... I always looked up to him, Aldridge. He was generous with his time, charming, and so willing to share his knowledge with a boy who succeeded to a title before he was ready."

Aldridge saluted Charles with his glass. "You saw a different side to him than his wife and children. In public, he was everything you say. *En famille*, he has always been erratic and tyrannical. I used to envy you and Hythe, and others of his disciples. But in the end, perhaps I had the better part, since I never expected enough of him to be disappointed."

Charles had nothing to say to that harsh assessment.

Aldridge offered him a wry smile. "I have shocked you. I solicit your pardon, Charles. I am a little overset myself."

"I do not wonder at it. That scene..." Charles could not complete the sentence, shaking his head as he remembered the indescribable rage that surged through him when he opened the door and saw the duke attacking Matilda.

"Would have been worse had you not happened along when you did. Another minute or two— I shudder to think I might have been too late. I am deeply in your debt, Charles. It must have been hard for you, to fight the man you so admire."

Not hard at all. He did not recall giving the matter a single thought. As soon as his eyes registered Matilda's plight, his only goal was to see her safe, and no past history with the duke would have stayed his hand even to murder, had that been needed.

"I hope I would always come to the rescue of ladies in danger," he said. It was not a lie, but it was at least a prevarication. Between his arrival in that doorway and the moment he took Matilda's hand after making her a cup of tea, his awareness had shifted; his sense of himself and his goals changing, as if he had leapt a hedge and landed in a whole new landscape, quite different from the first.

Matilda—he could no longer keep her at a distance, even in his own mind, by thinking of her as Miss Grenford—was his lady. His to protect and to serve. Whether he could ever be her lord remained to be seen. Most of the time, as far as he could see, she didn't even like him.

She had cried on his shoulder, it was true, but his was the nearest one available.

She had invited him into her quest to help her sister, but again, he was at hand and ready to help.

A knock on the door heralded the arrival of a footman with a message. Miss Grenford and Miss Jessica asked Lord Aldridge and

Lord Hamner to step up to the sisters' sitting room, as Miss Jessica had a story she had promised to tell today.

Aldridge raised one elegant eyebrow. "My sisters' *private* sitting room? Is there something you need to tell me, Hamner?"

Charles was already on his feet. "It is two days later," he explained, then realized how obscure the remark was. "Miss Jessica's friend in Clerkenwell asked her to keep her secret for two days. May I...? I don't suppose Matil— Miss Grenford wishes to come downstairs given..." he waved one hand in a helpless effort to convey bruising and shock.

Aldridge's sigh was near theatrical. "I suppose Sir Galahad should hear the end of the tale. This way, Hamner."

In the pretty sitting room, feminine without being fussy, Matilda had changed her gown for one with a high neck, and had further folded a light gauze scarf about her throat so that the bruises no longer showed. She was pale but composed, and met Charles's anxious gaze with a smile. "Thank you for coming."

Miss Jessica sat beside her sister, holding her hand. Just as well, or Charles might have appropriated the place, and if he had been that close to Matilda he could not have resisted touching her. He should probably keep his distance until he had the savage feelings aroused by seeing her in danger under some sort of control.

Charles took the seat to which he was directed, but Aldridge ignored the wave of Matilda's hand and sat on the arm of her sofa. Dropping his usual bored sardonic air, the marquis bent over his sister. "How are you, Matilda? Are you up to this?"

"Do not fuss over me, too, Aldridge. I will keep busy, and I will be perfectly well. I am more worried about Aunt Eleanor. The doctor said she is not badly hurt and will quickly recover, but what did he tell you?"

Aldridge patted the hand that was not resting in Jessica's. "The same. Do not be concerned, dear one. The doctor is not, and neither is Mama."

Matilda turned her eyes to Charles. "I need to thank you, my lord. I shudder to think what might have happened had you delayed coming to my aid."

Charles reassured her he was always at her service. Even if she took it as a mere form of words, he hoped that later he could convince her of his sincerity. Not today. Not while she was still recovering from the horror of the attack.

"I should leave you to your recovery, Miss Grenford," he offered, but she shook her head.

"Jessica promised that she would explain about the friend in Clerkenwell today, and I am determined to hear the story. I thought you would wish it, too. Aldridge also needs to know—if he has not already been informed by those he sets to watch us." She arched one eyebrow at the marquis, a smile playing around her lips, the gesture enhancing the slight familial resemblance between half-brother and sister.

"Watchers?" Jessica's eyes widened. "Aldridge!"

"For our safety," Matilda scolded, "and do not deny it has been necessary, Jessie."

Jessica blushed. "I do not know where to start."

"The beginning is usually an excellent place." Even the tone was that of Matilda's brother, though in a more feminine register.

Jessica raised her own eyebrow, but obediently began, "In October, I met a friend while visiting repatriated widows at St. Swithins. Do you remember Anne Pembroke, Matilda? Who disappeared during our first season?"

Matilda nodded. Aldridge said, "The Pembroke girl? Wasn't she brought out by an aunt then sent home in disgrace when she was caught kissing Amhurst's son in a garden?"

Charles nodded. He remembered the scandal. Amhurst had proclaimed that his son was already betrothed and, just like that, the girl was ruined.

"By my recollection," Aldridge said. "The betrothal came to nothing; if it existed in truth. I never heard the name of the supposed betrothed mentioned."

"Then Amhurst's son joined a Hussar regiment," Charles mused. "Unusual in the heir to an heir of an earl. I don't know what happened to the girl."

"She was sent to an aunt in Scotland," Jessica explained. "It is her I have been helping. Her and her son."

"Poor girl," he commented.

"You said she was with the war widows." Aldridge was leaning forward, his gaze intent. "Did she marry a soldier, Jess?"

Matilda frowned. "Two years ago, she had no eyes for anyone but Amhurst's son, Mr. Wharton, but I suppose if she was with child..."

"She married Wharton, Tilda. She ran away. A friend of Wharton's gave her money for her passage to Spain, and Wharton had servants and transport waiting for her when she arrived. He wed her as soon as she reached his brigade, and she followed the drum until he died of a fever somewhere in the mountains between Spain and France..." she paused, and then sprung the last of the story on them, her voice dropping to a thrilled hum. "just a day before the letter came telling him his father had died, and he was now earl."

Charles met Aldridge's eyes. Aldridge had realized the same thing as him and put it into words. "Amhurst's brother has been named Earl, but if his nephew married and had a son..."

Charles completed the thought. "Amhurst's brother was estranged from the previous earl, and living in obscurity. He has married on the strength of his new wealth and his title. I doubt he will like being supplanted by his great nephew."

"You may be sure of his displeasure," Jessica said. "Lady Amhurst, as she is now, wrote to him as well as to her own parents, but with no reply. After I spoke to the new earl's wife, though, they came and took her and the boy home to their townhouse, and I thought all would be well."

It wasn't. In pieces, interrupted by questions, Jessica told of Lady Amhurst approaching her in the street outside the hospital, begging for help. The uncle-in-law had refused to believe in her marriage, and had had her escorted from the house, but not before taking her son. "He may be a bastard, but he is family," the man had told her.

The distraught mother, convinced that the false earl meant the boy no good, had gone to her parents for help, but they, too, had turned her away, telling her that she had brought her troubles on herself and that the child was better off with the earl, his great uncle.

So, Jessica and Lady Amhurst had stolen the child back. Matilda's hair rose on the back of her neck as she listened to Jessica's audacious plan; arriving at the townhouse dressed as servants when the false Amhursts were entertaining, and sneaking up to the top floor, where they found little Sammie, hungry and cold, crying alone in a dark nursery. Lady Amhurst had gone into hiding, and Jessica had been searching for anyone among the soldiers or camp followers back from the wars for someone who had witnessed the wedding.

"The marriage should be noted in the regimental records," Aldridge told her. "Young Wharton would have needed permission from his regimental commander, both to wed and to keep his wife with him. I'll see what I can find out, Jess."

Jessica clung to Matilda's hand, her voice small. "I should have told you before. I have made a mess of things, trying to do it all myself."

"You were sworn to secrecy, you said," Matilda reminded her.

"She was so frightened, you see. She was still weak from being ill, and she was sure that other people in Society would reject her as her in-laws and then her family did. Amhurst told her that she could not prevent him from taking the child, as he was the head of the family."

"He cannot have it both ways," Aldridge said. "If the child was born outside of marriage, then his mother has sole authority over him. If inside of marriage, then he is the Earl of Amhurst, and his mother the Countess of Amhurst, and due all the respect of that position. Did Lady Amhurst's husband name a guardian for the boy? Things would be simpler if he did so, as long as he didn't choose his uncle."

"Three, but the only one in England hasn't replied to her letter. The other two are both still with the army somewhere in the south of France," Jessica said. "They're no use to her there."

On the contrary. Not only did that mean the uncle had no authority over the boy or his mother, but also no decisions could be imposed on the widowed Countess without first talking to one of the soldiers, and if it took a month or two, that was all to the good.

"It makes a considerable difference, Jess," Aldridge answered. "The uncle has no authority over the boy or his mother."

"True," Charles agreed. "Furthermore, no decisions about the boy's welfare can be imposed on the widow without first talking to at least two of the guardians."

Aldridge nodded. "Yes, and if it takes a month or two to get a message into the war zone and back out again, that's all to the good."

"See? I should have told you," Jessica repeated. "I thought I could do something good; something important by myself. Make a real difference. Instead, Lady Amhurst had disappeared, and who knows how she will manage?"

"If I remember Anne Pembroke, she will have a plan," Matilda soothed.

Charles agreed. "By your account, Miss Jessica, she escaped her family and ran away to Spain, followed the drum for two years, brought herself and her son back from Spain even though she was bereaved and ill, and then stole her son from his great-uncle's house. I would say she has considerable resilience."

Something Miss Jessica had said started a hare in his thoughts. Hythe had mentioned a widow arriving from somewhere overseas, and a letter that awaited him in London. Better to say nothing now in case one lost widow was not the same person as the other. He'd call on Hythe and check it out.

Aldridge had gone on talking. "Jess, you'll need to wait for her to get in touch. Meanwhile, we can make a start on resolving the matter. We can find out who the brigade commander is, and where he is, and make sure of the guardianship matter, at least. Hamner, we should leave the ladies to prepare for their evening entertainments."

Charles gave Matilda a concerned look. "Are you planning to go out? Even after... Are you sure you are well enough?"

"I would not miss it for the world," Matilda assured him. "Merchant of Venice is one of my favorite plays. And Jess and Percy are looking forward to it, too."

Charles had to leave it at that, since Aldridge made no demur and Charles did not have the authority to cosset Matilda as he would wish. The thought stole unbidden into his mind: not yet.

"Aldridge," he asked, "may I have a word before I go?"

CHAPTER 8

Aldridge took advantage of the misty thaw the next day to move the duke to Haverford Castle on the north coast of Kent near Margate. He had tentative guardianship, pending a final decision by a committee of the House of Lords and ratification by the Prince Regent. No one doubted the outcome. The attack on Matilda, the reports of several doctors, and Haverford's own raving incomprehension when he appeared before the hearing all favored the decision to place one of the kingdom's foremost duchies in safer hands.

"I'll be gone several days," Aldridge told Matilda. "I understand the roads are dreadful, so I do not expect to make good time. I hope Mama will keep to her rooms today, but I don't suppose you or I can insist that she does so."

Her Grace was resting, her dresser told Matilda. She wanted no fuss, and would be well directly. Matilda could not help a smile at the message, delivered in a flawless imitation of Aunt Eleanor's tone. "Please make sure I am told if she wishes us to visit, or if she has any tasks we may do for her," she said. "Oh, and do send me a message if she decides to get up."

The dresser, a long-standing and trusted servant, complained that even Miss Tilda would not be able to stop Her Grace if she took it into her head to overdo things, "but I will let you know, Miss Tilda, you can be sure."

"We need to make the most of the fine weather," Jessica declared, "Though I hope it doesn't last overlong. Every day of warmer temperatures makes the Frost Fair less likely."

She and Miss Cummins hurried off about errands to do with the charity event, leaving Matilda to take a pen and notebook down into the reception rooms to note what furniture needed to be moved into another part of the house, or remain for use at the auction, the breakfast, or the ball.

As they had it planned, the ballroom could be set up the day before, all except for fresh flowers, which would need to be delivered and arranged on the morning of the third of February.

The grand dining room would also be prepared on the second to entertain those guests invited to join the duchess for dinner before the ball.

Indeed, work on both rooms had already begun, as well as the withdrawing rooms for ladies and gentlemen, set up in parlors at the extreme ends of the central wing.

The other rooms—a long gallery, three major salons and a series of smaller parlors—would be needed for the afternoon's auction and Breakfast, if the ice did not allow the alternative venue. After each was cleared of guests, servants would need to rapidly make the necessary changes—to supper room, card rooms and a couple of rooms for quiet conversation.

Matilda had apprenticed to her guardian at enough major events to be able to write lists of the possible problems with ideas on how to solve them, and by early afternoon, she was satisfied that, whatever the weather did, they could cope.

She visited the duchess again, and this time was invited inside. Her Grace was dressed, but lying propped up on pillows on a sofa in her sitting room, her eye swollen nearly shut by a large purple bruise. Reassured that Matilda was fully recovered, she claimed that she, too, was on the mend.

"I shall be perfectly well by the auction and ball, my dear," she insisted, "but I know you will all fret if I get up too quickly. Indeed, I am still a little shaken, so I shall rest, and you shall be my deputy and run my messages."

"Of course, Aunt Eleanor," Matilda agreed, and explained what she had been doing. By the time she had displayed her list, the duchess had paled and was drooping on her pillows.

"Tell me what is most urgent for me to know," Matilda said, "then I shall go away and let you rest."

"Nothing, Matilda. You are doing an excellent job. Give me a kiss, my dear, and off you go."

Matilda returned downstairs to check a couple of details she'd thought of during her conversation with the duchess. As she came through the door from the family stairs into the grand entrance hall, the butler opened the door to Lord Hamner. She watched him stamp the snow from his boots and step inside, making a joking remark about the cold to the footman who came to collect his coat, muffler, hat, and gloves.

He had been wonderful yesterday. Indeed, ever since they met in the fog just after Christmas, the granite surface seemed to have evaporated: first in irritation, to be sure, but later that heat had turned to a more comforting warmth.

She shook her head at her own foolish heart. His change of attitude probably meant he had stopped blaming her for the kiss he had stolen at the house party at Hollystone Hall a year ago. No. She could not honestly call it stolen. She had both given and received, and she greatly feared she would do it again.

Except that his subsequent actions showed he would not consider her as a bride, and she would never dishonor the duchess's care for her by allowing a kiss from anyone but a suitor for her hand in marriage. At least, not again.

He noticed her and approached, smiling warmly. "Miss Grenford. I trust you are well? I called to enquire after you and the duchess. I also have some news for Miss Jessica."

"I am well, my lord. The duchess is recovering from her fall, and hopes to be up and about in the next day or two. Jessie has not yet returned from errands, but I was about to take tea. Would you care to join me?"

"I'd like that, very much." He followed her to the Rose Parlor, named for both the color of its draperies and the carvings and plasterwork. It was one of her favorite parlors for entertaining: small enough that it didn't need a score of people in it to make it seem cozy, but large enough that the maid who scurried after them for propriety's sake could take a seat on the other side of the room where she could not overhear their conversation.

"You have been hard at work, I see," Lord Hamner said, as she put her lists to one side and invited him to sit. While they waited for privacy, she told him about her preparations for the charity events, and the complications of not yet knowing the venue for the auction.

"Mother has been saying the same thing," Lord Hamner said, "but she is most impressed with your gift for organization, Miss Grenford."

Matilda blushed. "The credit goes to my guardian, my lord. Aunt Eleanor has seen me well trained."

A footman and two more maids carried in refreshments: tea, coffee, finely cut bread spread with cucumber relish, some of Monsieur Fournier's little iced cakes, date scones served with cream.

Lord Hamner surveyed it all with delight. "This is a feast, Miss Grenford."

She invited him to serve himself, while she fixed him the coffee he asked for. As he filled his plate, he asked, "If we are not to stand on ceremony, I wonder if I might beg you to call me Hamner. Or even, should you wish it, Charles."

Matilda paused, his cup in her hand, then gathered her scattered wits and passed it to him. "You are very kind, Lo– Hamner."

He shook his head. "Not kind at all. You called me pompous, Matilda. You had the right of it, but I am trying to amend. May I call you Matilda?"

Matilda cast a glance at the maid, but she had her head bent low over her mending and was did not appear to be taking any notice of them.

"Just when we are alone," Hamner cajoled. "Or am I being an idiot again? I thought... I hoped that you might be coming to care for me as I do for you."

"I had no idea." Matilda lifted her chin, her lips firming as she remembered last year's tears. "Have we not travelled this path once before, my lord? You made your opinion of me clear at that time, did you not?"

His clear blue eyes met hers. If she did not guard her heart, he would break it all over again, but he sounded sincere. "I was a fool, and worse than a fool. A pompous prig, you said, and that hurt, because you were right."

"You kissed me, then spurned me and proposed to another woman," she reminded him.

"Ah." The color rose in his face and he looked down at the coffee cup, dwarfed by his large capable hands. "You are Lady Felicity's friend. Of course, you know about that."

"What? You hoped to deceive me?"

"Not that!" The cup clattered as his hands shook, and he put it down on the side table. "I hoped I could explain it before you knew what an ass I had been. To burn for one woman and propose to another, as if they were interchangeable? My mother tells me I deserve for you to send me away and never speak to me again, but I hope to convince you that I have learned from my stupidity."

Almost without her volition, Matilda's head shook, slowly, more in disbelief than negation. "You despise the circumstances of my birth. You do not believe I would reflect credit to your name. Your words, Lord Hamner."

Hamner leaned forward as if he would grasp her hands, but stopped short of reaching for them. His voice vibrated with passion. "Do I regret that your birth has barred you from all the respect you deserve? Yes. You are the daughter of a duke, raised by a duchess, and a lady of uncommon intelligence, grace, and ability. You act always with propriety and dignity. You should take precedence with others of your rank, and I am indignant that you cannot. You would grace the name of the highest in the land. I was an ignorant fool to think otherwise, and an uncouth lout to say what I did. Though I hope my *actual* words were kinder, Matilda."

"Perhaps." She pursed her lips. "However, you agree that I took your meaning. As an apology for that kiss—I was humiliated, Charles, and I do not see how you expect me to forget it."

She only realized that she had slipped into calling him by his given name when his eyes lit up, but he did not capitalize on the error. "Not forget. But may I hope for forgiveness? In time? Give me leave to prove my sincerity by my devotion? I mean marriage, Matilda, in case you are in doubt. Yesterday, I saw you in danger, and I knew I could not be happy without you. I spoke to your brother, but he said some of what you have said, and told me that I would need to make my own petition to you. The choice of whether I am permitted to be your friend and your suitor is entirely yours."

"I do not know how to answer you." Hamner opened his mouth again, but Matilda held up her hand. "Enough. Lord Hamner, I shall think on what you have said, but we shall not speak of it again today. Aunt Eleanor appreciated your mother's help yesterday. Is she well?"

Hamner accepted her lead and they chatted for a few minutes about the work that Lady Hamner and Matilda had been doing together, and other matters to do with the Society.

"You said you had some news for my sister," Matilda said, after they had exhausted that subject. "Is it something you could entrust to me?"

"Good news, I hope. It was something the Earl of Hythe said to me a week or so ago, about a widow of a friend who was missing. I called on him this morning, and he confirmed that his widow is also Miss Jessica's. Not only can he attest to Lady Amhurst's marriage, he is the friend who sent her to her marriage, and Lord Amhurst appointed him as one of the guardians to the little boy. Once Miss Jessica's friend surfaces again, he will be happy to protect her and her child. Meanwhile, he intends to visit both her family and her husband's, and to start proceedings to have little Lord Amhurst declared his father's heir."

Matilda had not expected that. Jessica would be thrilled. "We owe you thanks again," she told Lord Hamner, and then, because he deserved a reward, "Charles."

CHAPTER 9

Two days of fine weather were followed by snow, and Aldridge didn't return home. Every lady of the Society was now hard at work preparing for the third of February. They had commissioned three reprintings of Lady Georgiana's leaflets about the plight of returned soldiers and sailors, and of the widows and orphans of those who hadn't returned. The Frost Fair was looking more and more likely, and Matilda and Lady Hamner had created and distributed detailed instructions for those who had volunteered furniture, carpets, drapery, braziers, and other equipment for the ice.

Those creating bunting to decorate the venue had doubled their production so that both Haverford House and the space on the ice would be draped in the Union Flag and the flags of the four kingdoms, regimental banners, and patriotic colors.

The three ladies in charge of organizing ticket sales (ten pounds for the auction and Venetian Breakfast, and fifteen pounds for the ball) had a minor panic when they discovered that the Society's enthusiastic volunteers had promised more tickets than had been printed, but a quick meeting with the main committee resolved that both venues could find room for another fifty people.

Matilda and Jessica added acting as messenger for the duchess on top of their other duties. Charles—her rebel mind had fallen on the name, and it was a struggle to remember to call him by the more formal 'Hamner'—Charles was a loyal escort, willing to take them wherever they wished at a moment's notice. He did not speak again of courting Matilda, but now and then she caught him regarding her with wistful hunger.

And he continued to call her by her given name.

On Monday the thirty-first, the Thames was a complete field of ice from London Bridge to Blackfriars Bridge. The watermen, who had been barred from their usual profession for most of the month by the dangerous ice floes, quickly organized to test and then to control access to the ice. When Matilda went down to view the area she and Lady Hamner had chosen for the Haverford marquee, they demanded payment for helping her and her party over the small rivulet that had formed at the bank.

"That is outrageous," complained Charles, at her elbow as had become usual.

"Na, jes' think about it," the waterman coaxed. Matilda focused to translate his thick accent into words she could understand. "People pay us to take them on the river. Doesn't matter whether it's wet or dry. We did the same twenty odd years back, and before that, I reckon."

"Were you here for the last Frost Fair?" Matilda asked. He certainly looked bent and wrinkled enough, what she could see of him in his greatcoat, cap, and scarf.

"That I were, me lady. And this bids fair to be a better one, it does."

Charles paid the couple of sixpences the man demanded, and then Matilda pointed out that he had now received the value of a boat ride. "Would you escort us, and tell us about the last Frost Fair, and what you expect for this one?"

They spent half an hour listening to the waterman's stories while they looked for a good site for the marquee and its subordinate tents—far enough from the main booths and activities of the fair that access was easy to control, and yet close enough that the ticket-holders could stroll the fair at their pleasure.

"That was clever," Charles noted, as they settled themselves back under the furs in his sleigh. "You've convinced the watermen to keep that part of the ice clear, and have negotiated a fee to make entry to the ice free to anyone who shows a ticket."

Matilda was pleased, too. "They shall do very well out of it: a lump-sum deposit before the event and another afterwards, and all they have to do is keep our space clear, let our servants onto the ice to set up, and pass people who show a ticket on the third of February. Not that I begrudge them. Imagine being unable to earn a living because the river you depend on freezes solid."

"You are a remarkable woman, Matilda Grenford," Charles said. Matilda tucked the comment away as she had the other compliments with which he lavished her. She had no doubt that he meant them, but she was still unsure about his change of heart.

Surely a man could not truly change such deep-seated opinions? He confessed himself that he was driven by desire. "To burn for one woman and propose to another," he said. Did desire last? If she married him, would he regret it? Would she?

She set her yearnings and her doubts to one side. The coming charity events were more than enough to think about, let alone keeping the duchess's injury (and its cause) from the world, and preventing Jessica from personally searching every gentlewomen's boarding house in London.

The sleigh passed the gates at Haverford House, the gate-keepers already familiar with it after several days of Hamner using it and the sturdy horses that drew it to squire Matilda around town.

Another, far more ornate sleigh, this one with a covered body and a team of three, stood at the steps. "Aldridge!" Matilda exclaimed, recognizing the troika that her brother, Lord Jonathan

Grenford, had sent to the duchess one Christmas when he was in Russia. Sure enough, the marquis was getting out from the equipage, tossing a laughing remark to his secretary, who emerged behind him.

As Charles brought their sleigh to a halt behind the Haverford troika, the marquis strolled along to greet them. "Matilda! And Lord Hamner, too." He handed Matilda from the carriage, and accepted the kiss she pressed to his cheek. "I am glad to see you home, Aldridge. You have made exceptional time!"

He gave the hand he had retained in his own a quick squeeze. "I could not miss the Society's auction and ball, Tilda. You shall have it on the ice as you hoped, I think."

"Yes. In fact," she waved a hand to include Charles in the discussion, "we have just come from there. All is arranged. I was about to bring Ch– Hamner inside to warm up with a mulled cider. Would you care to join us, Aldridge? Mr. Markinson, too, of course."

The secretary demurred, and trudged off to the heir's wing with a large case of papers, followed by a servant carrying the marquis's trunk, but Aldridge accompanied Matilda into the main house.

"Your suit prospers, then, Hamner?" Matilda heard him ask.

"She has at least permitted me to assist her with the Society's event, my lord," Charles replied. Something in his voice hinted that, if she turned, she would find him keeping a wary eye on her. It comforted her to know the uncertainty was not all on one side.

When Matilda asked a footman to order refreshments to the family parlor, she was told that the duchess and her sisters were already there. Her Grace had emerged from seclusion while Matilda was out, the swelling on her face barely noticeable, the discoloration concealed with powder. She greeted Aldridge with pleasure, and gave Charles her hand to kiss.

"Matilda, Jessica has just been showing your excellent work to Frances and me. I am very proud of you, my dear. Hamner, I believe you have been a stalwart support these past few days. I thank you, and the Society will be grateful."

Frances, at almost thirteen the youngest Grenford ward, was cajoling Aldridge to take her for a ride in his sleigh. "Lord Hamner took us to Hyde Park skating, but his sleigh is very small, so we had to walk. Can we not take the troika, Aldridge? Tomorrow?"

"Perhaps, kitten," Aldridge told her, trying not to smile. "If I can make the time, where would you like to go?"

"The Frost Fair, of course." She was bouncing with excitement, and full of stories told to her by her governess and the servants about the Frost Fair of 1795.

Aldridge amused them for a while with his own memories. He must have been a boy of fifteen, and the stories he trotted out for Frances were probably much sanitized. Before Matilda quite knew how it happened, Charles had not only been invited to go along on the expedition to the ice the next day, but was staying for a light meal. Somehow, without Matilda making any decisions about his place in her life, he had been accepted into their family circle.

In the end it was Charles, summoned by a message from Aldridge who could not, after all, avoid his ducal responsibilities, who took the three sisters down to the ice in the troika. If she had not already been in love with Charles, seeing his gentle way with Frances might have won her. The granite earl had gone as if he'd never been, leaving the charming, kind, courteous lord who had set stars in her eyes when he danced with her at her first ball.

He patiently took Frances off to see the elephant and have her fortune told while Matilda and Jessica took their turn answering questions at the Society's booth, making sure that every person attracted into the booth by Monsieur Fournier's delectable cakes and pastries left with at least one of Lady Georgiana's leaflets.

He insisted on paying for the four of them to have their caricatures drawn, first as individuals and then as a group, "to remember the day," he said.

He stopped a sputtering Lord Amhurst with a few stern words when the indignant man accosted them to demand to know which of them sent Lord Hythe to his doorstep with what the false earl called "a pack of damnable lies", and he sent Mr. Driscoll and a pack of his cronies scurrying away with a lift of an eyebrow and a glare that rivaled Aldridge at his most imperious.

By the time they made their way home, full of hawker food and beverages, the attendant footmen burdened with fairings, slightly silly with the experiences they'd tried and the sights they'd seen, first Frances and then Jessica had accepted Charles's invitation to call him by his first name. What could Matilda do but follow their example?

"What are your plans for tomorrow?" Charles asked. "May I be of service?"

"My duties for the auction and ball are all but over until the actual events," Matilda told him. "Tomorrow, Jessica and I will be preparing the food for our picnic baskets."

"With your own fair hands?" He smiled. "I shall be sure to take plenty of money with me to the auction." He intended to bid on her basket, then. Would he be impressed? In her spare time over the past week, she had consulted Cook, visited Madame Fournier, who had once been the duchess's secretary and was now married to a famous chef, and pored over recipes.

Still, cooking skills—while favored by the duchess—were not normally considered lady-like. Surely, he did not want a countess who cooked?

But he was telling Frances about trips with his mother and father to a cottage on their estate, where his father took him fishing and his mother made their meals. "Mother says that a lady should at least know the basics of every task she expects her servants to do, and I believe the same applies to a gentleman. I might not be able to get the shine on my boots that my valet manages, but if I travel alone, I am not completely helpless."

"That is what Aunt Eleanor says, too," Jessica told him.

They said goodbye to the earl and went upstairs to tell the duchess all about their afternoon. "Charles is very kind," Frances told her. "He said I might call him Charles. I think he wants to marry Matilda. I thought it might be Jessica, because the all men want Jessica, but I am sure it is Matilda. He looks at her." Frances adopted an expression that could only be called languishing.

Matilda glared at Jessica, who could not speak for laughing. "Frances, such personal remarks are not appropriate."

Frances looked at Matilda then decided to address herself to Aunt Eleanor. "I only want to know, Aunt Eleanor," she explained. "If Matilda marries Charles, will I be the bride's attendant, like my cousin Daisy was when cousin Susan married?"

"If that is your hope, dear Frances," Aunt Eleanor replied, "you might begin by not annoying your sister."

CHAPTER 10

Matilda, with a little help and advice from the cook, made pies and puddings, and roasted several different kinds of meat. She added cut cheese and fresh fruit to the basket that already held crockery, cutlery, condiments, and several types of drink.

Tomorrow, after she made the bread, she would make a salmagundi with cold chicken, hard-boiled eggs, anchovy fillets, beetroot, red cabbage, cooked tongue, celery, bright salad leaves, and cucumbers from the Haverford hot house.

Jessica teased that she was feeding an army, but she helped prepare the roasts, and would use some of the meat in her own basket. Jessica was also making gingerbread cake, pork pies, and syllabub.

They were in the thick of it when a message came down to say Lord Hamner had called. Matilda's impulse to cast down what she was doing and hurry to see him annoyed her almost as much as his arrogance in calling when she had told him she was busy.

"Please inform Lord Hamner that I am not 'at home'," she told the footman.

She glared at Jessica's grin, and Jessica, who had opened her mouth, changed her mind and turned back to the little shortbread biscuits that she was cutting out with a tin cutter shaped like a star.

It was Matilda's choice to refuse Charles, but she went to bed that night aching with something that felt like homesickness. The day had not been complete without him.

Charles was up early on the morning of the Ladies' Society Venetian Breakfast. Aldridge had invited him to break his fast at Haverford House so he could escort the young ladies to the ice to oversee the erection of the marquee and its attendant tents.

He walked the short distance to the mansion, since the ice made riding dangerous for both man and horse, treading carefully as he mulled over the words his mother had said the previous evening, as he daydreamed after dinner, imagining Matilda in the countess's chair and trying not to feel disconsolate at not seeing her for a whole day.

"When you propose to Miss Grenford, Charles—you do plan to propose, do you not?" She waited for his nod. "Tell her that I welcome her as a daughter-in-law. She worries about the circumstances of her birth, and she may need reassurance about my opinion."

"I do not care who her mother was," Charles began, indignantly, but his mother held up a hand to stop him.

"Nor I, and that is my point. I cannot imagine a match that would better please me. She will make a magnificent countess, but that is beside the point. She is good for you, and she loves you, and she will be a wonderful mother for the beautiful grandchildren the pair of you will make for me. I will be sure to tell her myself, but I cannot raise the issue with her until you have actually proposed."

"I am glad to have your blessing, Mother, but I would marry Matilda without it."

Mother laughed. "So I would hope."

It was too early to propose, was it not? She was starting to like him a little, but he could not fool himself that he'd won back the ground he'd lost at the house party just over a year ago.

Still, when he was admitted to the Haverford House family breakfast room, he could have sworn her eyes lit up at the sight of him, and she readily accepted his escort in place of her brother. "I will bring Her Grace down in time for the auction," Aldridge promised.

The area the watermen had set aside for the event was humming with activity. The marquee was up already, with streams of servants bringing in furnishing, carpets, and drapes to turn it into a sumptuous reception room, with a stage at one end for the auctioneer.

Charles found himself in charge of managing the furbishment of a number of smaller tents among a dozen set up to provide dining areas for the successful bidders. For the next several hours, he went from task to task as directed by young ladies of the Society, each of whom marshaled one part of the preparation.

At last, they paused for a hot drink and a collective sigh of satisfaction. The patronesses and elder committee members were beginning to arrive. Soon, they would set up the reception lines for the ticket holders, and the event would begin. Charles made his way to Matilda's side.

"Nearly time," he commented.

"I am afraid no one will come," she confessed. "I know it is silly, but there you are."

"I think only those who are recluses or infirm will miss it," Charles assured her. This evidence of the insecurity she hid under her efficiency and competence set him yearning to hold her in his arms and protect her from every chill wind. "You have sold hundreds of tickets, and I expect them all to be here. Such an unusual setting! It was a brilliant idea to hold the event here, and the marquee and tents look marvelous. Very comfortable, too. You and my mother are largely to be credited with organizing the venue, or so I understand."

Matilda blushed. "Your mother has worked very hard, and has come up with most of the good ideas."

"She says the same about you," Charles assured her. "She is most impressed with you, Matilda." Was this the time to pass on Mother's message? But no, they were being called to form the reception lines, and there were the first ticket-holders, queuing in the cold, dozens of them.

Even with three entry points, gatekeepers to check tickets, and three reception lines, it took more than half an hour to bring the bulk of the ticket holders inside; not just the usual supporters of the charity, but dozens, perhaps hundreds of the *beau monde* who would otherwise never put their hands in their pockets for the charitable cause in question.

Matilda, when she made her way back to Charles's side, suggested it was partly the potential for scandal in the nature of the auction. "Sale of a lady's time? Shocking!"

Jessica and Percy, who had joined them, laughed and declared, "But it is all for charity. Her Grace told Lady Jersey that the most proper of the *ton's* sticklers could have no objection to a lady offering food and the pleasure of her company in support of a good cause, and Countess Leuven agreed."

The duchess, any signs of her injury well concealed, opened the auction and introduced her friend, Brigadier General Lord Redepenning, known almost universally as Lord Henry. He explained how the auction would work, and in no time at all was knocking down baskets to the eager bidders.

It was fun to watch. Lord Henry had the crowd laughing with his quips, egging on the bidders, and cheering the winners. Some baskets went to acknowledged suitors and husbands. Even for those, the bidding was often fierce, and Percy Cummins' basket sold for the princely sum of one hundred pounds, the Earl of Trehallow outbidding everyone else, including Aldridge.

"Next," Lord Henry announced, "we have a basket packed by Miss Jessica Grenford." He lifted the lid, and made an artistic show of scenting the contents. "Gingerbread, ladies and gentlemen. And is this champagne? Much more, too. I cannot begin to describe the treats in store for the lucky winner."

The first bid of five pounds came from the other side of the room, and another followed, then another, until the bidding was up to ten pounds. Then Basil Driscoll put in a bid of fifteen pounds. Jessica looked around in alarm. Matilda cast a pleading look at Charles. He waited for Aldridge to intervene, but the marquis had been called out of the marquee by one of the servants on duty.

Another bid, this one for seventeen pounds. It was a friend of Trehallow. She'd be safe with James Marr.

"Twenty pounds," Driscoll shouted.

Charles waited for another bid. Nothing. Matilda met his eyes again and, as Lord Henry raised his gavel, Charles answered the plea.

"Fifty pounds!" The basket was knocked down to him, and Jessica came to take his arm. "Come with me," Charles begged Matilda, and led both sisters to the front, where Jessica's basket awaited.

Matilda's basket was one of the last to be auctioned. Lord Henry had been warning the remaining men to bid high or be left out, and the dwindling crowd had responded with some ridiculous bids. A basket by Margaret Bellham, a spinster on her seventh season, sold for 90 pounds, but then she was known to employ a famous cook.

Miss Cratchett, heiress to a mill owner, and one of those maidens about whom people say, 'but she has a lovely personality' was escorted off to lunch by Lord Aldridge, beaming widely, though whether at the lunch companion she had gained or the seventy pounds contributed to the charity it was hard to say.

Hamner waited with Jessica and Matilda. When Lord Henry announced Matilda's basket, Charles felt her tense beside him.

"Ten pounds," shouted James Marr.

"Fifteen," countered Charles.

"I say," said Vernon Mellbarrow. "He already has a basket and a lovely lunch guest."

"Nothing in the rules to say he cannot buy another," Lord Henry decided.

The Marquess of Welbrook bid twenty pounds, and James Marr topped him by another five.

"Thirty pounds." That was Driscoll, the evil swine.

Two of the bidders had their heads together. "It is unfair for Hamner to have two baskets," Melbarrow shouted. "If the lady will accept both James and myself, we are happy to continue bidding. Seventy-five pounds!"

"One hundred pounds," said Charles, firmly, following the strategy displayed earlier by the Earl of Trehallow. In triumph, he accepted his second basket of the afternoon, and marched off with the Grenford sisters, collecting his mother to play chaperone on his way out of the marquee.

CHAPTER 11

O ne of the footmen led Matilda's party to a table in one of the larger tents, where a half a dozen groups already enjoyed their meal.

Lord Marr and Sir Mellbarrow arrived, escorting Cecilia Fournier, and boasting about winning a basket by the best chef in London. "In Europe, gentlemen, if you please," Cecilia scolded, laughing. She winked at Matilda as she and the gentlemen passed the table. "My husband would not argue if you said 'in the world'!" They took a table in the far corner, and a few moments later Monsieur Fournier himself joined them.

"There were many more bidders than baskets," Charles commented. "The rest will be satisfied with food from the hawkers, I suppose."

"Not at all," Matilda explained. "As soon as the auction is over, a feast will be spread in the marquee for all those ticket holders who have neither contributed nor purchased a basket. No one will go hungry." It would be a varied offering, too, for no one had made merely enough for one basket, and the surplus food had all been donated to serve as lunch for the disappointed.

Charles smiled at Matilda and then glanced around the table, to include his mother and Jessica in his comments. "The Society is to be congratulated. I can see that winter Venetian Breakfasts with basket auctions will become the next thing for raising charitable funds.

"We shall have to put our thinking caps on for next year," Matilda told him. "Aunt Eleanor does not like to repeat herself."

Just then, they were interrupted. Mr. Driscoll must have purchased one of the last baskets. He and Lord Amhurst hurried into the tent with Miss Fairley, a timid wallflower who had only recently joined the Society and whose chaperone, a prune-faced old besom of an aunt, seemed determined to throw her at any gentleman who showed the least interest. Where was the woman? Surely, Matilda thought, she had not abandoned poor Miss Fairley to a reprobate like Driscoll?

"They are here," Driscoll said, and he plonked the basket he was carrying onto a spare table. He took a pace towards the table where the Grenford sisters sat with Charles and Lady Hamner, but stopped when Charles stood and met his eyes.

He turned back to Amhurst, saying in a loud voice, "I cannot believe we are expected to eat with such alley sweepings."

Charles, his fists clenched, took a step towards the horrid man, but Matilda put a hand on his arm and shook her head. "Pretend it is not about us," she murmured, keeping her voice low. "He wants to make a display. Ignoring him is the best strategy."

Lady Hamner smiled her approval. "Quite right, my dear. Take the moral high ground, I always say."

Jessica sighed. "So does Aunt Eleanor."

With some reluctance, Charles sank back into his seat and attempted to join in the renewed conversation, stopping frequently to glare at Amhurst and Driscoll. He was not the only one, as they continued to exchange remarks about the smell, contagion, and moral turpitude, pretending not to look at Matilda and Jessica, but making sure the entire tent knew who they were targeting with their attacks.

At the other tables, people glared or turned their backs, according to their natures. Matilda did her best not to look their way, but when she heard Miss Fairley sob, she could not help herself. A few yards away, the girl was attempting to shrink in her seat, face scarlet, and in tears. Before she thought about it, she was on her feet and marching over.

She completely ignored the two men, and held out her hand to Miss Fairley. "Will you join us, Miss Fairley? We have plenty."

Miss Fairley brightened and began to rise.

"We bought your time with your basket," Driscoll snapped, and Miss Fairley dropped back into her chair. "Go away, Miss Grenford." He sneered over the name, making it another insult. "A good girl like Miss Fairley doesn't keep company with the likes of you."

Charles had followed, and was at Matilda's shoulder. Mr. Marr and the Earl of Chadbourn approached, and so did a number of the other men in the tent.

Amhurst addressed the tent at large. "We are trying to eat our basket in peace. This woman, who should not be allowed in polite company, is causing trouble. Just like her sister did, taking the part of the trollop who tried to pass off her bastard as my nephew's son." Driscoll told him to be quiet, but he rounded on Jessica, his face in a snarl. "Where have you hidden her? I'll have the law on you. I'll ruin you, and your sisters."

Charles, Marr, and another man took hold of him, and dragged him towards the entrance to the tent, Driscoll having stepped aside with his hands spread. He continued to shout, "I'll have you drummed out of London. You'll be selling yourself in the streets by the time I'm done with you, bitch!"

Before they reached the heavy drape that kept the cold air from inside, it lifted, and the Lords Hythe and Sutton stepped through, followed by Hythe's sisters, Lady Felicity and Lady Sutton.

"May we take Wharton off your hands?" Hythe asked Charles.

"He has some questions to answer about his treatment of the true Earl of Amhurst and the child's mother."

"I am the true Earl of Amhurst, you fools, and the bitch that chased after that useless brat Samuel has undoubtedly frozen to death and her whelp with her." Amhurst screamed.

"On the contrary," Hythe told him, "Lady Amhurst and the earl are safe and well."

Felicity and Sophia skirted the men and crossed to where Jessica and Matilda stood, their eyes wide. "Her letter finally reached Hythe," Felicity explained. "He has all the proof she needs to put Mr. Wharton back into the hole where he belongs, and she is now staying with my sister and Sutton at the Winshire mansion."

Driscoll had started shouting now. The whole tent—perhaps half the fair—heard him break with his former bosom bow. "You lied to me. You told me the woman was deranged and didn't even know your nephew." The false earl was led away, with Driscoll following.

"I'll see my sister's marriage declared void, Amhurst," Driscoll yelled, his voice fading as they left the tent. "No, you aren't Amhurst are you, Wharton? You promised to make her wealthy and a countess and now you are nothing and I'm not going to let you drag her down with you!"

Matilda, managing to keep her voice level and calm, invited the Belvoir sisters to join her table, "and you, Miss Fairley, if you care to do so."

Several people helped them push tables together, and soon they made a merry party, putting the unpleasantness behind them, but interrupted every few minutes as one after another of the other diners came over to the table to ask after Miss Fairley's wellbeing or just to show their support with a friendly comment. Matilda was touched. Ever since she and Jessica had attracted the attention of bullies at school, she expected to be shunned when her origins were discussed. Not so, it seemed. This group, at least, accepted her despite those vile men.

After the discouraging start, they had a delightful lunch, and even Miss Fairley came out of her shell enough to talk about the gown she planned to wear at the ball that night, and to shyly agree to dances with several of the gentlemen.

Before she knew where the time had gone, Matilda was climbing back into the troika for the return journey to Haverford House. She parted with the Hamners at the banks of the Thames, but not before Charles had asked for a private word with her this evening before dinner. He was going to propose. She just knew it. What she didn't know was what she was going to reply.

Haverford House seethed like a stirred ants' nest, servants hurrying in every direction as they made the final preparations for the duchess's grand dinner followed by the charity ball. Charles followed the footman sent to conduct him through the ordered chaos to a private parlor in the family wing.

He had dressed with enormous care, driving his valet demented by changing his mind three times about his waistcoat, rejecting six cravats before settling on the seventh, and hesitating for twenty minutes on his choice of fobs. The valet would probably slit his wrists in despair if he could see how Charles had set his hair in disarray by running his fingers through it, and ruined the hard-won perfection of the cravat by tugging it further open because he felt it choking him.

Then the door opened. Matilda entered the room and he lost his breath again. She was magnificent in a violet gown that hugged her curves before sweeping out into a deceptively simple skirt that avoided fashionable ruffles in favor of more subtle stitching to add detail without fuss. The neckline was low enough to rivet his attention while still high enough to be demure by the current standards. She wore pearls at her neck, her wrists, dangling from her ears and glowing in her dark hair, and the blue eyes he met when he wrenched his attention from the snowy skin displayed by her décolletage had taken on a violet cast from the gown.

He gazed, losing track of time and space, until she said his name. "Charles?"

"I had a speech." His voice croaked, and he swallowed. "I do not remember a word."

With one hand, index finger outstretched, he traced an inch or so away from her face. "Why did I try so hard to resist you, you beautiful woman?"

It was the wrong thing to say. Her nostrils flared. "Because I am the base-born daughter of a harlot."

"I cannot remember why I thought that important," he confessed. "You are the beloved sister of the next Duke of Haverford, the ward of the current duchess, and a lady of impeccable education, training and manners. That is not why I love you, though."

Her eyes softened. "You love me?"

"That was part of the speech. It is the only bit I remember. I look into your eyes, and I forget my own name."

"Why?" Matilda asked.

"Why do I forget? No? Why now?" She colored, and he realized what she was asking. "Why do I love you? How can I explain something that has grown in my heart without my knowledge, even against my will?" He took both of her hands, and suddenly the words began to flow.

"I have been attracted to you since the first time we danced, but that is desire, and desire is a part of love but not the whole. I do desire you, my love, more and more each day, but I also admire you, I like being with you, I enjoy talking to you, I respect you. I want to see you every morning when I wake, spend my days with you, have the right to dance the first waltz with you at every ball, and go home with you every night. I want to see your belly rounded with our child, and watch you as you gently teach them the way I've seen you teach your little sister. I want you and only you as my countess and the mother of my children. I want to grow old with you, Matilda Grenford."

He dropped to one knee. "Miss Grenford, I esteem you with all my heart. Will you do me the very great honor of becoming my wife?"

He waited, his anxiety rising as she said nothing, despair taking over as tears rose and began to leak from her pansy eyes. Then she began to nod as she slipped to her own knees and reached out for him. "Yes. Oh, yes. Charles, I love you, too."

For more than a year, Charles had kept to himself the fact that the Haverford Ice Princess kissed like a flame. As he abandoned his own granite facade for once and for all, he rejoiced in her heat. This time was even better than the last, and the best was yet to come. Though perhaps not here in a family parlor where her brother or sisters could walk in at any time.

"I hope you do not want a long betrothal," he whispered, between kisses.

She broke off her attempt to completely unravel his cravat. "Not long," she agreed.

Her fervent answer demanded that he kiss her again, losing himself so deep he didn't know they were no longer alone until a voice behind him said, "I trust you are betrothed to my sister, Hamner, for it would be most inconvenient to start the evening's celebrations by killing you."

Matilda leapt to her feet, blushing, and Charles rose more slowly, to put a defiant arm around her waist. She leaned into his side.

"Do not tease the poor man," said the duchess. "Of course, he and Matilda are betrothed, and I am delighted, my dears, for I could tell you were made for one another."

Mother was there, too, declaring her own pleasure at the match, and Jessica and Frances were hugging their sister.

Charles tidied his cravat and his hair while Aldridge ordered champagne and talked about announcing the betrothal at the dinner in less than an hour. Mother had arrived early, but soon the other guests would be gathering.

Perhaps Charles had made a tactical error, asking for her hand before a dinner that would mean two hours of propriety in the company of others. And then the ball, another five hours, though at least then he'd have opportunities to touch her, to murmur endearments, perhaps to steal a kiss.

Matilda emerged from the tidying hands of her sisters and their eyes met in a long warm embrace. It was enough to soothe his impatience. Perhaps the duchess would rearrange her table so Matilda and her new betrothed could walk in together and sit side by side. And if not, he could be patient. He would have a lifetime to find countless ways of melting Matilda.

THE END

OTHER BOOKS BY JUDE KNIGHT

More Regency books by Jude Knight

The Golden Redepennings series

True love is rare and elusive, but they won't settle for less.

Candle's Christmas Chair (A novella in The Golden Redepennings series)

They are separated by social standing and malicious lies. He has until Christmas to convince her to give their love another chance.

Gingerbread Bride (A novella in The Golden Redepennings series)

Mary runs from an unwanted marriage and finds adventure, danger and her girlhood hero, coming once more to her rescue.

Farewell to Kindness (Book 1 in The Golden Redepennings series)

Love is not always convenient. Anne and Rede have different goals, but when their enemies join forces, so must they.

A Raging Madness (Book 2 in The Golden Redepennings series)

Their marriage is a fiction. Their enemies are all too real. Uncovering the truth will need all the trust Ella and Alex can find.

The Realm of Silence (Book 3 in The Golden Redepennings series)

Rescue her daughter, destroy her dragons, defeat his demons, return to his lonely life. How hard can it be?

Unkept Promises (Book 4 in The Golden Redepennings series)

Mia hopes to negotiate a comfortable marriage. Jules wants his wife to return to England, where she belongs. Love confounds them both.

Other Regency stories

A Baron for Becky

She was a fallen woman. How could the men who loved her lift her back to her feet?

Revealed in Mist

As spy and enquiry agent, Prue and David worked to uncover secrets, while hiding a few of their own.

A Suitable Husband

A chef from the slums, however talented, is no fit mate for the cousin of a duke, however distant. But Cedrica can dream.

Lord Calne's Christmas Ruby

One wealthy merchant's heiress with an aversion to fortune hunters. One an impoverished earl with a twisted hand. Combine and stir with one villainous rector.

House of Thorns

His rose thief bride comes with a scandal that threatens to tear them apart.

For more about these and for the rest of Jude's books, see https://judeknightauthor.

ABOUT JUDE KNIGHT

Jude Knight was always going to be a novelist, but life kept getting in the way, until she nearly lost the dream for fear of failing. Her mother encouraged her, and she wrote a thousand beginnings, but it took a huge life event to shove her into writing an ending.

In 2014, she entered her first contest, attended her first romance writers contest finished her first historical fiction novel, and published her first novella. Over a dozen books later, she's living her dream: writing historical fiction with a large helping of romance, more than a dash of suspense, and a sprinkling of humour.

Sign Me Up!
Newsletter: http://judeknightauthor.com/newsletter/

Learn more about Jude at:
Website and blog: http://judeknightauthor.com/
Bookshop: https://judeknight.selz.com/
Books + Main Bites: https://
bookandmainbites.com/JudeKnightAuthor

facebook.com/JudeKnightAuthor
twitter.com/JudeKnightBooks
pinterest.com/jknight1033
bookbub.com/profile/jude-knight

MY ONE TRUE LOVE

RUE ALLYN

My One True Love
By Rue Allyn

Lord Trevor returned from war to find his best friend gone. No one would tell him where she might be. Then he found her in the frosty London fog of January 1814 only to lose her in the next moment. Mary Percival saw him in the fog and ran. She knew he would hate her once he heard what others said. The memory of their friendship was too dear for her to survive knowing he despised her.

CHAPTER 1

December 27, 1813,
Outside Haverford House, London

Damn *the fog.* Major Lord Arthur Trevor PenRhydderch, twenty-first Earl of Trehallow, stared blindly down the alley beside Haverford House where he had seen the woman disappear. The lane had filled with a sudden fog so thick even the street lamps appeared as blurred yellow-gray discs. He could walk within an inch of Percy and never see her.

"Hallo, Trev, are you there?" An empty and hollow shout reached Trevor's ears from his friend, Lord James Marr, heir to the Earl of Strathnaver.

"Over here, James. Stay put and I will make my way back to you." He reversed his position and stretched a hand out until he found the solid surface of Haverford House. Using the wall as a guide, and any handrails when he found stairs, he began the slow trek back to his friends.

A yellow-gray disc of light appeared in the distance—approximately, he thought, where he had left his two friends.

"I bumped into a linkman," Sir Vernon Melbarrow called. "Brought him along to help us get to your townhouse."

The action struck Trevor as a trifle unnecessary, since they had been standing practically in front of his London home when he had taken off in pursuit of a woman he knew in his heart was Percy. He had not seen Miss Mary Percival Cummins in more than three years—his last visit home on leave from his regiment. But she had been blooming and happy then, anticipating her come out and the announcement of her betrothal. So happy, he had kept silent about his own feelings. It had been the right decision at the time. Now, things were different.

When Trevor returned home this past Christmas, Cummins's House had been shuttered and dark. No one would speak to him of Percy, so he had no idea what had happened to her. He wanted to know. She had been his best friend once. Even if she had never written, he believed that friendship still lived. That belief had kept him alive, determined to survive all battles and return to the home he knew. Except nothing was as he had known it.

"There you are." James's hand appeared on Trevor's arm, the wrist and sleeve disappearing into a shape darker than the cotton wool fog.

"Here, man," Vernon said to the fellow who earned his living by carrying torches to light the way for pedestrians in dark streets. A second darker shape that must have been Sir Vernon, twisted toward the glow. "Lead us up these demned steps, so we do not break our necks."

"Ya sur. Jes grab hol't me sleeve, and I'll have ye up in a trice."

"I've got you. Here, Trev, James," Melbarrow directed, "link your arms with mine. We'll be cozy as cats sipping some of Trev's good brandy in nothing flat."

And they were. At least his two friends were cozy and sipping brandy. Trevor hired the linkman to take him back to Haverford House. Percy had come from there, and he had called to her, but she had rushed down the steps, around the corner, and into the alley before he could approach. Then that fog had descended. If anyone knew Percy's whereabouts it would be the Duchess of Haverford.

But despite arriving with all possible speed, Her Grace of Haverford would not receive him. She asked him to return tomorrow at two, so he could not imagine she did not want to see him. She would remember Percy. Laughing, smiling, intrepid Percy, defender of the weak, always in search of adventure, and the best friend a lonely boy living on the Welsh border could have had.

Back he went to his friends, to the brandy, and to the fire that would banish the damp chill, and he hoped, any megrims from Percy running away from him. Why had she done it? Had she not recognized him? Possibly. Might there be some other reason? Something associated with the refusal of anyone at home to speak of her? He would have to wait until he met with Her Grace of Haverford tomorrow. Hopefully she would have answers for him.

☙❧

With that sudden fog chasing her, Percy rushed through the kitchen entrance of Haverford House and up the servants' stairs, making her way to the sitting room where most of the members of the *Ladies' Society for the Care of the Widows and Orphans of Fallen Heroes and the Children of Wounded Veterans* still sipped their tea. She burst into the room, praying that she arrived before Trevor.

"Is he here? Did Major PenRhydderch come in? Was he asking for me?"

"PenRhydderch? Do you mean the Earl of Trehallow, Miss Cummins?" Her Grace of Haverford looked over a large embroidery hoop on a stand, her hand suspended in the act of taking a stitch.

"Major PenRhydderch is the earl's brother."

"Hmm," muttered the duchess. "It seems you are not *au courant*. The twentieth Earl, your Major's brother, was killed in a carriage accident six months ago along with his wife and infant son. However, to answer your question, the major has not been here."

Percy suppressed a gasp. "How horrible for him. I'm sorry for his loss, but please, if he should enquire about me, please, Your Grace and ladies, claim that you do not know me and we've never met." It broke her heart to request such a deception, but Trevor was better off not knowing her.

The front door knocker banged loudly.

"Why on earth would we do that?" queried Miss Jessica Grenford, one of Percy's dearest friends.

"Because I ask it of you, and I have never asked anything from any of you."

"That is not sufficient reason for lying, Miss Mary Percival Cummins. Explain yourself," ordered Her Grace.

A knock fell on the parlor door.

"Enter," said her grace.

Percy braced herself.

A Haverford footman entered with silver salver in hand. He walked to the duchess, bowed and extended the salver toward her. "Your Grace."

The duchess took the card from the salver, peered at it for a moment, then returned the card to the salver. "Tell the Earl of Trehallow that I am occupied at present but will be happy to receive him tomorrow at two in the afternoon precisely."

"Yes, Your Grace." The footman straightened and left the room.

Percy released her breath. "Thank you, Your Grace."

"You will note, my dear, that I did not prevaricate. Now sit," The duchess pointed to an empty chair directly opposite her. "Explain, please, why you would ask any of us to deceive the earl."

Percy sat and spent a good while arranging her wool muff in her lap. The silence stretched. She raised her gaze and searched the faces of the women she considered her friends. She saw nothing but polite interest. No judgment, no avid curiosity for gossip. She would have to trust them with her shame.

CHAPTER 2

By the morning of January seventh, Percy was heartily sick of being housebound. Had it not been for the Duchess of Haverford's insistence on sending a half dozen footmen with torches to accompany Percy home the day the fog had begun, she would likely be wandering still or more likely frozen to death.

Hovel though it was, Percy was grateful she had this small shelter, which sat at the end of an anonymous lane in the shadow of Newgate prison. She paced the small square of floor, eyeing the lone window every now and then to see if the rate of snow had slowed. She had missed almost seven days of work as almoner for the Benevolent Pauper's Hospital of the Apostles. In addition, she had missed volunteering after work as aide to the nurses in the section of the hospital given over to wounded military enlisted men.

She had gotten the work through the auspices of Miss Jessica Grenford, a friend from their years at school together, and one of the few people acquainted with her from the past who had not shunned her completely. Jessica had petitioned the Duchess of Haverford, one of the sponsors of the hospital, to find a position for

Percy. The Duchess had insisted upon an interview. It had been one of the most trying times of Percy's life. Almost as bad as the day when her distant cousin had cast her from her home because, he claimed, he could not have a brazen and wanton woman like her near his own sweet and innocent daughters.

But Her Grace of Haverford had been most kind, finding not only the almoner's position for Percy but also this small home, which only took half her salary in rent allowing her to purchase enough food and sundries to sustain her. She owed much to the duchess and her family, so when Percy received Her Grace's invitation to join the *Ladies' Society for the Care of the Widows and Orphans of Fallen Heroes and the Children of Wounded Veterans*, she had not hesitated. However, she had also decided never to put herself forward but to act solely in a supporting role for the great ladies who also belonged to the society.

Another glance at the window showed that the snow finally slowed, permitting a trickle of cloud dimmed light in through the window. "Excellent," Percy said to the black mouser who had taken up residence with her. "I'll get my outdoor things and be off. Do not get into any mischief while I'm gone, Midnight."

The cat yawned and licked a paw.

"Yes, yes, I know. I own nothing from which you could make mischief. Nonetheless, you must heed me, for who knows, some day in the future a miracle will occur, and you and I will reside in a comfortable home with plenty of food and drink for both of us." Her stomach grumbled, as if on cue. She would stop at the bakery and splurge on some day-old bread.

Finally ready to leave, she opened the door and gasped. Her shoulders slumped. Yes, there was light, but snow was piled to mid-thigh height directly in front of her door, with no sign of the stairs, the walkway, or the street. Several yards distant, she saw some enterprising boys with shovels knocking on doors. The wind brought her some of the words said by the nearest lad.

"Clean yer stoop and walk, Missus O'Leary? Only a penny."

The neighbor eyed the boy and the snow and then nodded. "Come and get yer penny when 'tis done." She turned to close the door and saw Percy staring at where the boy had begun to clear away the snow.

"Boy," shouted Percy's neighbor, turning back to wave him forward. He tromped through the path of his earlier footprints. "First, clear the walk and stoop next door, and I'll have two pennies for you. This young lady needs to be about her business, and I ain't goin' out for an hour or so yet."

"Alright, missus." The boy saluted then moved over to clear Percy's walk and stoop.

Percy's eyes watered. "Thank you, Mistress O'Leary."

"Think nothing of it, Dearie. 'Twas you that brought Mister O'Leary the medicine that cured his croup and let him go back to work. I know what you sacrificed to get it too. Getting' yer walk and stoop cleared is the least I can do to say thank you."

"I was happy to do it."

"I know. And I'm happy to return the favor."

It did not take long before Percy was trudging down a cleared pathway in the middle of what was probably her street. The baker had no day-old bread, in fact he had nothing at all to sell. He had been unable to get out to acquire more coal, so the fires that heated his ovens had gone out. He was waiting now for one of his sons to return with enough coal to fire one of the ovens and promised Percy that when she passed by on her way home she could have a fresh loaf of fine white bread for the same price as day old, seeing as how he probably would not have many customers today.

Still hungry, she thanked him and went on her way. It would not be the first time she had had to wait out a full day before she could eat. Assured she would not starve, she ignored the protests of her stomach and hurried on to work.

Despite the snow and the difficulties of traveling about, there was a line of ten men waiting outside the office where she interviewed the sick and injured to determine if they were poor enough to be treated at the Benevolent Pauper's Hospital of the Apostles. She rarely turned anyone away. London had far too many poor, and far too many of those were wounded veterans or the families of dead soldiers. It angered her that a country as wealthy and rich in resources as England would not care for those who sacrificed so much in its defense. She and Her Grace had had many discussions on the topic. Percy liked to believe that those discussions had in part prompted the latest project taken up by the Ladies' Society.

She thought of all this as she opened her office and set about preparing for her first client. Finally ready, she motioned the first man to come in and sit in the chair beside her desk.

"Now, Mister… ?"

"Brunson. Dick Brunson."

She noted the name. "What is your occupation?"

"I ain't got none. I used t' be a soldier in the 37th foot. But I lost me 'and fightin' t' Frenchies. T' army let me go afore me wound was 'ealed proper, and I ain't been able to find work since. Me stump's beginnin' to fester, and I'm afeared for my family. If I die or can't work ever, who'll look after them? Even if you lets me in the 'ospital, what will become of 'em while I'm in 'ere?"

"First we will talk about your needs, then you can give me your family's address, and I shall send someone who can help."

"Ye will, Miss? 'At 'd be ever so kind."

Percy smiled at him. "It is my job, Mr. Brunson. I'm here to help you with your health and any issues that might impact it. Now, can you tell me the name of your commanding officer in the 37th foot?"

And so the interviews went, hour after hour, with the line getting progressively longer then shrinking until around four in the afternoon, with the sun beginning to sink, only two people remained.

Trevor could not believe his eyes. He had found her. He had

watched Percy for over half an hour as she sat in that dim, dank little office interviewing man after man. Documenting their needs and statistics for the hospital staff and sponsors.

"Wot'd y'say Major. Think she'll shut the door on us? It's after four, and the sign says the office closes at four."

If Percy had not changed, she would never shut the door on anyone in need. But what if she had changed? He still did not know what had happened to cause her to end up here as almoner for the hospital.

"Do not worry, Corporal. I'll make certain that we are seen today and not a minute later."

Corporal Ritten's sister had almost waited too long before braving the last of the blizzard to make her way to Major Lord Trehallow's home and ask his help. Her brother needed to have a shrapnel fragment removed from his leg so he could walk well enough to seek work. They had heard that the hospital sometimes treated wounded veterans with little or no income. She wanted to know if the major would be good enough to go with her brother to see the hospital's almoner and smooth the way.

Trevor had been tempted to simply pay for the surgery and nursing during recovery, but the merest hint of such charity would put Ritten's back up. He would not take charity when there was a perfectly good hospital that would take him at little or no cost.

So they stood and waited. Trevor watched his erstwhile friend asking questions and scratching away at paper as the interviewee spoke.

"Excellent, Mr. Longworthy. Come back on Tuesday next with this document." She dusted the paper she had been writing on, handed it to Longworthy and smiled. "Our oral surgeon holds his clinic that day, and he'll be able to tell you if surgery is needed or not, and to recommend treatment for those teeth that bother you."

"Is that all, Miss?"

"Yes sir, Mr. Longworthy. You will get treatment for those teeth, but you must be seen first to have the problem correctly diagnosed."

The man stood and pulled on his forelock. "Thank'ee Miss. I'll put them cold compresses on every day like you told me."

"You're welcome, Mr. Longworthy." She stood and gestured the man out then bent to search in one of the drawers of the small desk.

"Next," she called.

"'At's us, Major."

"Indeed. You first, Corporal."

"But there's only one chair. Majors shouldn't stand when there's a chair."

"Majors always stand when their men are wounded. You're the one with an injured leg that you should not have been standing on for the past hour."

They moved into the office and Ritten sat, heaving a relieved sigh.

Percy had not even looked up after taking more paper from the desk drawer, arranging it neatly to one side, fixing the nib of her pen, dipping the tip thriftily in the inkpot and asking, "Name, please?"

"Corporal William S. Ritten, late of the 25th Lancers."

"And what is the problem, Corporal Ritten?"

"It's me leg, see." He lifted the limb as if to show her.

She looked up, saw Trevor, blinked, then stared.

"Oh 'at's silly of me. Ye can't see through me pants, can ye?" Corporal Ritten smiled.

But he could have been in Timbuktu for all the notice Percy took.

"You?"

"Yes, me."

"How?"

"In my carriage."

"Why?"

"Corporal Ritten has a wound gained in the service of his

country that is not healing properly. The Army will not treat him because he is no longer a soldier."

"I see." She straightened the spectacles resting on the bridge of her nose. "I'm certain Corporal Ritten can speak for himself. But you, sir. In what capacity are you here?"

Why had she not said his name? He had an odd desire to hear *Trevor* from her lips. Did she not wish to acknowledge their friendship? He wanted answers to those and so many more questions. Even Lord Trehallow, his formal title, would be better than a plain 'sir.'

"I asked th' major t' be 'ere, Miss. I'm not sure I can answer all the questions right, and I don't read but a mite. If I 'afta sign summat, th' Major can read it and tell me what I'm signing."

Percy's gaze shifted to the Corporal. "Very wise of you to seek assistance. Now let us see if we can get you some help for your leg."

Trevor studied her as she questioned Ritten. Not once could he detect any sign of condescension or impatience. She acted as if she were conversing with an equal. That much, at least, had not changed. Percy had never stood on ceremony with anyone.

"There," she said. "Finished. All we need now is your signature. I shall send a message round to your home when the surgery is scheduled."

"I'm ever so grateful, Miss. If my leg can be fixed, I can look for work again. M'family's 'bout starved, even though me wife takes in washing when she can get it. This weather's made finding work all but impossible."

"As it happens," Percy said. "I am in need of an assistant." She placed the dry end of her pen against her lips and pursed them in thought.

Trevor stared at her mouth, recalling the one time he had thought of kissing her. Knowing nothing would come of it, he had rejected the idea, thinking that he might frighten her and spoil their friendship. He wished now that he had taken the chance. He covered a shrug by leaning against the nearby wall. He had not kissed her, and regrets now would change nothing. He forced himself to stop maundering and pay attention to Ritten's problem.

"So, if you would be willing to learn to read better, I could hire you at least temporarily to assist me both before and after your surgery."

"I ain't got money for lessons, Miss."

"I would be happy…" Trevor stepped forward to offer payment.

"The hospital will cover the costs of your training, and I would teach you myself, as you will be my assistant. You will be able to apply your lessons all the sooner, if you are in this office with me."

Trevor had to resist dropping his jaw along with Ritten.

"You'd do that for me, Miss?"

"The hospital will do it. I simply represent the hospital in the matter. As almoner, part of my job is to help our clients find work suitable for their abilities. Wounded leg or no, you seem perfectly capable of reading to me."

"I'm ever so grateful. When…"

"What does the position pay," Trevor queried.

Percy named a figure that was reasonable but not excessive.

"It's a good rate, ain't it, Major?"

Percy held the pen parallel to the desk surface both hands clenched in a white-knuckled grip around the stem. She was worried. Why?

"Aye, Ritten." By its lack of excess, the salary named considered the man's pride as well as his more basic needs. "It is an excellent amount, as long as there is promise of more should you prove deserving by your performance."

She gave a quick nod. "Of course. With time and good perfor- mance, Corporal Ritten might even be considered for promotion."

Trevor smiled. "It is the chance of a lifetime, Corporal. Snatch it quick before she takes it back."

"Ye'd not do that to me, Miss. Would ye?"

"Of course not. But you will have to sign some documents." She bent her head and rummaged in one of the desk drawers. "Ah, here they are."

She straightened and placed a small stack of paper on the desk surface. "You may take these with you. The Major can help you with reading and completing the documents. Bring them back at eight o'clock on Monday next. As long as all is in order, you may start work then."

Corporal Ritten stood as straight as he could and snapped a salute. "I'll be here, Miss. Thank you."

"You are most welcome, Corporal."

"Ritten, wait for me in the carriage. I would like to thank your benefactress privately."

The corporal gave one glance from Trevor to Percy. "Aye, Sir," he said, then limped out of the building.

Trevor opened his pocket watch to check the time. "It is well past your closing time. We've kept you over long. May I offer to see you home?"

"That is not necessary."

"Perhaps not, but dark is falling and London at night is no place for a respectable woman. Unless you have another escort, I must insist."

She pressed her lips together and stared at him for a long moment. "Very well. I'll join you as soon as I've cleared my desk and donned my outer clothes."

"I'll wait." He was not about to let her out of his sight without knowing where and how to find her again. He and Percy Cummins had unfinished business, though she did not know it. He would learn what happened to her, and then hopefully persuade her to become his wife. Barring that, he would insist she allow him to help her resolve whatever trouble had befallen her.

Percy settled herself on the rear-facing seat opposite Corporal Ritten.

"Are ye joining us, then, Miss?"

"The Major insisted on escorting me home."

The door opened and Trevor stuck his head inside the coach. "I'll need your direction, Miss Cummins."

She did not want him knowing where she lived. She shook her head and dropped her gaze to her fingers clenched in her lap. She dared not look at him. One glance at the concern in his deep brown eyes might have her betraying all good sense and throwing herself into his arms to weep out her troubles. He would feel honor bound to solve all her problems. She could not allow that.

"For the coachman," he continued.

"Haverford House," she blurted. She did not have to go inside, and if Trevor insisted on seeing her as far as the foyer, she would let him. The footmen were all familiar with her comings and goings. No one would question her if she left through the kitchen the minute Trevor left through the front door.

But Robert Burns had been right in his poetic address To a Mouse, "The best laid schemes o' mice and men, gang aft agley." Her plans went awry the moment she crossed the threshold. There, in the midst of the foyer, stood Jessica and the duchess herself.

"Trehallow, my lad," the duchess said. Jessica followed, crossing to where Trevor and Percy stood just inside the now closed front door. "What a pleasant surprise, and you've brought our Miss Cummins back home with you. We had begun to worry about you, dear." The duchess—who did not prevaricate—lied through her teeth. "Go on up and change. We shall wait dinner until you come down."

Jess took Percy by the arm and compelled her to walk to the stairs. There she spoke a few quiet words to a nearby footman. Percy was being whisked away up the stairs before she could blink. What was Her Grace thinking?

"You will join us for dinner, Trehallow. I insist," Her Grace decreed.

"Then I could not possibly refuse. I'm so…"

Percy followed the footman around a turn in the stairs and the rest of Trevor's words were lost.

Moments later, over her protests that some mistake had been made, the footman opened the door to a large cheery chamber with striped hangings on the walls and bed. A chest of drawers and a nook holding a small desk lined one wall. A huge wardrobe occupied most of the other wall and windows marched across the far end. The drapes were drawn against the chill of the winter night and a fire burned in the grate.

Percy had scarcely taken in the furnishings and the thick paisley carpet on the floor when the door opened and two women entered. Each of them carried a stack of fabric that together were nearly as tall as Percy herself. They set the material down on the bed and she saw that the piles were made of dresses, lingerie, stockings, gloves and shawls with assorted other garments thrown in.

"I am Her Grace's dresser," said a woman with posture even more regal than that of the duchess. The dresser gestured to the other woman, just barely out of her teens. "This is Jenks. She'll act as your maid while you are in residence. You may address all questions about the household to her, and, if any difficulty arises, do not hesitate to call upon me or the housekeeper."

Jenks curtsied. "So pleased to meet you, Miss Cummins."

"If there is nothing else, Miss?" asked the dresser.

Percy swallowed and shook her head.

"Then I will leave you. Jenks will show you the way to the main stairway as soon as you are ready to join the rest of the party." A soft but final sounding click followed the dresser's departure.

"If you're ready, Miss, we brought a lovely burgundy lace over cream satin gown. I'll arrange your hair with velvet ribbons that match the lace. It will be ever so lovely with your dark blonde hair, milk white skin, beautiful blue eyes."

Percy stared at the maid as she approached.

"Here, let me help you out of that day dress."

Grateful for Jenks' chatter, Percy allowed herself to be twisted this way and that. She listened with only half an ear, turning most of her attention to the predicament she was in and how to extricate herself.

Her Grace of Haverford could not possibly want to house a woman of Percy's reputation. She eyed the stacks of clothing on the bed. Nor could Her Grace want to give all of those clothes away. Even if Percy could afford them, she had no place to keep them, nor the means to maintain them. The fabrics, delicate and elegant, were totally inappropriate for work, so she had no place to wear such riches.

She sighed. Until she could speak alone with the duchess and learn her intent, Percy could do nothing. She focused instead on the ordeal of dining with people who would no doubt give her the cut direct if she were not a guest of the Duchess of Haverford.

CHAPTER 3

The following afternoon, Trevor handed Percy down from James's sleigh to the straw-strewn entrance to Hyde Park with Miss Jessica Grenford and James following. The promenade had been cleared of snow, and straw spread to prevent walkers from slipping on any remaining icy patches. The snow had been piled head high on either side of the path wide enough for four people to walk abreast. The end result blocked most of what watery sunlight filtered through the clouds and gave the effect of treading behind the earthworks on a battlefield.

Behind them, Miss Jessica whispered loudly, "James, you know our purpose here is to keep each other distracted so that Trehallow and Miss Cummins may become reacquainted."

James replied, though Trevor could not hear what he was saying. A quick glance behind showed the other couple falling back enough that conversation could be private but the proprieties would be maintained.

He and Percy walked in silence nearly half the length of the promenade, the only sounds coming from the crunch of straw on the frozen ground beneath their feet and the low murmur of the other couple's voices.

He wanted to ask her what happened. Why she had become this silent almost shy person, when that was so alien to the lively, curious, intrepid Percy he remembered. But he could not find the words.

"How have you been, Percy?" was all he could manage.

"Well enough with the duchess's patronage."

Was she completely dependent on the duchess? That would not sit well with the Percy he had known. "I was sorry to hear of your parents' passings. That must have been a very difficult time for you."

She shrugged. "I prefer not to speak of it."

So she would not talk about her family. "How did you come to know the Duchess of Haverford?"

"Jessica and I were at school together. She insisted I come to her and the Duchess after… after my father died. Mother was too ill to travel, so I came by myself. Her Grace has been all that is kind and helpful. Mother remained at Cummins House under the care of my cousin Donald. I hoped she was well cared for, since I could not be there to see to her comfort myself."

Which implied that, without the Haverford's help, Percy might not have been able to provide for her mother at all.

"I am very sorry I was not there to help, Percy. But surely your cousin gave you and your mother a home?"

Percy looked at him, her expression hard, her lips pressed together. "As I said earlier, it is not a time I care to discuss. You, too, have suffered great losses. You must miss your brother and his family terribly. I am very sorry for your loss."

"You well know that Edmund and I did not agree on much of anything. I was as glad to go off to the army as he was to see me go. But that does not mean I do not miss him, Belinda and the babe, whom I never got to meet. They were the last of my family, and I miss that terribly. Especially at this time of year. Why did you run away when I called to you last week?"

He had not meant to ask her, not now, not like that. Not when he was vulnerable and swamped with painful memories. But his mouth had spoken the words without his brain giving the order. It had been his heart, that bruised and almost broken organ, that needed to cling to some shred of the life he once knew.

She did not speak.

He waited, then waited some more.

"I did not want you to know where I was."

He was glad she had not tried to lie, to attempt a false innocence. Glad she had not said something like, "Why, I do not know what you're talking about. Until you brought Corporal Ritten to the hospital, I had not thought of you in more than three years."

"Why?" he asked. "You've no family. I've no family. We were friends once, as close as friends can be to being family. Did you think I had forgotten?"

"No." She shook her head and looked off into the distance, then down at the ground, anywhere but directly at him.

"Do you wish I had?"

That brought her head up, and she paused in mid-stride, turning to face him. "No, never. After… after father died, I wished for you almost every day. For the one person I knew would understand."

"You still had your mother then."

Percy started to walk again. "She was ill. It was all I could do to comfort her. Most of the time I could not."

"Your mother was the warmest of women. How is it possible she could not get comfort from her own daughter?"

Again, a long silence.

"I would really rather not talk about this."

"Please." He halted them both. "I need to know, Percy. What happened? Why are you in London? Why did you not marry that man—Baron Blanchard—as your father had arranged? Why are you not home in Deebridge? Why could you not comfort your mother?"

She uttered a bitter laugh. "So many questions. I must think carefully so I do not get the answers mixed up."

Now he shook his head. "They all have the same answer, do they not?"

She tilted her head to look at him. "You figured that out, did you?"

"Yes. Whatever happened to you was life changing. You are Percy, my good friend, and the woman I, ahem, respect and admire most in the world, but you are also different. You are quiet, as if some spell had been cast that leached all the vibrant, intrepid, curious life from you and left you a shell of your former self."

That bitter laugh again. "You are still the same blunt Trevor. You never would let me get away with any deception I tried to pull on you. Yes, you are right. I am a changed woman. I have to be."

"Why?"

"I cannot, will not tell you now. It is too personal to speak of when we are in company." She glanced at where Jess stood tittering at something James said. "It would cast a pall over the day, and our friends do not deserve that."

"I understand." He wished he did not. "But you will tell me."

"Yes."

"When?"

"Monday. I've a half day and can speak with you in the afternoon."

"At Haverford House?"

She swallowed. "Yes. I can ask Her Grace for permission to be private with you for the few minutes it will take to tell my tale."

She was so woebegone, her tone colorless and flat. He wanted nothing more than to take her in his arms and croon away her woes. But only a husband, brother, or father could do that. "Then I will wait until Monday."

"Come on, you two," Jessica called. "I swear my extremities are frozen. Let us go home and have some hot tea. I know cook made orange scones this morning."

"I remember those orange scones as if it were yesterday." Trevor smiled. "They are delicious. I also remember that Aldridge once told me how you ate so many you made yourself sick." He and Percy rejoined their friends.

"I was six."

"I suppose you think that is an excuse," James remarked, a smile on his face.

"No," Jessica laughed. "But it is an explanation."

They returned to the sleigh. Trevor handed the ladies up and followed his friend onto the rear facing seat.

Jessica continued to chatter, but Percy fell silent. He studied her whenever expressing polite interest allowed him to let his gaze drift over her.

She looked like his friend, the Percy he had known growing up, yet she did not. His friend had possessed an inner fire, a view of the world that saw excitement, adventure, and joy in every-thing from the smallest flower to the grandest landscape. She had had no trouble and taken much pleasure in sharing that enthu-siasm with everyone she met. This woman, this Percy, kept her expression carefully blank. She held herself stiffly, as if afraid of some sort of attack, and never, never—in the few days since they had become reacquainted—put herself or an idea forward without being directly addressed. She had promised to tell him what had happened, but would it make any difference? No matter how terrible, he believed nothing could make him think less of her. He wanted his old Percy back, but had not a clue how to help her.

After braving sporadic snow showers and the hazards of icicles two feet long or more, Trehallow was ushered into a small sitting room at Haverford House that Monday, but only Her Grace occupied the room. Tea was laid out before her.

"Your Grace. I am given to understand that Miss Cummins is not yet returned from her work at the hospital."

"That is so, Trehallow, my boy. Sit down and have some tea. I have a number of things to discuss with you."

"I'm honored, Your Grace, but perhaps I should take my sleigh and go to fetch Miss Cummins. If the delay is due to the impassible streets, that is."

"It is not. I have no notion what has delayed Miss Cummins, but I have already sent a sleigh with the supplies she requested and three footmen to assist her. I assure you, she is safe and well, which is all that good manners requires you to know." The duchess spoke evenly as she poured tea and handed him the cup and saucer. However, reproof was clear in her expression when she gazed at him as he took the saucer from her hand.

What could he possibly have done to offend one of the most influential women of the *ton,* and how could he fix it? He was used to charging into battle, even when his regiment appeared to be outnumbered, so, best to be frank. He doubted he could outmaneuver a social general as expert as Her Grace. "Have I offended in some way, Your Grace? If so, I most humbly apologize."

She smiled at him. "I always knew you were a good boy. Kind from the moment your mother lifted you from your cradle."

There, she had managed to tell him he had been behaving childishly and compliment him at the same time. "You are very kind to say so. I was unaware that you knew my mother."

"I was acquainted with her through your maternal Aunt Geraldine. She and I made our come out the same year."

He had fond memories of his aunt and her husband, Admiral Scattergood. He had not seen them in more than a decade, the admiral being posted to the West Indies. "Aunt Geraldine is a favorite of mine. Had she been here, I might have been more *au courant* and thus avoided gaining your disfavor. Since that is not the case, may I know the nature of my offense?"

Her Grace sipped her tea, taking her time.

His neck cloth shrank as he waited. He wanted nothing more than to run a finger along the inner edge to loosen the abruptly tight linen.

"In truth, it is not so much me personally whom you have offended as Miss Cummins. Since she is not here, and I stand some-what *in loco parentis* to her, I have decided, with her limited permission, to confront the problem for her and save her any distress."

"I am glad she has such a friend in you. The last thing I would wish for her is distress of any sort."

"Hmm." The duchess sipped.

He followed suit, waiting for her next move.

"Yet, I believe you have caused Miss Cummins much distress in the past three days."

"It was never my intention to do so."

"Nonetheless. The young lady returned in a conflicted state from her outing with you, Jessica, and Strathnaver's son, James."

"If I caused that, I am most heartily sorry."

"Good, I hope you will tell her so yourself, when you attend the theater with us on the twenty sixth for Keane's debut performance as Shylock. I have seen him in the provinces, and we are in for a treat."

"It will be my pleasure to do so. Yet, I am not quite clear about the offence for which I am apologizing."

"As to that, I have Miss Cummins's permission to suggest that you not press her to reveal the events of the past three years that have led to her residence at Haverford House."

Yet Percy had promised to tell him. As far as he knew, Percy had never gone back on a promise. This had to be a plea for more time. Because he loved her, he would give her all the time in the world.

"Your Grace, you must know that Percy, er, Miss Cummins and I have been friends from the cradle."

"Yes, yes, my boy, I'm aware. Your estates share a boundary in a somewhat isolated corner of Wales near the river Dee. Naturally, children of gentry and nobility would become friends in such circumstances. However, as her friend, I am surprised you insisted on asking forceful questions about a time in her life when you were not present."

His neck heated, and the cravat all but strangled him. Her Grace stressed *not present* as if he had committed a crime for choosing to serve his country rather than see the woman he loved wed to someone else. He sipped his tea to regain his composure. "You are right, I presumed too much upon our past friendship. I do indeed owe Miss Cummins an apology."

"Excellent. I thought you might see reason. Now, as to the second matter I wish to discuss. What precisely are your intentions toward Miss Cummins?"

The duchess's question should not have surprised him, yet it caught him off guard. He had not thought his interest in Percy so obvious, but then the duchess was known for her keen perception. He had been in company with Her Grace and Miss Cummins at dinner the other night, and he had been seated beside Percy at the table. Her Grace had been several seats distant at the foot of the table, but she must have seen something that he hoped no one else had. "I have the utmost respect and affection for Miss Cummins. In fact, I hope to offer for her hand in marriage as soon as possible."

One brow rose. "Your affections are engaged that deeply?"

"They have been for some time, but circumstance prevented me speaking before now."

"Ah. More tea?"

"No, thank you, Your Grace." He set his cup aside.

"I gather you wished to wed Miss Cummins before her engagement was announced three years ago."

"That is true. I hesitated too long, and when I learned of the betrothal, I could not honorably speak."

"A mark of a true gentleman."

"Do you know what happened? Obviously, Miss Cummins did not marry."

"It is not my story to tell, Trehallow. Though, if you intend to propose, I will encourage Miss Cummins to confide in you before you ask. Once you hear the tale, you may decide not to offer for her."

He found himself offended at the thought that he would place past events over a life-long friendship. "I can imagine nothing that would change my mind."

"Yes, well. Apparently you could not imagine that demanding answers of an old friend would be offensive."

"I take your point."

"Excellent. Then take this one as well. Miss Cummins is of age, but that does not mean she has no one to look out for her. If she should accept your proposal, I ask that you speak with Aldridge regarding the settlements."

"I thank you and him in advance. I would not wish Miss Cummins to have to deal with that."

"Oh, do not get me wrong. She has a level head for business matters and is well able to look after herself. One of the reasons she was offered the position of almoner at the hospital is her ability with accounts and management. She was well trained, better than most young women her age. However, both Aldridge and I have become fond of her, and somewhat protective, since she lost her parents."

"I am glad she has such caring friends. Is there anything else?"

"Only a request that you not propose before our Venetian Breakfast on February third. Miss Cummins is an essential person in this current project of our Ladies' Society. She might refuse simply on the grounds that she would not wish to disappoint us when we are counting on her. Now that I think about it, the project, which involves improving the lives of our neglected veterans and the dependents of our valiant deceased, might interest you."

"I am not certain…"

"Tut tut. I will not hear any objections. Think of it as a means for attracting Miss Cummins's interest. You do know her brother died at Salamanca?"

"No, I knew he fell in battle, but not which one."

"Then you can see why this project is not only essential to the good of the nation but also to Miss Cummins's personal well-being. I will send word as soon as I know exactly when your assistance is required."

"I am happy to be of service to you and to such a good cause. I think, too, I would be a fool not to take the advice you so generously give. Since the welfare of the men I fought with and their families is a topic dear to my heart, I am happy to assist where I may and would not think of taking Miss Cummins away from such excellent work. I've waited more than three years, Your Grace. Another few weeks is not too much to ask. It will give me more time to lay the foundation for my proposal."

"An excellent notion, Trehallow. Now, I have much to do before this evening's entertainment, so you had best be about your business."

He took his leave, wondering as he waited for the sleigh to be brought round, exactly how best to convince Percy that she wanted to marry him. One large obstacle stood in his path. The past three years, and the events therein that had led to Percy's present circumstances. Planning a strategy for any campaign was deucedly difficult, if one did not know the lay of the land. He had until February third. He would have to spend those days easing his way back into the comfortable friendship he and Percy had once shared. But how best to do that? The project the duchess spoke of would help, for it was another link between him and Percy.

CHAPTER 4

W ith a scant two hours remaining before Her Grace, family and all guests sat to dinner, Percy told the coachman to let her off at the kitchen gate of Haverford House. It was closer to the mews, and she might be able to get to her chamber without confronting any of the family. Much as she loved Jess, and grateful as she was to Her Grace and her family, she found being in company stressful. She never knew when someone who had heard of her indiscretion would snub her or, worse, make snide comments designed to hurt and belittle.

Had it not been for Jessica's insistence—and Her Grace's machinations—Percy would never have dared show her face in London, let alone take up residence at Haverford House. She had resisted the suggestion most strongly when she had first come to London and sat discussing her very limited choices over tea with Jessica, Matilda, and Her Grace.

Percy made her way up the servants' stairs to the third floor and the bedchamber she had been assigned. She had the duchess to thank for her position at the hospital and for the Newgate house as well as the generously low rent. She had been allowed to keep her pride by paying her own way and at the same time put a pittance away toward her future. This business of residing at Haverford House and giving nothing in return for her board and keep must stop. She could not bear to be the object of pity, charitable or otherwise.

However, the duchess had thus far evaded every attempt at a private conversation, and the longer Percy stayed at Haverford House, the more difficult leaving would be. She would have to enlist Jessica's help. No one was better than her friend at creating devious plans designed to outwit the cleverest of opponents. And Her Grace was more clever than most.

Removing her outer garments, Percy moved to the charming vanity, where she took the pins from her hair and massaged her aching scalp. Between today's crisis at the hospital and the diffi-cult ride home, she was worn to the bone. She could plead a very real headache and request a tray in her room to avoid dinner. But how ungrateful that would be. She picked up her hair brush to stroke away as much of the day's stress as possi-ble, then she would lie down for just a few minutes. Jenks would wake her when it was time to dress for the evening meal.

"Percy, Percy, wake up."

The mattress jounced and jiggled in time with the sound of Jessica's voice.

"Nooo, I need to rest." She rolled away from the gleam cast by whatever light her friend had brought into the room.

"You can rest later." Jess pulled at Percy's shoulder. "I have the most exciting news."

Percy kept her eyes closed. "Whatever it is, I am sure it can wait until after dinner. For now, I just want to rest."

"I suppose a proposal of marriage could wait, but I do not see why. Please, Percy, I simply have to tell you."

Percy struggled upright, planting her hands behind her on the mattress to keep herself from yielding to exhaustion. Jessica's energy was draining what little vitality Percy had managed to recover in the few moments she had been asleep.

"Never tell me Driscoll has spoken to Aldridge and gained his approval."

Jess rolled her eyes. "Nothing so silly as that. Even if Driscoll had honorable intentions, which he does not, you know I would never accept. The man is a dirty shirt."

"Then who is it? You flirt with half of London, Jessica."

"And none of them propose. Though part of that might be they are all frightened of my very ducal half-brother. It is most amusing to see him interrupt his own profligate activities to come the proper guardian and defend me against his fellow reprobates."

"Hmmm." Percy scrubbed one hand across her eyes. "When you put it that way, I can see the charm of the activity. However, if no one is proposing for you, then what are you talking about. Is Hamner asking for Matilda?"

"Not Matilda, silly. You."

Percy leapt from the bed as if it were on fire. "What in the world are you talking about? I do not know any gentlemen well enough for one of them to propose, and none of my few male acquaintances would be foolish enough to ask for my hand. Especially once they know the cause of my lost reputation, which I would tell any suitor, since it is only right that a man with marriage on his mind knows exactly what he is getting into with me as a wife."

"But it is true. I overheard Her Grace discussing it with the gentleman just this afternoon."

A chill ran down Percy's spine. She knew of only one gentleman who was supposed to call this afternoon. Of course, it could have been someone else. It had to have been someone else. "You've been eavesdropping again."

"Well, how else is one to learn anything worth knowing? Besides, it is not my fault if someone left the door between the small parlor and the library open."

"Jessica, I love you most dearly. However, if you do not learn to respect the privacy of others, you will come to a bad end. I'm sure of it." She moved across the room to stare out the window where snowflakes drifted throughout the night.

"Well, I am not so certain. Are you not in the least curious to know who is planning to propose to you?"

Wrapping her shawl about her to ward off the chill from the window, Percy sighed. "It could only be one person."

"You know? You knew all along that Trehallow plans to propose? Why have you not shared this news?"

She gave Jess a level stare. "Because I did not know, and I am completely taken aback that he would consider marriage with me. But then, I'm fairly certain he does not know what happened to cause me to leave Wales." She turned back to the window, seeing in her mind's eye the confusion and hurt on Trevor's face when she refused to confide in him. He had gotten her promise to tell him all today, and she would keep that promise, delayed though it might be by weather and circumstance. "He will change his mind once he learns the truth."

Jess rose and took Percy by the hand. "Come sit by the fire; you'll catch a chill standing by the window for so long. Sit, and tell me why Trehallow must learn the truth, as you call it."

"Because any man deserves to know the background and history of the woman he considers asking to be his wife."

"Nonsense."

"No, not nonsense. A marriage based on deceit is doomed to failure, and hiding a truth is as much a deception as a lie."

"I cannot agree with you."

"Nonetheless, it is true, and I'll not waste my breath arguing with you." Nor would she allow Trevor to waste any more time imagining that she would be a good match for him. She would send a note to him—his townhouse was just down the street—requesting that he come to Haverford House for tea. She could offer to show him the Long Gallery and give him the truth there.

"Excellent. Such an argument would put us firmly at odds

because I do not agree with you. Nor do I believe that His Lordship is the sort of man who would care a tuppence for what others think. He was your friend once. Your dear friend, as I recall. You told me of him when we were in school."

"Yes, he was a friend but never more than that. He was a second son lacking any expectations, and my father would not have welcomed Trevor's suit. That never became an issue, because Trevor never asked for my hand. Nor did he at any time indicate feelings more tender for me than those appropriate to a dear friend of long-standing."

"Perhaps not. From all I hear, he is a true gentleman. As such, he would not have wished to distress you or cause discord between you and your father."

Percy smiled. "Trevor was always kind to everyone around him, and very thoughtful. It is one of the traits that I am certain made him an excellent officer. But kind or not, friend or not, I am not a suitable wife for a belted earl."

"Hmph." Jess flounced from her chair to the door. "Much you know about it. I'll wager my best bonnet you're wrong, and the two of you will be wed by March." She opened the door to leave. "Well?"

"I would take that wager, had I the means to pay on the very odd chance that I lost. Now go away. Jenks will be here any moment to help me dress for dinner."

"I will, but if you are not wed to the earl by March first, I'll give you that bonnet anyway. You'll need something as consolation."

Percy smiled despite the small ache in her heart, and waved her friend away before turning to stare into the flames.

Her heart should not hurt at all, knowing that soon Trevor would think as badly of her as the rest of the *ton*. There had been a time, before she had learned of the arranged match with Baron Blanchard, when she had daydreamed of marrying. More often than not, the someone who figured most prominently in those daydreams had been Trevor. She had known then that they would never make a match of it. More reasons than ever stood between them now. She must quash ruthlessly any small hope that Jessica's nonsense had fostered.

❧

Her Grace's summons arrived with Trevor's morning post on Wednesday, January twelfth. For that day, she requested he devote the afternoon to escorting Miss Cummins to a variety of locations where they would interview veterans for positions in households throughout the *ton* and businesses throughout London. Her Grace also included a list of other tasks, each with the date and time he was expected to escort Percy on her missions. Her Grace was giving him plenty of opportunities to fix his interests with Percy. He had hopes that, after days of time spent with his love, Percy might be willing to consider his proposal when the Duchess's restriction expired.

She was on the outer stairs of the building when Trevor arrived, with her maid Jenks in tow to preserve the proprieties. One look at his friend's face told him something troubled her greatly. Nonetheless, she allowed him to hand her up into the carriage.

"I told Her Grace that an escort was completely unnecessary on this occasion."

"I am happy to help and certain that the Duchess had good reason to provide you with an escort."

"Yes, she mentioned something about having a gentleman with military experience adding weight to any offer of employment for veterans."

"She is right to think so. Our veterans are proud of their service to their country and used to doing for themselves. Without assurance from an officer—even one who sold out—many men would see the opportunities you offer as little more than thinly disguised pity. This is especially true of those men with permanent injuries or disfigurements."

"I am well aware of the sensibilities of such men. I deal with them and their pride every day at the hospital without assistance from any man."

She might as well have said without any assistance from you.

"And you handle those men very well, as I observed when you interviewed Corporal Ritten. Speaking of the corporal, how is he working out as your assistant?"

"Excellently, considering that due to the weather he has only been employed for two days. His ability to remember the smallest detail more than compensates for what he lacks in reading and writing skills. His experience as a soldier gives him credibility with applicants. He is a God-send, allowing me to take time from my position as almoner to perform tasks for the Ladies's Society."

"And you have just proven Her Grace's point. Having a soldier with you lends credibility to your offer. I will also point out that the men who apply to you at the hospital come to you. They've already made the decision to seek help. Many of those we will interview together will have to be convinced that we have their best interests at heart."

A small line formed between her brows. "You have a valid point, which makes accepting your escort a trifle easier. Nonetheless, I am sure you have better things to do than dance attendance on me and two or three dozen veterans a day for the next week or two."

He relaxed against the squabs, grateful that she was not going to resent his presence. "Truth be told, I have been at loose ends since returning to town and am grateful to Her Grace for finding me an occupation, one which is dear to my heart. I find myself furious with the government every time I learn of a former soldier going without shelter, food, or adequate clothing."

"Your sentiments do you credit, my lord. Perhaps when the time comes you will consider putting your title behind the bill that is being drafted. Aldridge believes he has found someone to propose it, since he is not yet in the House of Lords."

"Please, call me Trevor?"

She cast a glance at Jenks who appeared for all the world to be asleep. "It would not be proper."

He acknowledged her concern by lowering his voice. "It is perfectly proper for friends to call each other by their first names. Are you saying we are no longer friends?"

"Of course not. I treasure the memories of our childhood friendship, but we are no longer children."

"We were not children the day you told me of your engagement. You used my first name then. 'Oh Trevor,' you said. 'I have the most exciting news.'"

She looked out the window for a long time. "Now that you've brought it up. I suppose you would like me to honor my promise and tell you what happened three years ago, even though the day of the promise is passed."

He took her hand. As she had done on the day they had walked in Hyde Park, she did not withdraw it. "Only if you wish to tell me. I was wrong to press you as I did. I apologize for causing you the slightest distress."

She withdrew her hand. "Perhaps another time.

A quick glance at Jenks showed the maid to be wide-awake.

"Of course. You need never speak of it if that is what you wish."

The sleigh pulled up at their first stop, and the conversation was suspended.

CHAPTER 5

On the afternoon of January eighteenth, Percy waited for Trevor at the entrance to the hospital. Why, oh why, had Her Grace seen fit to force him on her? It was not as if Trevor was the only gentleman available to act as escort. The duchess was related to half of England and godmother to the other half. She knew plenty of gentlemen who could fill the bill. What could she possibly hope to gain? Her Grace was known to manipulate people when she thought there would be some benefit. But nothing good could come of keeping Percy and Trevor together.

The past days had been excruciatingly awkward for Percy. Trevor and Jenks would arrive promptly at one o'clock to collect her. She and Trevor would exchange insubstantial pleasantries until enough interviews had been conducted that discussion of her work would occupy the remainder of the day. Every now and then, as happened today, Trevor would compare the circumstances of the widows, orphans, and veterans to events in battle or, oddly, their shared childhood.

"It strikes me," he said, as they returned to the carriage—Jenks having preceded them—"That the children in that family are as lonely and neglected as you and I were."

"Yes. Their mother must work, which leaves the older child—not that six is very old—to care for the younger ones. Our only disadvantage was that our brothers were much older and could not be companions in our youth. However, we had a definite advantage with living in the country and financial security that those poor folk have never had."

"So, you understand how insecure the lot of enlisted families can be."

"Without a doubt. My brother often wrote of the difficulties of the enlisted men, and we would send what assistance we could manage. My mother or I would write to our female friends among the *ton* in London. Jessica brought the problem to the attention of Her Grace."

"This project that so occupies the Ladies' Society is one of fairly long standing."

"Indeed. Gathering statistics and verifiable anecdotal information to support our efforts in the political arena has occupied most of my time for the last three years, the rest of the ladies being occupied with other aspects of our project." She leaned forward as she warmed to her topic. "Too much time has been required to document and enumerate the problems of widows, orphans and veterans. But I have completed my part of the task, and the duchess has turned over the compilation of my data to others on the committee. When all our documents and petitions are ready, Aldridge will find someone to sponsor a bill in parliament. The bill will address the issue in a more permanent way than can be done, even with the large sums the Ladies' Society has been able to and continues to raise. Once the bill is before parliament, we will be able to move on to other projects where the need is just as great or..." She let her words trail off, for Trevor was smiling at her.

She frowned, straightened, and cast him a warning glare. "Tell me, pray, what is amusing about our activities?"

The smile disappeared. "Nothing. Nothing about the poverty and squalor among the veterans and the dependents of our deceased heroes is at all amusing."

"Then what causes you to smile?"

The corners of his mouth lifted. "I smile because I am happy. Your enthusiasm makes me happy. You've not been so vocal about any subject since the day I took Corporal Ritten to your office. How is he, by the way? He has not contacted me for help."

She relaxed a bit. Confused by the cause of his happiness, she gratefully put it aside to examine in the privacy of her chamber at Haverford House. "The Corporal is doing very well. He picks up reading as if he were a sponge. He is very careful with the formation of his letters, which means his writing is slower than is useful at present. However, he shall have plenty of time to practice after his surgery in mid-February."

Trevor frowned. "That long from now? Could it not be arranged sooner?"

"I understand your feelings, but other cases truly are more urgent than his. In addition, the weather has created a backlog due to the impassibility of the roads throughout England. Deliveries of supplies have been delayed, and medical staff prevented from traveling. Since Corporal Ritten has waited this long without doing permanent damage to his leg, it was agreed that his procedure could wait several weeks."

"Have precautions been taken to prevent further injury and infection?"

"Absolutely. He sees a nurse before relieving me at work every day. Otherwise, I would not allow him to work." She smiled. The Corporal's success was a visible reminder of the benefits the Ladies' Society project would produce. Being part of that gave Percy no little satisfaction.

"Just as well then. His family needs the income, and he needs to feel like the provider he is."

"Do not worry for him, Trehallow. He is eager to learn and diligent. He'll have many opportunities once his work for me is recognized." She sat back, falling silent as the coach approached Haverford House. Corporal Ritten needed the work and could replace her as almoner. All she had to do was to decide whether to leave or stay in London. If she remained, she would have to find new employment, and she had no idea where or how to do so. She hated applying to Her Grace again, but what other recourse did she have? No reputable agency would accept her resume, and without some sort of connection, no employer would be bothered to interview her. Perhaps using her savings to buy passage on a ship bound for the West Indies might be best.

"Do you plan to spend the evening in the sleigh?"

She blinked, turning her head to see Trevor holding out his hand to help her down and escort her inside. "I'm sorry."

She accepted his assistance.

"Think nothing of it. You fell into a brown study for a bit there, and I had not the heart to disturb your thoughts."

After he assisted Jenks from the sleigh, Percy took his arm up the stairs and into the foyer. "That is very thoughtful of you, your lordship. But then, you always were thoughtful."

"Not enough so, evidently, or you would not continue to '*my lord*' me."

She rolled her eyes and smiled. "One has nothing to do with the other. I challenge you to give me one good reason why I should be less formal with you than I am with any other gentleman."

He blinked at her as the butler removed her cloak and took her bonnet and gloves.

"Have I rendered you speechless?" she asked.

He swallowed and shook his head but did not speak.

"Perhaps when I see you tomorrow, you will have found your ability to speak and dreamed up a response." She laid a hand on his cheek before turning away and mounting the stairs. "Goodnight, Lord Trehallow.

Trevor's gaze followed her until she disappeared around a turn in the staircase. She had smiled, like the Percy he had known of old. Not just now, but in the carriage. And she had been positively beautiful when describing what had been done, what was being done, what needed to be done to help the veterans and dependents of deceased heroes.

He had wondered with the first smile if she was beginning to thaw, if his intrepid Percy was beginning to emerge from hiding. Now he was certain. It augured well for his hope to make her his wife.

"I see you are smitten." Aldridge's drawl broke into Trevor's thoughts.

He turned to face the Marquis. "And what if I am?"

"It is nothing to me." He gave an elegant shrug. "But if you distress the young lady again, you will upset my mother and my sister. That in turn shall upset me to the point where I might be called upon to teach you a lesson—a painful one."

Trevor, equal in height and breadth to Aldridge though a couple of years younger, looked him up and down as if inspecting a subaltern. "You might find that more difficult than you imagine. I know a great deal more about fighting and self-defense than when I was a school-boy."

"Neither of us is a child, Trehallow. Any fight between us would be settled as adults. But let us hope it does not come to that." Aldridge laid an arm across Trevor's shoulders. "What say you join me for a pleasant evening of cards and lovely women?"

Trevor shook his head. "I am honored by the invitation, but I find of late that such activities hold little interest for me."

The Marquis raised a brow. "You are indeed smitten. Make certain to see me about the settlements before you make an offer."

"I've promised your mother not to speak before the day of her Venetian Breakfast."

"Just about two weeks from now. When you are ready, send round the name of your solicitor."

"I shall." Trevor bowed and wished the Marquis good night.

"And a good night to you as well."

Less than two weeks. Was there enough time? He had best send for his solicitor and perhaps examine the Trehallow family jewels. If nothing there was suitable for Percy, he would have to visit a jeweler and all of that took time.

CHAPTER 6

He saw her for each of the next eight days, except for the nineteenth, when the snow fell so heavily it threatened to destroy most of the roofs in London. They had been to visit widows, lancers, hussars, grenadiers, orphans whose mothers had also died or simply given up their children out of desperation to those who offered food, shelter, and clothing. They spoke with relatives, pastors, government, and military officials who had the processing of any small benefits due to the veterans and the dependents.

Some of those he and Percy tried to help were grateful. An equal number were too proud to accept obvious help and a delicate dance of persuasive language was required to lead those stiff-rumped veterans and widows to the blessings that could be had with the assistance of the Ladies' Society.

By the twenty-first they had cleared all but a few names from the lengthy list of those in need. Before he left to collect Percy that day, Her Grace sent over a note and two pairs of ice skates—one for a man, one smaller for a woman. "Take Miss Cummins skating on the Serpentine. Jessica, Matilda, Hamner, and a party of other young people will join you. Send Jenks home and have your sleigh return for you."

Lord above, Her Grace was a managing old girl, but he had to thank her. She was handing him a chance to steal a few private moments with Percy.

The afternoon had been splendid, despite an occasional snow shower. Percy had been reluctant at first, then, after he showed her the note, his beloved became increasingly eager. Once out on the ice with a group of friends, she had danced, and pirouetted, raced, and glided with a freedom he only remembered. His friend was indeed coming back.

"What say we get some hot chocolate and roasted chestnuts from those enterprising vendors at the riverside," suggested Percy. Several of the other ladies nodded their agreement.

"A splendid idea," endorsed Lady Theodosia Mansfield. "I am all but worn out with skating. I doubt my limbs could take much more."

Trevor cast about to find Hamner and the Misses Grenford, but they were out of sight. Hamner must be with the ladies, so Trevor did not worry and agreed with the plan for chocolate and chestnuts.

"Then let us escort you to the benches where you may exchange skates for boots before we warm ourselves with Montezuma's best," said Vernon, who had gained the privilege of escorting Lady Theodosia that day.

"Last one to the benches is a warty toad," shouted Percy as she took off across the river.

Her lead was too great for anyone to catch her, but Trevor gave it a try, knowing they would have a few seconds of blessed privacy before Lady Theo and Vernon caught up, for they followed at a very leisurely pace.

He came to a halt in front of a laughing Percy who sat at on a bench and picked at the ties holding the metal blades to her shoes.

"Allow me." Trevor made an exaggerated bow and nearly lost his balance.

Percy giggled. "Wilt thou be my white knight and save me from yon gnarly monster." She pointed at her feet.

"'Twould please me greatly to defeat said snake and any others that dare to incommode my lady fair." He grasped her left foot and began to unravel the knots.

She tilted her head and fluttered her eyelids. "La, Sir Knight, you could turn a lady's head."

"Not a difficult thing to do with a slut, a wanton whose loose behavior killed her father and destroyed her fiancé's heart."

The snide tone dripped icy droplets of contempt.

Percy froze.

Trevor lifted his head and saw her spirit shrivel, as he looked higher to identify the speaker. "Mr. Cummins. What terrible event brings you to London?"

"A pleasure to see you, Lord Trehallow," Cummins said, impervious to the implication that his presence was not wanted "I would think a hero of the Peninsula could find better company to keep."

Trevor rose, leaving Percy with one skate on and one off. "You low-life scum. You will apologize to Miss Cummins immediately, or I'll give you the thrashing you deserve."

"Good show, Trevor, my man," Vernon said. "But I do not think Cummins is worth your time and effort."

"Miss Cummins's honor and reputation is worth every effort. I am waiting to hear that apology."

Cummins looked down his long nose. He only succeeded in making himself ridiculous, since he was shorter than Trevor by a head. "I would not waste my breath. Good day, ladies." He pointedly nodded at every female present other than Percy.

One by one the women turned their backs, giving him the cut direct. Their escorts joined them. Only Trevor saw the angry glare Cummins cast toward the group and the red-eyed fury he bent on Percy's bowed head.

"Get out of here, Cummins," he warned.

"Oh, I'm leaving, but your little doxy, my cousin, will regret she ever attempted to associate with her betters."

Trevor watched until the man was out of sight, then knelt before Percy. He was glad to see she had not allowed the cur to bring her to tears. She had never been one to weep in the face of brutes. Then Trevor saw how pale she was, how listless her gaze. Her lips trembled, and her shoulders quaked. Perhaps a few heated tears would be better than the chill of such a passionless demeanor.

He quickly untied her second skate and lifted her into his arms. "Miss Cummins is chilled to the bone. I'm taking her to the sleigh. Lady Theodosia, could you and Vernon acquire some hot chocolate and chestnuts for her. I am sure it will help to warm her."

He left with "of course," echoing behind him.

He settled Percy in the vehicle, spread a blanket across her, then sat beside her, taking her once more into his arms. It was a measure of her distress that she uttered no protest.

He desperately wanted to know what it was that Donald Cummins believed to cause him to maltreat his cousin so. But Percy did not need to be pressured for information now. She needed comfort and support. She needed to know she was loved and respected. Anyone who thought less of her did not matter. With all of that running through his head, along with ways to strip the skin from Donald Cummins, Trevor kept silent. He held Percy close, rubbing her arm and stroking her hair.

❧❦❧

By pleading a cold, she managed to avoid Trevor until the evening of the twenty-sixth. She missed work, but she had no expenses, living on Her Grace's charity. Besides, a week past she had given her small house to a widow with five children. The children had been delighted with Midnight, and the widow grateful to have a reliable mouser. The rent there had been paid through the end of

February. By then, the widow would hopefully have found work. Percy had not a clue what she would do to survive once the Ladies' Society latest project was complete. However, since encountering her cousin, remaining longer in London was not an option. Not if she wanted to leave behind the scandal attached to her name. Leaving would be best for Trevor too. She could not allow him to propose. She was completely inappropriate as an Earl's choice of wife. Society would ridicule him mercilessly, and that she would not allow.

She stared into the mirror as Jenks finished dressing her hair. All attempts to cry off from the excursion to the theatre met with strong resistance, especially after Aldridge had decreed Her Grace would remain at home. Jess had pointed out that, with Her Grace absent, it was more vital than ever for Percy—indeed the entire Grenford clan—to make a bold show. If Percy were seen in company without Her Grace's presence, most of the gossip would be put to rest.

"You've more friends than you know," said Jessica, who watched Jenks work. "You have spent the last three years of your life trying to atone for something that was no fault of your own. You have been all that is kind, generous, hard-working and dedicated, doing more for others when you ask nothing for yourself. That has not gone unnoticed by those who matter."

"There you are, Miss Cummins." Jenks gave the coiffure a pat. "You'll be the brightest light in the theatre tonight. No one would dare imply you lacked honor."

Percy tried to smile. She did not want to hurt Jenks's feelings or Jessica's, but they were both wrong. Nothing she could do would ever atone for her part in her father's suicide, or her mother's grief. Her cousin's vituperative comments may be based on gossip, but with her father's death coming on the heels of that gossip, she had never had the strength of will to deny the dirt cast upon her reputation. Three years later, she doubted anything could restore her honor.

Jenks answered a knock on the door.

"Lord Trehallow is below, Miss Cummins," said a footman. "Lord Hamner has also arrived to escort the Misses Grenford. The Marquis regrets that he cannot accompany you to the theatre."

"Thank you," murmured Jessica. "Tell the gentlemen we will be down shortly."

Percy rose. "Time to face the dragons."

"Here is your cloak, Miss. And the duchess said to be certain you took this ermine muff with you."

Percy sighed and accepted the muff then allowed Jenks to drape the cloak over her shoulders before adjusting the clasp that held the garment's edges together. Jenks performed the same office for Jessica, and all too soon, they descended the stairs to find the gentlemen waiting in the foyer.

"You look stunning tonight, Miss Cummins." Trevor took her hand and pressed a careful salute to her fingers. She wanted to linger with his lips touching her. Instead she snatched her hand away, burying it in the muff. She saw hurt frown briefly on his face, and her heart ached. Better a small hurt now. If she depressed his attentions, he might suffer less when she told him she was leaving London. Where she would go, she had no idea, but by then, perhaps, Trevor would be glad to see the last of her.

The ride to Drury Lane passed all too quickly; much Percy supposed, as a condemned man's walk to the gallows might seem too short.

Trevor handed her down from the sleigh and took her arm. She blinked at the size of the crowd. Edmund Kean's reputation had preceded him from Exeter, but this showing was excessively small.

"I thought we might be the only people to brave the bitter cold just to see a play," Trevor remarked. They mounted the steps and made their way through the scanty crowd to the Haverford box. Their party had little difficulty when others began to notice the notorious Miss Cummins. Women swept their skirts aside, turning their backs. Men leered, not very discreetly until they noticed Trevor's angry frown.

"Please, Lord Trehallow, ignore them. To do otherwise just draws more attention," Percy pleaded.

He bent his head to meet her gaze. "Of course. Since it pleases you, I will ignore their rudeness."

"It must be the weather keeping people from attending tonight. Kean is reputed to be an outstanding actor. His London debut has been much anticipated since it was announced months ago," Jessica said.

Percy mentally thanked her friend for changing the subject.

"Yes," Hamner agreed. "I hear he is better than Garrick and Kemble."

"We shall discover how talented Kean is for ourselves very soon."

A footman opened the door to the box.

"Trehallow, you and Percy take the front seats," ordered Jessica.

"But…"

"Nonsense, my friend. No objections will change my mind. Her Grace would be ashamed if you were to cower in the shadows."

Percy nodded her acceptance and allowed Trevor to seat her at the front of the box.

Talk among the sparse number of patrons in the gallery below rose to a crescendo. From the gallery and the opposite boxes, entirely too many stares were bent on Percy.

The evening's host came on stage and pleaded for quiet. Mr. Kean would not allow the stage curtains to be withdrawn until the crowd indicated its readiness for the performance with complete quiet.

The audience settled, though Percy was aware of continued stares until the curtains opened.

When the curtains closed indicating intermission, Percy turned to Trevor. "Kean's reputation is well deserved, Trevor. That performance shall become legend. Mark my words. However, I find myself famished, and energized both. Could we walk out and get refreshments?"

"An excellent idea," Jessica approved. "I, too, find myself excited and hungry. But I wish to be here to greet any friends who choose to visit. Would you get plates for us? You'll have to be quick, for I suspect Kean's performance has had a similar effect on the entire audience." She pointed to the gallery where people were streaming up the aisles to the lobby.

※

Trevor blinked. Percy had used his given name. Without any hesitation or prompting. Nor was she subdued and reluctant as she had been when the evening started. What had changed? He doubted anything in Shakespeare's Merchant of Venice had inspired his love to drop her unnecessary shame. He did agree, however, that Kean's performance was inspiring. Perhaps she was simply transported out of the personal darkness that suppressed her naturally buoyant and intrepid spirit.

Regardless of the cause, he was pleased and happy to see again the inner fire that had always shown bright and strong in his best friend. Pray heaven they encounter no one rude enough to cause his love to sink back into unwarranted guilt. He helped her rise and escorted her from the box. Jessica had been correct. It seemed the entire audience had come for refreshments and to discuss the performance thus far. Everywhere he turned he heard Kean, Kean, Kean as well as stellar, immortal, truly gifted, and many other accolades. No one spoke Percy's name. No one noticed her enough to turn aside and give the cut direct.

Her Grace had been right to insist that Percy attend tonight's performance. They approached the refreshment stand. "What delicacy appeals, Miss Cummins?"

"Oh, I should not, but I would love some of the gingerbread and perhaps some champagne. But you need not purchase…"

"It is my pleasure, my dear." He raised her hand to kiss her fingers.

"I've no doubt my cousin sees to all your pleasures, Trehallow." The man in front of them, turned with his purchases, revealing her cousin's disgusted sneer.

"How dare you, sir." Trevor began.

"Indeed, cousin." Percy stepped in front of Trevor. "How dare you cast aspersions where you have no knowledge of any dishonorable behavior on my part?"

Percy's interruption startled Trevor so much he lost his speech.

Donald swept his gaze around the room, suddenly grown quiet. Skirts rustled as women stepped back forming a space in which Trevor, Percy, and Donald confronted each other. However, Trevor noted, no one turned their backs. Too avid for gossip to give the cuts they imagined Percy deserved.

"I had the tale direct from your former fiancé, Baron Blanchard. How on the eve of your betrothal, you were found in intimate circumstances with a stable boy. You always did let your passions rule you, and, as I predicted, it led to your downfall."

"You predicted nothing." Percy challenged the man's lies. "You and I had never met in person until my father's funeral. You did not know me then, and you do not know me now. You believe any tale that suits you. Even if the tale misrepresents the facts."

"Facts. Facts!" Donald nearly shouted. "You were found by your fiancé *in flagrante delicto*. That is a fact. Your fiancé could not face the shame of being cuckolded before he was wed and fled the country. That is a fact. Your father killed himself from shame, and your mother, whom I sheltered when you deserted her, died of grief. Those are the facts, cousin. One more fact remains. I denounce you and your licentious ways. Neither belong in the Cummins family."

Trevor watched Percy go white and tremble. He prepared to catch her should she faint at the bile her cousin spewed. But just as Trevor raised his hand to comfort her, her face flushed. The only remaining white was on the knuckles of the fists at her sides.

Before he could blink, she drew back and punched Donald in the nose.

He fell like a stone.

"You broke my nose," he said. Though the words sounded more like *Do boke ma nofe.*

The crowd tittered.

"That, cousin, is the least of what you deserve for spreading lies and rumors of an event you know next to nothing about. That stable boy attacked me. But I defended myself, and he achieved nothing but a kiss on the cheek. Baron Blanchard appeared after I had managed to put the cur on the floor with a knee to his..."

Gasps from the onlookers drowned out Percy's description of how she had felled her attacker.

"My fiancé chose to believe the stable lad's lies over my truth. My father, incensed on my behalf, suggested that Blanchard leave the country or he would reveal information about the Baron's dealings with slave traders. My father..." A sob escaped her. The first sign of emotion other than anger. "My father's suicide was due to shame that he had attempted to repair our family's financial difficulties by wedding me to such a bounder. As for deserting my mother, you are the person who forbade me the house. You said you would toss my sick mother in the street if I did not leave immediately. Then when she died, you refused to permit me to attend the funeral. Those, are the facts, cousin. And now, I repudiate you. I would not be a member of your family if paid a million pounds."

She swept her skirt aside as she stepped around the man on the floor to place her order at the refreshment booth.

On the floor, Donald mumbled what sounded like curses and *you'll regret this.*

Trevor looked down on the man. "If you know what is good for you, you'll not come near Miss Cummins again. Should I hear of you or anyone spreading more lies about her, I will find you and break much more than your nose." Having issued his warning, Trevor turned on his heel and kept close to Percy's side. Quiet murmurs ran through the crowd. After receiving their refreshments, Trevor turned, helping Percy around Donald who still sat where he had fallen. And one by one the crowd began to applaud until the noise was louder than that given Kean when the curtain fell at intermission.

"How brave." "How terrible for her." "Always knew Donald Cummins was a toad." A torrent of similar comments followed Percy and Trevor to the Haverford box where they found Aldridge speaking with his sister.

"Word is spreading rapidly that Kean's Shylock is well worth braving the cold and snow. I had planned an evening with friends, but the friends decided to come here. I wanted to know if all of you agree with the praises being sung about Kean?"

"Percy!" Ignoring her half-brother, Jessica leapt from her seat and flung her arms about her friend. "I just heard what happened. Is it true?"

Aldridge raised a brow. "I did notice some sort of ruckus around the refreshment stand as I arrived. However, I knew any news of interest would come to my sister first, so I did not bother to stop."

She kept her focus on Percy. "Please say that you truly knocked Donald Cummins down and broke his nose."

"Jessica, such an interest in violence is unseemly." Percy admonished, but she was smiling. "I did. I've set the record straight finally."

"What made you do it?"

Trevor wanted to know, too, and eagerly waited for Percy to respond.

However, at that moment, the host came on stage and called for quiet from the audience.

"We will talk after the performance," Percy whispered to the party at large, but she looked only at Trevor.

Aldridge took his leave to return to his own party.

Trevor pushed aside the small disappointment at the delay. His love had recovered her courage. He prayed the mouse she had been for the past three years was banished forever. He wanted this brave, righteous, good-hearted woman to be his wife and raise their children. But that would have to wait, if he was to keep his promise to Her Grace.

Percy glanced out the window of the small parlor. A thin mist had formed, softening the hard edges of nearby buildings and blurring the lines of branches and street pavers. Would the mist deepen to a fog like that which had ushered in the frost a month ago? She prayed not.

A knock. A footman entered. "The Earl of Trehallow to see you, miss."

Trevor entered.

"Have Jenks fetch my cloak, bonnet and muff, please." Percy asked the footman before he left.

"What is amiss, Percy?" Trevor took her hands. "Your note said you needed me urgently."

"I'm sorry if I made it seem like I was in dire straits. I need your escort and help, and I worried that the mist would thicken and make travel impossible."

"Since you have every reason to worry about that, let us go now. You can tell me what you need as we move."

She nodded. They met Jenks in the foyer. She helped Percy with her outer garments while the footman returned Trevor his greatcoat, hat and gloves. Then Jenks followed them into the coach.

"What direction shall I give the coachman?" Trevor asked as he handed Percy and the maid into the sleigh.

"The Royal Artillery Barracks, Woolwich, please."

"That is more than twelve miles from here. We shall be lucky if we get back before dark," protested Trevor. "Besides, no lady should be seen at an army barracks. Do you not think... That is, given yesterday evening's events, you might be best advised to permit me to do this for you?"

Percy tried not to be angry with him. "I cannot act the coward now that I have finally found the courage to put my cousin in his place. I have a direct commission from Her Grace who has made an appointment for me to meet with Master Musician George McKenzie. I must go in person. You are coming with me to help me plead my case."

Trevor gave the coachman directions then settled back beside Percy. "I cannot like it. What in the world is so important that Her Grace must send you on this errand?"

"The orchestra she engaged for the breakfast and the ball was advised of the possibility that we would hold the breakfast outside. They have withdrawn all services. The manager insists that the weather is not good for the instruments, and any music performed in the present cold would be most unpleasant."

"I see. So, Her Grace wants you to carry her request for the Royal Artillery Band to perform."

"The Royal Artillery Band is the most highly regarded orchestral group in the land. And as a military unit, it is much used to playing out of doors and in the most difficult of circumstances."

"I've heard George McKenzie is a formidable man," Trevor remarked.

"I think I've proven my ability to manage the most formidable of circumstances. I doubt even a master musician can intimidate me now."

She took pride in the statement. For too long she had allowed her cousin's opinions to rule her life. She had been a fool to do so and blamed her grief over her father for stealing her good sense and pushing her into a pit of guilt and shame. Her mother's passing only added to the emotional burden.

Trevor took her gloved hand in his. His warmth and strength seeped into her chilled fingers. "I'm very happy to have my friend back."

Percy stole a glance at Jenks who smiled and gave one short nod. "Oh, Trevor, thank you. You know that you contributed greatly to my ability to throw off blame I should never have accepted."

"I think you did it all on your own."

"No, hear me out. It was not until you came back and persisted —I suspect with assistance from Her Grace—in renewing our friendship that I began to realize perhaps I was not as horrid a person as cousin Donald claimed."

"Yet you did not confront him after skating on the Serpentine."

"It is difficult to explain. But that day I enjoyed myself more than any day since before my betrothal ball. I was so used to believing I did not deserve to be happy that, when Donald came along, I could not reconcile my pleasure with my guilt. It took me a while to realize his sneers and untruths stole my joy, not anything I had done.

"I avoided you and almost everyone else and had made up my mind to leave the country. But I had committed to attending the theatre. I have never let Her Grace down and did not want to do so last night."

"You have always been steadfast to your friends."

"Then at the theater, Donald started spouting his filthy insults, and instead of cowering, I was incensed to the point of violence. I had nothing to lose, since I thought I would be leaving England. But my friends were not leaving, and Donald's bile would cover them with inescapable scandal. So, I struck him. With that one punch, I felt a powerful sense of relief, as if a great burden had fallen from my shoulders to the floor with my cousin."

"It was a burden you should never have carried."

"Perhaps, probably, no—certainly. But even afterward, I was both thrilled and appalled. I needed time to consider my actions and the impact they would have on me and those I love."

Trevor's grip on her hand tightened a bit, and his gaze met hers. "Dare I believe that I am among those you love?"

"Well, of course. You, Her Grace, Jessica, Matilda and a host of others, even Aldridge." She glanced at where Jenks sat frowning.

"May we speak of this on another occasion?" He released her hand.

Jenks smiled.

Percy dropped her gaze. "Perhaps."

"What could happen to make you certain?" He longed to place a finger under her chin and lift her face so he could see her eyes.

"I… I do not know. I need time to get used to being more myself, before, before speaking of conditions or promises."

"Should I go away?"

"No, no. Please. Stay and be my friend. Bid on my basket and dance with me at the ball. Let us discover together what we might mean to each other."

"Certainly. Now tell me what you plan to put in your basket and if you will make it yourself? As I recall, the Cummins's house cook taught you to make the most scrumptious apple tarts."

"I will make everything in my basket, save for the wine. Her Grace gifted me with an excellent vintage on my last birthday. I have not felt like drinking it until recently. The Venetian Breakfast is exactly the sort of occasion to open that bottle." She smiled.

Trevor smiled back at her. "But first we will have to brave the dragon, George McKenzie, and persuade him to bring the Royal Artillery Band to Mayfair for Her Grace of Haverford.

CHAPTER 7

Persuading Master Musician McKenzie proved as easy as mentioning the Duchess of Haverford. So, when February third dawned bright and clear, Trevor entered Haverford House at the very early hour of eight o'clock with a spring in his step. He had hope that Percy might actually consider his suit.

"Her Grace requested you join the party in the breakfast parlor," said the footman who took Trevor's cloak, hat, and gloves.

"Thank you. I'll find my way." In the breakfast parlor the ladies were seated around the table with cups of tea and small plates of food. He served himself from the buffet then joined the men who stood ranked around the room holding plates and eating quietly as Her Grace issued orders like the master strategist she was.

All too soon the room emptied, and the company made its way to the ice where the frost fair had appeared and grown in size over the past two days. The sun shone dimly through the fog. The people of London watched in awe as an army of Haverford servants augmented by those of various great houses, erected a sumptuous marquee on the ice at one end of the makeshift town. The tent dwarfed the booths and shelters around it, being as it was as large as the Haverford ballroom with a ceiling almost as tall.

Trevor saw some of the ladies arrive to watch just as men began carrying in rolls of carpeting to cover the ice. And more men followed with chairs, and tables, and crates, which—he had been told—contained linens for the tables, cotton to drape the walls, furs and woolen shawls in which to snuggle, and much, much more.

Around the marquee, a score of other tents, large and small, sprouted and grew under the ministering hands of a swarming army of workers. Trevor was one of them, assisting with laying rugs and assembling tents. At the edge of the area, he observed the guard of returned soldiers—some with obviously healed wounds—set up a perimeter of ribbons and bollards.

All was complete by noon. Trevor was dismissed along with all the other gentlemen, so they could clean themselves up from their exertions and dress for the auction and breakfast.

He thanked heaven for the military experience that allowed him to bathe and dress quickly, arriving back at the large auction tent in time to watch the band assemble and Brigadier-General Lord Redepenning direct the placement of the baskets.

Alone or in pairs, the ladies of the society drifted in, and soon all were ready to greet the paying guests. Trevor stood at Percy's side collecting tickets and telling Miss Jessica Grenford what names to record as being present.

At five minutes to one, with the number of ticket holders dwindling, he suggested they find chairs near the podium, passing by the display table on the way so that Percy could point out the basket on which he should bid.

She had just taken his hand when he heard Donald Cummins sneer. Percy turned to look.

"Are you certain," Cummins addressed Miss Jessica Grenford, "that none of the food will cause the purchasers to become ill? I know some of the, er, ladies have expertise in areas other than cooking."

Cummins, bruises spreading from beneath the bandage covering his nose, stared directly at Percy.

"Please, let me handle this," Trevor murmured in her ear.

She nodded.

"I am surprised you dared show your face here, Cummins." Trevor placed himself between the cousins.

"I purchased a ticket. I have every right to be here."

"Before you insulted Miss Cummins, perhaps. Miss Jessica, let us refund Mr. Cummins his purchase price. I'm certain he would prefer to dine elsewhere today."

She had the cash in Cummins' hand before he could protest. "Good day to you." Her voice was treacle sweet.

"Her Grace will hear about this," said Cummins.

"I will tell her myself," responded Percy from behind Trevor.

"You." Cummins sneered. "You will get everything you deserve. I'll make sure of it."

"You had best leave. Unless you wish to have your nose broken a second time," threatened Trevor.

Cummins left.

"Good riddance to bad rubbish," Miss Jessica stated.

From deeper within the tent, the band began to tune up.

"Let us hurry, Trehallow," Percy urged. "Jessica, we'll save you a seat. Lord Marr and Sir Melbarrow would be vastly disappointed in us both if we did not bring you."

"Thank you, Percy," replied Jessica. "However, I am promised to sit with Hamner and Matilda. Why do you and Trehallow not join us?"

"I would like that very much. Trehallow, think you your friends will forgive you for neglecting them?" asked Percy.

"I'll just step away to tell them then re-join you with Hamner's party."

As well as the usual supporters, the marquee was crowded by dozens, perhaps hundreds of the *beau monde* who would never otherwise put their hands in their pockets for the charitable cause in question. The unusual setting was undoubtedly a draw card, and the talk the Society's members had been assiduously spreading about how fashionable people would all be present.

The potential for scandal in the nature of the auction helped, too. Sale of a lady's time? But for charity, the members had all explained, insisting that the most proper of the *ton's* sticklers could have no objection to a lady offering food and the pleasure of her company in support of a good cause.

The excited clatter of voices dwindled to a hum when Brigadier-General Lord Redepenning stepped up onto the stage at the rear of the marquee, accompanied by Her Grace, the Duchess of Haverford.

Her Grace spoke first, briefly explaining the purpose of the Society, encouraging everyone to open their purses and be generous, and then handing over to Mrs. Beresford, as the chairwoman of the Society's organizing committee.

Mrs. Beresford confined herself to welcoming them all before inviting Lord Henry (as he was known by all but his subordinates in the Horse Guard) to begin the auction.

Lord Henry briefly explained how the auction would work: the winner of a basket also won the right to share the contents with the lady who donated it. The usual rules of propriety prevailed, and no lady would lunch unchaperoned, unless, of course, her basket was purchased by a close family member.

A footman in Haverford livery handed Mrs. Beresford the first basket, and she brought it to Lord Henry.

He mimed opening the top, held it to his nose, and gave a deep theatrical sigh. "Magnificent. Your Graces, my ladies, my lords, gentlemen, I give you a picnic basket that, if it tastes as good as it smells, will be a rare treat. One made even pleasanter, dare I say, by the company of the lovely Lady Priscilla Fenton."

He lifted the label again, and added, "Oh, and it says, her elder brother and his wife." Speaking over the laughter, he added, "Ah, well," which set them off again.

The bidding was fast, and no one was surprised when Lord Wrathall, who had been courting Lady Priscilla for the last several months, allowed himself to be cozened out of nine pounds ten shillings for the privilege of walking off with the basket and the lady.

Three baskets later, Lord Henry moved to a heavily-laden basket from the Chadbourn kitchens. A hush came over the crowd when he announced the lady to be Lady Georgiana Hayden. From somewhere, Trevor heard an incredulous stage whisper, "The Recluse of Cambridge? Does Sudbury know she is here?"

He turned to the source in time to see Sir Horace Malford, red in the face storming toward them. "What are you thinking?" he hissed at Lady Hayden. "Your mother will…"

"Quiet in the ranks," Lord Henry called out. "Are you bidding, Sir Horace?"

"I will not be a part of this disgrace," the man snapped.

"Then I suggest you sit down, Horace and be quiet," Lord Henry retorted.

Lady Hayden stood tall and proud as only a duke's daughter could, only the faint flush to her cheeks showing her distress as Horace sputtered, people tittered, and no bids were forthcoming.

"Really," Hamner said in a loud aside to Miss Matilda Grenford, "is the man calling an event organized by Her Grace the Duchess of Haverford a disgrace?"

"Twenty guineas," a commanding voice from the rear said. All heads turned to see her brother, the Marquess of Glenaire, look unwaveringly at Lord Henry.

"Ah!" Lord Henry said. "Offered by a man who has undoubtedly experienced picnics prepared by Lady Georgiana and knows their worth." He held the gavel as his eyes scanned the room and the comments and laughter stilled. Finally, he brought it down. "Sold to the Marquess of Glenaire."

Baskets by Miss Flora Penhurst and Lady Emma Frampton went for nine pounds and eighteen pounds, the second with much competition between Lieutenant Branson and his greatest friend and constant rival Beau Fishingworth. Both were left open-mouthed when a last-minute bid by Viscount Sterling topped their budgets and took away the prize.

"The next basket," said Lord Henry, accepting it from Mrs. Beresford and checking the label, "has been lovingly packed by Miss Cummins. Do I have five pounds, gentlemen?"

Trevor cast the opening bid of ten pounds

"A very stiff opening bid," said the general. "I wish I could bid on this one myself. Apple tarts, mincemeat pies, a bottle of very excellent wine, and numerous other delectable treats."

A voice in the back of the tent called out twenty pounds. Trevor turned and tried to discern who was bidding against him.

Someone behind Hamner made a ribald remark about what else came with Miss Cummins' basket. Jessica made to spin around, and both Percy and Matilda stopped her. Hamner turned instead, glaring the grin off the idiot's face.

Trevor fisted his hands, but refrained from starting a donnybrook at the auction. He would punish the offender soon enough.

"Twenty-five pounds," came another bid, from directly to Trevor's left. He countered immediately with thirty pounds, only to be topped by a bid of thirty-five pounds. He knew the last voice and glared the Marquis of Aldridge. Aldridge grinned, and winked. He raised one eyebrow, waiting for Trevor's counterbid.

"One hundred pounds," yelled Trevor, and gave Aldridge a level stare, daring him to bid higher. It was a dangerous gambit. Aldridge's pockets were very deep. But it worked. Aldridge spread his hands in defeat.

Into the deafening silence prompted by the truly outrageous bid —one could keep a modest household on such a sum—Lord Henry said, "Going once, going twice. With no further bids, sold to the Earl of Trehallow. Sir, pay the purser to my left and claim your prize."

"Come, I need to speak with you." Basket in hand, Trevor

escorted Percy, with Jenks following, to one of the smaller tents nearby where successful bidders could partake of their winnings away from the hubbub of the bidding. They were lucky enough to find one unoccupied. Percy asked Jenks to stand in the tent opening, just so others would see that the proprieties were being observed.

Finding himself surprisingly shy now that the moment had come, he waited until they had consumed nearly all of the food and poured the last of the wine. *What if she said no?*

"You said you wished to speak with me, Trevor."

His name on her lips shook loose his fear. Nothing would be gained by further delay. He took her hand and plunged ahead. "Percy Cummins, my love, would you do me the honor of becoming my wife?"

Her eyes were wide, and her fingers trembled where they touched his.

"You cannot be surprised."

"I can." She protested. "I am. So much has happened since you left for the army. You know most of it now, and yet you still wish to marry me. I'm amazed."

"I wish you were not amazed, Percy, although I think I understand why you might be. What is important to me is whether amazed or not, you are pleased?"

"I am uncertain."

"Do you need time?"

She nodded.

"A lot of time?"

She shook her head.

"Excellent. I find myself impatient for a positive answer. Is there anything I can do to influence you one way or the other?"

"No, in fact I would like to end this conversation now. Please take me home to Haverford House and do not speak privately with me until the ball. I will save you the first waltz, and if my answer is yes, the last waltz as well."

"It is, and always will be, my pleasure to serve you, Percy."

She nodded her thanks but refused to speak. He left her with Jenks at the Haverford doorstep. He stood staring at the house like an idiot for a long while after the door closed.

Percy lay down to rest the minute she gained her bedroom. But her mind circled like a mad thing, and she could not rest. She called for Jenks and a bath, then took her time dressing for the ball. As dinner approached, she was still considering Trevor's proposal, so she sent her regrets to the duchess and requested a tray in her room. As Jenks placed the final pin in Percy's coiffure and twitched the folds of the pale teal and russet gown, she finally knew her mind.

"You're a picture, you are, Miss Percy."

"Thank you, Jenks. You must take most of the credit."

Jenks colored.

"Now I have a question for you."

"Yes, miss."

"Were I to offer you a position as my dresser, would you be willing to leave Her Grace's household for mine."

Jenks' eyes went wide. "Do you mean that nice young earl has finally popped the question and you've accepted him?"

"The gentleman has asked. But I have not yet answered him. I have something I need to know before I give my final answer. Given that I accept, I will need a dresser. I would like that dresser to be you."

"This is ever so exciting. It would be my pleasure to be your dresser, Miss Cummins."

"Need I tell you not to say anything to anyone before you learn from me what I've said to the earl?"

"No miss. Her Grace has trained us all to be discreet. We never talk amongst ourselves unless it is common knowledge."

"Thank you, I appreciate your discretion. You need not wait up for me tonight." Then Percy swept out the door of her chamber. She arrived at the entrance to the ballroom and joined the receiving line with the other members of the Ladies Society. Her dance card filled as gentlemen passed through the line. She would have very sore feet by the time the evening ended. But the hope in her heart would ease any physical pain.

Trevor approached and bowed over her hand. "My felicitations to you and the rest of the ladies for your efforts on behalf of the veterans, widows, and orphans. Rumors say that you have raised well over one hundred thousand pounds." He took her dance card as he spoke.

She smiled at him. "I have not been told the precise number. Her Grace is keeping it a closely guarded secret to announce with several other items just before supper."

"I see you have saved me the first waltz, but the last waltz still has no name beside it."

"Yes," She took the card from his grasp. "I'm saving that dance for the man I love."

His color faded the slightest bit. "May I know which lucky gentleman to congratulate?"

"Take me in to supper. I should know by then."

He inhaled a long breath.

She knew she was cruel to tease him so, but she did need to know for certain before she finally consented.

She enjoyed every dance, but none so much as her waltz with Trevor. He was about to hand her over to her next partner when she put her hand on his arm. "Sir Melbarrow, please forgive me. I find myself in need of some air and would like his lordship to escort me. We are old family friends and have much to catch up on."

Vernon bowed his acceptance and walked off.

Trevor escorted her to the balcony just beyond the doors at the end of the long gallery. She leaned against the balustrade gazing out at the snow-covered gardens below. He came up behind her, placing his hands on the balustrade one on either side of hers, sheltering her from the cold with the warmth of his body.

"What is it we need to catch up on, my old family friend?" His breath tickled her ear.

"I want to know if you recall the night I told you of my betrothal."

"I have tried to forget that night for more than three years."

"Why?"

"You have always been my one true love, Percy. I might have spoken my heart that night, but you told me of your engagement, and you were so excited. I had nothing to offer you save the possibility of a successful career in the army. I refrained from speaking my heart. I told myself that I must be satisfied knowing you would be cared for and hopefully cherished by someone with the means to do so."

"I thought as much." She paused choosing her words carefully. "I always said you were too noble by half."

"Yes, every time I suggested that you were acting on impulse and might regret the consequences of your actions."

"And you were right. I very much regret the consequences of my kindness to that young stable lad. Almost as much as I regret not telling you I have always loved you."

She felt him stiffen. Then his hands lifted to her shoulders and turned her around to face him.

"We have been a couple of noble fools."

"Yes." Happy tears welled in her eyes.

"Do you think it is time we stopped being so foolish and for once give in to impulse?"

"Well, if we have to think about it…"

His mouth found hers in a kiss that seared her soul.

"Goodness," she said when he finally stopped for breath. "I always liked action better than words. Would you like to sign your name on my dance card for the last waltz?"

"It would be my great pleasure." He stepped away placing her card on the balustrade in order to sign.

"No! Do not—" Percy shoved at him.

❧❧❧

"What?" He lifted his head only to be blinded by the flash of a pistol firing. His ears rang. He saw Donald Cummins throw the pistol at him. "Percy?" His voice sounded tinny and distant. He could not see Percy.

People began to pour out onto the balcony.

He blinked looking around, and then down, because something rested on his feet.

"Percy! My God. Someone fetch a doctor."

She lay still and pale, crumpled on the chilly flagstones. He sat, gathered her into his arms, pleading with her to wake up.

People moved around him. He did not know who nor did he care. A hand on his shoulder drew his attention briefly. James was mouthing words at him. Trevor turned his attention back to Percy, noting in passing that Aldridge and a few others were herding guests back into the ballroom.

"Here."

His hearing returned in a blast of sound. A folded kerchief was thrust before him. He took it and applied it to the wound high on Percy's left shoulder. He used both hands, letting her body rest against his thighs. But the hand that had been supporting her back came away drenched in blood.

"Use my neck cloth." James thrust the wadded-up linen into Trevor's hands. With his friend's help he managed to press the second pad to the exit wound. Moments later the doctor appeared.

"Excellent, excellent. Pressure is the best thing to stop the blood flowing. You must let us take her inside now."

He did not want to let go. Fear unlike anything he had known gripped him. "She will die."

"She shall die for certain, son, if you do not let me see to her."

"Let the doctor do his job, Trevor. He is my personal physician, and I hire only the best," said Her Grace.

Where she had come from, he had no notion, but he nodded his agreement.

Percy was lifted and gently laid on a rug then lifted again by the corners of the rug and taken through a set of doors that led to some room other than the ballroom.

The terror that had held him immobile became molten fury. He surged to his feet. "Where is Donald Cummins? He did this. I'll kill him."

James did his best to hold Trevor back but was dragged along, protesting. "Cummins has already been dealt with."

Trevor shook off James's hold then turned on his friend. "But, I need to…"

"No. You. Do not. Attack Cummins and it will only hurt both you and Miss Cummins. Aldridge has everything well in hand. Cummins will get his due. You must focus on Miss Cummins. She needs you by her side more than she needs you going off half-cocked and committing murder.

"James," ordered Her Grace. "You will see to Trehallow. Get him some brandy and clean him up before he goes in to see Percy. If she sees all that blood on him, he shall scare her silly."

Trevor looked down at himself. His shirt and waistcoat turned red with Percy's life. The thought nearly felled him.

"Come along, my friend." James gripped Trevor's sleeve, tugging him toward the house. "Must follow Her Grace's orders you know. Would not want to scare Miss Cummins."

"She lives?"

"Last I knew. Let us get you cleaned up, and we shall find out."

Clean and, in his opinion, too much later, Trevor sat in a chair at her bedside, with Jenks seated in the opposite corner waiting for her to wake up.

Then at long last her eyes opened, and she looked at him. "Hello."

"Marry me now," he blurted, unwilling to risk another day without her at his side.

"No." Unsurprisingly her answer was weak.

"I could not bear it if I were to lose you."

"I hurt like the very dickens, Trevor, my love. However, I am not going to die."

"You nearly did."

"But I did not. I am very much alive and will continue that way. Besides, as the bride, I get to set the date. I refused to be married from my bed, nor will you carry me down the aisle."

He resigned himself to waiting.

His patience was rewarded.

Percy, wearing a stunning bonnet—formerly Miss Jessica Grenford's best—wed Trevor in the warmth and sunlight of the Haverford gardens on the twentieth day of May, 1814. They retired to his home in Wales and lived the rest of their lives in peace and happiness. Every year, when the third of February raised its chilly winds, they sat by the fireside, toasting the Frost Fair and the one true love it brought them.

THE END

Book3: *Knight Defender* ~ A MacKai Family Novel

To defend his home, Baron Raeb MacKai must give his heart to his greatest enemy.

Regency

The French Duchess

If Marielle, Duchess of Stonegreave isn't a traitor, why do the men who love her usually end up dead?

Contemporary

Her Cadillac Cowboy

Will Josh McKinley have to give up the car he treasures in order to win Sarah Carson's heart?

The Catnapped Lover

Completely revised

Adam would have won his bet, if it hadn't been for Deirdre Clancy and that blasted cat.

Erotica

The Widow's Revenge

A vow of revenge becomes a promise of love when a mysterious widow plots to ruin the man responsible for her husband's death

Off Limits

Only the sea could draw two passionate people of such opposite backgrounds together, and only US Navy regulations could keep them apart

Hazard Duty

No sailor is going to get Ros Duncan and her dreams. She doesn't care how handsome he is.

ABOUT RUE ALLYN

Author of historical and contemporary romances Rue Allyn is insatiably curious, an avid reader and traveler. She loves to hear from readers about their favorite books and real-life adventures. Crazy Cat stories are especially welcome. Contact her at Rue@RueAllyn.com. She can't wait to hear from you.

Keep up with Rue Allyn by subscribing to her newsletter and get a free download of one of Rue's books.

Learn more about Rue at:
Website: https://RueAllyn.com

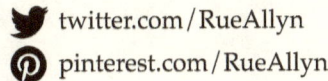

twitter.com/RueAllyn
pinterest.com/RueAllyn

LORD ETHAN'S COURAGE

CAROLINE WARFIELD

Lord Ethan's Courage
By Caroline Warfield

When a young woman marches into an alley full of homeless former soldiers, Ethan Alcott feels something he thought dead stir to life: his sense of honor. Efforts at charity put the chit in danger; someone needs to take her in hand.

Lady Flora Landrum discovers that the mysterious one-armed ruffian she encountered in a back alley is Lord Ethan Alcott, son of the Marquess of Welbrook; her astonishment gives way to determination. As Ethan comes to admire Flora's courage, perhaps he can reclaim his own.

CHAPTER 1

T he smell of fresh bread turned his stomach, as the smell of gin no longer did, but not as much as the unwanted sympathy of women too foolish to stay where they belonged. Ethan hunkered deeper into a corner of two walls that met unevenly in the back of a warehouse next to Finnegan's Pub. Perhaps she would pass and leave him be.

She did not. Ethan Alcott, so old at heart that he no longer knew or cared if he was twenty-eight or twenty-nine in chronological years, looked at the fresh-faced babe in the woods and wondered vaguely where her keepers might be.

She stopped by the man slouched against the wall a few feet down, and handed him bread wrapped in paper. *Not enough to trade for whisky. Perhaps she isn't completely ignorant,* he thought.

He folded the remains of his left arm across his chest and stared at his knees, knowing from experience that if he ignored her she would pass him by; at least, she would if he waited long enough.

He could see the tips of two expensive-looking half boots peeping out from under what he suspected was her maid's cast-off gown. Men in this alley would kill for the boots alone. Lady Bountiful went down on her heels in front of him and reached out to hand him her gift. *Stupid, that.*

His good hand—the remaining one—darted out and seized her wrist before he thought. "Don't ever reach so close to a desperate man. Down on your haunches like that you are easy prey for any man who wants you on your back with your skirts up. Did your mother teach you nothing?" he snarled. His words may have been crude, but he spoke so fast he forgot to strip Mayfair from his voice and pronunciation. Let her make of that what she would. He shoved her hand aside and sank back into his defensive position.

The woman leapt to her feet and Ethan watched a pair of serviceable men's boots hurry to her side.

"Lady Flora!" a young voice shouted. "Be you well?"

The youngest most easily persuadable footman, no doubt.

"Well enough, John. This gentleman doesn't wish to accept our gift," she replied, acidly. She had dropped her offering in his lap when he grabbed her wrist. He ignored it. Neither pair of boots moved. He glanced up through lowered lashes to see a pair of deep blue eyes studying him as if he were a puzzle to solve.

I'm nobody's damned problem to solve. Go away, he demanded silently.

"Who are you," she asked. He kept his eyes downcast.

"Come now, Lady Flora," the lad said. "The earl won't be pleased if you linger." The footman may have been as young as he sounded, but his scared face and missing ear were utterly unexpected.

"Chadbourn would not be pleased if he knew I was even here, John, and you know it. What he doesn't know won't hurt him."

Chadbourn! Good God. A blasted earl. Ethan searched his memory. He served with the heir in the Peninsula. Will Landrum had been a good soldier. A decent man. Should keep a better watch on his sister.

"Besides," the chit went on, moving down the line. "My brother doesn't notice anything I do. He's too busy figuring out his new duties."

The earl then, not the heir. Neglecting one of those duties though. *Someone needs to take this chit in hand.*

Her voice trailed away, and eventually the two of them disappeared into the icy London fog. He reached down then and picked up the offering she dropped in his lap. He stuffed the bread in his mouth with a shaking hand. *Excess of gin or cold?* The weather had gotten sharp; he didn't remember a winter as cold as this one, but then, he'd never lived on the streets before. It must be approaching January, he thought. If he didn't find shelter soon, he probably wouldn't survive until spring.

Do I care? The question occupied him for a moment. He certainly had choices, as none of the other wretches sheltering behind the warehouse who hoped to beg at the rear door to Finnegan's Pub did.

Choices. He didn't deserve them and couldn't be certain he still had them. Would his father welcome him if he saw his son like this? If he knew what Ethan had done? The thought of facing it all kept him in this alley; gin—when he could get it—kept the thought away.

He wrapped the remains of the blanket he had stolen around his shoulders as tightly as he could and tried to force all thought from his mind. The hardest thing to banish was the memory of the woman's blue eyes and one final thought: Someone needs to take that chit in hand.

He squeezed his eyes shut and sought sleep. Somewhere deep inside him the desire to survive stirred to life, broke open, and began to plant roots in the dark.

⚜

Lady Flora Landrum, youngest sister of the current earl, arrived at Chadbourn House via the back gate to avoid the neighbors' prying eyes. The knocker on the front had been removed from the door, indicating the entire family had departed. The neighbors all knew the earl wasn't in residence, living as he did in bachelor rooms at the Albany, and they also believed Flora had left when her sister's family departed for the country. She hoped they would continue to believe it. Let them see a servant hurrying in via the tradesmen's entrance. The empty rooms and skeleton staff in the supposedly-closed townhouse suited Flo just fine.

"Leave those boots here for the boot boy; you don't want to tramp on the good rugs what with where those have been. I'll have your bath sent up right quick, Lady Flora, and Martha will bring those rags down to me," Mrs. Potter said, standing arms akimbo, frowning at Flo.

The boot boy had left with her sister Sylvia, as had most of the servants; Flo took off her boots and left them by the door anyway. It had been ridiculously easy to stay behind when her sister's family left for the country. Emery, Sylvia's husband, ignored her, and Sylvia had been too lost in her 'morning tonic' to notice. Mrs. Potter — the cook and, when the house was officially closed, housekeeper —made no secret of her disapproval, but wouldn't give Flo away.

The woman's frown sent a shiver of guilt through Flo, but she raised her chin and sailed past toward the front stairs. Flo refused to regret her decision. She could not endure any more of Emery's ill treatment of his family. She'd been shunted to his household right after Father's funeral the previous September. To her shame, she knew she ought to confront her brother about it for Sylvia's sake, but to do so would be to reveal that she lived alone with a few servants in the earl's massive townhouse and no companion to give her respectable cover. Besides, Will had been sunk in his own grief and overwhelmed by the duties of his new station.

A half hour later, she lowered herself into hot, lavender-scented water and willed every tense muscle to relax. The errand had been ill advised; she'd put herself in more jeopardy than she expected and accomplished little good. She found the men behind

Finnegan's Pub as she'd been told, but this lot seemed so far gone even bread did not help. Those men broke her heart, even the nasty man who had grabbed her arm.

If her brother had done naught else, his efforts on behalf of returning veterans had woken her up to the plight of men flooding home from the Peninsular War. When she hid in her room and stayed behind, it had been for their sake, or so she told herself. Living on her own at Chadbourn House, she had freedom to do her part—if only she could find truly constructive ways to help.

She believed she could to do more for those poor men who had given so much for the country. *But what?* She sank back down into the warm water, allowing it to soak the stench of the alley from her body. It couldn't remove her memories of what she had seen, however.

Images in her mind returned over and over to the one-handed man lying in the corner. When his eyes flew open, the force of his anger almost knocked her on her heels. Those eyes startled her as much as his grip on her wrist. His gaunt sunken cheeks, ashen pallor, and slumped shoulders had not prepared her for the strength of his reaction.

She couldn't clear his eyes from her memory. She'd been shocked by the profound grief in those rich brown eyes, visible even when mixed with raging fury. The sight stabbed her in the heart.

The last of the tension in her back melted away, and she let her head fall back against the rim of the tub, relaxed and drowsy. One other detail filtered to the surface, his voice. His accents didn't belong there; they sounded more like those of an educated gentleman, and that puzzled her. She sighed and let the mystery float away. She'd never see him again anyway.

CHAPTER 2

E than shivered behind the mews to the rear of Chadbourn House, able neither to return to his hiding place nor to approach the earl. He held the stump of his damaged arm against his chest with the other, trying to keep the chill at bay. It had snowed the night before.

Many months had passed since anything as inconvenient as duty had bothered Ethan, and now that it had, he didn't care for the feeling at all. Belief someone should tell the earl his sister put herself in jeopardy drew him there; old fears held him back. He might have hovered next to the mews until he froze to death and they hauled his unloved carcass to a pauper's grave—or sold it to the body snatchers—if he hadn't been spotted.

"You there, looking for a meal? Speak up; I almost missed you in the fog."

Ethan gaped at the groom who came toward him wiping his hands. He didn't know if the man meant to accuse him of stealing or offer him bread.

"Y've come to the right place; follow me." The man didn't wait; he started toward the house. "What regiment?"

Ethan, thoroughly confused, followed him. "Regiment?"

"Aye, where'd you serve, man?"

How can he tell I'm a soldier?

"Veteran, aren't ye? Why else would you hang outside the earl's kitchen?" the groom held a door open for him.

Ethan stepped up, and mumbled under his breath, "Light Division," as he passed.

"Craufurd's? God love y'!"

Warmth wrapped itself around Ethan as they entered the kitchen. "'Nother 'un Mrs. Potter," the groom called. "Served in th' Light Division. Not many o' them left," he added mournfully, on his way back out the door.

A plump woman gave Ethan a swift no-nonsense examination before he could speak, and scowled at his appearance then waved a dripping spoon toward a table in the corner. The savory stew she set on the table so overwhelmed him that he almost forgot who he was, much less why he came.

Ethan attacked the stew, shoveling it in as rapidly as he could swallow. "Easy now," the woman chided. "No point in making yourself sick." She set a plate of warm bread down next to him. "Craufurd's was it? My man died at Cuidad Rodrigo."

Ethan kept eating, more slowly now, his stomach clenching. He hadn't come to share war stories. *Cuidad Rodrigo*. The words almost drove him back out the door. "I've come to see the earl," he said between bites of bread.

"He isn't here," she said. "If it's work you want—"

"It's not," he muttered. He knew the ways of the upper ten thousand. No earl was 'in' until he knew who asked and what they wanted. "I won't keep him long. I'll just say my piece and be gone." He considered in bitter humor that he ought to have brought his calling card.

The one-eared footman he saw in the alley came in carrying buckets of water. "Another hungry veteran, Mrs. Potter?" he asked. "What's his regiment?"

"As you see," the cook responded. "Served with—"

Ethan had enough bad memories. He rose to his feet. "Tell the earl I have a message, and I'll—"

"He isn't here," Mrs. Potter repeated.

"You can see his man of business if you want work, though," the footman added.

Ethan did not want work, and he most certainly did not want to revisit bad memories with the oddest collection of servants he'd ever encountered.

"What I have to say is for his ears only. I know the earl isn't 'in'. I'll only take a moment to give him my message and be on my way."

Both servants stared at him as if he were simpleminded.

"It isn't how it's done," the footman muttered.

Years past caring how things ought to be done, Ethan lost all patience. He stalked out the door to the family quarters, with the footman scurrying behind.

"You can't go there!" the boy shouted. A stern looking butler started down from the front of the house, and Ethan turned down a hallway, surprised at his spurt of energy. A study was bound to be off the back corridors, and if he made enough of a scene the earl would show himself. He yanked open a door and stopped dead in his tracks.

"You!" the speaker and sole occupant of the room stared at him in astonishment. He had wandered into the library, and stumbled onto Lady Flora.

Standing in his rags, smelling like the back-alley rat he was, Ethan did the only logical thing. He stood as straight as he could, looked at her directly, summoned his most aristocratic diction, and said, "I must apologize, my lady, but I'm here to speak to the earl." His tutors would have been proud.

"My brother isn't here," the lady replied, bafflement causing her to appear too adorable for Ethan's peace of mind.

"I tried to tell him, Lady Flora, but he run off."

The lady studied Ethan even as she assured her servant he had done no wrong. *He certainly did! The lad should have tackled an intruder before he let him anywhere near the lady.*

"Who are you?" she asked, as she had the day before.

No one you should know. "My business is with the earl."

She breathed deeply, wrinkled her nose—probably at the way he smelled—and addressed the butler who had joined them. "Kindly show this gentleman out the tradesmen's entrance, Swift, and see that he has my brother's direction."

The butler raised weary brows. "Could cause an uproar, Lady Flora." Younger than most of his profession, and the man looked more like a burly prizefighter than a butler, one more oddity in this house's strange staff.

"We knew one would happen eventually," Lady Flora replied, with a sad smile at the butler.

What sort of uproar? Ethan let the men drag him out, too puzzled to struggle and more determined than ever to speak to the earl.

❧

The following morning, Flo still pondered the questions that continue to plague her: what to do with her useless life, and how to make a difference. Taking chocolate in bed, she cataloged her options. The world urged marriage as the answer to a young woman's prayers, but Sylvia's plight had soured her on that idea.

However, a thought came to her regarding the misery of returning soldiers. She decided to visit the Benevolent Pauper's Hospital of the Apostles. That would be a safer activity, and she had no doubt she could find something constructive to contribute there. She jumped out of bed with renewed energy.

"I'll take my usual on a tray in the library," she called to John the footman on her way down the stairs without pausing to hear his reply. She often took breakfast in the library, the one room kept warm all day for her. She continued on her way, humming under her breath, pushed into the room, still humming, a wide smile on her face in anticipation of a productive day, and stumbled to a stop.

Her brother sat in his favorite leather chair, a cup of coffee at his side, and a fierce glare marring his handsome face.

"Lady Flora Margaretta Landrum, what in God's name have you been up to?" he demanded without preamble.

"How—oh never mind, you were bound to find out sooner or later. As you see, I'm not 'up to' anything. I merely stayed behind when Emery forced Sylvia to decamp for home, driven no doubt by creditors or an irate husband, I care not which. You really must do something about that man; Sylvia fades by the day, sunk in misery." An attack, Flo had found, was frequently the best defense.

"I didn't come here about Sylvia," the earl replied. At thirty-two, William Landrum, Earl of Chadbourn, was newly come into his title and weighted down with grief and new responsibilities. He had no patience for games. "What the devil were you doing behind a squalid pub with no more protection that a half-deaf boy with no sense of danger?"

Damn. How did he find out about that? She swallowed hard. "Don't insult John! He fought at Talavera. He tried to talk me out of it. Aren't you glad he followed me?"

"You're changing the subject again. You put yourself—and John —in danger for no good reason."

"No good reason? Since you returned from Spain you've thought of nothing but the plight of our soldiers. Even..." Tears choked her momentarily. "Even when Father was dying, the two of you talked as much about the shame of our country's neglect as you did about the everlasting estate and its needs. You fought with Emery about it, on the rare occasion you bothered to speak with the bounder at all—and I know he's been no support in Parliament. Am I not supposed to care? Am I to sit idly in gentile mourning while families starve and wounded men go uncared for?"

Her brother stared back momentarily stunned by her outburst.

She drew breath and went on. "You pushed me onto Sylvia and

wiped your hands of me. Problem solved. I will not be at the mercy of Emery Wheatly! Look at what he does to Sylvia. I saw her in her bath, Will. Bruises everywhere. Bruises! Never where you might see them. She has given up. Since Father's death she retreats into her tonics and gloom. And Charles—had you spent any time with the boy you would see what a frightened little fellow he has become. You can't—"

"Enough!" her brother roared surging to his feet. "Do you think I didn't notice, Flo? But Emery has all the rights. I even tried to get Sylvia to come home. Once she was under my roof… but she kept telling me nothing was wrong. What can I do? He won't even let Charles stay here, though I've begged him."

Flo bit back tears. "There's more, Will. You have to listen to me."

Her brother, up until recent months the best of men, had never shouted at her before. He struggled to compose himself, and nodded to her to continue.

"He attempted to strike me once." She rushed on at her brother's stricken look. "A swift knee to his privates—that move you taught me—disabused him of the notion. Besides, he knew I would tell you, and you would kill him."

He had his arms around her then. "Damn, Flo. Why didn't you tell me?"

She wiggled free. "I would have, but then they left, and I was here, and…"

"You didn't want me to know you were on your own."

She bit her lip, unable to answer.

"I've obviously not paid the attention I should. I'm sorry, but what am I to do? I couldn't send you to Louisa in Philadelphia. Even if we weren't at war—which we are—it is too far away. It never occurred to me he could be so stupid as to harm you. I thought you would be safe until Aunt Imogene came down from Yorkshire. She promised she'd be here in a month."

"Can't I just stay here alone?" She knew all too well that would not be permitted. The tears broke loose, and his arms were around her again before she could stop. She sobbed quietly into her brother's coat, while he murmured, "I'm sorry, I'm so sorry," over and over.

"What am I going to do with you?" he asked rhetorically. "I won't send you back to Sylvia—" Her heart lifted, and she opened her mouth to thank him, but he waved her off. "If I move back, this becomes a bachelor establishment. I've been providing temporary quarters for men who need it. Am I to push them out?"

"You could leave them at your rooms. Or move them here. There are more bedrooms, and you could assist more of them." She bounced upright on a wave of enthusiasm. "I could help."

Will looked at her dubiously. "If you think I'd house you with a group of ex-soldiers, you need more supervision than I realized. Even if I'm here, I can't watch you every moment."

"I don't require watching."

"Your behavior suggests otherwise. I'm going to have to find a respectable companion to stay with you here, one who can't be wrapped around your fingers as our servants obviously are."

"Thank you, Will. Even some horrid dragon would be better than Emery and Sylvia. But know this: I won't stop trying to help our soldiers. I'm going to the Benevolent Pauper's Hospital of the Apostles today. It should be safer, and—"

"Absolutely not; they care for the sickest of the poor, not just injured soldiers. I'll not have you falling ill." An idea lit his face. "The Duchess of Haverford and some of her friends have begun organizing projects to help. You'd do well to meet with her."

She wrinkled her nose. "I read about that. *The Ladies' Society For The Care of the Widows and Orphans of Fallen Heroes and the Children of Wounded Veterans.* Have you ever heard a more ridiculous name? It must have taken them several meetings just to name the blasted thing while they sat around over tea and cakes. I want to do more than talk, more than knit scarves to send to Spain."

He grinned at her. "The duchess would agree. You'll like her. Glenaire's sister is involved."

"The Countess of Ardmore? She spends her time spewing bile and lording it over the entire *ton*. Glenaire's mother believes all of England is beneath them except the royal dukes and maybe the Haverfords. The countess is worse."

"Not her. His older sister, Georgiana."

"The Recluse of Cambridge? I've never seen her in town."

He shrugged. "Her parents removed to the country, and Richard convinced her to spend some time in London. You'd like her, I think. Eat your breakfast and think about it." Servants had been waiting patiently at the door.

Food did help. They ate in companionable silence. "One thing, Will," she asked at last. "How did you find out I was at Finnegan's."

"Ethan Alcott came to me."

"Ethan Alcott? Who is that?"

"The Marquess of Welbrook's second son. You met him, I gather."

Her brows drew together, until a peculiar suspicion surfaced. "Is he missing one hand by any chance?"

He peered back sadly. "French saber."

"Filthy, bug ridden, malodorous..."

Will grinned. "That's him. Or it was when he appeared on my doorstep. I'm making progress with that last point." His smile quickly dropped. "Less progress on the state of his mind."

CHAPTER 3

Leaning back against the seat of Chadbourn's town carriage, Flo let hope fill her. The meeting of the Ladies' Society had been nothing like she expected. The duchess, strong minded and intelligent as they come, laid out their plans like a general. They would approach the problem strategically, using social events to lobby for votes in Parliament, writing letters and pamphlets to sway opinion, creating projects to raise funds, and expanding their work to include the unemployed and wounded veterans themselves, traveling in groups to volunteer at hospitals and less savory places. That last one made her smile. Will would not be able to argue, if her efforts had the duchess's support.

Lady Georgiana Hayden, ten years older than Flo and unmarried, had been a surprise. Nothing like her sister, the vile Countess of Ardmore, she led the pamphleteer efforts of the group. Lady Georgiana's reserve made it difficult for Flora to warm up to her at first, but the subject of overbearing brothers helped, and Flora quickly realized warmth and no small amount of shyness lay under the stern exterior. An idea took hold, one Flo couldn't shake.

Lady Georgiana would make a perfectly acceptable companion.

Unfortunately, the lady only planned to be in London until the Season began, but perhaps Lady Georgiana would consider moving to Chadbourn House until Aunt Imogene arrived.

The more Flora considered it, the more the idea pleased her. So much in fact, that she couldn't wait to tell her brother. The coachman attempted to dissuade her when she ordered the carriage to the Albany, where the earl intended to stay until he arranged housing for his temporary guests, but she had her way.

The gentleman at the desk below stairs was less easily persuaded. "Brother you say? I've heard it before. Young woman, this bachelors' establishment is no place for you. I suggest you tell your mother—"

Flo opened her mouth to object one more time, but a voice from the stairs interrupted her.

"I'll handle this, Martin." The man came down the stairs, approached her, and muttered under his breath, "Have you no sense of appropriate behavior?"

She whirled around at the arrogant speaker, ready to put a flea in his ear, but stared instead.

Thin to the point of gaunt, the man's clothes hung on his lean frame. In clean, perfectly respectable clothing, with neatly trimmed hair, and sporting a black sling—one she knew covered a missing hand—she almost didn't recognize Ethan Alcott. Lord Ethan Alcott, she reminded herself. His face had been scrubbed, but his complexion retained an ashen look. His eyes, however, held her transfixed, those rich brown eyes in which his obvious anger once again failed to mask a deep well of sorrow.

"L-lord Ethan?"

"At your service Lady Flora. May I escort you home?" He flicked a glance at Martin who watched them avidly. Belatedly, it occurred to Flo that the man at the desk was the sort to sell tidbits to *The Teatime Tattler* and its ilk.

"I was hoping to speak with my brother," she said.

"He would undoubtedly be happy to wait on you at home, once he returns." The brown eyes held hers unrelentingly.

Flo gave in. "Kindly convey my wish to speak with him when you see him, my lord," she said dismissively, trying to ignore the arm he winged for her to take.

"I will do that as soon as I see you home." He didn't budge.

She took his arm with poor grace—casting a smile dripping honey at the gaping doorman—turned to Ethan, and hissed, "Unnecessary."

"Oh, I think it is. I won't return Chadbourn's kindness by neglecting to protect his sister." He all but tossed her into the carriage. Flora's maid, Martha, stared wide-eyed when he climbed in behind her. He smiled at the sight. "At least you show a particle of sense."

Flo refused to speak to him; at least, she tried. "Your escort is unnecessary."

"It *is* necessary, if I'm to make certain you get home safely, even if it is to an establishment in which a young lady ought not to be living on her own. You've caused your brother enough trouble, and me as well."

"You? What have I ever done to you?"

He leaned back and squeezed his eyes shut. She didn't think he would answer. She flounced to one side and stared out the window, imagining painful ways to remove this interfering troublemaker from her carriage.

"You called me Lord Ethan."

Flo turned back incredulous. "I called you by your name? Oh, the horror of it."

"Martin heard you. He'll puzzle out my father's name soon enough."

"Why would you care? I should think he would be pleased to know that the son of the Marquess of Welbrook resided at the Albany."

"If Martin knows, the Marquess of Welbrook will know soon enough."

Their eyes held for a long moment while she thought it through. "You're hiding from your family," she concluded.

"Did you think they arranged my accommodations in the alley behind Finnegan's Pub?"

"Of course not. Where do they think you are?"

"I have no idea. Missing. Presumed dead. No idea."

"But how? Why?"

This time she was certain he would not answer. Obviously, his life did not concern her. The carriage turned onto one of London's most fashionable squares. With the house still ostensibly closed, the carriage went around to the mews, where the groom opened the door and handed her down. Ethan aided her maid, earning some sympathy from Flo.

She looked up at the coachman. "Return Lord Ethan to the Albany," she said, daring him to object.

He stood his ground for a moment. Finally, he spoke. "I woke up on a troop ship among the wounded. Enlisted men. No one knew who I was; it seemed simpler to leave it that way."

She had no answer for that. He bounded back into the carriage and was gone.

◈

Drinking late into the night, as gentlemen do, Ethan sat with the earl in an awkward sort of companionship. Grateful as he was for food and shelter, he still fought the instinct to run and hide. Will's prodding didn't help.

"Your brother is a good man; I've worked with him as your father's representative on legislation. Why not approach him first? I could invite him here."

He knows Edmund? The thought made him uneasy. The earl meant well, but he didn't understand, and Ethan didn't have the energy to make him do so. Even well fed and clean, he felt dead inside, as if he died at Badajoz. Will Chadbourn spoke to a dead man; why would he wish that on his father or brother?

Will sat back with a sigh and reached for the bottle. "Stubborn man," he muttered, pouring them each another glass.

"When did you come home?" Ethan asked in attempt to turn the subject.

"After Cuidad Rodrigo."

"You were there?" Ethan gasped, perhaps not so dead after all.

Will nodded sadly. "We've both seen ugly things, Ethan. Those at home don't want to know; they want to hear we survived." Something in Ethan's face must have warned him not to continue down that track because he changed the subject. "Swift told me you were with the Light Division."

"Your staff has an unusual interest in war."

"Most of them fought or cared for those who did. The Light Division at Cuidad—bad business that."

Ordered to storm the breach in the city's defenses, the Light Division was decimated, suffered staggering losses, including that of their brilliant commander, Robert Craufurd.

Ethan attempted a shrug. "We made it into the cathedral square." What was left of us.

"You took the French surrender," Will said.

Both men stared into the fire, and Ethan found comfort in knowing Will shared the images of bodies piled high in ditches, and men climbing over them to storm the walls. Even Wellington had been sickened—and then Badajoz.

"Did you tell your father? What we saw; what really happened?" Ethan asked.

"No," Will replied. After a pause he went on, "I was called home because he had become ill. There seemed little point." He turned and looked at Ethan directly. "They don't really need to hear it if they weren't there, but that's no excuse not to speak with your father—or at least your brother. They deserve to know you're alive."

Ethan refused to address his family situation. "How is it they let you serve? You were the heir."

"Did your brother ask to serve?" Will sounded genuinely interested.

"When I left, he professed envy. I don't know what passed between him and Father. There was never a question, but that he was being prepared to be Marquess. I could be spared. You were an only son, though."

"It took some effort, but my father had a perfectly able nephew as spare. Still, once he fell ill, I was needed."

"You weren't at Badajoz." Silenced deepened between them. It had been worse than Cuidad Rodrigo in ways Ethan wouldn't discuss, in ways he could never tell his family. "You should have left me as I was," Ethan said after a while.

CHAPTER 4

F lo pulled a thin blanket up around the shoulders of a young soldier. The matrons at the Benevolent Pauper's Hospital of the Apostles had told him he would be released in the next day or two. The Ladies' Society had been able to pay his way home to Yorkshire, and she had helped him write a letter to his mother warning her of his arrival.

She joined Lady Georgiana Hayden and the others in the lobby of the hospital before departing. The older women had insisted that safety of numbers made their work possible, and she had quickly realized the wisdom of traveling in groups when a man whose mind had been damaged attempted to attack one of their members.

Once in the Chadbourn carriage, Flo felt her shoulders relax. The experience had been exhausting. Across from her, Lady Georgiana seemed lost in thought. The woman had agreed to stay at Chadbourn House for a month or two and had proven to be easy company.

"They all brag about their glory," Flo said, sick at heart. They bragged, but their pitiful state belied their words. In spite of her resentment of Will's insistence on a companion, this morning she was enormously grateful for company.

"I suspect they must," the older lady replied.

"Their eyes though—haunted, every one of them. The letter I wrote for Robby Porter was full of cheer, but his eyes told a different story. They've seen terrible things."

Lady Georgiana's face mirrored Flo's own sorrow. "I suspect both seen and done things that haunt them."

"Done?" The thought startled Flo.

"War is an ugly thing. It demands inhuman amounts of courage, and can be soul destroying."

"You mean they may have turned coward? They bring shame home with them?" Flo asked, trying to think it through.

"Sometimes, yes. But war can strip off the veneer of civilization. Men are driven to savagery of which they didn't know themselves capable."

"But not all of them surely, and the war is necessary, is it not?" Flo asked. "The Corsican is a beast, and if they don't defend us what will happen?"

"Necessary, perhaps, but the longer it goes on the more it eats at them. They see and do things they can't talk about at home—both on the battlefield and off."

Flo mulled that thought over for a while. Her companion's sympathetic voice interrupted her reverie. "We're not meant to know, and they're not to be condemned by those of us who weren't there."

"No, I suspect not. Who knows what we would do in that situation? The women of Spain have suffered greatly," Flo murmured. The papers spoke of hunger and disruption, but she could guess what undefended women on their own might face.

Lady Georgiana nodded gravely. "We can only care for them, while they heal."

"Shame would be a terrible burden, would it not?" Flo

remarked, not requiring an answer. The image of Ethan Alcott's deeply sorrowful eyes came to her.

What had those eyes witnessed? Things he dreads his family knowing, I'll wager.

Another thought came to her. Her sister never spoke to Flo about her marriage. Flo assumed it to be fear; now she wondered if it was shame, an even more debilitating emotion. *Shame festers when hidden*, she thought, and it brought Ethan Alcott to mind again.

How will we help him heal? she wondered. It didn't occur to her to question the determination that she and Will between them would try to do just that.

She looked across the carriage, and saw the sorrow in the older woman's face. "I've never known a lady to speak so honestly about war, Lady Georgiana. You must be close to someone who serves."

The pale blue eyes opened wide. She seemed to accept Flo's concern. "I knew someone long ago. He was a gentle soul; I worry what nine years of war have done to him. My brother—" she waved a hand— "has had no news."

No news or none he can repeat. Lady Georgiana's brother, the Marquess of Glenaire, was a fixture in the war office with a reputation for knowing all that could be known. Flo reached across and took the woman's hand in sympathy, bringing a shy smile.

"Please call me Georgie. If we're to live together for several weeks, we can't stand on formality. May I all you Flora?"

"Flo," she replied beaming at her new friend. "I'm so glad you're with me."

Alighting from the carriage at Chadbourn House, Flo made a decision. She would talk to Will about her new realization and about Ethan Alcott.

❦

Ethan looked down the dinner table at Lady Flora's enthusiastic face and let her joy raise his spirits. He'd argued with Will about coming to dinner at Chadbourn House, but Will convinced him a small family dinner would be just the thing to help him "remember how to be civilized." *If only he knew.*

"The duchess believes, of course, that the government must act. She plans to use every social event this Season to persuade your titled peers to vote for relief," the chit went on as if government neglect of its soldiers was news. "That's why Georgie is drafting pamphlets we can distribute to the papers and on the street. Isn't she brilliant?"

The companion—sister of the Marquess of Glenaire if he understood correctly—looked uncomfortable. "Hardly that. The need is obvious," she said. "And they are from the committee, not me." She would do well to remain anonymous if, as he suspected, she was Sudbury's daughter. The old duke would stand in opposition to a support bill. Her brother, a power in the war department, probably agreed with the old man—although, if he was Will's friend, perhaps not.

Lady Flora almost bounced in her seat and went on. "We can't wait for that, in any case. The duchess says we must do what we can in the meantime." She nattered on at some length about baskets to fatherless families and visits to hospitals. At least she now had the stern Lady Georgiana and the others at her side.

Thoughts of the men he'd come back with dropped a pall on Ethan's mood. Many had no one to see to them, and no skills beyond fighting even if there was work to be had.

"What do you think, Lord Ethan?" Her question caught him out; he had drifted out of the conversation and into his shadows.

"I apologize, Lady Flora. I was woolgathering." The manners his mother drummed into him came to the fore.

"The ladies plan a Venetian Breakfast before the duchess's annual charity ball at Haverford House to benefit the cause, and there may be a Frost Fair if the weather holds another week or two. If there is, we can host the breakfast on the ice before the ball. All of London will go, of course, and it will be a perfect venue for distributing Georgie's pamphlets and raising awareness. There's to be an auction of picnic baskets as well."

"That ought to be well received. Everyone loves treats." Ethan clamped his mouth shut after that banal comment. *Baskets, indeed, as if that will do the men good.*

"The proceeds of that particular effort will go to widows and orphans. We've collected names of women in desperate straits, and plan to distribute funds, which we believe will be rather more useful than charity baskets," Lady Georgiana explained. "In addition, we expect a public auction to draw attention to the problem."

Wiser than I gave them credit for. "Admirable," Ethan murmured. The footman brought the fish course, and he gave his attention to his dinner.

"She didn't explain all of it," Flo said. "Each lady will contribute a picnic basket and then share the meal with the gentlemen who are successful bidders. There's talk of sharing a dance at the ball afterward. Will you come?"

Ethan's head bobbed up. Lady Flora's startled expression made him aware of his scowl, and he attempted to soften it. He glanced at Will to see the earl smiling benignly at his sister. *Doesn't the fool mind she plans to auction her company off? Even if it is for a good cause...*

Lady Flora broke eye contact when he didn't answer her question. A sudden thought seemed to possess her quicksilver mind, and she changed the subject. Perhaps he'd embarrassed her.

"Will! How could I forget? We had a letter today from Louisa. I can't imagine how it got through." Lady Flora turned to Lady Georgiana. "My sister lives in Philadelphia and mail, as you can imagine, has been difficult. In fact, hers makes it clear she hasn't received many of mine."

"Is all well with them?" Will asked.

"Yes! She sent news that she expects a happy event in the summer, and that Samuel is thriving. He is two years old already. How I wish I could see him."

"There's been little fighting near her, thank God. The major conflict so far has taken place in Upper Canada," Will said.

"Heaven help the Americans if Napoleon surrenders. Now that Wellington has invaded France the end may be close. When that happens, there'll be troops to spare to North America." *Putting Lady Flora's sister in the line of fire.* Ethan regretted his outburst as soon as he said it. His dinner companions stared at him; none seemed able to reply. He had been right; he wasn't fit company for ladies.

Will turned the conversation to family matters, news of cousins and happenings among the tenants at Chadbourn Park. Ethan drew breath. He had naught to contribute.

"Flo, about this Frost Fair—do you think Charles would enjoy it?" Will asked. "It might be a good excuse to ask Emery to let him visit us. I can offer to send my secretary to fetch him."

Lady Flora positively glowed at that. "He would love it, Will. Do it! The Frost Fair will be wonderful." The glance she sent Ethan at mention of the fair skittered away. She sobered just as quickly. "It is unlikely he will come, however," she murmured.

Surely the foolish woman isn't angling for an escort! She can't be that idiotic.

The conversation drifted about, making no demands on Ethan, while he tried to squash visions of promenading on the icy Thames with Lady Flora on his arm. The ladies relieved him by rising to leave the gentlemen to their port.

"That wasn't so terrible, was it?" The earl raised a questioning eyebrow.

"I'm sorry about my hasty words about the North American war. I—"

Will waved his apology away. "You only spoke the truth, and the ladies would puzzle that out sooner or later."

"Still, not fit conversation for family dinner. Lady Flora dotes on your nephew?"

"She worries for him," Will replied. "My brother-in-law is a cold fish." He grimaced. "You and I were blessed in our fathers." He leaned toward Ethan. "You ought to give him a chance. I know what happened at Badajoz. He doesn't need the horror, only that his son fought, suffered, and is home."

The blood drained from Ethan's head and his sight blinked out for a moment. "How—"

"I had Glenaire enquire. But gossip among former officers is enough to give anyone a general picture of the horror. The battle was bad enough, but the aftermath—England's shame. Wellington dispatched troops to restore order."

Glenaire enquired... How much does he know? Ethan swallowed bile. "We— I— In the end we tried to stop it. Some of us tried. It wasn't enough. Those poor people."

"You have been pronounced missing, presumed dead."

"Glenaire again? Interfering bastard," Ethan growled.

Will chuckled. "He is that; all for our everlasting good, of course. He believes the war department is now obliged to inform your father you are alive."

Ethan paled and gripped his glass. "Did you save that to pounce on me over port?"

The earl went on. "I convinced him not to, that you needed time to do it yourself. But Ethan, he's right."

Ethan's eyes strayed to the wall above Will's left shoulder while his mind darted through bits of this painful conversation. "Wellington sent in a detachment to restore order the next morning?" Ethan asked at last, half his mind wondering how he might disappear again.

"Yes—too late and it wasn't effective." Will stared into his drink. "I heard it didn't stop until he erected a gallows in the cathedral square," he murmured.

"Did he? I—"

"You were gone by then, weren't you?" Will murmured gently.

Ethan would not answer that. "Shall we go back to the Albany?"

Will rose. "As soon as we say good bye to the ladies." He started for the door before saying offhandedly, "You need to say it, Ethan, whatever it is. Get it off your soul and move on." He didn't wait for a reply.

Flo listened to Georgiana with half an ear for almost an hour, her vision darting to the door.

"They may leave without saying good-bye," Georgie pointed out.

Her companion's sympathy brought heat to Flo's cheeks. Had her growing interest in Lord Ethan Alcott become obvious? "He hated being here," she said.

"He struggled with polite conversation," Georgie agreed.

"Will is trying to bring him back to, to—not society precisely," Flo couldn't quite find the word for what she meant.

"Humanity? Or at least, comfort in human interaction? I don't think any of us completely understand the darkness he has been in."

Flo nodded. "Perhaps light is the word I meant. Bring him back to the light where there are other realities besides war."

Before Georgie could reply, the door opened and the men stepped in but did not sit. "We'll take our leave of you ladies," Will said.

"Yes, thank you for dinner," Lord Ethan added, rather, Flo thought, as a schoolboy might repeat his tutor's lessons in etiquette. He studied the floor, waiting for Will with a coiled tension that put her in mind of a man about to bolt.

"I'll see you to the door," Flo said, raising a defiant chin to her brother, who bit back a grin. Lord Ethan's startled glance told her he'd rather endure a tooth extraction than her company.

She returned his scowl with her best smile, strolled toward the men, and took the arm Lord Ethan failed to offer. Will pretended not to notice. At the door, her brother remembered papers he meant to fetch from his study, turned, and, before Flo or her companion could react, left them.

Suddenly alone with him, flustered and uncertain, Flo removed her hand from the poor man's arm. His ill-at-ease demeanor left her searching through her catalog of polite small talk: books he can't have read, gossip he likely missed, social calendars he wasn't on. She rejected the weather out of hand.

"How are you finding my brother's rooms at the Albany?" she blurted out finally. *Better than the alley behind Finnegan's no doubt.* Her face burned at that bit of stupidity, and she feared she looked as red as she felt.

"Well enough," he responded, looking desperate.

She longed to ask what he planned to do with himself, longed to know how he felt about her brother's interference.

"Your brother means well," he said, as if he read her mind.

"He usually does," she answered ruefully. "Brothers think they know best. They can be the very devil…" For one moment she saw sympathy in his eyes as if he, too, knew that brothers could be— *Of course.* She reached over and put her hand on his arm.

"Your brother must care about you very much. Whatever you've seen and done, secrets fester. You have to get it out. Go to your brother. You—" Only Will's reappearance stopped her babbling; the panic in Ethan's face alarmed her.

Will frowned from one to the other but didn't ask uncomfortable questions. "The carriage has been brought round," he said, bowing to his sister and stepping out. Lord Ethan ran after him as if the hounds of Hell nipped at his heels.

CHAPTER 5

The following morning, before the ladies did more than begin their breakfast, Will stormed back in to Chadbourn House.

"He's gone," he announced breathlessly, pinning his sister with a ferocious glare. "What in the name of all that is holy did you say to him last night, Flora Margaretta Landrum? He slipped out during the night, and no one at the Albany even saw him go."

Flora froze and Georgie set her serviette in her lap. "That poor man," she murmured.

Will began to refuse the coffee John the footman offered, but changed his mind and sat with a sigh. "A few moments to break my fast won't make any difference," Will muttered. "The irritating wretch doesn't wish to be found."

"But we must," Flo exclaimed coming out of the daze his announcement caused. She heard her voice quiver and took a deep breath. "We can't let him harm himself, or fade away in some back alley."

"Not *we*, I," her brother corrected, ignoring her scowl. "Where did you find him that first time?"

"Behind Finnegan's Pub by the docks."

"Damn. I'd hoped I had it wrong; I already checked there." He took another swallow of his coffee deep in thought.

"I told him he should speak with his brother," Flo said, belatedly answering the question he asked when he arrived.

Will dropped his head back and stared upward. "That makes two of us then. Perhaps we pushed him too hard and too fast."

"When I told him secrets festered and he ought to share them, he panicked. His eyes looked wild," she said.

Flo watched her brother accept a plate of eggs and toast and tuck into it. "How can you eat at a time like this?" she demanded.

"Starving myself won't help Ethan, and I suspect I'll need my strength today."

"Well said, Will," Georgie said, standing. "With your permission, I think I'll alert my brother. He can set runners looking for him. Unless you've already done so?"

"Glenaire was my next stop. Thank you for doing it for me, Georgiana."

Brother and sister watched her leave. "So where will we go next?" Flo asked as soon as they were alone.

"Flo..."

"Don't coddle me, Will. I won't sit here and pace while you search for him. Besides, when we find him—and I won't say 'if'—it may take both of us to talk him out of whatever darkness he's retreated into."

Her brother studied her so intensely she fought the urge to wiggle in her seat. "There are things he won't tell me, fears to tell his family, and most emphatically will not tell a lady," he said.

She nodded slowly. "I'm not so frail a flower as you gentlemen believe, nor so lacking in imagination that I can't guess what may happen in time of war, and if it appears my presence hinders rather than helps, I'll withdraw. That's all I can promise. I'm going with you."

Her brother held his hands up in a gesture of surrender. "So, my warrior princess, where do you think we should go next?"

Flo bit her lower lip. "What if he went home?"

Will's eyes went wide. "Do you think so?"

She shrugged. "I think we need to speak with the Marquess of Welbrook."

❧

Welbrook's butler pushed the door shut against the biting winter wind. He frowned down at Will's card, disapproving, no doubt, of the early and unfashionable hour, but Flo thought he sensed the importance of the visit.

"The Marquess is, I fear, out of town. Would you wish to see the young lord?"

The young lord. Flo's heart sped up.

"Kindly ask Viscount Penrhyd for a moment of his time. Tell him it is of utmost importance."

Penrhyd? Ethan's brother, no doubt. Flo tamped down her expectations. Would the butler have told us if Ethan had come here?

While the butler went in search of the viscount, a footman took their wraps, shaking the snow on the marble tiles of the foyer, while another showed them to a withdrawing room to wait.

Flo examined her surroundings, trying to see Ethan Alcott in this room. While not the most sumptuous house in London, his father's home bespoke good taste and comfort, warmth of body and spirit. *Why would anyone prefer to lie in the gutter than to live in this place?*

"Chadbourn?" A deep voice interrupted her musing. Viscount Penhryd stood in the doorway. He shared his brother's lean frame and black hair, but lacked his intensity. When his gaze swept over Flo, his puzzlement deepened. "What brings you here at this hour?" He gestured toward comfortable chairs near the fire.

Will glanced at Flo. They had hoped to find Ethan here and

hadn't discussed what to say if he wasn't. Will obviously agonized over what to tell this young man, and how much.

"Lady Flora Landrum. May I present Viscount Penrhyd? Penrhyd, my sister, Lady Flora."

"I'm honored," the viscount said politely, with the trace of a bow; his eyes didn't leave her brother.

"Lady Flora belongs to the Ladies' Society for the relief of our soldiers and their families."

"I am aware of the ladies' efforts. Have you come for a contribution or to lobby for votes?" The man continued to look baffled.

Flo felt the same. *Where is Will going with this?*

Her brother cleared his throat uneasily. "In the process of providing relief to some particularly indigent veterans a few weeks ago—" He stopped and glanced at Flo, and back to the Viscount. "The thing is Penrhyd, have you heard from your brother?"

The Viscount went rigid. "What are you saying Chadbourn? Ethan went missing over a year ago. My father is considering formal mourning. We'd have initiated it, but my mother won't hear of it."

"It is well, you haven't my lord," Flo said softly.

"Perhaps you best begin at the beginning," the viscount told them, gripping the arms of the chair so tightly his knuckles appeared white.

"What my brother started to say is that a few weeks ago I happened upon some of the poorest, most wretched of our returning men."

"I know they exist, Lady Flora. It is England's shame, but what does it have to do with my brother."

"One of them shocked me with his educated speech. He took offense at my presence in such a place." She felt her face color and cast her brother a pleading glance.

"The man, quite rightly distressed by a lady's presence in such a place, felt obliged to come to warn me about my sister's foolish start endangering herself." Flo dropped her eyes to her lap under

Will's ferocious frown before he glanced back at Penrhyd. "The thing is, it was Ethan."

"You mean you found him visiting the poor veterans?" the viscount rasped hoarsely."

"I mean he lay among them, as one of them." Flo wondered frantically if she ought to describe the filth and the stench, the missing hand. She decided not.

"I don't understand. Why would Ethan be there? If he's home, why hasn't he come to us?"

"None of us completely understands, Penrhyd. War does things to a man." Will told the viscount everything up to the point his brother disappeared the previous night. "He won't thank me for coming here," he concluded. "This is the very thing he ran to avoid."

The viscount sank his head to his hands, supported by his elbows on his chair's arms. "We've been sick with grief and worry. How can he have done this to us?"

"You can't be more miserable than Lord Ethan himself," Flo chided.

He raised his eyes to hers. "You're right of course. What must he have been through to put him in such a state?" He turned to Will, "You say he woke up among the enlisted wounded on a ship with no one recognizing him?"

Will was saved answering by a scratch at the door.

"Enter," the viscount said.

The butler bowed to his lordship. "I hope I'm correct to disturb you. There is a man huddled in the garden. Normally I would send him on his way, but I thought—" Will surged to his feet.

The old bounder listened at the door, Flo thought. *Thank goodness.* She rose as well, and passed her brother at a run.

It took the viscount a moment or two longer, but when he realized why she ran, he bounded for the door behind the Landrums.

CHAPTER 6

The cold had stiffened Ethan's bones and numbed his injured stump until he thought he likely could not rise even if he wanted to—even if he had somewhere to go. He knew he should move lest the cold take his worthless life, but the ice around his heart seemed to have frozen all motivation as well.

Odd, he thought idly, *that the cold of Mayfair could kill a man as thoroughly as the icy streets of the east end.* His father's garden smelled better, however, even with the flowers dead and the hedges withered and brown. His feet had found the garden with no conscious decision on his part after an hour or more of aimless wandering in the dark streets of London on the coldest night in Ethan's memory. Now he hunkered between the cold stone of the garden shed and the unforgiving wall, unable to move.

The early morning sun rose weak and grey, but enough to pierce the fog and illuminate the place as if through a veil, and memory seized him. From his haven between the two walls he could see the edge of a stone bench, one he and Edmund used as a pirate ship or galloping steed as the mood seized them in boyhood. One of the balconies two stories up would open to his brother's room, the other to what once was his. Memory left him with a hollow longing.

He had left Chadbourn's rooms in a panic, thinking to get as far away from the overbearing Landrums as possible. They pushed him, brother and sister, to open his soul to his family, something he could never do. It would hurt them too badly. Yet, here he was. Perhaps the warmth and obvious affection of the Landrum family made him sentimental. Perhaps he'd allowed Lady Flora's earnest plea—and her gentle gaze—to penetrate the protective shell he inhabited.

He tossed about for somewhere to go—anywhere but here—but found none. He knew he ought to return to the Albany, but he found it harder and harder to think clearly. Before he could make the effort to rise, the back door of the elegant townhouse flew open and a flash of blue pushed past two men and down the steps.

His heart stuttered at the sight of Lady Flora Landrum turning her head from side to side, searching the garden until she jarred her coiffure loose and one chestnut lock tumbled over her ear. A spark of warmth curled itself around his heart. The foolish chit. She'll catch her death without a cloak. The irony of the kettle calling the pot black brought silent laughter up from his depths until it almost reached his mouth. He longed to spar words with her.

"Next to the shed," a voice said. When she marched in his direction, he pushed himself painfully to his feet.

"Ethan!" A man ran past her calling his name just as his knees buckled. He fell forward into his brother's arms.

I can't stay. I have to go. I'm not fit. No words came out of his mouth. The instinct to run drained from him, and he collapsed against Edmund's shoulder. His brother brushed Chadbourn's help aside. Ethan felt himself lifted and gave in to the feeling of safety.

"Ethan, you bloody idiot. We've been terrified for you; I can't tell you how happy I am to have you home," his brother said, carrying him inside.

For now. Until you know everything.

The warmth of the drawing room overwhelmed his senses, sudden change as painful as it was welcome. Edmund laid him on a settee, tenderly placed the arm missing a hand across his chest, and stood back. He studied the ruin of Ethan's arm for a moment, jerked away, and ran about shouting orders. Ethan only vaguely heard him.

Someone, Chadbourn he thought, stood behind the settee and began to rub his back in an attempt to make his blood flow. One thing came to him clearly through the haze: Lady Flora kneeling beside him, her eyes on his, holding his hand.

"Whatever it is, Ethan, you can't fix it by destroying yourself," she murmured, and the sound of her voice saying his name filled him with another sort of warmth.

What was it I need to fix? The thought flitted in and out as blankets arrived to wrap him, and someone began stripping off his frozen wet clothing.

"Out with you, Flo," Chadbourn called. "Let us get him dressed in warm clothes and covered."

"No!" he tried to hold onto her hand as if it was his lifeline and failed.

"Moments only; I won't let them keep me out," she whispered, pulling away.

Rude hands forced him into a thick nightshirt and dressing gown, warm socks, and a cocoon of a wool blanket. All the while, one of them rubbed his back.

Edmund came down on his knees and began rubbing Ethan's legs, but Chadbourn stopped him. "I saw it once in the Pyrenees. A man almost died from his companions' over eager help. The surgeon explained that we have to warm his middle first. You sent for a doctor?"

His brother loomed over him, rubbing his belly and shoulders. "Yes, I sent a man running. Warm up, damn it, Ethan!"

A more welcome voice came to his brother's side. Lady Flora dropped down next to him, cup in hand. "Sip it slowly; it will help you," she said. The lady forced tea, hot and dark, on him while he struggled to remember her earlier words. *What was it I need to fix?*

"My lord, the carriage is ready and I am prepared to travel. Do you wish to add to your message that Lord Ethan has returned?" The voice came from the door.

Edmund stood to face the speaker. "No just— Wait; let me think. Tell my father Lord Ethan has returned to us ill, a physician has been summoned, and he is in my care. Assure him he will be well, however."

Father! Like the sudden heat of the room his father's name both warmed and hurt him. *What was it I need to fix? So much, oh so much.*

৩ৡৣঌ

Flo fidgeted in misery; she found the Welbrook drawing room uncomfortable, filled as it was with memories of her last visit. Georgie had agreed with some reluctance to accompany her during proper calling hours, and that only after Will approved this visit.

Will himself had called daily, feeling obliged to mind the well-being of someone he'd taken under his wing. She knew this because he had moved back to Chadbourn House once he no longer had Ethan as a guest at The Albany.

He reported a sad case of lung fever, the doctor's dire warnings, and finally, last night, a turn for the better. All the while Flo fretted and fumed. She had to see for herself, and had almost given into temptation to storm the Welbrook house. Only with Ethan's improvement did her brother relent.

Now she fretted with impatience, while the butler went to see if the family was "in." After what felt like an eternity Viscount Penrhyd himself greeted the ladies.

Flo gave what she hoped was a creditable curtsy, and said, "May I inquire, my lord, if you've recovered from the shock of my last visit?"

His smile held only a hint of sadness. "Good shock is easy to bear. I'm well, but I think, perhaps, you actually came to see my brother."

His blunt talk flustered her, and she studied the toes of her slippers, murmuring, "Georgie and I are concerned about him." She peeped up and continued, "He was my brother's guest before…"

"Before he came home. I know we have you and your brother to thank for that. He might have died on the streets without you."

"Is he well? My brother told me a lung fever laid him low, but that he's improved." She held her breath.

"In body, yes. His fever has gone, thank the powers that be," Penrhyd said fiercely.

The information lifted her spirits, but worry persisted. "And his mind? Has he spoken to you?"

"About his ordeal? No. We don't know any more than your brother told us. He wants to see you."

"Me?" she squeaked.

"Father and I were in the sickroom when they told us you had called. He overheard and asked—nay, demanded—to see you."

Flo glance over to find Georgie frowning deeply. "My lord," Georgie said, "I'm not sure it would be proper."

"Strictly speaking, perhaps not. But if you could bring yourself to accompany Lady Flora, and my father and I are present, it might be acceptable. It would give my brother comfort."

Flo used her eyes to plead with Georgie, barely controlling the urge to bound up the stairs.

Lady Georgiana sighed deeply. "Very well. For a few moments."

The viscount escorted the ladies upstairs into a room at the back of the house. The rare sunny day poured light through windows overlooking the garden. A tall man rose from a chair next to the bed at their entrance.

Flo hardly registered his shock of white hair and a face that matched his sons', seeing only the man on the bed, even as she heard Viscount Penrhyd introduce her and her companion to his father, even as she dipped a proper curtsy to the marquess.

"This is my savior, Father." Ethan's voice sounded weak, but it didn't waver. He reached out his good hand to her, and the old man moved to stand against the wall with his elder son.

Flo dropped into the chair his father had abandoned and took the offered hand in hers, studying his pale face and haunted eyes for signs of improvement. "Are you, then? Saved that is?"

He broke eye contact at that. "I'm here," he murmured. "Isn't that enough. It is what you wanted."

"I'm not the one who can say so, my lord."

He turned back to her then. "You are merciless."

"On the contrary. You are the one who must show yourself mercy. And I suggested you talk with them, not that you sit in an icy garden until you made yourself ill."

"I can't—"

"Lady Flora, my son has just recovered from severe illness. This is not the time to press him."

She smiled back to the marquess. "I understand, my lord. Perhaps in time Lord Ethan can put down the burdens he carries." She would have risen, but he held her hand fast. She turned back to see his intense gaze bore into her.

"Now," he said.

"Now?"

"Not later. I may not have courage," he said.

She realized he meant to unburden himself in front of her, and felt like an intruder. *Surely this is a private family moment.* She turned to Georgie who took a step closer.

"It may be best if we leave you to rest," Lady Georgiana interjected.

Ethan ignored her; his eyes bore into Flo's. "You saw me in that alley. I will tell you what put me there."

She stared back, unable to gainsay him.

"I can only do this once. Be my courage."

She nodded then and gave his fingers a gentle squeeze.

His eyes never left hers, though surely his message was meant for the two men listening avidly behind her. "What do you know of Badajoz?"

Behind her Georgie gasped; Flo searched her mind. "It was a great victory bought at great cost."

He squeezed his eyes shut, and she thought he had withdrawn from them again, but she heard him murmur, "More than you can imagine, and it wasn't the first."

"You don't have to do this, Ethan," she whispered.

"Exactly right," his father said. "The things you remember are not fit for ladies, I'll warrant, in any case, son."

The grip on her hand didn't weaken. She replied to the marquess without taking her gaze from his son. "Sometimes, shame is harder to recount than horrid memories."

"My son is no coward!" The old man's words, wrenched from his soul, echoed off the walls.

His fears, no doubt. "Yes. I think not," she agreed out loud. "There are other reasons for shame." Ethan's eyes blinked open, filled with surprise at her insight and yet the bleakness she saw there almost made her faint. His gentle press to her fingers kept her steady.

"After the surrender," he began, but he choked on his words.

War can strip off the veneer of civilization... The memory of Georgie's words flooded Flo's mind with horrific images. "The troops wouldn't stop at surrender," she guessed. After a long silence she added, "You tried to stop it."

His brows shot up and he growled. "Don't give me credit. Not at first. I burned and destroyed with the enlisted men." He turned to the wall, and his voice dropped to a dull rasp. "We gave everything and the damned city... They wouldn't surrender, and we were enraged by the dead on the walls, enraged..."

She heard a sob behind her. The marquess.

Ethan turned back to her suddenly. "I came to my senses. I did, but not soon enough." His eyes flitted over her shoulder toward his father and back to Flo "So much shame overwhelmed me that I stripped off my tunic, my insignias of rank. I threw it all down."

That at least explains how he came to be on the boat among the common soldiers.

"What happened next, Ethan?" his brother asked.

Ethan's gaze stayed on Flo's. "I started back to camp. I had no coat, no gun, no sword. I—" He swallowed deeply. "I came upon an officer—a major no less—and a mob in an alcove. They— She—" He took a shuddering breath. "I had to stop them. I tried, I tried, I —" His gaze came into focus as if just realizing who held his hand. He couldn't go on.

"Enough!" The marquess said. "My son needs to rest."

Flo gave into impulse and leaned in to kiss Ethan's forehead. "Be well, my lord," she said. Still leaning over him she whispered, "Whatever happened, you can't fix it now, but you can help the other veterans. You can, but not as a starving wretch."

She turned to leave, but had no words for the two grieving men behind her beyond a whispered, "Thank you."

As she got to the door, she heard one more thing from the man on the bed. "It wasn't a French saber." She turned to see him raising the arm without a hand. "Not a French saber," he repeated.

Our own men turned on him! Buzzing filled her ears.

CHAPTER 7

Two days after her visit, Ethan received Chadbourn from a chair in the sickroom when Edmund accompanied him up.

"Goodness, Ethan. You look like a changed man." Will sounded confident, but Ethan didn't miss the concern in his eyes.

"Food and warmth." Ethan attempted a smile; the unfamiliar sensation made it brief.

"The ladies sent this to relieve your boredom. If you find it equally tedious, I won't tell."

Ethan took the small volume from the earl and glanced at the title. "'*Pride and Prejudice, By the Author of Sense and Sensibility,*'" he read. "I haven't heard of either book."

"Published only last year and already in a second edition," the earl replied. "The ladies dote on it, but I have to admit I liked it as well. Volumes two and three will be forthcoming if you enjoy this one, and perhaps even if you don't."

Ethan couldn't miss Will's intense study, and dreaded what it might mean. Edmund pulled up a chair to sit with them, and Ethan was glad.

A note had been tucked in the book. Ethan showed it to the earl with a raised brow. Chadbourn gestured upward with a hand, and so Ethan opened it and read. "Lord Ethan, I hope this finds you better. Rest your fevered mind with some pleasant reading. It is my hope that that may help. Lady Flora Landrum."

"A bit dramatic," the earl mumbled.

Fevered mind, indeed. "Thank her for me," Ethan told him. He suspected the earl had read it before presenting it, protective brother that he was, and indeed, Chadbourn appeared to choose his next words carefully.

"I gather you unburdened yourself yesterday." He attempted to sound casual and failed.

Edmund's gaze sharpened, and Ethan's gut clenched. He didn't like to remember his conversation with Flora, and he dreaded the loss of Will Chadbourn's newly-formed friendship. He glanced at his brother. "My only defense is that I needed a buffer between my words and my family. I could speak looking at her face; not my father's."

"And my sister pushed you to speak," the earl sighed, leaning back in his chair.

"She did." He leaned toward Chadbourn. "Will, please know I didn't speak in detail and I stopped short of—"

"Something a lady shouldn't hear? How did you lose your hand? Flo told me you said, 'he wasn't French.' What in God's name happened?"

"If she repeated everything I said, you may surmise I came upon a group of men abusing a woman."

"He stopped short of actually spelling that out, Chadbourn," Edmund interjected.

"You should realize the ladies are capable of surmise as well, however," the earl said.

Ethan grimaced at that. "Only it was a young girl, not a grown woman and the mob was led by an officer, one without honor." The darkness began to descend again, tempting Ethan to hide.

Edmund leaned forward and touched his arm. "What did you do, Ethan? You said you tried."

"I ran into the middle of them screaming like a banshee—unarmed and in my shirtsleeves. The officer took offense when I intervened." He raised his damaged arm. "I don't remember much after that. Shocked faces. I can only pray the distraction made a difference."

"You're lucky you didn't bleed to death," Will said. "I'm guessing at least someone in that mob was shamed enough to take you to the surgeons. Who was the officer?"

"Major Lord Alfred Hartford," he spat with a grimace.

Will let out a string of curses. "Incompetent bastard," he concluded. "I always loathed him."

"The Duke of Warrington's youngest? I should kill him!" Edmund said. He sighed at Ethan's horror. "I wouldn't, of course, but you ought to have brought it to authorities."

"His father is the regent's crony," Will reminded him. "They will protect him—but you knew that, Ethan, didn't you? Is that why you stayed hidden?"

"Perhaps that was part of it. If I speak up now, nothing will happen to him, and I can't bear it," Ethan shouted.

Will and Edmund's eyes met. "What?" Ethan demanded. "I won't go to Horse Guards with this. If I spill my guts there, I'll look like a weakling, and he'll get off."

"There may be other ways," Edmund said.

"It can't hurt to look into the major's whereabouts," Will added.

Silence stretched between them. The earl patted his knee and rose to leave, but Ethan had one more thing to say. "Your sister said something else yesterday. She reminded me that I can do nothing to change the past—and I hope you both accept that we can do little about the bastard that did this—but I can still help the others. She meant the men on the street. Is that what you do?"

"What do you mean?"

"I've seen the one-eared footman and the pugilist butler. I spoke with that soldier's widow you call a cook. How many more have you employed?"

"Not enough, though Chadbourn Park is thick with them."

Ethan sat back pensively. "We can do the same—hire veterans that is. What do you think, Edmund?"

"One-eared footman?" Edmund asked.

"There's a one-legged footman at Chadbourn Park," Will answered with a wry grin. "He manages."

"You'll need staff at Brookside when you're well," Edmund told his brother.

"The farm grandfather left me?"

Edmund nodded. "I've tried to keep an eye on your steward, but I fear it is understaffed and sadly neglected. He turned to address Will. "We can hire veterans, but there must be more we can do."

"There is. Not least is badgering the government to take responsibility. You—both of you—might find the tracts from that Ladies' Society interesting, even more so than that book in your lap. But you need to be well—body and soul, Ethan, at least as can be. Think about it."

Ethan might have despaired in the next several days if it weren't for the steady stream of good wishes from Flora—he heard her brother call her Flo, but she had become "my Flora" to him. He kept that bit of nonsense to himself, though the household knew he looked forward to her missives, often delivered by Chadbourn himself. A box of sweet cakes from the Chadbourn kitchen came with a tract on the need to employ returning soldiers written, so Will assured him, by Lady Georgiana. A potted orchid came with one on destitute widows. Volume two by the "Author of Sense and Sensibility" came with a flier about a coming event.

Flora is getting her Frost Fair after all, he mused. A smile began with a twitch of his lips and grew to engulf his heart.

Viscount Digby Osgood stood on a stool lacing a brightly painted sign to the canvass in front of a newly created booth. It read: *The Ladies' Society For The Care of the Widows and Orphans of Fallen Heroes and the Children of Wounded Veterans.*

"Why you managed to get it all on one sign after all. I am impressed!" a voice called. Flo looked out to see Lady Constance Whittles gazing up at Lord Osgood with adoring eyes. A footman accompanied her, and they both carried boxes of pamphlets.

Lord Osgood hopped down and helped carry them inside the tent where Lady Constance helped Georgie and Flo unpack tracts and arranged them on a long table stretched across the opening. Flo had been pleased with the location, well removed from some of the more raucous establishments, on a street with a vendor of hot cider, one hawking pasties, and another selling woolen scarves. They were only six places down from Mr. Clemens, editor of *The Teatime Tattler* and his printing press. If they needed copies, they could apply to him quickly.

"I wonder if that is the best place for the table," Flo said. "The duchess suggested we make every effort to engage people in conversation. The written word is good, but the personal approach is better." She glanced sharply at Georgie, "Not that your writing isn't wonderful."

Georgie returned a wan smile. "No offense taken. I know better than any the limitations of printed words. Shall we pull it back? I believe Her Grace plans to send sweets from Fournier's of London to entice people to linger."

"I do believe it might be better against the wall," Lady Constance suggested.

"I have to agree," Flo answered with a smile.

"Allow me, ladies," Lord Osgood said.

"Cakes from Monsieur Fournier's renowned restaurant are treasures that will draw this man in—and many others no doubt," Lord Osgood told them, as he helped them suit action to words, pulling the table to the side of the booth. The young man helped the ladies in many of their endeavors, motivated, Flo suspected, by his obvious interest in Lady Constance Whittles.

"Thank you, Lord Osgood," Lady Georgiana said.

Flo knelt to warm her hands at the small brazier they had brought. She had removed her mittens for the work, and the fierce cold had not abated one whit. *Good, I suppose, if we're to socialize and work on this ice!*

"Help me unroll this rug," Georgiana said. Flo and the viscount jumped to assist. They had found a thick, if somewhat worn, wool rug in the Chadbourn attics. At least they wouldn't have to stand on ice when their turns came to be in the booth.

Lady Constance looked around the tent. "You two seem to have everything well in hand. Perhaps I can lend some assistance elsewhere.

"I believe I will accompany Lady Constance," Lord Osgood said, "unless you ladies have further tasks for me. Will you need escort home?"

"Chadbourn plans to return for us," Georgiana told him.

"Where is he?" the man asked. "I was expecting to see him; I understood he planned to help today."

"Something changed, and he went to visit at Welbrook House," Flo said biting back the temptation to mention Ethan's name. She had no idea what announcements about his return the family planned to make.

When he left with a proper bow and jaunty wave, Flo voiced concerns to Georgie who stood beside her watching him leave. "What is my brother up to, do you think? We've hardly seen him these few days," she said.

"He told you he planned to speak with other veterans. One suspects soldiers reminisce most honestly when they gather for drinks and none of us are there to inhibit their memories," her friend suggested.

Flo nodded. "It is a closed world, isn't it? I suspect he has been seeking information about Ethan's injury. Perhaps he was able to pry something loose. He certainly seemed in a rush to get to Welbrook's house after breakfast this morning."

"We'll find out soon enough—or not if the gentlemen choose to protect our delicate ears," Georgie said, drawing a rude snort from Flo. "Come help me finish unpacking," she said.

Once the pamphlets were arranged to their satisfaction and camp stools unfolded, Georgie decide to tack copies of the flier about the charity auction to the tent poles on either side of the entry.

"What do you think you're about, Missy?" a rude voice demanded.

Flo rushed to the opening. Georgiana stood frozen in place with her back to the speaker. The expression on her face alarmed Flo.

"Good to see you too, Uncle Horace," her tone dripped sarcasm. She pulled herself up to her full height and slipped into what Flo had come to recognize as her Lady Georgiana Hayden-daughter-of-ducal-splendor persona. She stood an inch taller than the rotund, florid-faced man. Flo would not have wanted to be on the receiving end of that glare. It outdid even her sister, the Countess of Ardmore.

"Lady Flora Landrum, may I present my maternal uncle, Sir Horace Malford."

"Landrum? Chadbourn's chick?" He cast Flo an assessing gaze as if determining the value of her fur-trimmed redingote, the size of her dowry, and her precise place in any order of precedence he might be forced to endure. Just as quickly he dismissed her and focused on his niece.

"Does your mother know about this abomination?" He indicated the fliers with a movement of his shoulder. "Does she even know you are in London? When I saw her at Mountview, she said—"

"I do not live in my mother's house nor under her rule, Uncle. I am of age. You will do well to remember that. I'm in London at

Glenaire's insistence. As it happens, I am a guest at Chadbourn House."

Cheeks quivering with indignation, he sputtered. "We shall see, we shall see when I report to your mother what I've seen here. Ladies' Society, indeed, as if a Hayden would dirty her hands."

Georgiana did not answer; she held her ground and pinned him with an aristocratic glare until he shrunk a bit, and hurried away, shaking his head.

Flo darted out a hand to Georgie's arm when her friend sank back. "Are you well?"

"Certainly. Horace is such a worm. He toadies to my mother who married above herself to his everlasting delight." She didn't look well, and didn't meet Flo's eyes. She brushed her hands together. "My, but it is cold."

"You look unhappy."

"It is just that I need to leave London sooner than we planned. And I need to warn the duchess that Sudbury may cause trouble." Her father, a powerful duke, was a friend—or at least a rival—of the Duke of Haverford.

"She'll sort it out." A thought struck Flo. "Am I right that you have your own household in Cambridge?" The thought filled her with awe. The ladies began pulling on their mittens.

"Yes, I do. Both my mother and I prefer it that way," her friend answered grimly.

"I envy you your own establishment. You can do as you please."

"Hardly! But it is a kind of independence, and I have my work. Don't envy me. You are fourteen years younger and have many options ahead of you."

"You mean the blasted marriage mart? I had a season. As much as I grieve for my father, I'm glad mourning will spare me the next one. Besides, I told you about my sister Sylvia; she has quite put me off marriage."

"Don't be so quick to assume it is that way for everyone.

Marriage just didn't happen for me. Come, let's go find that hot cider while we wait for Chadbourn."

Mention of her brother made her think of Ethan. "Do you suppose Lord... Edmund will attend the Frost Fair—perhaps even our auction?"

"Don't see why not. In spite of what my uncle believes, all of London will be here. Even my brother plans to attend."

"I suppose Lord Ethan won't be well enough." Flo mumbled.

Georgiana bit her lip to suppress a grin, and took Flo by the arm. "It seems unlikely—but you may well see him again at some later time."

I can hope. I can always hope, Flo thought.

⚜

"Dead?" Ethan repeated for the third time.

"Glenaire checked official records, and yes, Alfred Hartford died crossing the Pyrenees into France. No one I know witnessed it, but multiple sources reported it," Will told him.

"It seems too easy," Edmund said, eyes on his brother who still stared at his lap.

"Perhaps not," Will mused. "The stories are consistent that he died after a fall hundreds of feet from a cliff edge." He also watched Ethan. "One rumor is that he jumped."

Ethan looked up sharply at that. "Guilt?"

Will shrugged. "There were plenty of reports about despicable behavior before, during and after Cuidad Rodrigo and Badajoz, but Hartford didn't strike me as man burdened by guilt."

Ethan sighed. "I suppose it doesn't matter."

"Another rumor is that someone pushed him."

"Who?"

"No one named names, but he was widely despised by his men, perhaps the very men you saw him with," Will said.

"The ones who took Ethan to the surgeons?" Edmund suggested.

"Someone participating or someone who witnessed it, yes," Will agreed.

"Or it may have been an accident," Ethan murmured.

"Perhaps. The Almighty exacting His own justice?"

"At least I don't have to fear what I would do if I encountered him in London," Edmund said. He studied his brother, who seemed lost in his own thoughts. "Sorry you can't exact revenge?" Edmund asked him.

Ethan shook his head. "This is tidier. I can't say I'm sorry the toad is dead."

"He didn't get a funeral. I gather they left him to the predators in the mountains. Perhaps you can bury him in your memories," Will suggested.

Not bloody damned likely. Yet, the ugly memories felt a little less raw knowing Hartford died, as so many brave men did on the walls of the city. Something else hung in his mind though. "The girl —I suppose we'll never know what happened to her."

"Probably not. I spoke with everyone I trusted who was at Badajoz and heard nothing."

"Thank you for trying," Ethan said. He tried to force a smile, "and thank Lady Flora for this." He held up Volume Three of the novel he had been reading.

Edmund walked Will downstairs. Just as they parted, Will pulled something from his coat. "I almost forgot. The ladies most specifically asked me to give this to you, Penrhyd."

"A charity auction on the ice?" the viscount laughed. "We're invited to the Haverford Ball of course, but this is something else entirely."

"All of London will be there. They are bound to raise quite a bit. Will you come?"

"Father can sit with Ethan, so I suppose I'm free to come," Edmund said.

"You can't keep treating him as if he'll fall apart—or disappear."

"We're just happy to have him back. Sooner or later he'll pursue his own life again, but for now we want to be close."

"Fair enough. Perhaps I'll see you tomorrow." He left with the nod of his head.

CHAPTER 8

The sun peeked dimly through the fog the morning of the Ladies' Society Venetian Breakfast. The people of London watched in awe as an army of Haverford servants, augmented by those of various great houses, erected a sumptuous marquee on the ice at one end of the makeshift town that had grown up along the Thames. The tent dwarfed the booths and shelters around it, as it was as large as the Haverford ballroom with a ceiling almost as tall.

Lady Flora and her companion arrived to watch just as men began carrying in rolls of carpeting to cover the ice. Her brother had abandoned her to Georgie's company as soon as they arrived, mumbling something about a message from the Marquess of Glenaire.

She watched more men follow with chairs, and tables, and crates that Flora knew contained linen for the tables, cotton to drape the walls, furs and woolen shawls in which to snuggle, and much, much more.

Around the marquee, a score of other tents, large and small, sprouted and grew under the ministering hands of a swarming army of workers. Mrs. Potter and a newly hired footman arrived from Chadbourn House with two overflowing hampers of food, one labeled *Lady Flora Landrum* and one *Lady Georgiana Hayden*, and carried them into the waiting tent.

More servants set up a perimeter: an insubstantial barrier of bollards and ribbons, reinforced by a guard that Flora knew to be returned soldiers and sailors, recovered sufficiently from their wounds to serve in the cold of a single day but no longer fit for foreign duty. The Society had found rooms for them all.

Flo and Georgie strolled among hundreds of the *beau monde* who crowded the marquee—many of them people would never otherwise put their hands in their pockets for the charitable cause in question. With every step she scanned the crowd looking—

Flo felt foolish, realizing she searched the crowd for the sight of Lord Ethan Alcott, who she knew lay well-cared for at Welbrook House and whose health could not be risked on the Thames ice. She determined to be happy about the size of the crowd and the success of the auction, whomever her luncheon companion may be.

The unusual setting had undoubtedly drawn many to the event, that and the talk that the Society's members had been assiduously spreading about how all fashionable people would be present. Flo wondered if their idea that each lady offered her company along with the lunch basket had caused enough titillation to draw others to witness the scandal.

Good. We can use the money!

They passed some particularly sour-looking matrons, and she looked up to see Georgie's eyes dancing as one tried to discuss the impropriety without ever—God forbid—criticizing the Duchess of Haverford herself.

It came as a relief when Brigadier General Lord Redepenning stepped up onto the stage, accompanied by Her Grace.

The duchess spoke first, briefly explaining the purpose of the Society, encouraging everyone to open their purses and be generous, and then handing over to Mrs Beresford, as the chairwoman of the Society's organizing committee.

Mrs Beresford confined herself to welcoming them all before inviting Lord Henry (as he was known by all but his subordinates in the Horse Guard) to begin the auction.

Flo glanced nervously around the room. Her brother had promised to be here for the bidding, but she saw no sign of him, nor did she spy the distinctive white-blond head of the Marquess of Glenaire towering over the company.

Lord Henry briefly explained how the auction would work: the winner of a basket also won the right to share the contents with the lady who donated it. The usual rules of propriety prevailed, and no lady would lunch without a chaperone, unless, of course, her basket was purchased by a close family member. With the lady's permission, the successful bidder might also claim a dance at the ball to follow in the evening.

A footman in Haverford livery handed Mrs. Beresford the first basket, and she brought it to Lord Henry.

He mimed opening the top, held it to his nose, and gave a deep theatrical sigh. "Magnificent. Your Graces, my ladies, my lords, gentlemen, I give you a picnic basket that, if it tastes as good as it smells, will be a rare treat. One made even pleasanter, dare I say, by the company of the lovely Lady Priscilla Fenton."

He lifted the label again, and added, "Oh, and it says, her elder brother and his wife." Speaking over the laughter, he added, "Ah, well," which set them off again.

The bidding was fast, and no one was surprised when Lord Wrathall, who had been courting Lady Priscilla for the last several months, allowed himself to be cozened out of nine pounds ten shillings for the privilege of walking off with the basket and the lady.

Three baskets later, Lord Henry moved to a familiar heavily-laden basket from the Chadbourn kitchens. A hush came over the crowd when he announced the lady to be Lady Georgiana Hayden. Flo heard an incredulous stage whisper behind her, "The Recluse of Cambridge? Does Sudbury know she is here?"

She turned to the source in time to see Sir Horace Malford, red in the face, storming toward them. "What are you thinking," he hissed at Georgie. "Your mother will…"

"Quiet in the ranks," Lord Henry called out. "Are you bidding, Sir Horace?"

"I will not be a part of this disgrace," the man snapped.

"Then I suggest you sit down, Horace, and be quiet," Lord Henry retorted.

Georgiana stood as tall and proud as only a Hayden can, but a faint flush to her cheeks showed her distress as Horace sputtered, people tittered, and no bids were forthcoming, afraid of drawing the wrath of the Duke or Duchess of Sudbury.

Flo heard the man standing by Matilda Grenford comment, "Is the man calling an event organized by Her Grace the Duchess of Haverford a disgrace?" He did not bid, however, and Flo's heart ached for her friend, who looked stoically ahead.

"They are all afraid of Sudbury," Flo whispered. Georgiana said nothing.

"Twenty Guineas," a commanding voice from the rear said. All heads turned to see the Marquess of Glenaire look unwaveringly at Lord Henry.

"Ah!" Lord Henry said. "Offered by a man who has undoubtedly experienced picnics prepared by Lady Georgiana and knows their worth." He held the gavel as his eyes scanned the room, and the comments and laughter stilled. Finally, he brought it down. "Sold to the Marquess of Glenaire."

The Marquess paid his shot, accepted the basket, and came to offer an arm and an encouraging, if muted, smile to his sister and lead her away. Will came to stand by Flo when they moved on.

The bidding continued briskly, and they had no time to speak. She saw Viscount Sterling scoop Lady Emma Frampton and her luncheon on offer out from under Lieutenant Branson and Beau Fishingworth. Several others went quickly, ten pounds here and twelve there, until the Earl of Trehallow shocked the company by outbidding the Marquis of Adlridge by the outrageous sum of one hundred pounds for the privilege of luncheon with Miss Cummins.

"Going once, going twice," Lord Henry intoned, "With no further bids, sold to the Earl of Trehallow. Sir, pay the purser to my left and claim your prize."

After an awed pause caused by the earl's bid, the auction continued, and Flo began to grow anxious until at last she saw her basket lifted to the table. Her brother would buy it, of course. That would be proper.

She bounced on her toes when the general intoned, "A lovely basket from Lady Flora Landrum, sister of the Earl of Chadbourn. Do I spy lemon cakes? The Chadbourn House kitchens are famous for them. Shall we begin bidding at ten pounds?" Silence.

"Oh, I say," a man called. "Lemon cakes are my favorite. Ten pounds."

Flora's one season had been brief, providing few suitors, and she feared her state of mourning offended the highest sticklers. Would she have many offers? When some tentative bids, from Lieutenant Branson and Beau Fishingworth among others, began to push the price upward, she sighed with relief.

Will smiled down at her. "Fifty pounds," he called.

"Seventy-five." For a heart stopping moment it sounded like Lord Ethan Alcott's voice, but of course that was impossible. Flo turned this way and that, looking for the source while Lord Henry called for more bids.

"Eighty," her brother called with a devilish grin and a wink. Flo's jaw dropped.

"One hundred and fifty." A collective gasp came over the crowd.

"Another generous bidder!" Lord Henry laughed.

Chadbourn smirked, "More than I expected."

It wasn't the highest bid that day, but far more than most. Flo felt her face heat. She barely heard Lord Henry close bidding. With one hand on her brother's shoulder she craned her neck to see who came forward.

Lord Edmund Alcott, Viscount Penrhyd sauntered toward the table to pay and collect her basket. No wonder she thought she heard Ethan! He sounded much like him.

"Lady Flora, Chadbourn," the grinning viscount greeted them.

Flo sank into a proper curtsey, eager to thank the viscount for his generous bid and equally eager to ask him about his brother's wellbeing.

"Chadbourn, would it be acceptable for me to escort your sister out of the marquee? I have something to show her."

Flo saw the twinkle in her brother's eye and peered from one to the other.

"Of course, Penrhyd. I will follow in due time." Will winked. He actually winked.

Bemused, Flo let herself be led away.

❦

Ethan watched through a break among the tents as Lady Flora—his Flora— took his brother's arm and exited the marquee housing the Venetian Breakfast. Edmund led her down the makeshift street toward the landau where Ethan waited with escalating frustration. Bundled in blankets and swathed in shawls like some damned infant, Ethan sat across from his father who examined him from the rear-facing seat as if he feared Ethan might fall ill at any moment.

"I won't collapse, I promise," he muttered.

"This is a fool's errand, Ethan. We can invite the earl and his sister to dinner, and she may thank you then," the old man grumbled. "I'm grateful to her for bringing you back to us; I'm happy to assist her in any way, but not at the expense of a relapse."

Ethan ignored him and shifted once more toward his brother and the woman on his arm. He had planned this carefully, sending Edmund as his surrogate, demanding the open landau, and requesting her maid who sat meekly in the far corner, for propriety's sake. He wouldn't quit now.

Flora and Edmund approached two open cafés; she glanced about with obvious confusion when they passed them, and seemed to be on the verge of asking questions when they reached the front of the landau.

Her brows rose as if to ask, you brought me to see a carriage? When she peered up at the coachman her eyes widened.

"John?"

The biddable one-eared footman spoke up. "I've had a promotion, Lady Flora. His lordship offered me work as coachman like I've always wanted."

"Does my brother know?"

"The earl said as how I should better myself, and that it opened a position for another man in need of one."

Flora's smile warmed Ethan more than the hot bricks his father had placed beneath his feet. Unfortunately, she smiled at Edmund not Ethan. "Well done, my lord. I suspect your tiger is new as well," she said, indicating the man who had clambered down prepared to open the landau's door. She couldn't have missed the man's pronounced limp.

Edmund cleared his throat. "We've made a start, my lady," he said, "but that isn't why I brought you here." He drew her to the side of the landau, looking past her at the passengers in the vehicle, and she turned her head in response. Ethan unwrapped his face to smile back at her.

Her gasp almost choked her. "You shouldn't be here!"

"My thoughts exactly," Edmund murmured in her ear, "but he wouldn't be swayed."

She appeared dumbfounded, unable to think what to say.

"Did we do well, Edmund?" Ethan asked.

"I believe the ladies were pleased with your purchase," his brother responded.

"His?" Flo asked.

"The same. This is the gentleman entitled to your time and attention, Lady Flora, but he will most likely not take the opportunity to dance at this evening's ball. I think you best have your meal and conversation some place warm."

"Yes, and quickly please. We have bespoken a private parlor at Farley's hotel," his father added, smiling kindly. "Your brother will come to accompany you home to change for the ball in two hours, and this young man—" he glanced pointedly at Ethan "—will go home where he belongs."

As Edmund helped her up, he said, "You might encourage my brother to wrap back up before his lungs take a relapse," he said. He handed the basket he bought up to Ethan.

To Ethan's pleased surprise, his father rose and stepped down to stand by his older son. "Well, Edmund, do you suppose there are still more of these lovely baskets to be had? Shall we go check?"

Flora's gaze flitted between the men's departing backs and the carriage, noticing Martha's familiar face peering shyly back over a warm cloak and shawl for the first time. She shot Ethan a frown. "An open carriage and my maid for propriety? The Alcott gentlemen have arranged everything neatly among themselves. With my brother's help, I suspect." She took a place on the forward-facing seat next to Ethan, taking the basket and handing it to Martha.

He grinned shamelessly, feeling smug. "We did—rather well I think."

The carriage lunged forward. "And I can see I have no excuse not to let you take me where you will," she sighed, coloring adorably.

When Ethan continued to grin like a fool, she pursed her lips primly. "Your scarf," she said, indicating the garment in question with a graceful gesture.

He obligingly covered his mouth. His "Thank you for obliging me," came muffled through the cashmere.

"Apparently, you are my mystery purchaser. I'm obliged, aren't I?"

Obliged. It wasn't at all what he wanted. His heart sank. "I won't hold you to this part of the bargain if you prefer to return to your friends."

"No, I—" she tossed about for something to say, and blurted out, "How could you manage the outrageous sum you paid us?"

The smile he couldn't quite shake deepened when the roses in Flora's cheeks intensified at her own boldness.

"I'm not a poor man, Lady Flora," he told her. *Far from it.* "Though given how you found me, you are justified in thinking so."

"Flo."

His brows shot up, unable to respond.

"Nothing about this entire afternoon has been decorous—not much in our entire acquaintance come that. You may as well call me Flo, Ethan." She held his gaze, chin high, daring him to nay-say her.

"Flora, I think." *My Flora.* "It suits you better. Flo doesn't convey your beautiful essence."

Her rigid posture relaxed, and the tenderness in her eyes drove his growing attraction to the edge of his control. He fought the urge to take her in his arms in the midst of the Frost Fair, watching maid and onlookers be damned. He wrapped his good hand tightly around his other elbow, while their eyes held, the sounds and smells of the fair receded, and the landau continued toward the edge of the ice so slowly it almost felt like no movement at all, reinforcing his sense of a moment out of time.

The noise of hawking vendors penetrated when they turned a corner, bringing him back to his senses, and he relaxed his arms.

"I'm not a poor man, Flora," he repeated. "My brother has been banking and investing my funds during the years I was gone. The tidy sum is a pleasant surprise. It may enable me to begin that business you set me to."

"What business?"

"Thinking about the other men. Doing the good I can do, rather than worrying about the things I can't fix."

Her luscious lips widened into a broad smile.

"You brought me back, Flora. Not just from the streets. Your words brought me home."

Overcome, her eyes dropped to her feet, but her hand slid across the seat to grasp his. They continued to their destination in silent accord.

CHAPTER 9

Their two hours sped by in the cozy room he had arranged with its crackling fire, well-set table, and comfortable chairs. Flo's respect for Ethan grew when he insisted Martha and the other servants be served in the same warm room at a table in the corner. He did it for her sake, of course, and Flora loved him for it.

Love him? Is that possible? She knew it would be true soon enough if it wasn't already.

At first the conversation had been awkward, while they sorted through the fair, their family, and the bitter weather. Turning to winters they recalled from childhood led to shared stories, one piled quickly upon the next, until Flo laughed out loud over one particularly funny story about him and his brother sneaking out one snowy January night to find the owl that lived in the Welbrook wood. It became less amusing when he explained they had become locked out.

"I might have frozen to death then and Edmund with me. You would think I would have learned something," he said shaking his head. "Father discovered us gone, of course, and locked the break-fast room window we'd used to escape. We pounded on the kitchen door hoping to alert the night porter, but when the door swung open we met the wrathful visage of our father."

Ethan's smile didn't quite meet his eyes this time, and Flo cataloged signs of exhaustion—sunken eyes circled in purple, slumped shoulders.

"I'm tiring you," she said.

"I'm weary," he admitted, "but I can sleep at my father's house. I'll be cossetted and cared for, don't doubt it. It does grow late, however, and we haven't talked about your work with the Ladies' Society."

"Or your plans," she said. "Do you have something in mind?"

"You saw my new coachman—don't raise your brows at me, Flora Landrum. I hired him myself. I admired his loyalty to you. I have an estate. It is rather far north I fear—Cumberland, in fact—but lovely country."

His voice lulled Flo even as his eyes held hers, and he leaned across the table toward her. She followed his lead, drawn as if by a magnetic force until their hands touched.

"Brookside is mine outright from my grandfather's will. Edmund saw to it for me, but he fears it will need work before it is ready for..."

He peered at her quizzically.

"For what, Ethan?"

"For residents. A home. For a family, that is, for me to..." He stumbled over his words.

A family... Flo's heart beat until she thought he must see it pounding.

He broke away to look at a spot over her shoulder. "That is— what I meant to say is—it will take work, and I can employ people. Your brother has no doubt he can supply willing and able men. He has already recommended a housekeeper, a sergeant's widow, a woman to be reckoned with. She'll leave for Brookside in a few days to see to the house."

Flo sat back, stricken. "You're going to the country? The Season will commence in a few weeks!" *Cumberland is so far*, her heart protested. *And what did you mean a family?*

"Won't you still be in mourning in the spring? I assumed you had no interest in the Season. Your brother thought—"

Her breath caught. *He considered me in his plans. He spoke to—* "You spoke to Will about me?"

He hesitated. "Yes," he stammered. "He thought our families might… a house party in October."

Is he dancing around courtship? Why can't men just say what they mean? She opened her mouth to ask him bluntly. Before she could speak, the door opened after a preemptory knock and her brother entered. If he approved Ethan's suit or even this *tête-à-tête*, his face told a different story, and he wasn't alone.

Turning in his seat, Ethan gaped at Will's companion. Though Ethan had never met him, white blond hair, ice blue eyes, and extraordinary height marked him as the famed Marquess of Glenaire himself.

The Marble Marquess removed his beaver hat and nodded at Ethan's companion. "Lady Flora, Lord Alcott, well met," he said with perfect manners.

Ethan started to rise, disconcerted when he had to lean on the table to steady himself.

"Don't stand! I will be brief." The marquess gestured Ethan down, and Chadbourn joined them at the table. Glenaire remained standing.

"Excuse me for barging into a private moment uninvited, but Chadbourn thought you would want to hear what I discovered as soon as may be." The pale eyes glanced at Flora. "He gave me permission to speak in front of the lady." Ethan found the hint of disapproval of that permission curious.

Flora said not a word. After a questioning glance at her brother she had kept her attention on the marquess who stood holding his hat with both hands.

"You know I looked into the, er, incident at Badajoz. I will have a written record drawn up and see to it you have a copy, but of course it is unlikely word of Lord Alfred Hartford's role will be made public."

"Chadbourn told me he met with an unfortunate accident."

"Just so. It took me longer to be certain of the outcome of the incident. There was a witness, but I made inquiries about one vital detail. It took several days for a brief message from a, uh, friend in Spain to arrive, sent as it was via carrier pigeon in response to my questions. Details will follow, but it may set your mind at ease to know that the young lady lives. She has taken refuge in the Convento da Madre de Deus in Esparança and the sisters there report that she is well."

Ethan squeezed his eyes shut, feeling moisture pool in them. He hadn't realized how much it mattered until that moment.

He held his injured arm to his heart. It wasn't in vain. *I managed one good act.* "Who—how?" He opened his eyes, stunned to see the Marquess studying him with something like respect.

"I do not know. Perhaps the men who saw you to the surgeons took her there as well. Your courage does you honor, Lord Alcott. Now, if you'll excuse me, I have pressing business." With a slight inclination of his head, he left them.

Ethan turned to see both Flora and Will watching him, worry stark in their faces. "Thank you for your concern, but I am well. The memories sit heavily in my mind, but I can bear it. This was welcome news." Joy bloomed on Flora's face, and she reached across to grip his injured arm. "He's right, you know. You men are coy about the details, but I am sure Glenaire is right. What you did showed immense courage and honor."

"Glenaire is always right," Will grumbled. "And this is one of those times I'm thankful for it."

"Chadbourn," Ethan said, sounding formal suddenly, "Will you permit a few moments alone with Lady Flora?"

Will peered closely at his sister. He must have seen what he needed there, because he rose and nodded his head. "You have five minutes, Ethan. Use them well." He nodded at the servants to follow him out.

Flo stood and watched John and Martha troop out after her brother and waited with heart pounding to hear what Ethan had to say.

He pushed himself up with one hand and circled the table before she could rush to help him. He came so close she inhaled something earthy and male, the scent of wool and sandalwood. Distracted by his nearness, she almost missed his words.

"Did you mean what you said?" he asked.

"About courage? Of course."

"Flora, I'm not well, nor am I whole." He raised the mangled arm. "But—"

"I care nothing for your missing hand, Ethan, except as a badge of honor. You must know that." She placed both hands against his waistcoat and studied his eyes, unsure what she hoped to find there.

"I will recover—the doctors are confident, and I'm stronger every day—but it will take time."

He sounded as if he were pleading. "What are you trying to tell me?" she demanded.

"When your mourning is over, and I am well, may I call on you?"

She took a step back, arms akimbo and flashed him stern frown. "Is that all you want to say? 'Call on me?' Where is your courage when I need it?"

He came closer to her. "I have no right to say more, but if you can be patient…"

Flo heaved a sigh of exasperation and closed the distance between them, grabbing his shoulders, and meeting his lips with her impatient ones. After a heartbeat he returned the kiss with an achingly tender one, using his damaged arm to pull her close while he feathered his graceful fingers across her cheek.

"Much better," she sighed against his neck, "But know this. I can wait out my mourning and your illness, but do not ask me to be patient." She spat each of the last words out one by one. "I am not a patient woman when I know what I want, Ethan Alcott, and I want you."

He kissed her again, this time deeply, passionately, possessively. When she moaned and pulled him closer, he pulled back, tipping his forehead onto hers. "Your brother believes you deserve a Season. I agree. If you still want this in a year…"

"God save me from men and their honor," she muttered into his cravat. "I'm not promising an entire year. My time of mourning ends September third. I expect to see you at Chadbourn Park that very day." She grabbed his lapels and gave him a shake.

"I will court you properly," he swore.

She rolled her eyes. "If you insist, you may make it a courtship, but Ethan, don't be too proper." Then she kissed him again, and he forgot to reply.

EPILOGUE

As it turned out, Emery Wheatly, Duke of Murnane and Flo's much despised brother-in-law, broke his miserable neck during a drunken ride that fall, plunging them all back into mourning.

Flora, impatient woman, refused to let that stop her. They were married in a simple family ceremony by Christmas.

THE END

OTHER BOOKS BY CAROLINE WARFIELD

The Earl of Chadbourn finds love soon after this story in *A Dangerous Nativity*, a book in which his nephew Charles also appears. You can read how Lady Georgiana finds happiness in *Dangerous Works*. As to the Marquess of Glenaire, his story is *Dangerous Weakness*. One reviewer said of him, "There is nothing so entertaining as watching a man who is always in control lose that control." Even young Charles finds true love, but his journey is long. Watch for him in Caroline's **Children of Empire series**.

You can find all her books here: https://www.carolinewarfield.com/bookshelf/

ABOUT CAROLINE WARFIELD

Award winning author Caroline Warfield has been many things: traveler, librarian, poet, raiser of children, bird watcher, Internet and Web services manager, conference speaker, indexer, tech writer, genealogist—even a nun. She reckons she is on at least her third act, happily working in an office surrounded by windows where she lets her characters lead her to adventures in England and the far-flung corners of the British Empire. She nudges them to explore the riskiest territory of all, the human heart.

Sign Me Up!
http://www.carolinewarfield.com/newsletter/
Facebook Street Team: https://www.facebook.com/
groups/1655563474529075/

Learn more about Caroline at:
Website: http://www.carolinewarfield.com/
Email: warfieldcaro@gmail.com

facebook.com/carolinewarfield7
twitter.com/CaroWarfield
bookbub.com/authors/caroline-warfield

A SECOND CHANCE AT LOVE

SHERRY EWING

A Second Chance At Love
By Sherry Ewing

Can the bittersweet frost of lost love be rekindled into a burning
flame?

Viscount Digby Osgood returns to London after a two-year
absence, planning to avoid the woman he courted and then left.
Can she ever forgive him and give them a second chance at love?
Lady Constance Whittles has only cared for one man in her life.
Even after he broke her heart, it remains fixed on him. Can they
truly take up where they left off?
Charity projects and a Frost Fair on the Thames bring them
together, but another stands in their way. Will he tear them apart?

CHAPTER 1

Whites
29 December, 1813

Viscount Digby Osgood perused the morning post, barely reading the words. He had dreamed of *her* again and had thought of little else ever since. Memories flitted across his mind of the blonde haired, green-eyed beauty who had captured his attention.

Had it really been two long years since he had seen her before being forced to travel on business for his father? He had been a cad the last time he had been with her, but what other choice had he had? Telling her not to wait for him and watching her tears had haunted Digby to this very day and his return to London only caused more anguish. Where was she now? What was she doing? Coming to his club might get her out of his mind, he had reasoned. But it had been a useless endeavor and the gentlemen sitting with him at his table offered no solace in his dilemma.

His three companions had been schoolmates at Oxford. Lord

Richard Cranfield was nursing a brandy, and, at this ungodly hour, one could only assume he was just as troubled as Digby with some unstated matter leaving him annoyed. Lord Milton Sutton stared mindlessly into the flames of the hearth, completely lost in thought to those around him. Lord George Chadwick inspected his waist-coat for some flaw, as if his valet would ever let him leave his town-house without being impeccably dressed. Digby quietly chuckled. George spent more coins on his wardrobe than most women of high society.

He gave a heavy sigh before folding the newspaper. "We are a fine group," Digby declared addressing his friends.

"Quite right," George agreed with a wide grin, completely misunderstanding Digby's meaning, for he beamed while tugging the lapels of his jacket into place. *Yes, George. We all know how dapper you look,* Digby thought attempting to hide his amusement.

Milton tore his gaze from the fire. "We need Frederick here to lighten our moods.

Richard swore. "And listen to him going on about how fabulous married life is? No, thank you. I would rather suffer here in silence."

Digby could not agree more, but still… "You should be happy for him and Margaret. At least one of us has found someone with whom to share our lives."

A snort escaped Richard. "Eh gads, man! I have a mistress who makes me happy. I hardly need a wife meddling in my affairs and demanding my attention seven days a week."

George signaled a passing servant for a drink. "A wife would ruin all my fine plans to remain carefree," he chimed in. "Thank-fully, my father tends to spend most of his valuable time on my brother, who will inherit the duchy. The unlucky bastard."

Digby did not miss the brief glimpse of pain that swept across his friend's face. "How is he, by the way?" he asked. "I have not seen him in ages."

George waved his hand in the air before inspecting the lace at his wrist. "Fine, I suppose. David and I have little in common, as you well know. Father wishes for him to marry and continues to parade eligible ladies before him, all willing to overlook the fact my brother would rather be working the land himself instead of enjoying the season. Why, he actually came to dinner the other night with dirt on his shirt. What woman would stand for that in her husband?"

Richard took another sip of his drink. "Any woman who is looking to be a duchess one day, that is who."

George's brow rose. "Well, I suppose you have that right. Still, I shall enjoy my bachelorhood and leave wedded bliss to my brother and any of you fools who think love is an emotion worth being shackled to a wife for the rest of your lives."

The men laughed. Digby thought George was probably more concerned a wife would outshine him with her wardrobe. George would never be able to stand it.

Milton rose. "All this talk of getting hitched is turning my stomach. How about a game of cards? Anyone care to join me?"

As the men began to stand and head toward one of the card rooms, Frederick, Viscount Beacham, entered the room as though they had conjured him up from thin air. The men exchanged greetings before their friend turned his attention to Digby.

"Can I detain you a moment, Digby?" Frederick asked before turning back to the rest of their friends. "I will not keep him long, gentlemen."

Richard laughed. "See that you do not. I feel lucky this morning and am looking forward to lightening Digby's purse."

Digby watched the three men leave before sitting back down and motioning for Frederick to take one of the vacant seats.

"We do not see you here much these days, Freddy," Digby said slipping easily, now that they were alone, into the nickname he and Frederick's wife Margaret used. Since he and Frederick were childhood friends, Digby knew no offense would be taken.

"Raising a family tends to occupy me these days. Mind you, I have no complaints," Frederick said with a smile.

"Margaret's sister Sophie is still staying with you?" Digby asked.

"Yes, and she just adores her nephew. If she had an allowance, she would most likely spend every bit of it spoiling him rotten."

"She was always such a delightful child."

"She is wonderful to have around."

"It was good of you to take her in when you married Margaret. I was surprised their father allowed it so willingly."

"The vicar knew how Margaret was more of a mother to Sophie than an older sister. I am glad to have her with us. But that is not why I am here. Margaret sent me."

Digby's heart skipped a beat. *Oh no!* Please do not let him mention *her* name. Digby would not be able to stand it.

"Here to take my money too, I suppose," Digby laughed, although the sound stuck in his suddenly dry throat.

"Not today."

Digby's brow rose at the implication. He might as well get this over with. "And..."

Frederick leaned forward in his chair. "And she wants to know when you are going to get over this ridiculous notion Lady Constance does not wish to see you now that you have returned to England."

Constance... her name whispered across his soul like a long-lost friend. Memories of their brief time together during the Christmas holiday two years ago once more flooded Digby's mind. He had become fond of her, even going so far as to say he was falling in love. They might have made a go of it had his father not insisted Digby travel on behalf of the family shipping business.

"It has been two years," Digby declared aloud. "I am certain she is spoken for." Those words turned his stomach sour. The thought of Constance with another was the reason he tried to avoid her at all costs since his return.

"Margaret has informed me Lady Constance has recently been seen in the company of some lieutenant, although his name escapes me at the moment."

"All the more reason to let her live her life without my interference."

A snort left Frederick's lips. "Margaret and Constance have been friends for years. You know how women talk. My wife does not care for the man, and you know what a good judge of character she is."

"Again… all the more reason to let her live her life without me, especially if she will become engaged to the man," he repeated scowling with the thought of Constance with anyone other than himself.

"Really, Digby! Do you think I would be here if she were engaged to be married?"

Digby thought of the tears running down Constance's face when last they spoke. A brief flicker of hope he might recover what he had foolishly lost leapt into his heart "I am certain she must hate me."

"There is only one way to find out. Head over to the Oxford Street Book Palace and Tea Rooms. I understand Miss Amelia Clemens has hired Lady Constance to help her with the place."

"Miss Amelia? Is she not the sister of that dreadful man who spreads gossip in that rag *The Teatime Tattler*?"

Frederick laughed before standing and pulling on Digby's arm to do the same. "Do not hold that against the woman. She cannot help she is related to such a vile man. I understand from Margaret that your lady is working the morning shift today, so get going. I shall be happy to take your place at the card table. And do not get lost in that bloody fog outside. The roads are barely manageable"

One moment Digby was happily going to play a game of cards with his friends and the next he was throwing on his coat and hat before hailing a hack. He gave the address of the bookshop to the driver before sitting back in the carriage seat wondering at his fate.

He would have been appalled to know that, upon Digby's departure, Frederick turned to the betting book at White's to pen in the projected date of Digby's wedding to the fair Lady Constance.

CHAPTER 2

L ady Constance Whittles put the leather book onto the shelf before inspecting the next one. Pushing her cart, she made her way to the end of the aisle and began looking for the spot where the tome needed to be replaced. She hoped she looked as though she was engrossed in what she was doing. It was either that or having some sort of conversation with the man who followed her around the bookstore expecting her to hang on his every word.

He was an attractive man, with his blond hair and blue eyes, but there was more to a person than their looks. Besides... the lieutenant had become overly possessive of late to the point where Constance was ready to break off her association with him. She was weary of him turning up whenever she was about town as if he had prearranged their meetings. They had only gone to dinner and the theater once, with her Aunt Penelope acting as chaperone, yet the gentleman behaved as though they had already spoken their vows. Marriage was the last thing she thought of... at least to this particular man.

There was only one person who owned her heart. She wished Digby felt the same. She knew she needed to move on—after all, it had been two long years since she last saw him—but her heart still cried out for him no matter how much she wished otherwise.

"I cannot tell you what a pleasure it is to be here with you today, Lady Constance," the gentleman said, moving a step closer to her and speaking as if it was mere coincidence they were here together.

"Lieutenant—"

Her voice cut off when he had the nerve to take her hand and actually kiss her knuckles instead of the air between her hand and his lips. A gasp escaped her.

"I have asked you on many occasions to call me Terrance," he murmured in a husky tone. Uncomfortable in his presence, her skin crawled.

She needed to distance herself from him. She pulled her hand away. "And I have previously expressed I could not presume such an informality, *Lieutenant*." His brow rose with the emphasis of his rank and not his given name.

"Surely you can make an exception," he crooned before reaching for her hand again.

Constance moved away and quickly took hold of the cart, wheeling it around the corner of the shelves. He continued to follow her. "I think not," she answered lifting her chin a tad higher. "Besides, this is hardly the place for a social call, Lieutenant. I happen to be working."

"A frivolous hobby I am certain you cannot possibly enjoy," he scoffed. Constance did not miss the brief look of annoyance that quickly skimmed across his features. He continued to seal his fate with every word he uttered. "Any wife of mine would be expected to remain at home and see to—"

The sound that interrupted him bordered on a hysterical laugh. "Then I am lucky we are not wed, for any husband of mine would understand why I enjoy being here helping Miss Amelia."

The lieutenant began sputtering at his apparent blunder. "L–Lady C–Constance, I meant no disrespect."

"Perhaps we can discuss this later at my aunt's townhouse,

Lieutenant Abernathy. I really must return to my duties." Constance took another book, placing it on the shelf. She thought ahead about the conversation that would happen. Her aunt would provide reinforcement when Constance told the lieutenant she would no longer see him.

"I will wait in the tea room, and we can continue our chat when you have a moment to spare," he said, with a wave of his hand. He gave her a short bow and left her standing. Whatever had she seen in this braying ass?

The front bell rang, breaking off Constance's unladylike thoughts. She left the cart and quickly made her way to the foyer of the store where she was pleasantly surprised to find a familiar face smiling at her. It was as if she had conjured the man up from thin air. She was so delighted to see him that she forgot herself.

"As I live and breathe, Digby Osgood." She watched his eyes widen before his spectacles began to fog up as the warm air of the shop hit them. His cheeks were red, probably because of the cold outside, and she hid a smile at her imagination, which almost thought he was blushing because she addressed him so informally. She should not have been so presumptuous and quickly corrected her mistake. "I mean… Lord Osgood."

Reaching inside his coat, he pulled out a linen handkerchief and began wiping his glasses before placing them back on the bridge of his nose. "Lady Constance," he said just as formally. He gave her a welcoming smile before removing his hat. "It has been too long."

Her breathing elevated just seeing Digby again, and she moved behind the desk to try to calm her thoughts. Still… she could not prevent herself from taking in the sight of him. His black hair curling at the edges was slightly damp where his hat had not covered his head from the falling snow. A slight cleft in his chin had always fascinated her whenever they had been together in the past. His face reminded her of the sculptures she had seen in her aunt's garden; classical and timeless. But it was his vivid blue eyes that were her undoing. He gazed upon her as though asking if he was assuming too much by being here. The silly man.

"Too long indeed. There are not many who would brave such inclement weather to venture outside," she finally answered hoping her assessment of him did not appear rude. "What brings you into the bookshop today? We have a new mystery if that is what you are looking for."

"Not today," he said while continuing to stare at her.

"Then if you have not come for a book, you must wish for some tea after being out in the cold," she declared as she raised her arm toward the tearoom. "Feel free to pick any table."

"I am not here for tea, either, my lady."

Her breath leapt into her throat. *Could he possibly mean…?* "Then whatever brings you here today, my lord."

"You."

It was a simple statement filled with as much hope as Constance herself had been feeling for two long years. "Me?" she finally gasped as her hand went to her throat.

"Yes, you," Digby replied stepping forward. "I had hoped you would forgive me and allow me another chance to make up for the feelings I hurt when we last spoke."

"There is nothing to forgive." Her words rushed from her lips before she even realized it.

"There is not?"

She gave him a warm smile, knowing she had already forgiven him years ago. Her heart had not changed where Digby was concerned. "No, there is not, my lord."

A rush of air left his lips as though he had been holding his breath while awaiting her answer. He stepped up to the desk and reached for her hand, kissing the air between his lips and her knuckles as any proper gentleman would. "You are very gracious, Constance. I must admit I was afraid you would hate me, considering how I left things between us."

She gave his hand a gentle squeeze. "I could never hate you,

Digby." A blush rushed to her cheeks at the tone of her voice. They had been on a first name basis two years ago and somehow it seemed right to call him by his given name. My word, she had missed this man.

"Then perhaps you would allow me to escort you to a meeting at the Duchess of Haverford's residence next week on the third. I understand she is in the process of forming several committees to organize an event for *The Ladies' Society for the Care of the Widows and Orphans of Fallen Heroes and the Children of Wounded Veterans.*"

Constance laughed. "You must be joking? Why, you will never get all that on any kind of a banner."

Digby joined her and laughed. "I would never make up such a tall tale, my lady."

"No one in their right mind would, although it does sound like a worthy cause."

"I could not agree more, which is why I have offered my services to the gentleman's auxiliary, whose responsibilities will include making sure you ladies are able to do your work in this dreadful weather. I knew this was just the sort of event that would be of interest to you."

"You know me so well. I would be happy to accompany you, Digby."

"Wonderful," he replied with a smile. "If your aunt could join us and act as chaperone, then I could pick you both up around noon, if that is acceptable."

"I will eagerly await next week, my lord."

Digby took her hand again and bowed over it. "As will I, my lady."

His gloved hand felt warm in hers. When Digby's thumb gently caressed the back in a small circular motion, Constance's heart leapt at the possibility that all was not lost. Her eyes went to his in a long lingering glance as pleasure swept across her entire being. She smiled, and he returned it with a smile of his own. Constance could not remember when she had ever been this happy... until the spell was interrupted. They quickly broke apart.

"I say, Lady Constance, is this gentleman bothering you?" Lieutenant Abernathy bellowed as he left the tearoom and rushed to her side. The few patrons who escaped the fog outside looked up from their books at the disturbance he was causing.

"Not at all and please lower your voice," Constance advised sternly before remembering her manners. "My apologies. Lieutenant Abernathy may I present Lord Osgood, who is an old friend."

The two men shook hands but, from the looks they exchanged, neither cared for the other.

The lieutenant all but dismissed Digby to give Constance his full attention. "I did not realize the time, my dear, and must return to my duties." His endearment caused Digby to raise his brow. "I will return to accompany you to your aunt's later this afternoon so we can continue our conversation as promised."

"I can meet you there, Lieutenant," Constance said.

"Nonsense! I cannot have a woman I care for walking the streets alone especially in this dreadful fog. It will be my honor to walk you home, *my* lady."

Constance flinched with the emphasis on that one word but she would in no way let this man intimidate her. "As I said, Lieutenant Abernathy, I shall meet you at my aunt's at four o'clock in time for afternoon tea. You know the address."

The lieutenant's mouth turned into a grim line of displeasure. "If you insist," he at last muttered between clenched teeth.

"Yes, I do."

He bowed before her. "Then I shall see you at the appointed hour. Osgood," the lieutenant said informally before continuing as he motioned toward the door. "Shall we leave the lady to her duties?"

"I still have business with Lady Constance but, by all means, do not let us keep you from returning to your regiment," Digby answered, before leaning on the desk with one elbow. He was now so close that Constance could smell the briefest hint of the cologne he wore. She almost sighed in pleasure.

Lieutenant Abernathy opened and closed his mouth several times before he snapped his lips shut and stormed from the bookstore.

"Be careful with that one, my lady," Digby warned. "I may have only just met the lieutenant, but there is something in his demeanor that does not sit well with me."

"I must say, I agree with you. After this afternoon, there will be no further reason to associate myself with him. I have seen for myself we would never suit."

"I am relieved to hear you say so and will look forward to next week," Digby replied, before donning his hat and bowing low over her hand. She felt the warmth of his breath and her heart began hammering away inside her chest. What this man did to her!

She murmured a soft goodbye and watched as he left the bookshop. She swore she could still feel the heat of his hand in hers hours later.

CHAPTER 3

Lieutenant Terrance Abernathy waited impatiently in the parlor of Lady Penelope Whittles's townhouse. The room was richly furnished and was a clear testament to the wealth that could be his if he played his hand right.

He had learned of Lady Constance by mere chance while attending an evening charity event during the last season. But between the ongoing war and trying to find a way to contrive an introduction, meeting the woman had taken far longer than Terrance would have liked. The waiting had tried his patience.

A spinster niece living with her spinster aunt, or so he had learned while listening in on a conversation between the Danver sisters. They had been so busy whispering the latest gossip they had no idea Terrance was eavesdropping by the open balcony door. As he overheard their conversation, he learned Lady Constance's father had abandoned her at a young age, apparently upset he did not have a male heir. She had been living with her aunt ever since. When her father had been lost at sea, Lady Constance inherited all her father's wealth.

Terrance looked about the elegant room again. Once he

married Lady Constance and was discharged from the army, he would be living in luxury for the rest of his life! Constance's money would see him out of debt and also ensure he would never need to worry about pinching a few pockets for a few extra coins.

The ring he had purchased was a modest one, and unless Lady Constance took the piece to have it inspected, she would be none the wiser that the main gem was fake. Terrance smiled at the thought of Constance as his wife. She would be thankful he ended her status as spinster and embrace life as an officer's wife. He would also ensure she quit working at that ghastly bookstore. Yes... the lady would become most biddable. Terrance would expect nothing less from a woman he took as his wife!

The front door opened, and Terrance heard Lady Penelope request tea be brought to the salon where he now sat. The clicking of nails on the marble foyer floor caused Terrance to grimace, wondering what type of dreadful animal was crossing the foyer. He did not have long to wait as a white fluffy mutt on a leash came into view along with the two ladies of the house.

He quickly hid his annoyance regarding the obnoxious canine, who began yapping in his direction. Terrance came to his feet and offered them a bow. "Lady Penelope... Lady Constance," he murmured over the noise. "A delight to see you this afternoon. Thank you for inviting me to your home." He did not miss the brief exchange the two women gave one another.

Constance handed the leash over to a servant. "Please take Mitsy and give her some water, Janet. She must be thirsty after her long walk."

The maid bobbed a curtsey and took the dog from sight. Terrance's ears were thankful for the silence—or was he? The stillness in the room became deafening while the women continued their assessment of him. Lady Penelope at last took a seat on the sofa before she motioned for Terrance to sit across from her in a vacant chair. Disappointment flashed when he realized he would not have the luxury of sitting next to Lady Constance, who went to sit next to her aunt.

Lady Penelope began asking him questions regarding the places he had traveled while on duty for his country. The weather was next, along with other mundane idle chit chat, until a tea trolley was rolled into the room.

"Constance, would you mind pouring, dear heart?" Lady Penelope asked, while her niece handed her a plate of delicate little cakes. She offered them to Terrance but, with a wave of his hand, he declined.

"Not at all," Lady Constance replied before raising her eyes to Terrance. "Would you care for cream and sugar, Lieutenant?"

"Just the tea. Thank you, Lady Constance," he said. When she held out his cup for him to take, his hand lingered over hers, and her eyes widened before she began to frown. Why was she acting this way? Surely he had convinced her he had feelings for her.

Terrance took a sip of his tea, wishing it was laced with a bit of liquor, but there was time for that later. Once the ladies had their refreshments, Lady Penelope set her cup down on a nearby table.

"Ladies..." Terrance began to make his intentions known regarding Lady Constance. "I came here today in the hopes that—"

Lady Penelope raised her hand, halting Terrance's words so the remainder of a sudden stuck in his throat. "If I may interrupt your thoughts, Lieutenant."

"Of course, my lady," he said while he sat back, waiting for the woman to continue. Lady Constance set her own cup down and folded her hands in her lap and cast her eyes in the direction of her aunt. This could not be good.

"My niece has informed me that, while she has enjoyed your company of late, she must decline any further invitations that might advance your possible relationship with her."

Terrance's cup rattled in the saucer and he set the china down with shaking hands. Was it his imagination, or did the woman actually find him unworthy to see her niece?

"I do not understand," he said hoping for an expanded explanation so he might decide how to change the lady's mind.

Lady Penelope picked up her cup again and took a sip. "It is really quite simple. Her heart lies elsewhere, Lieutenant." Lady Constance at last gazed upon him with what appeared an apologetic smile.

Was that also pity he saw reflected in her eyes? "Surely you must know of my feelings for you," he said, trying not to sound like some pathetic fool. "Why, I had hopes that you would become my wife."

Lady Constance gasped. "How can you possibly have feelings for me after one evening to dinner and the theater? You barely know me." Her lips snapped opened and closed several times before she spoke again, after she appeared to collect her thoughts. "I apologize, Lieutenant, for my rudeness. Until recently, I had thought the man I had come to care for no longer had feelings for me. I did not wish to continue to give you hope that somehow—"

Lady Penelope reached over to pat her niece's hand. "There is no need to go into details, my dear. I am certain the Lieutenant can understand the importance of keeping ones heart guarded, and you have no need to voice aloud the particulars of such a personal matter."

Terrance had a vision of that clod Osgood from earlier today at the bookshop. Be damned! The woman could not possibly be interested in such a bookish-looking man, could she? Terrance stood, knowing he was being dismissed, although the women were too polite to ask him to leave.

He bowed. "I wish you the best, Lady Constance," he said, trying with all his might not to show his frustration at what he had lost. "Lady Penelope..."

"Good day, Lieutenant," Lady Penelope replied, with a nod of her head.

Terrance made his way to the door where a footman offered him his hat. The door almost shut on his backside as Terrance left. He took his leave of the townhouse and hailed a hack to drive him back to the inn where he was staying in preference to the barracks while his regiment was in London. His mind whirled with ideas for turning this situation to his favor. He was confident in his ability to re-coup his losses and still win the hand of the elusive—but wealthy—Lady Constance.

CHAPTER 4

Digby took out his watch fob for what seemed like the hundredth time and gave a heavy sigh. Only fifteen minutes? Truly? Time certainly was not accommodating his desire to return to Constance's company. Why did the minutes seemingly crawl like a slug moving along a forest floor? He put the watch away even while a drink was being pressed into his hand. He took the crystal glass, nodding his thanks to Richard. Digby was surprised his friend was in attendance along with the other gentlemen currently waiting for their ladies at Haverford House.

Digby lifted his glass in a silent salute before taking a drink. "What brings you here today, Richard? I did not think this was the sort of thing to draw your notice."

Richard scanned the room before answering with a shrug of indifference. "You have that right, Digby. But my mother insisted I escort my sister Josephine here today since she was unable to do so herself. Other commitments, or so she claimed."

"Your sister is now of a marriageable age. I am uncertain where the years have gone. As for your mother, well…" Digby's words trailed off, not wishing to appear rude by continuing his thoughts.

Richard waved him off. "Neither of us need to make excuses for her, Digby. We grew up together; you know her as well as I do. My mother has not changed over the years. Once all the arrangements have been made for this event the Duchess is organizing, my mother will be sure to be *seen* at every aspect of it. She can barely spare time for her children, let alone something so mundane as actually attending meetings to plan something that does not revolve completely around her. As for Josephine, no one will ever be good enough for my sister."

"Since I am an only child, I will have to take your word for it," Digby replied, wondering how Richard and Josephine survived having parents who basically let servants raise them. He supposed that was not so uncommon in the *ton*, yet his own parents were always loving and caring where their son was concerned, even putting their own needs aside to ensure Digby had the finest education.

Richard motioned for a passing servant to refill their glasses. "What are you doing here, Digby?" he asked, before taking another sip of his brandy.

"I offered my services to the duchess in whatever capacity she may need. This event will benefit so many, and the monies raised are for a worthy cause," he answered."

"And…" Richard drawled. He hid a smirk, leaving Digby in no doubt his friend knew exactly why he was here.

"And I also accompanied Lady Constance Whittles and her aunt to attend the committee meeting."

Richard laughed. "About time you made up with the lady. Saw her a couple times after you left town. She looked completely crestfallen."

"It certainly was not my intention to hurt her feelings," he said. He took another sip of the drink and felt the liquor burn down his throat. The distant murmur of feminine laughter echoed through the hallway and Digby attempted to hide a smile, knowing Constance was most likely enjoying herself. "Perhaps one of the women here might be of interest to *you*?" Digby hinted, taking another sip of his drink. "The de Courtenay sisters arrived. Lady Constance was having a pleasant conversation with Miss Miranda before their meeting started. From what I overheard, she is still available."

"Are you mad?" Richard hissed, a look of alarm crossing his face. "You could not possibly have forgotten that scene at Hollystone Hall the Christmas before last? I am actually surprised she would show up here of all places after her fiasco with Aldridge and Gren. The scandal Miss Miranda caused still makes my head spin. My father would die on the spot if I even considered her for a wife!"

"She must have redeemed herself in the eyes of Society by now," Digby suggested.

"If her efforts to find herself a wealthy husband have subsided, it is not to my knowledge. That particular young miss wants a title, but there is no way she will get mine. Besides, I understand she is now setting her cap for a duke. Becoming a countess would be beneath her aspirations."

"Do not be so hard on yourself, Richard, or her," Digby scolded. "Surely there must be some lady you have your eyes on as a possible wife?"

"No one suitable and up to the standards my parents expect, unfortunately, and that is the reason behind my recent sour mood."

"So no particular lady has caught your attention as yet."

"You *have* been away, Digby." Richard scowled, although he did not deny he had been seeing someone, or go into details about her. "Take a look at the gentlemen waiting with us? It is fair to assume the ladies who are present are either spoken for or already paired off with one of the men here."

"We shall find someone for you," Digby said, placing his hand on his friends shoulder.

"I am not really looking for a wife, Digby. Still plenty of time for all that, I suppose."

"If you say so."

"I do. Let us drop the subject and move on to something more pleasurable. How about a game of billiards while we await the ladies?"

Digby shrugged. "Why not? Given the time, the ladies will still be a while."

Digby followed behind Richard, nodding to several acquaintances as they made their way to the billiard room. He might as well occupy his time doing something to keep his mind off Constance, otherwise he just might embarrass himself by invading the meeting with the ladies!

๛

Constance waited in the foyer while a servant went to fetch her pelisse. Her aunt had stayed behind in the meeting room to finish up a few details, and Constance hoped this would give her some additional time alone with Digby. Her heart leapt when she saw him leaving the front parlor. She could barely contain her breathing as he came ever nearer to her side. How she loved this man.

"Your aunt—" he started to say, bowing over her hand.

"—is momentarily delayed," she finished with a smile.

He leaned forward to whisper in her ear. "Come with me," he urged, while gently taking her elbow.

She gave a quick glance around and nodded. None of the other people gathering in the foyer paid any attention to them. They were too preoccupied with their own conversations or going on about the details of the event to follow next month.

Constance and Digby did not go far and she was thankful he escorted her into an open room with no door, thus ensuring her reputation remained intact. A nook not visible from the hallway gave them a semblance of privacy and she could only wonder what this man who owned her heart would do next. She did not have long to wait.

"You may think this is too forward of me, Lady Constance," he began.

She let a light laugh escaped her. "We have known one another far too long to be so formal, my lord, at least when we are alone together."

He brightened her day with his smile and brought her closer. "Constance… you do me a great honor."

"The honor is mine, Digby," she breathed in a soft whisper, resting her hands lightly on his forearms.

"During my time away, a day did not go by that I did not think of you. The hurt I caused you at our parting has weighed heavily on my mind for two long years."

"I have already forgiven you for all that, Digby."

"Yes, I know, and I am most grateful you can forget my foolish-ness. This may be too fast, since we have only just reunited, but I wanted you to know I still care for you, Constance."

She reached up to cup his cheek. "Digby, surely you must know you still own my heart?"

"You give me hope for a future together," he said in a husky tone.

"Nothing would make me happier."

She thought she was prepared for when Digby bent down to place his lips upon her own. The kiss was gentle at first, a testament to what they truly felt for one another. But as she stepped closer, wrapping her arms around his neck, everything changed. Digby pulled her into his arms and every fiber of her being burst in sheer joy. He deepened their kiss, and she was more than willing to follow his lead. Tingling sensations stole down her spine and Constance knew in this very instant that she had not lost his love. Surely, if Digby could kiss her like this then he would certainly wish for them to wed at some point in their future.

A low moan of desire escaped her and she felt his arms tighten around her waist.

"Lord Osgood!"

They quickly broke apart as if a bucket of freezing water had been thrown at them. The Duchess of Haverford stood at the entryway to the room staring at them. Constance thought she witnessed a brief glimpse of humor at the corner of her eyes before a look of stern disapproval marked her features.

Constance dropped into a curtsey and Digby bowed. "Your Grace," they murmured in unison. They stole a quick glance at one another and a blush rushed across Constance's cheeks.

The Duchess stepped into the room. "I hope your intentions toward this young lady are honorable, Lord Osgood."

"Yes, of course, Your Grace. I hold Lady Constance in the highest regard," he said, before stealing another look at her.

"Do not disappoint me then. Lady Constance… I believe your aunt is ready to depart and I know she does not like to be kept waiting." The duchess swept away.

Constance was not sure if she should feel embarrassed or giddy with relief that their reprimand was so lightly given. "I suppose we should go."

"I wish we could stay," he said and the look he gave her stole her breath away again.

"As do I," she declared before Digby leaned down to quickly steal another kiss.

He offered her his arm, and she gladly took it as they made their way into the hallway. "Now tell me all about what you and the other lovely ladies have planned for us next month."

"Oh, Digby! You will not believe what we have in store. The Duchess plans for a Venetian Breakfast. The ladies will provide baskets to be raffled off. The gentleman whose bid wins the basket will enjoy the lady's company for lunch and also receive the honor of a dance," she exclaimed with excitement.

"Dare I hope it might be a waltz?" he asked while helping her with her coat.

"We shall see. There's also to be a ball that night here at Haverford House."

"And will you give me a hint about which basket you have made, my lady?" he whispered with a twinkle in his eyes.

Constance blushed before she laughed. "I believe, my lord, that would be considered cheating."

"All is fair in love and... well... you know what they say." He gave a merry laugh and once more offered his arm. As they made their way into the foyer, her aunt's raised brow told Constance another reprimand would be forthcoming. Still, she would not think of such things for now. Not when Digby was escorting them into his carriage and making sure they were comfortable. Nor would she think of it during their ride back to her aunt's townhouse while Digby kept them amused with stories of his childhood.

The ride was far too short and Constance was disappointed her time with Digby was at an end. She had to endure Aunt Penelope's lecture on propriety and keeping her reputation intact. Once it was over and she could leave the room, Constance gave a heavy sigh of relief. She could only hope the days would pass quickly until she could enjoy Digby's company again.

CHAPTER 5

Terrance trudged his way through the heavily falling snow. The docks and streets were mainly deserted. He must have lost his wits to be out in such inclement weather. He should be at the inn where he was staying, with a drink in hand and a fire at his feet. Instead, he had pressed his luck that perhaps an unwary traveler or two would be out and he would be the richer for their carelessness.

He tested the pouch clutched in his fingers. The sailor he had run into near the docks had still been drunk, making him an easy mark when Terrance bumped into him. Mumbling an apology, Terrance had relieved the drunkard of his purse before he even knew what happened. Hoping the man was still intoxicated enough to not remember the collision, Terrance had hurried away from the sailor knowing they usually travelled in groups. No sense running into any of the man's friends.

He finally stopped and leaned up against a brick building. Opening the leather pouch, he counted the coins. A larger amount than he had suspected! Why, that fool must have been carrying all his wages and the monies would see Terrance's room paid for at the nearby inn for the next few weeks. What luck!

His attention was drawn to the sound of horses. An elegant carriage rolled up to the local hospital across the street. Wondering who would be visiting the wounded and sick on such a horrid day, Terrance walked across the road and hid himself in the alleyway between the two buildings. Thinking he might find himself a little richer, he stepped forward only to sink further back into the shadows when he witnessed a burly footman stepping down to open the door of the carriage. He did not want to mess with someone of that ilk.

Terrance was just about to leave when he heard a familiar voice.

"I do not know why you picked such a day to visit wounded soldiers, Constance."

Lady Constance stepped down onto the snow-covered walk. "Because they need cheering, Aunt Penelope, today more than ever. I am certain no one will think of visiting them with such horrid road conditions. Besides, we made all these cakes for them to enjoy. I would not want them to spoil."

Lady Penelope gave her niece a kiss upon her cheek. "I suppose you have that right, dearest. Personally, I am looking forward to sampling Monsieur Fournier's delicacies at the Venetian Breakfast the Society ladies are planning"

"The Duchess is sparing no expense for our event. Between the ticket sales from the breakfast, auction, and ball, we will be able to donate a considerable amount to our causes," Constance beamed, while directing two footmen to help carry their baskets.

"I understand Lady Georgiana Hayden is working on having pamphlets printed to inform people of our various causes. Why, it also appears a Frost Fair may take place if—"

Whatever Lady Penelope planned to say next was cut off as they entered the hospital.

Terrance scowled when the door closed behind the women and he took the time to once more count his coins. Pushing off the brick wall, he pulled his coat closer together and made his way toward his inn.

He began planning ways to ensure he landed on his feet rich as can be, along with wiggling his way back into Constance's good graces. If he could manage to purchase tickets to the event, he was certain he could win Constance's favor. It was either that or he would need to find another gullible lady with a considerable dowry before his next deployment or his money ran out.

CHAPTER 6

Constance sat on the park bench while Digby tightened the laces of her skates. The Serpentine at Hyde Park was filled with skaters despite the heavy snow and she was nervously hoping to appear graceful and not a clod on the ice. Constance had been pleasantly surprised when Digby, Frederick, Margaret, and Sophie had shown up at her aunt's, saying they were whisking her away for a day on the ice. Considering how bored she was due to the recent storms, she happily agreed to the outing.

"All set," Digby declared, offering his arm. "Shall we take a turn, my lady?"

"I would be delighted."

The sound of Margaret's laughter as she and her husband drew near caught Constance's attention. "Come join us, Constance," Margaret called out. "You are missing all the fun!"

Constance got her bearings as she stood. "I must admit it has been some time since I have indulged in skating, Digby." Her legs wobbled, and his arm went around her waist to steady her.

He pointed to Margaret's sister as she easily twirled about the ice. "If Miss Sophie can do it, then so can you. Just embrace your inner child, Constance," he teased.

She laughed. "It is not my inner child I am worried about, Digby, but my womanly dignity, if I end up face forward on the ice."

"You are safe with me, my dear," he said, while he began helping her skate along the frozen lake.

She gave a heavenly sigh. "I have no doubt about that, my lord."

They had made several turns about the lake and Constance was just beginning to feel confident in her ability to remain upright when an unexpected person whisked up next to her, making her teeter in place. Digby's arm tightened around her, preventing her fall. The gentleman was uncomfortably close. "Lady Constance," Lieutenant Abernathy said, with a tip of his cap and a sly grin, before he moved quickly on.

Digby skated with her toward the side of the lake. "Are you alright, Constance?"

Her breath heaved while she attempted to force air back into her lungs. "Yes, I believe so."

"I really do despise that man," Digby murmured as they watched the Lieutenant skate up to Lady Abigail Danver.

Constance rested her hand upon Digby's forearm, drawing his attention to her instead of the lieutenant. "Do not give him the time of day. Truly… he is not worth any expense of energy, and the extra attention only flatters his already overinflated ego."

"If you insist."

"I do. However, I wonder if I should warn Lady Abigail about him? I would hate for her to become entangled with the likes of him. You were right when you said he was trouble."

They began to skate again before Digby finally responded, as though he had been collecting his thoughts. "Has he been troubling you, Constance?"

Her hand tightened on Digby's arms as if she stood in need of his strength. "Not really, but he seems to be turning up a lot lately whenever I am about. I swore I saw him a couple of weeks ago when my aunt and I visited a local hospital, although I could be mistaken."

"I do not like the sound of that," Digby fumed. "Perhaps you are in need of a guardsman of sorts."

"You sound as though I need a few knights in armor with swords at their side to protect me," she laughed, trying to make light of a situation that was far from humorous. She was very concerned about the lieutenant of late and hardly thought it was a mere coincidence that he appeared wherever she did. He must be following her.

"I am certain I could find a helmet and breastplate in our attic somewhere. I am just as clear that a good rapier would do the trick." Digby chuckled before he looked at her fondly. "I am serious, Constance. I worry about your safety."

"I was perfectly safe, Digby," she said, patting his arm. "My aunt and I had Marshall with us. No one—and I mean no one— would mess with him. Besides, the Duchess warned us to be certain we have several footman with us for protection, if we venture to the shiftier side of town."

"Be sure to heed her warning. As long as you continue to have your footmen with you, then I will worry less. I hope you know you can always count on me to lend assistance."

"I am sure you will be busy as the Duchess's event draws near. I heard she was hoping we could possibly change the venue to the ice if the Thames freezes over in time. I would love to attend a Frost Fair!" Constance laughed, and Digby joined her.

"With the amount of floating ice on the waterways and London Bridge near impassable, that outcome might be possible," Digby replied. "You still have not told me what your basket will look like. How will I know which one to bid on?"

She gazed upon him before offering him a bright smile. "I

suppose I could give you a hint. I plan to bake a pie," she said, mischievously.

Digby groaned. "That is hardly a hint at all, my lady. I am certain several ladies will plan to fill their basket with a pie."

She laughed, watching his brow crinkle in concentration. "Then I guess you shall be making a considerable contribution to our cause, good sir!"

His lips twitched in merriment. "Yes... I suppose I will," he said, before he once more whisked her along the ice.

Constance could not have asked for a better day, despite the lieutenant's presence at the lake. She did her best to forget him but also decided to pen a note to the Danver sisters to be wary of a particular soldier. She would hate for anyone to fall into his grasp.

CHAPTER 7

Digby alighted from his carriage in front of the Theatre Royal on Drury Lane and offered his hand to assist Constance. "Watch your step, my lady. The walkway is icy," he warned, taking her elbow and calling back inside. "Freddy, be careful or you shall end up on your, er, dignity."

Frederick chuckled before he, too, left the carriage and helped his wife descend safely onto the walk. "And make a spectacle of myself in front of the ladies? I hardly think such a tragedy will happen," he mocked, before skidding on the ice. "Bloody hell!"

Digby laughed as he watched Margaret grab her husband's arm to prevent him from falling. "I did warn you."

Margaret giggled. "His pride is hurt, Digby," she said, as she linked her hand in her husband's. "Come along, my lord, and let me see you inside."

Frederick muttered another soft curse before he and Margaret began having a hushed conversation between them.

"However did you manage to procure tickets to tonight's play, Digby," Constance asked as she observed several other couples making their way inside. "I was not aware there were any performances tonight. I thought this theater was on the verge of bankruptcy."

"My parents were given tickets, but mother was feeling unwell so they offered them to me and my guests. I understand only a select few have been given this rare opportunity."

"What is the play called?"

Digby looked at the playbill. "We shall be seeing The Merchant of Venice. Edmund Kean is having his London debut performance as Shylock." He began escorting Constance to his parents' box with Frederick and Margaret following close behind. Once they were settled, it was indeed clear there were not many in the audience. It would feel almost as though they were being given their own personal show, although Digby did observe several critics in attendance.

Constance leaned forward in her seat. "The Earl of Trehallow is in the Duchess' box. He was at Haverford House with you, was he not, Digby?"

"Yes, he has also been enlisted to help Her Grace."

"Miss Amelia Clemens and her brother Samuel are also here," she continued. "I wonder if she has heard any more news about whether the event will be moved to the Thames."

"The ice would need to be tested to ensure it is safe enough for that to occur. I would be more concerned with what Mr. Clemens' review will say come tomorrow's edition of *The Teatime Tattler*," Digby said. "A bad review and the theatre will be closed for sure."

"I doubt Mr. Clemens would purposely give the play and performers a bad review, Digby," Constance scolded him, with a tap on his arm.

"We shall see come the morning. Since he normally reports on the latest gossip about the *ton*, those he targets never come out the better. I sincerely doubt his scruples, or lack thereof, would prevent him from ruining the play if that is his intent."

"Perhaps during the intermission I can persuade Miss Amelia to have a brief discussion about the event. If we are to move everything to the ice, we will be scrambling to ensure everything is in place.

Digby laughed. "Somehow, I have the distinct impression the Duchess will handle all the details of such an excursion like a well-trained general, my dear." Digby lifted her hand and placed a kiss upon her knuckles.

Constance's cheeks reddened and they shared a smile before the play began. He had a hard time paying attention to the performers with Constance at his side.

⚜

Constance finished her conversation with Amelia and began searching the busy foyer for Digby. She had forgotten her fan in his box and he had excused himself in order to retrieve it for her. Laugher filled the room as people continued to enjoy the intermission. Couples were still conversing, but some were heading back to their seats, leaving her the impression the play would resume shortly. The crowd began to thin out as she renewed her search for Digby. He could not have gone far.

"Good evening, Constance," a voice purred in her ear. The gentleman slid his arm around her waist and pulled her up against his body before Constance could mutter a protest.

A gasp escaped her as she recognized the voice. She quickly pulled out of his embrace and turned blazing eyes upon him. "How dare you, Lieutenant?" she hissed. Her chest heaved, and her temper flared when his eyes slid down the length of her body.

"I asked you to call me Terrance," he murmured, taking a step closer to her.

"I have told you previously that I could not," she fumed, "nor did I give you permission to address me so casually."

He began to circle around her as though she welcomed his attention. "You look lovely tonight, my dear. What a shame you are not gracing my arm this evening. We would make a striking pair.

Do you not agree?" His wicked smile only reaffirmed Constance's opinion of this man.

"*We* are not together now nor shall we be so in the future."

"Do not be so hasty, my pet." He bent down to once more whisper in her ear. "I am certain I can please you more than your current escort."

He stood upright again, and Constance raised her arm to slap the disgusting smirk from his face. He caught her wrist and held it firmly. "My, oh my! We are feisty this evening, Constance," he drawled stepping closer to her.

"You will maintain your distance, sir!" she warned through clenched teeth, pulling on her arm. He at last let go.

He waved his hand in the air. "I will see you soon, my dear. Until then, I really should return to my seat. Must not keep a lady waiting." He gave her a short bow and left her standing there while the orchestra played a chord announcing the play was to begin again. Those who still milled around began making their way back inside.

Her nerves shattered, Constance ran to the women's with-drawing room to check her appearance. She patted her hair back in place and looked at her reflection. Though she was pale, with the slight hint of blush in her cheeks, she felt nauseous from the anger bubbling inside her. She took several deep breaths to regain her composure before quickly leaving the room. In her distracted state, she stumbled into Digby who reached out to steady her.

"Constance! Are you unwell?" he asked, concern for her welfare flooding his face. "You look pale. Should I take you home?"

Constance forced a small smile, but she was sure he saw right through her façade. "No, I am all right."

Digby reached up to cup her cheeks with his hands, "You do not have to lie to me, Constance. Whatever is the matter?"

"The lieutenant is here—" she began.

Digby's faced changed, and his brow furrowed. "What the devil is he doing here?"

"It is not a matter of why he is here, because that is not what I am interested in. It is how he acted with me."

"What do you mean?"

"He was bold in his conversation with me, ungentlemanly, and forcefully grabbed me." Constance rubbed at her wrist. "He made me uncomfortable, the way he talked as though I was his possession." Angry tears began to form in her eyes as she confessed.

Digby's jaw clenched. "I shall kill him."

"Digby, no. He is not worth it."

"But what he said to you—it is unforgivable. A gentleman would know the difference."

"He is no gentleman, and he does not deserve our attention. What matters is that you and I are here. Only we matter."

"If you are sure... perhaps we should leave?"

"No. I will not let a buffoon ruin our evening."

Digby kissed her forehead. "If you are sure..."

"I am. I just want to forget the whole fiasco happened," she muttered. Digby began escorting her back to their box.

"I have a feeling that will be easier said than done, my dear."

Digby was doing his best to suppress his anger, but Constance could see it in the dangerous tones of his voice, the set of his jaw. She could understand the emotion and could only wonder what in the world the lieutenant would attempt next.

CHAPTER 8

Digby stood on a stool lacing a brightly painted sign to the canvas in front of a newly created booth. It read: *The Ladies' Society for the Care of the Widows and Orphans of Fallen Heroes and the Children of Wounded Veterans.*

"Why, you managed to get it all on one sign after all. I am impressed!" Constance said with a laugh, as she came up to the booth. Her arms were laden with a fairly large box and her footman Marshall carried an even heavier load.

Digby quickly hopped down from the stool. "Let me help you with that, Lady Constance," he said, taking the box from her and bringing it into the tent where Lady Georgiana Hayden and Lady Flora Landrum were organizing their pamphlets.

"Thank you, Lord Osgood. Lady Georgiana... Lady Flora, how nice to see you," Constance began by acknowledging the two women, who were also part of the Society. "You found a nice spot for your tent. It is far enough away from the more... er... unruly establishments but also close enough to some of the vendors who might provide hot cider or other necessities if we grow too cold."

Flora welcomed her with a smile. "Thank you for bringing the rest of the pamphlets, Lady Constance. I do not know what we would have done without your help."

"Marshall, you can set your boxes there," Lady Georgiana instructed, moving out of the way before she continued. "This is the perfect location, especially with Mr. Clemens and his printing press for *The Teatime Tattler* just six booths away if we need extra pamphlets printed."

Digby cleared his throat. "That is convenient," he said biting his tongue to keep in his opinions about the editor. If Mr. Clemens was volunteering his services to help with this event, then Digby could certainly think only kind thoughts about the man... at least until the event was over. He had no doubt Samuel would return to his old ways. After all, people paid good monies for his gossip rag.

"I wonder if that is the best place for the table," Lady Flora pondered, while she began tapping her cheek in concentration. "The duchess suggested we make every effort to engage people in conversation. The written word is good but personal is better." She turned to Lady Georgiana "Not that your writing isn't wonderful."

Lady Georgiana offered her a smile. "No offense taken. I know better than any the limitations of printed words. Shall we pull the table back?"

"I do believe it might be better against the wall," Constance suggested.

"I have to agree," Lady Flora answered with a smile.

"Allow me, ladies," Digby said before pulling the table to the side of the booth.

"Thank you, Lord Osgood," Lady Georgiana said. "I believe Her Grace plans to send sweets from Fournier's of London to entice people to linger. We can place them here for everyone to see."

"Cakes from Monsieur Fournier's renowned restaurant are treasures that will draw this man in—and many others," Digby said. Having tasted the chef's cooking and cakes, he had no doubt the ladies' booth would be filled with people.

Constance looked around the tent. "You two seem to have

everything well in hand. Perhaps I can lend some assistance where the Venetian Breakfast will take place tomorrow."

"Let me accompany you, Lady Constance," he offered. Lady Flora giggled and Lady Georgiana smirked, causing his lady to blush. "That is, if you no longer require any further assistance from me."

"We can handle things now, Lord Osgood," Lady Georgiana declared. "If we have need of you, we shall know where to find you."

He gave the women a bow. "I am at your service, ladies. Lady Constance," he offered her his arm. "Shall we?"

She smiled at him, blushing sweetly. They left the tent to make their way across the iced-over Thames to lend whatever assistance might still be needed for tomorrow's preparations.

❧

The big day had at last arrived and Digby once more escorted Constance across the frozen Thames. The morning sun shone through the fog, the rays of light almost magical. A veritable village had sprung up almost overnight on the ice as vendors readied their own booths for the customers who would buy their wares.

"I am glad you have Marshall with you," Digby said, as he peered back over his shoulder to see the man several steps behind. The footman knew his job well, as he kept a close eye on his charge and the surrounding area.

"He has become a bodyguard of sorts," Constance whispered. "Aunt Penelope insisted when I told her what happened at the theater, but we have also offered his services to ensure those attending the breakfast have paid for the privilege of being in attendance."

"I understand the Duchess has commandeered a whole section of the ice on the outskirts of this town that has suddenly appeared."

Constance giggled. "Just wait until you see what is happening, Digby. It will make your head spin!"

As they neared the area, it was not hard to miss the crowd who had gathered to witness the spectacle before them. It was as though all of London had turned up to see the goings on. An army of Haverford servants and others from various noble houses had erected a sumptuous marquee on the ice. The tent dwarfed the other booths and shelters around it and must have been as large as the Haverford ballroom itself! Men carried rolls of carpeting to cover the ice and more followed with chairs, tables, and crates.

"What is in the boxes?" Digby asked.

Constance laughed. "Oh, just little things like linen for the tables, cotton to drape the walls, furs and woolen shawls to keep warm... that sort of thing."

A chuckle escaped Digby. "As usual, Her Grace has spared no expense and thought of everything."

Constance pointed to several soldiers who stood near a makeshift barrier of bollards and ribbons. "She even thought of a guard of returned soldiers and sailors who have recovered enough from their wounds to serve for the day. That is where Marshall shall also help if he is needed."

"Her Grace is a marvel," Digby mused.

"She is at that," Constance agreed. "Perhaps we can steal away for a while to see the booths. Once the auction and breakfast starts, I fear I will be occupied until after the bidding."

"I heard there is an elephant walking the ice."

Constance's eyes widened. "Really? Oh, Digby, we must go see it."

"Then let us see if we can find the beast," he said, giving her a wink. He enjoyed making his lady happy. He would do anything just so she would smile upon him again and again.

CHAPTER 9

The tent was crowded, not only by the charity's supporters, but with hundreds of the *beau monde* who would never normally spend their coins for such a cause. Thanks to the Duchess's efforts to ensure that anyone who was anyone knew of this worthy event, those of Society turned out in droves wanting to be seen.

Scandal was also being whispered in the air, due to the nature of the auction. The sale of a lady's time, if you won her basket, was most improper, but the committee members had insisted the money being raised was for a good cause. Surely the *ton*'s elite would understand their reasoning.

Constance stood at the side of the tent close enough to the stage if she needed to lend assistance but also for when it was her turn for her basket to be auctioned. She gave Digby's arm a slight squeeze, and he smiled warmly at her. Their day together thus far had been dream-like, and she could barely contain her excitement for the rest.

Busy conversations of the enthusiastic patrons diminished to a low murmur when Brigadier General Lord Redepenning stepped onto the stage at the rear of the marquee, accompanied by Her Grace, the Duchess of Haverford.

Her Grace spoke first, briefly explaining the purpose of the Society. Constance was hardly surprised when the duchess encouraged all who were present to open their purses and be generous for the action that was about to begin. She then introduced Mrs. Beresford, as the chairwoman of the Society's organising committee.

Mrs. Beresford limited her time to welcoming everyone before asking Lord Henry, as he was known by all but his subordinates in the Horse Guard, to begin the auction.

Lord Henry briefly explained how the auction would work: the winner of a basket also won the right to share the contents with the lady who donated it. The usual rules of propriety prevailed, and no lady would lunch unchaperoned, unless, of course, her basket was purchased by a close family member.

A footman in Haverford livery handed Mrs Beresford the first basket, and she brought it to Lord Henry.

He mimicked opening the top, holding it to his nose, and gave a profound theatrical sigh. "Magnificent!" he exclaimed. Your Graces, my ladies, my lords, gentlemen... I give you a picnic basket that, if it tastes as good as it smells, will be a rare treat. One made even pleasanter, dare I say, by the company of the lovely Lady Priscilla Fenton."

Lifting the label again, he added, "Oh, and it says, her elder brother and his wife." Speaking over the laughter, he continued. "Ah, well." The crowd's merriment filled the tent yet again.

The bidding was fast. No one was surprised when Lord Wrathall, who had been courting Lady Priscilla for the last several months, allowed himself to be cozened out of nine pounds ten shillings for winning the basket and, no doubt, the lady's affection.

Three baskets later, Lord Henry was holding up Lady Georgiana's basket. A none too gentle voice calling the lady the *recluse of Cambridge* magnetized the crowd before Sir Horace Malford came storming toward Lady Georgiana. Constance, worried for her friend, caught Lady Flora's look of concern from across the stage. Constance stepped forward but Digby held her back.

"What are you thinking," Sir Horace hissed at Georgie. "Your mother will—"

"Quiet in the ranks," Lord Henry called out. "Are you bidding, Sir Horace?"

"I will not be a part of this disgrace," the man snapped.

"Really," The Earl of Hamner said in a loud enough tone for all to hear while he stood next to Miss Grenford, "is the man calling an event organised by Her Grace the Duchess of Haverford a disgrace?"

"Then I suggest you sit down, Horace, and be quiet" Lord Henry retorted.

Constance smiled as she watched Georgiana standing there proudly, her chin lifted higher. Only the faintest blush to her cheeks showed how truly upset she was by Horace's outburst. People began whispering among themselves when no bids were offered from the crowd.

"Twenty guineas," a commanding voice from the rear called out. Everyone turned in their chairs to witness the Marquess of Glenaire, Lady Georgiana's brother, look unwaveringly at Lord Henry.

"Ah!" Lord Henry said. "Offered by a man who has undoubtedly experienced picnics prepared by Lady Georgiana and knows their worth." He held the gavel as his eyes scanned the room until the comments and laughter became a dull hum. Finally, he brought it down. "Sold to the Marquess of Glenaire."

The basket of Miss Cummins was brought forth next and a bidding war began to ensue between the Earl of Trehallow and the Marquis of Aldridge, the Duchess's son. Trehallow would not stand a chance against Aldridge, for the Marquis' pockets ran deep.

Outrageous sums for a basket bounced back and forth between the two men but Constance's attention was suddenly drawn to the man standing beside her. Digby bent down to whisper in her ear. She sighed, listening to the husky tone of his voice.

"You could have told me you would be standing with your basket," he murmured. His hand went to her back in a soft caress.

Her attempts to stifle her giggle failed. "What fun would that be?"

"You, my dear, are a bit of a mischievous minx, I fear," he teased with a roguish grin.

"And you love me for it" The words rushed out. Her eyes widened by what she had just let slip. How could she have voiced her inner thoughts aloud? Her cheeks heated at her assumption. "I mean I—"

"I do love you, Constance," Digby said, his eyes twinkling in delight. "I never stopped loving you while I was gone from your side."

"You do?" she asked in surprise. They had never confessed their feelings before, although Constance had always hoped that one day they would do so.

He took her hand and kissed it. "Yes, I do."

"Digby…" Her voice was a breathy whisper as she gazed up into his eyes. "I lo—"

"One hundred pounds!" Trehallow yelled levelling his stare directly at Aldridge. It was almost as though the earl was daring the Marquis to go higher with his bid. But Aldridge refrained, spreading his hands in defeat while Lord Henry quickly closed the bidding.

Constance shook her head. "A person could run a modest household with the amounts of some of these bids."

"I would gladly pay a substantial amount and more to win your basket, Constance, and I have the money here to prove it."

She playfully swatted his arm. "Do not dare pay such an outlandish amount. I can bake you a pie and all the rest of the contents any time."

"Yes... but the money would be well spent and go to a good cause," he reminded her of their purpose here today.

She gave him a warning look, but a laugh escaped her. As basket after basket sold, some of the crowd began to thin as the winners left with their ladies to partake of the delicacies to be found within their prizes. The Duchess had also provided a luncheon for those who had not been able to win a basket once the auction ended.

With a nervous fluttering in her stomach, Constance went to stand close to the stage, knowing her basket would be next. After the previous winner collected his prize, she began to ascend the stairs but her footsteps faltered when she saw an unwelcome character entering the tent. Lord Henry rushed over to take hold of her elbow before she disgraced herself by falling as she tripped on the last step.

"Are you unhurt, Lady Constance?" he asked quietly as he brought her forward to stand next to him.

Her eyes met Lieutenant Abernathy's as he calmly strolled closer to the stage and took an empty seat. He smiled. She scowled.

"Lady Constance?" Lord Henry said again as she turned her attention to him.

"Yes. I am fine, my lord. Shall we begin?" she asked. Her eyes met Digby's. His clenched fists told her more than anything he could have voiced aloud.

CHAPTER 10

Terrance fingered the coins he held in his hand. A lucky game of dice had landed him twenty pounds, a veritable fortune and far more than he had earned picking pockets in recent days. He had almost stayed for another round, the urge to gamble his winnings surging through his veins like fire. But he withstood the temptation. Taking his winnings, he had quickly left the docks to make his way through the Frost Fair booths until he came to the tent holding the charitable auction.

Forced to pay the ungodly sum of ten pounds for admittance into the festivities, he grumbled a curse but paid the soldier guarding the entrance. Terrance's purse was much lighter, but he was now one step closer to winning Lady Constance. She had become an obsession with him, much like his gambling habit of late. He vowed to have her whether she was willing or not.

Further luck was in his favor as he entered the tent in time to witness her stepping onto the stage. A light laugh escaped him. It was not the basket he would be bidding on, but her. He took a seat toward the front, ignoring a warning glare from Osgood. Terrance adjusted his coat, knowing he looked his best while in uniform. That fop Osgood was incapable of looking anywhere near as good, and Terrance gave Constance a snide grin. She would be his, and she would enjoy their time spent together.

Lord Henry stood center stage and peered into the basket. "Pie… among other delicacies, gentlemen." His brow rose as he gave Constance a bright smile. "Raspberry, my lady?"

"Yes, of course, Lord Henry. My Aunt gave me her favorite recipe, so I know whoever wins my basket will enjoy the pie immensely."

Constance smiled sweetly toward the audience, and a part of Terrance stirred to life. If only she would look upon him with those incredible green eyes of hers!

"Rightly so," Lord Henry beamed. "Who shall start the bidding?"

Terrance raised his arm. "Two pounds," he called out, and several sniggers were heard at the paltry starting bid.

"Three pounds," another voice at the rear of the tent placed his bid.

A third gentleman, whom Terrance did not know, stood. "Really, Chadwick? Surely this lady's basket is worth more than that. You spent as much with your tailor just for the buttons on your waistcoat!"

Laughter burst throughout the tent causing Terrance to grimace. The nobility had an odd sense of fashion, which he resented, especially considering his own meager attire when not in uniform.

"Four pounds then. That should make Sutton happy." Chadwick stood to be heard above the continuing laughter. "I do appreciate a good raspberry pie. What say you, Osgood?"

As Osgood stepped forward, Terrance leapt to his feet. "Five pounds," he called out before turning to stare at his rival.

Osgood smirked, and Terrance had a feeling in the pit of his belly that he would not come out the winner this day. Osgood then proceeded to take a linen square out of his jacket, clean the lenses of his spectacles, and then return them to his face as though he had all the time in the world.

"Lord Osgood," Lord Henry called out. "Do you plan to place a bid for this basket that is as lovely as the lady who provided it today?"

"I do plan to bid on Lady Constance's basket, although if I bid too high an amount I may be out of favor with the lady."

"Come, come, Lord Osgood! Remember the cause of the Society," Lord Henry cajoled to Terrance's annoyance, obviously hoping for a higher bid.

"Very well," Osgood said. "Ten pounds."

Terrance fumed, knowing full well he could not cover the next bid. "Fifteen!" He gulped at the amount, wondering where he would find the funds to pay for Constance's company.

"Twenty pounds," another voice chimed in and everyone turned to see Lord Richard Cranfield standing as he, too, placed his bid.

"Let us see how far you are willing to go to win the company of the lady, Richard," Osgood called out with a laugh to the latest bidder. "You know I will go to any lengths to win this basket!"

Osgood and Cranfield began placing bids, one higher than the next. Terrance remained in his seat, a disgusted scowl most likely permanently etched across his face. But it was the smile of satisfaction on Lady Constance's features that set Terrance over the edge of his sanity. He could see for himself how pleased she was that Terrance was no longer placing his bid along with the other men.

"Sold to Lord Osgood for the sum of one hundred and twenty-five pounds. Pay the purser to my left and claim your prize," Lord Henry said as he closed the bidding.

Osgood went to the stage and offered his arm to Lady Constance who handed over the basket.

"Your prize, my lord," Constance said with another bright smile.

"You are the true prize, my lady," Osgood was heard to say.

Terrance stood, knocking over his chair. He took one last look at the couple and stormed from the tent. He would have to come up with another idea to get to Constance. In the meantime, he would head back to the docks and see if he could double his money with what remained of his winnings. Unless luck continued to be on his side, he highly doubted he would be able to cover the admission to tonight's ball.

Digby leaned back in his chair and watched while Constance sliced a piece of the raspberry pie he had won. Her basket had indeed been filled with every delicious delicacy for a proper Venetian Breakfast including a lovely red wine. While they ate their lunch, Constance had explained how her aunt dried the berries while they were in season so they could enjoy her favorite pie any time of the year. But it was Constance's company and listening to her laugh as they sat at their table and ate that set his heart to take flight. He could not ever remember being so happy.

Momentarily distracted from the woman who had been holding his attention, Digby was surprised to see Chester, eighth Duke of Eastly entering the tent. He rarely left his estate. The duke made his way across the room until he reached a table where Miss Artemis Synclaire sat. His sister Lady Theodosia Mansfield was close by along with Lady Harriet Ross who gave the duke a salute with her glass. Digby could not tell if the duke was amused or not, but Digby's eyes widened when the duke hooked an umbrella on the back of his chair before he took his seat. If that was *the* infamous umbrella belonging to Lady Ross, Eastly was doomed!

Constance handing over a plate to Digby and nodding to the next table brought his concentration back to his lady. "Would you mind, Lord Osgood," she said, while keeping their conversation formal for those around them.

"It would be my pleasure, Lady Constance. Lady Penelope, would you like some pie?" he asked the lady sitting across from them. Constance's aunt was close enough to observe the rules of proper conduct were adhered to but not so close to prevent him and Constance from speaking somewhat privately.

"You are too kind to share your dessert with me, Lord Osgood," Lady Penelope said taking the plate. She returned to her conversation with the other ladies seated with her.

"Your aunt is too kind to allow us our own table," Digby said taking his own plate.

Constance giggled. "She may not have married, but she certainly understands we want time to ourselves. She is not that far away in the event you do not behave yourself."

"I would never dare," Digby answered.

Lady Penelope leaned toward their table. "See that you do not, young sir," she warned, giving evidence she was more than capable of hearing everything being said.

Digby gave her a nod before trying a piece of pie. "Scrumptious, Lady Constance," he said before taking another bite. "This must be the best raspberry pie I have ever tasted."

"You will turn my head with your compliments, Lord Osgood," she exclaimed then watched him with an amused smile before she burst out in laughter.

He gazed behind him but did not see anything of interest to cause her to laugh. "What do you see that amuses you so?" he asked with a grin of his own.

Constance smiled again handing him a linen napkin. "I believe you have something on your chin."

Aghast he had allowed the juice from the pie to drip down his chin, he took the linen. "Forgive me," he said hastily before wiping the stain away. "I suppose I just like a good berry pie."

They finished their dessert in silence and before long they heard an orchestra tuning their instruments.

"I believe I also owe you a dance, my lord," Constance said.

Digby rose from his seat and offered her his arm. "I thought the dance was for this evening at the ball."

"I am certain you will be able to claim one there, too, but the duchess has set up an area where we can dance on the ice."

"That could be dangerous," he declared with a chuckle.

She laughed. "She has placed carpets down to prevent anyone falling. Never fear, my lord. Your dignity will remain intact!"

As he took his lady into his arms, he could have given a heart-felt prayer to God above that he had redeemed himself as far as Constance was concerned. She fit there so perfectly, that, as he began to twirl her around among the other dancers present, he could envision her in his life for the rest of his days.

"It has been far too long since I have been able to dance with you, Constance," he said in a husky tone.

"Yes, it has," she replied as she gazed up into his eyes. "Have I told you how much I missed you while you were gone?"

"No, you have not."

She gave a pretty blush. "I suppose it is a bit unladylike to make mention of something so personal."

"I am humbly grateful you feel comfortable enough to confide in me. I, too, have missed your company these past two years."

"It seemed like it was forever…" Her voice held all the emotions he had also felt while they had been apart.

"I have to agree. I wish I could steal you away so I could kiss you," he said giving her a small smile. "I spoke no falsehood when I told you I loved you back at the auction."

A becoming blush raced across her cheeks. "I love you too, Digby," she finally answered. She had never looked lovelier in Digby's mind.

"Then perhaps you will not mind if I speak to your Aunt to ask for her blessing, since your father has passed on." He held his breath, waiting for her answer.

She took a deep breath, her eyes twinkling with delight. "I would like that very much."

Relief swept through Digby as though a heavy weight had been lifted from his mind. As he whirled Constance around this makeshift dance floor, he began to wonder what their evening would bring.

CHAPTER 11

Haverford House was overflowing with the elite of Society. The women had taken extra care with their newly-fitted gowns while jewels sparkled from their necks in the candlelight. The men appeared resplendent in their jackets and neatly tied cravats. Servants carried trays of champagne to the guests who drank from the crystal flutes as though there was a never-ending supply to be consumed. The duchess had seen to every detail for the evening, and those present had not complained at the cost of attending her evening ball. Many would sell their very soul to be seen at a Haverford event.

Constance and Digby were never far from one another. She had enjoyed their dance together and wished for several more. She had been so pleased when he even took the time to escort her aunt upon the dance floor. Constance watched them leave the ballroom together. *Those two were up to something,* she thought. They returned a short while later, and Digby raised his hand in a silent invitation to their second dance. Although she asked, Digby refused to tell her what they had discussed. The curiosity was going to kill her but no matter how much she pleaded, Digby remained quiet, saying she would learn soon enough.

She spotted his parents near the balcony doors, and they raised their glasses toward her in a soundless salute. She returned the gesture before focusing her attention on anything that might need seeing to. Constance was unsure why she was worried about the little details for the ball. The duchess and her committees had planned things well. With the auction alone, they had raised a considerable amount of money for their charities. The ball just might double their fundraising efforts. Like a well-run ship, there was nothing for Constance to do but enjoy herself, and she planned to do just that.

The orchestra began again, and Constance willingly placed her hand in Digby's before he tucked it into the crook of his elbow with a slight pat and squeeze. They had taken three turns around the dance floor before he casually led her away from the ballroom.

"What are you up to, Digby?" she asked breathlessly, when he pulled her into a vacant salon. It was a comfortable room with a shelf of books against one wall. Candles lit the room in a warm glow, and her heart began to flutter in her chest when he took her into his arms. The distant music from the ballroom could still be heard as he began to gently sway in an ever-so-slow dance. There was no one else but them. The ball was all but forgotten.

"I have spoken to your aunt," he said. She swore his eyes shone with so much love that her heart was about to burst.

"You have?"

"Yes, I have."

"And?"

"You must know how much I care for you, Constance," he declared in a solemn voice. He took her hand to give the back a kiss before he continued "You have given me a second chance at love. I never thought I would ever earn your trust again."

"I never stopped loving you, Digby. You owned my heart two

years ago, and those feelings never changed. If anything, your absence only made me love you more."

He watched her intently while running a finger down her cheek until he slightly lifted her chin. He brought his lips down to meet her own, and their breaths mingled together on a heartbeat before he completely claimed her. Deepening their kiss, he took possession of her very soul, and she never wanted this moment to end. He brought her closer as her hands wound their way around his neck to play with the edges of his hair. She felt every part of him, and she could only ponder what life had in store for their future together.

Distant clapping from the ballroom caused them to break apart, but not before Digby leaned down to kiss the tip of her nose. Nervously, she smiled before blushing most probably the shade of the brightest red rose. Her hands went to her cheeks, and she could feel the heat caused by this man who had proclaimed his love for her.

He began fumbling inside his jacket.

"You never said what you and Aunt Penelope discussed," she said to form some sort of conversation to ease her embarrassment.

"Why, she gave us her blessing, of course," he said with a broad grin.

"She did?" Constance gasped out in relief.

"She did indeed, my love." He pulled out an emerald ring surrounded by diamonds. "This was my mother's. My father gave it to her for their engagement, although I must admit this gem pales in comparison to your lovely eyes. Will you become my wife, Constance, and make me a happy man?"

Tears welled in her eyes. "Yes! Oh, Digby! Yes, I will marry you," she exclaimed in excitement.

He placed the ring on her finger, and he once more kissed her to seal their promise to one another. "Shall we go tell our family and friends our good news?"

"By all means, Digby."

As they returned to the ballroom, conversations grew when the news spread of their sudden engagement. The rest of the evening became a blur, but Constance knew, without any doubt in her mind, that their life together would be a happy one.

CHAPTER 12

Two days later, Digby and Constance came up to the banks of the Thames and began reading the sign in front of them. The large chalked boards gave proof the river was still safely frozen, and the booths still erected upon the ice were testament to that. They began wandering and inspecting various stands and made several small purchases, since they had not had a lot of time to do so while working for the charity event before. Hot cider kept them warm, and to be extra certain Constance remained that way, Digby purchased a colorful wool scarf for his lady.

A loud booming crack sounded beneath their feet, and Constance's look of startled surprise had Digby holding her arm tighter.

"Do you suppose the ice is still safe?" she asked in alarm, clutching his elbow.

"I would like to think so, but perhaps we should make this excursion shorter than we originally planned. We should still have the time to walk past the remaining booths if you like," Digby replied. He looked up toward the sky even as the wind picked up, and it started to snow.

As they continued to stroll arm in arm, they were surprised to see a booth where someone was roasting a sheep. A crowd had gathered to watch the exhibition, but, to Digby's mind, this was tempting fate. Constance mentioned she would like to see if the elephant was still near, but the animal was no longer on the ice. For that, Digby was grateful. As they approached the end of the booths near the bank of Cheapside, several children were having a snowball fight. Their laughter rang out, and Constance turned to Digby with a smile.

"You know, some of those gingerbread cookies looked good a few stalls back," she said, her eyes twinkling in delight.

Digby chuckled. "If my lady wants gingerbread, than I shall get gingerbread."

"Perhaps you could…"

He laughed again. "Are you thinking the children would like some as well?" he asked. He grinned, knowing her answer.

She laughed and the sound of her merriment went straight to Digby's heart. "Be sure to get plenty so the children can enjoy their treat," she coaxed with a squeeze of his arm.

Digby looked around the area. "Perhaps you should come with me. I do not like the idea of leaving you alone."

Constance waved him off. "I shall be fine. You will hardly be far, and I want to watch the children play."

"I will be right back, my lady."

Digby reluctantly left her side and made his way to the stall where they had seen the cookies. He ordered a dozen and waited for them to be wrapped. He could still see Constance in the distance, making her way closer to where the children continued to throw snow at one another.

"Digby! Surprised to see you here alone," Milton said. "Thought for sure Lady Constance would be in your company."

He turned to see his friend and George coming up to the stall. Digby pointed in the distance to where Constance stood. "I was just purchasing some cookies for the children at my lady's urging."

"She has a kind heart, that one does," George declared. "You are lucky to have found her, Digby."

"I am lucky indeed," Digby agreed as he returned Constance's wave even as they heard another loud crack.

Milton gave Digby a pat on his shoulder. "We best make our way off the ice. That is the second time I have experienced that sound, and I do not wish to take any chances."

"I had best get Constance," Digby said as he took his purchase.

He had taken only a few steps when a deafening boom was heard beneath his feet followed by a crack appearing. He watched in horror as the ice opened up, and Constance fell through. The children began to shriek.

"Digby!"

Her scream tore at his heart as he saw her hanging on to the edge. He began to run, slipping and sliding on the ice beneath his feet, knowing he would never get to her before she sank beneath the water. The weight of her dress and coat would pull her under for sure!

Terrance had just come from his inn in Cheapside and was heading toward the Frost Fair when he heard the faint cries for help. As he wandered through the people beginning to gather, he heard the whisperings that a woman had fallen through the ice. He picked up his pace, removing his jacket as he approached the edge of the hole, preparing to jump in if he needed to. The woman's head bobbed under the water, and he made a quick grab for anything to help her out. He managed to catch hold of her arm and pulled with all his might. The woman gasped for air when she reached the surface, her lips a faint shade of blue from the cold.

"My God! Constance," he said in alarm. He tugged on her arm, and she tumbled into his embrace from the force of his efforts. He looked around for the coat he had dropped nearby and wrapped her tightly in it. Quickly, he picked her up in his arms. He needed to get her warm, and his inn was the first place to come to his mind. She was now *his*, and he had every intention of keeping her.

"Abernathy!"

He turned as his name echoed across the frozen river and quickened his pace. Be damned, that bespectacled oaf would not take his prize from him, nor would Osgood's dandy friends who ran behind him.

Terrance continued his way across the river and had almost made it to the bank when Osgood came up behind him.

"Just where do you think you are taking my lady?" he growled before taking Terrance's arm and turning him about.

"She is hardly yours, Osgood," Terrance sneered.

"As of two nights ago, she is. We are engaged."

"No!" Terrance hissed as Osgood began to pry his hands from around Constance. He could feel his grip loosening from around the woman.

"Give her to me!" Osgood said as she all but fell against him. "George! Milton! Take Constance and get us a carriage while I deal with this vermin."

"Digby?" Constance murmured, her voice shaking from cold. "What happened?"

"Go with George and Milton, my love," he said kissing her forehead.

"Damn you, Osgood!" Terrance howled before rushing toward his nemesis.

Digby managed to land a solid punch square on Terrance's jaw. His head reeling from the impact, he saw Digby shaking his injured hand. Terrance leered. *This should be easy*, he thought.

The two men began circling each other before they began throwing punches. Terrance was surprised Osgood had enough force to actually cause him pain. He had always thought of the man as too soft. Still, Terrance landed several well-aimed punches of his own, but it was not until he heard the sound of his nose crunching and tasted blood at his lip that he began to think he would be on the losing end of this fight.

Whistles began to sound in the distance, and Terrance noticed several watermen constables from the river police making their way toward them. With one last swing of his arm, his fist connected with Osgood's cheek, causing the man to lose his footing and slip on the ice. His head gave a sickening smack when he landed on the ground, and Terrance felt this was a good time for a hasty exit.

As he fled the Thames to hide out until the area was clear, his last thought was to find another woman with a hefty dowry. Lady Constance was too much of a bother and was obviously lost to him.

CHAPTER 13

L eft languishing in her room for several days, Constance was determined to see how Digby fared. After his fall on the ice and the lieutenant's hasty retreat, Digby's friends had carried him from the Thames. Constance had given the driver her aunt's address, arguing that her residence was closer than Digby's.

He had a bump on his head that the doctor said would heal, and since Digby had briefly awoken, he was confident the patient would be on his feet in no time. But since the doctor's departure, Digby had come down with the flu, and Aunt Penelope had insisted he remain in the guest room. The poor man had been bed ridden with a fever, and Constance was at her wits end to see for herself that he was well taken care of.

She pleaded her case to her aunt. He was her fiancé after all, but Aunt Penelope informed her, in no uncertain terms, that Lord Osgood's care would be at the hands of the servants and the doctor only. She was, under no circumstance, allowed in the room. Constance protested again but to no avail. Her aunt was most adamant that she protect Constance's reputation at all costs, as well as keep her healthy. Hence, she was banished to her room.

She heaved a heavy sigh and closed her book. She had had enough of her attempts at embroidery. Her usually nimble fingers had fumbled with the needle until she had made a mess of the piece she had been working on. Even the thread was in knots. Her attempts at reading had only caused her to re-read the same page at least four times. That she could not remember what the book was even about testified that her mind was clearly on the man down the hall.

Tossing the book aside, she left her room. Silently, she made her way down the corridor until she heard Digby's door opening. Scooting behind some drapery, she watched a servant leaving the room. Conveniently, he left the door partially open. Constance smiled. Surely this was a sign for her to enter. An open invitation…

Constance poked her head inside the door to ensure she was alone. Not seeing another servant, she went to the bed to peer down at Digby. His face was flushed, with perspiration on his brow and upper lip. She pushed back a lock of his wavy black hair and felt for herself the fever radiating from him. He was burning up. Constance took up a cloth lying next to his spectacles, dipped it in a basin of cool water, and placed it on his forehead.

Digby tossed his head back and forth. "Too damned hot," he mumbled and tossed off the sheet covering his body.

Constance gasped, seeing he only wore a pair of drawers. She could feel the blush creeping along her cheeks as she quickly looked away from his naked chest. Curiosity getting the better of her, she took one last peek before she heard someone in the hallway. Upon hearing footsteps coming closer to the room, she pulled the sheets back over Digby's burning body, despite his protestations and attempts to pull them off once more.

In his hysteria, he once again pulled the covers off as Constance found a place to hide. The door opened, and another servant came to check on him. The sound of the creaking floor echoed in the room. From her hiding spot behind the curtain, she could see the servant pull the blanket back over him and set a cool cloth on his forehead. This seemed to soothe Digby, as he did not try to take the covers off for a third time. The servant left, and Constance tip-toed back over to her beloved. She bent low, placing a kiss on his forehead.

"Be well, my love," she whispered.

She slowly walked to the door, wary of the creaking floorboard the servant had stepped on, and opened the door. Seeing no one in the hallway, she hastened from the room. Once safely behind her own door, she sunk to the floor, wondering when they would be married and when she could be Digby's wife in every way.

Digby opened his eyes. He felt as if he had been run over by a carriage. His vision was blurred. Where had his spectacles been placed? He fumbled around for them on the bedside table and slowly put them on. Once he could see clearly again, he took in his surroundings. He was in an unfamiliar room, but one thing was very familiar to him. Constance slept on the loveseat, a surprise to him. He watched as her shoulders rose and fell with every breath. She was stunning, even in sleep, and all he wanted to do was take her in his arms.

"Constance," he whispered softly. His throat was raw, his voice raspy at best.

His lady's eyes fluttered open, and her gaze fell on him. A smile turned up her mouth softening her features, and she threw the blanket off to rush to his side.

"At long last," she cooed. "Your fever has broken."

"Fever? What fever?" Digby looked down at his naked chest. In his gentlemanly modesty, he pulled the covers up to his chin, so as not to frighten the woman before him. "Uh… forgive my indecency."

"You have been ill, my darling. I insisted you be brought to my aunt's since it was closer than your own townhouse. Your parents have been sick with worry and have been here to check on you several times." Constance motioned to a maid sitting near the door and began giving her instructions. "Janet, please see that a message is relayed to Lord Osgood's parents informing them he is now on the mend."

Digby ran his hand through his hair and winced, noticing the knot on his head. "And why is my head so sore?"

"You had an altercation with Lieutenant Abernathy after my fall through the ice. He is responsible for you hitting your head when you, too, fell. The doctor believed you would not have a concussion as your head injury was not that severe. We have been assured the sleeping you have done was due to a nasty bout of the flu. We took every precaution, however, in the event your illness was more severe."

"You did?"

"But of course," she said busying herself by fixing him a cup of tea. "Here, drink this. It will make you feel better."

He took the cup and sipped, peering at her over the rim. Looking about the room, he was again surprised to notice they were alone. "You... took care of me yourself?" he asked, afraid of what the young woman may have gone through while tending him.

She blushed, most becomingly he thought. "I did what I could, when my aunt allowed it, Digby, although my aunt protested that others could see to tending you and my reputation was at stake. I told her I did not care a fig for my reputation. My main concern was that you were properly nursed by someone who loved for you."

He set the cup down. "I am most thankful for your ministrations, my lady." At a loss for words, he became embarrassed. The dear young woman had seen him at his worst.

She seemed to understand his dilemma. She hesitated but an instant before reaching out to pat his hand. "You are most welcome."

Digby felt the back of his head again. "I cannot believe I let Abernathy get the best of me," he mumbled feeling the fool for falling on the ice in the first place.

"You both took quite the beating, but I will admit that, if it had not been for the lieutenant reaching me in time to pull me from the river, we may not have had the opportunity to plan our wedding."

"I am unsure how I can ever repay him, even though I have disliked the man from the moment we met."

"There is no need. Aunt Penelope sent a reward for his services, although I doubt his intentions were honorable at the time. Your friend Lord Sutton saw to delivering the reward himself, and gave him a warning to never cross paths with us again. I believe the lieutenant is asking for a reassignment. I am certain we have seen the last of him."

"I need to repay your aunt."

"There is no need, Digby."

They were silent for a moment, each lost in thought. "I should have never left you alone. What happened to you is all my fault."

"No one could have predicted the ice would crack. After my incident, everyone at the Frost Fair began to quickly pack up their booths. The Thames is once again a flowing river."

"But we heard the cracks and should have taken it as a sign. I am so sorry, my love, for not being close enough to rescue you myself," Digby said taking her hand.

"You have nothing to apologize for, my dearest Digby. Besides… you did rescue me. You gave us a second chance at love by finding me again. No woman could be happier than I am at this very moment. I love you very much."

"I love you, too," he whispered.

She leaned forward and kissed his cheek before standing and smoothing down her hair. "I must look a fright after sleeping the night away in a chair," she laughed gaily.

"I have never seen you look lovelier, Constance." Her eyes lit with happiness at his words. She gave a slight nod and made her way towards the door.

"I will have a servant bring you up something to eat. Nothing too substantial since you have been ill for so long."

"I am in your debt, along with Lady Penelope, for your tender care. It was certainly not how I was planning to spend the day," Digby replied, wondering how he would ever make it up to her. It was a lot to ask to take care of someone who had apparently been so sick.

She opened the door to leave but turned back one last time to look upon him. "I will look forward to another evening at the theater once you are on the mend, good sir, along with a lifetime of happiness in the years to come."

Her answer dispelled his worst fears that she would not forgive him for allowing her to fall through the ice. "You can count on it, Constance," Digby said as he watched her leave.

Digby lay back down on the pillow and closed his eyes. A smile crept along his face and when he dreamed, he dreamed of the woman who meant all to him. A lifetime of happiness she had said… it was indeed something he would look forward to.

EPILOGUE

August 1814

Constance snuggled up to Digby in their bed. His arm brought her closer until her head rested on his chest. His heartbeat was strong, and she smiled, thinking of how he had made all her dreams come true.

"Do you think everyone is this happy on their wedding day, Digby?" she asked while running her fingers along his chest playfully.

He took her hand and brought it to his lips. "No one could be as happy as we are today, my love," he whispered.

"Maybe Margaret and Frederick," she mused. "They have a happy marriage. Now if we could only find matches for your other friends, life would be quite grand."

A rumble of laughter cracked from his lips. "I believe Richard, Milton, and George are fine as they are, Constance. Leave them to their bachelorhood."

He rolled over and began nibbling at her neck, causing Constance to giggle.

"I will enlist Margaret's help to find them all suitable brides," she continued with a guilty smile. "They just do not know what they are missing."

Digby looked up from kissing her. His brow rose when she burst out laughing. "Do not dare, my lady!"

"I want them to be happy too," she said as he began kissing the other side of her neck. "Are you trying to distract me, my lord?"

He began moving lower and Constance gave a low throaty moan. "Is it working, my dear?" he asked with a husky tone that left her wanting more.

"Yes," she whispered. "Make love to me once more, Digby, and never leave me again."

"It is my fondest wish to keep you forever by my side," he whispered, before sealing his vow with a heavenly kiss.

Hours later as she watched her husband sleep, Constance remembered their wedding day and how happy she was to have finally married the man of her dreams. He fulfilled each and every desire she could have ever wished for. Maybe having a second chance at love was not so bad after all. It had brought her Digby, and for the rest of their lives, she could be thankful she had him to love.

THE END

OTHER BOOKS BY SHERRY EWING

Medieval & Time Travel Series:

To Love A Scottish Laird: De Wolfe Pack Connected World

Sometimes you really can fall in love at first sight…

To Love An English Knight: De Wolfe Pack Connected World

Can a chance encounter lead to love?

To Love An English Knight: A De Wolfe Pack Connected World - Release date December 28, 2019

Can a chance encounter lead to love?

If My Heart Could See You

When you're enemies, does love have a fighting chance?

For All of Ever: The Knights of Berwyck, A Quest Through Time Novel (Book One)

Sometimes to find your future, you must look to the past…

Only For You: The Knights of Berwyck, A Quest Through Time Novel (Book Two)

Sometimes it's hard to remember that true love conquers all, *only after the battle is over*…

Hearts Across Time: The Knights of Berwyck (Books One & Two)

Sometimes all you need is to just believe…

A Knight to Call My Own

When your heart is broken, is love still worth the risk?

To Follow My Heart: The Knights of Berwyck, A Quest Through Time Novel (Book Three)

Love is a leap. Sometimes you need to jump…

The Piper's Lady in Never Too Late, A Bluestocking Belles Collection

True love binds them. Deceit divides them. Will they choose love?

One Last Kiss: The Knights of Berwyck, A Quest Through Time (Book Five)

Sometimes it takes a miracle to find your heart's desire…

Regencies:

A Kiss For Charity: A de Courtenay Novella (Book One)

Love heals all wounds but will their pride keep them apart?

The Earl Takes A Wife: A de Courtenay Novella (Book Two)

It began with a memory etched in the heart.

Nothing But Time: A Family of Worth (Book One)

They will risk everything for their forbidden love…

One Moment In Time: A Family of Worth (Book Two)

One moment in time may be enough if it lasts forever…

Under the Mistletoe

A new suitor seeks her hand. An old flame holds her heart. Which one will she meet under the kissing bough?

Learn more about Sherry Ewing's books on her website at www.SherryEwing.com/Books

ABOUT SHERRY EWING

Sherry Ewing picked up her first historical romance when she was a teenager and has been hooked ever since. A bestselling author, she writes historical and time travel romances to awaken the soul one heart at a time. When not writing, she can be found in the San Francisco area at her day job as an Information Technology Specialist.

Sign Me Up!
Newsletter: http://bit.ly/2vGrqQM
Facebook Street Team: https://www.facebook.com/groups/799623313455472/
Facebook Official Fan page: https://www.facebook.com/groups/356905935241836/

Learn more about Sherry at:
www.SherryEwing.com
Sherry@SherryEwing.com

facebook.com/sherryewingauthor
twitter.com/sherry_ewing
instagram.com/sherry.ewing
bookbub.com/authors/sherry-ewing
pinterest.com/SherryLEwing
goodreads.com/goodreadscomsherry_ewing
youtube.com/SherryEwingauthor

THE UMBRELLA CHRONICLES

CHRONICLES

Chester and Artemis's Story

AMY QUINTON

The Umbrella Chronicles—
Chester and Artemis's Story

Beastly duke seeks ~~confident~~ *any* woman who doesn't faint at the
sight of his scars. Prefers not to leave the house to find her.
There comes a time in every bachelor's life, when his good-natured
but meddling sister gets it into her mind to play matchmaker. And
on every occasion, they contact none other than Lady Harriett Ross,
self-proclaimed Motley Meddler, the Mistress of Destiny, and
Wielder of the Infamous Umbrella.
Enter the Duke of Eastly. A man with just such a sister. He has
scars, thinks society is nonsense, and prefers to stay far away from
any and all shenanigans. But he could never resist his sibling, who
tells him a sorrowful tale of woe, of a dear friend's shy plight ahead
of an important auction at the Frost Fair of 1814. No worries. He
has the perfect solution. Help is on the way!
Enter the friend, Miss Artemis Synclaire. The precise opposite of
timid and shy. And as such, she won't stand for the *Beast's* asinine
resolution. She'd rather dine with an elephant (which could
actually be arranged) than deal with a man such as he.
Can two such stubborn people ever bend enough to discover
they've found their perfect match?

CHAPTER 1

2nd February 1814
Eastly House, London

C hester Mansfield, 8th Duke of Eastly, groaned at the sound of knuckles rapping smartly against his study door. "Whoever it is can bugger off," he growled.

Despite his warning bellow, Chess heard the door behind him open and a soft, feminine voice answer, "Brother, mine, I'm in desperate need of your assistance."

Chess turned away from the window in time to see his sister, Lady Theodosia Mansfield, march across his study without concern for his gruff pronouncement.

Next, she'd begin pacing a circle before his desk, as was her usual habit when she wanted something of him.

He tensed as he recognized a yearning to smile, the action pulling at the scar bisecting his lips at the corner of his mouth, and forced his habitual glower lest she think him easily manipulated to her whims.

"Oh?" he queried and clasped his hands together to prevent

himself from automatically reaching for the top drawer of his desk where he kept coins and bank drafts. He swallowed and added, "In need of funds?"

In truth, he might as well accept the fact that after all these years, he'd deny his beloved sister nothing. He knew it. *She knew it.* Hell, she never appeared the least bit afraid of him. For that point, he wasn't entirely sure why they continued to play this game of maybe.

Perhaps, it was simply tradition.

She paused her habitual pacing and bit at her lip, twisting her fingers before her. "Er, not precisely." Then, she clenched her hands into fists and carried on her circular campaign.

He snorted. "What does the Society for Brats want now?"

She tossed him a scowl as she passed his desk for the second time, to which he had to smother the urge to laugh, and she asked, "Have you been speaking to Miss Jessica Grenford, of late?"

He raised a brow. They both knew the answer to that question. He didn't *do* polite society. His knuckles turned white as he fought the urge to brush his hand over the scars trailing down his face.

More importantly, he'd never betray Miss Grenford's privacy, for she was a friend who at times, applied to him for assistance on delicate, private affairs. It was all above board, but no one would ever believe it of either of them.

Worse, his sister might take it into her head to promote a match.

Satisfied, his sister continued, "*The Ladies' Society for the Care of the Widows and Orphans of Fallen Heroes and the Children of Wounded Veterans* is having an auction. Tomorrow." He always marveled at how she could recite the atrocious name with utter accuracy and always in one breath. He called it the Society for Brats just to hear her say it. He dipped his head, encouraging her to continue. "Well, a Venetian Breakfast, an auction, and a ball." She stopped her pacing, her eyes alit with excitement, "and all but the ball is to be held on the Thames. On the ice. At the Frost Fair. The ball will be held at the Duchess of Haverford's home, naturally."

"Naturally," he mocked.

She ignored his sarcasm, her eyes taking on that dreamy quality, something he recognized but hadn't felt since he'd become a man full grown, a long time ago. He was nearly thirty-nine now. Damn.

Theo's voice trailed off for a moment, and he envied her her... hope. Deeply uncomfortable with the thought, he cleared his throat, and she shook her head, continuing, "We're raising money to help our cause through ticket sales for admittance to the activities and through the auction."

Hesitantly, he asked, "And what are you auctioning?"

"Oh, I'm so glad you asked, Chess."

He snorted.

"All the ladies are preparing baskets of food. The gentlemen will bid on their basket of choice, and the winner will receive the basket, of course, breakfast with the lady who prepared the basket, and a dance with said lady at the ball." She clasped her hands together. "Isn't it marvelous?"

He compressed his lips. Marvelously horrific. But he didn't say that aloud, though she understood his thoughts completely, for she stuck out her tongue, and the side of his mouth twitched despite himself.

"And you want me to..." He narrowed his eyes and crossed his arms, making it perfectly clear she should remember he did not go out in society.

She lifted her chin. "And one of the ladies, a friend, is...well, she's *painfully* shy."

"No." He shook his head, lest she misheard him.

She ignored him and continued, "The Smatherly sisters refer to her as Mouse, it's all very vulgar and mean." *Better than Beastly...* He rubbed at the back of his neck, and then looked up as her eyes rested on his, softening a bit. He scowled, and she continued, "Needless to say, I'm concerned, more importantly, *she's* concerned, her basket will receive no bids... It's going to be nearly impossible to convince her to come..." He had no doubt his sister would succeed to that endeavor; she was a force to be reckoned with in her own right.

Nevertheless, "No."

She folded her arms. "Her name is Miss Artemis Synclaire."

He refolded his. "Never heard of her."

"Well, of course not." Theo pursed her lips.

Chess raised a brow? He was not in *total* seclusion. Still, he began, "You know I don't—"

Theo leaned on his desk. "Surely, you're clever enough to figure out a way, brother mine." And with that, she batted her eyes, the vixen, settled a voucher on his desk, then spun on her heel and waltzed out the door.

Lady Theo pulled the door closed with a soft click, then looked up and locked eyes with Aunt Harriett, matchmaker extraordinaire, wielder of *The Umbrella*, coconspirator in little white lies, matriarch and manipulator of *the ton*.

They shared a knowing smile, exchanged a saucy wink, and Lady Theo said, "Your turn."

CHAPTER 2

Lady Harriett Ross walked into the duke's study as if she owned the place, her favorite pink crocheted shawl wrapped snuggly about her shoulders, her ever-present black umbrella clutched in her left hand. She pointed *The Umbrella* toward the duke, who was staring at her, mouth agog, from behind his desk. "Chester, lad. You're a dear for seeing me with no notice; I'll settle myself by the fire, thank you very much. But first, hold this."

He dipped his head, "Lady Harriett…"

She noted the wary look that lingered in the duke's eye as she tossed him *The Umbrella* right over his orderly desk, giving him no chance to refuse. He snatched it out of the air, deftly and without hesitation. Had he heard of her infamous Umbrella? The one that put the fear of God in bachelors everywhere?

Harriett grinned from ear to ear the moment she presented her back. And as she settled herself in a wingback by the fire, she added, "I am pleased to hear you are going to help your sister and poor Miss Synclaire. That one is such a *timid* dear, but so very nice. Soft, quiet. And light as the spring air, with dark hair, doe eyes. A dear lamb." Harriett settled her feet on the fender and ignored the duke as he rummaged around the room behind her. She imagined she could hear him grinding his teeth and rolling his eyes, and she grinned once again.

Without a word, the duke handed her a tumbler of Scotch whisky and settled *The Umbrella* against the arm of her chair.

No matter. She'd cracked tougher nuts. Besides, he'd already accepted It. That was usually enough.

Harriett suppressed a sigh of satisfaction. God, she loved knowing men were doomed.

She carried on. "You know, there aren't many men who would do the like for their sister. Your actions are the mark of a true gentleman. A man of character."

The duke cleared his throat, and with a deceptively lively voice, said, "Lady Harriett, thank you kindly for the timely reminder."

"Aunt Harriett, son, Aunt Harriett to friends," she returned.

Harriett sipped her whisky as she watched the duke pull the bell pull.

They'd barely touched on the subject of the weather lately—extreme fog, snow, and ice—when a knock at the door sounded and the duke called, "Enter."

A rather precise man, with a narrow build and face, entered carrying a portable desk. He walked with brisk precision and approached the duke directly, "Your Grace."

"Aunt Harriett, this is Mr. Dorian Simmons, my secretary. Mr. Simmons, Lady Harriett Ross, Aunt to the Marquess of Dansbury."

The secretary bowed to Harriett who replied, "Delighted, young man, delighted."

"Simmons, I have an important task for you." The duke marched back to his desk with a long stride, his steps sure, and reached into the top drawer. He pulled out a velvet pouch and picked up a card from the desktop. "I want you to take this voucher and, tomorrow, attend the Frost Fair, specifically, the auction being put on by the...by the...by the Ladies' Society for something about the Widows and Veterans or other."

Simmons cleared his throat. *"The Ladies' Society for the Care of the Widows and Orphans of Fallen Heroes and the Children of Wounded Veterans?"*

The duke snorted. "Aye. That's the one."

Simmons accepted the voucher. "Is that all, Your Grace?"

"Of course not. Take this money and bid on the basket for Miss Artemis Synclaire. Win it. Fifty pounds should do it, I think."

Why that clever beast of a man.

"Is that all, Your Grace?"

"That is all."

"Excellent." Mr. Simmons bowed. "Your Grace, Lady Harriett." And he exited the room. Even the door closed with a precise click.

The duke settled himself with his own tumbler in the chair next to hers, a self-satisfied smile on his face.

He was that proud of himself, eh?

Harriett watched, laughing to herself as he took a sip of whisky. *The poor misguided fool. Tsk. Tsk.*

Harriett patted her hair, ensuring her vibrant red curls were still pinned to perfection, and settled in for a worthy battle of wit and redirection. The man wouldn't know what hit him.

Aloud, she said, "I say, that's that. Well done, Your Grace. Well done."

She watched from the corner of her eye as the duke's smile fell, and his gaze darted to her. He hadn't expected agreement. Poor man. She stifled a grin. And carried on…

"You're so right. It's ridiculous for a sister to think her brother, a busy man such as yourself, would drop everything to attend a frivolous little auction." She waved the idea away with a flick of her hand.

The duke pulled at his cravat. "Indeed."

"It's not as if the appearance of a reclusive duke would do all that much to boost Miss Synclaire's esteem in the eyes of the *ton*. A quite hopeless case, really."

The duke cleared his throat.

"And besides, your presence would likely do quite the opposite, pull attention away from that poor, sweet thing, what with the name calling—what do they call you? Oh, right, Beastly. No duke should have to put up with such juvenile attacks, simply because of a few scars…"

"Quite so," he grumbled.

"Miss Synclaire couldn't possibly understand. Well, I suppose she could, you know, Mouse and all that, but compared to a *duke*…and *Beastly*…"

The duke pulled at his cravat again and turned up his tumbler, swallowing the entirety of his whisky in one large gulp.

Lady Harriett took a delicate sip of hers, masking the grin that threatened.

The duke ran a hand through his hair, seemingly unaware of his actions.

"Even if the auction tent, the marquee, will be massive—as big as the Haverford House ballroom—and have plenty of pennants and flags and hidden corners from whence an ascetic duke could watch, discreetly, from afar—I daresay could become lost in such a place—it's simply too much to ask. No. You did the right thing, Duke." Harriett added with a decisive nod.

She stood then, and the duke followed suit as manners dictated. She picked up her Umbrella and walked to the door.

"I'm so glad we had this talk, son. I'm glad you're doing the right thing. Don't let your sister twist you about her finger. And don't, definitely do not, go to that auction tomorrow. It's not something you truly want to see. Nothing exciting, at all, really… Besides, only fools would venture out in such foul weather, snow piled in heaps as tall as carriages on either side of the road. Only rough men with hearty constitutions should even consider going out in it. Perhaps, I should put a word in to Eleanor about rescheduling the auction. It would be far wiser for *gentle*men, and ladies, I daresay, to stay inside by the toasty warm fire and put their feet up and risk nothing."

She opened the door, then promptly closed it again and spun around, her Umbrella held aloft before her. "Do you know what this is?"

If he said a black umbrella, she would throttle him with the bell pull.

He grinned as if the thought crossed his mind and said, "I've heard the rumors, and I've seen the betting books at White's. Every man who touched It became engaged within a fortnight."

She nodded. "One-hundred percent accuracy, lad. You would do well to remember that."

Then, Lady Harriett very deliberately leaned *The Umbrella* against the wall and marched out the door, closing it a little harder than was absolutely necessary.

❦

Inside the study, Chess pulled off his cravat and tossed it on the desk. "Dammit."

The Umbrella rolled to the floor.

CHAPTER 3

Miss Artemis Synclaire sucked in a breath as Brigadier General Lord Redepenning, Lord Henry to most and today's auctioneer, leaned on his walking stick and turned to the table behind him.

Hers was the only basket left. She'd spent the better part of an hour admiring the bunting and flags of England, Ireland, Scotland, and the Union. Dreading this very moment.

She shuffled her feet, all nerves, and even though carpets covered the ice and the tent flaps were closed against the chill, she could still feel the frigid cold of the frozen water beneath her feet, seeping through her layers and into her shoes, which didn't help her unease. Beneath the tablecloth, she wiggled her toes, willing heat into her feet.

Lord Redepenning peeked inside her hamper and performed an exaggerated sniff, which had all the younger ladies giggling once again. "Mmm…," he said, "I believe I smell plum pudding, a fine roast, and—*sniff*—something with a definite spice, something exotic, I think." He glanced over his shoulder to Artemis, who, with a smile, dipped her head in acknowledgment. He then hefted her basket and brought it to the smaller table up front, next to his podium.

He checked the air again. "Do I detect coffee?"

Once again, Artemis dipped her head.

He winked in return. "An interesting choice, Miss Synclaire..."

Artie glanced over one table to Lady Theodosia Mansfield, who crossed her arms and fingers and practically bounced in her chair with excitement, leaving Artie to wonder what had the girl so impossibly enthused.

Artie turned back to her own table, where she sat alone, and smoothed the table cloth before her, waiting for the auction to begin.

Lord Henry's careful voice reached out. "Do I have one pound for this lovely basket of delights?"

Basil Driscoll, a man of dubious reputation, raised his hand, and Artie glanced to Theo, who looked alarmed. Whispers floated over the air, and Artie did her best to ignore them. Everything would work out in the end, she was sure. It was not like she was expected to be alone with the man. And she certainly wasn't afraid.

Lord Henry nodded and looked out. "How about two pounds? Do I hear two?"

A tall, thin man stepped forward, hand raised. "Two pounds."

Lord Henry asked, "And you are?"

The man bowed, his ears turning red. "Mr. Dorian Simmons, secretary to the Duke of Eastly; I'm bidding on his behalf."

A collective gasp echoed around the room, and the harsh word, *Beastly*, could be heard on faint whispers beneath the din.

Artie darted a glance to Theo, who'd turned beet red and wore a look of utter embarrassment. "Your brother?" Artie mouthed.

Theo winced. "Sorry," she mouthed back.

Artie turned away and crossed her arms. She'd never met the

elusive duke, despite her friendship with Theo, but her friend was forever singing his praises. Reclusive beast or not, *Theo's brother or not*, how dare the man think he could bid on her basket and not even bother to make an appearance. What? Was she expected to eat her own basket by herself? Would the secretary take off with it, take it to the elusive duke, and leave her here alone?

Not if she had anything to say about it, even if she ended up having to fight off the advances of that fiend Driscoll as a result.

Lord Henry spoke up. "Do I hear three?"

Artie stood, ignoring Theo, who whispered sharply, "Artie. What are you doing?" and said, "Lord Henry, I'm afraid I cannot accept the last bid."

Lord Henry smiled. "Come, dear. Surely you do not believe the rumors…"

Artie shook her head. "That is not my point. I will not accept a bid from a man who could not even bother to make an appearance or offer in person."

She genuinely couldn't abide the type of man who never lifted a finger but to order others around, particularly the servants or any that sort of man felt were beneath them. She imagined Eastly as a man pale from lack of sun and weak from dearth of exercise. Though that image didn't fit the painting Theo had drawn in Artie's mind. In Theo's eyes, her brother was a veritable saint, the very image of perfection in manners, in mind, in form. Apart from the scars, of course. And strong. The outdoorsy, sporting type.

But perhaps, Theo didn't see her brother as he truly was, rather maybe, she saw him through eyes filled with love.

Driscoll snickered.

Theo dropped her head into her hand.

Lord Henry glanced warily at Driscoll and said, "But Miss Synclaire, it's for a good cause—"

Artie could feel the eyes of everyone in the room darting back and forth between her, Lord Henry, and Mr. Simmons. Her cheeks heated, and she lifted her chin. "Nevertheless—"

Driscoll shouted, "Three pounds!"

Everyone gasped.

Mr. Simmons pulled at his cravat and quickly rejoined with "F-four pounds."

Lord Henry glanced to Artie, who crossed her arms and turned to the secretary. He may have pulled at his cravat, but she read determination in his eyes. He would not fail his employer. Well, then.

Artie turned back to Lord Henry. "All right. If Mr. Simmons wins the basket, I shall dine and dance with Mr. Simmons. *Not* His Grace. Clearly." The din of voices grew louder at that pronouncement. Artie held up her finger and raised her voice. "And another thing—"

"Three. Hundred. Pounds!"

The new voice was deep, part growl, part thunder, and it rumbled through her, bringing a tingle to her fingers and warming her from the inside out. It was an altogether peculiar sensation, and Artie spun around, seeking the source of that soul churning sound.

Out of the shadows stepped a great hulking *beast* of a man. Hair, thick and loose, all tawny shades of gold and brown, and far too long for fashion, but quite marvelous all the same. Bulging arms threatened the seams of the black velvet jacket he wore snug to the waist. He donned a burgundy waistcoat... but the rest of his ensemble was all black...the snug trousers, Hessians—even the tassels were black, cravat, shirt...

He was delicious. And large. And mighty. And entirely too *virile.*

His lips were full, though an angry scar bisected them in the corner, which was a relief, or the man might have been too overwhelming. Too handsome. Just, too much.

The word Beastly floated on the air once again, and suddenly, Artie knew: this was the reclusive Duke of Eastly.

And definitely not weak or wan.

It dawned on her that, if anything, Theo had *downplayed* her brother's characteristics; well, at least her brother's physical, *er,* qualities.

Lord Henry slammed his mallet on the podium, making Artie jump and the hammer crack. "Sold!" he exclaimed.

Artie ignored the chaos and sucked in a breath. For at the moment, she only had eyes for a beast.

CHAPTER 4

He hadn't intended to reveal himself. Nor to offer such an outrageous sum.

But he'd found her, in a word, magnificent.

Her eyes glimmered with intelligence and audaciousness; her posture suggested confidence and courage. Fire, wit, mettle, beauty...everything he'd ever dreamt of in a woman. He'd spoken before he'd even completed those thoughts. Who could blame him? He was only truly surprised there hadn't been an all-out war for the opportunity to procure her basket.

She could have packed boiled turnips (he'd rather drink from the Thames), and he'd have still bid the same.

As Eastly entered the luncheon tent and approached her table, he spared a quick glance toward his sister, who had the good grace to offer him a sheepish smile. He'd deal with her later.

Then he caught sight of Aunt Harriett, who winked and raised her cup to him. He'd deal with her, too.

He focused on Miss Synclaire.

He was already consumed with the daring woman before him.

And she returned his gaze with such intensity, he momentarily forgot all about his scarring, not to mention the whispers of *beast* dripping from everyone's lips. A first.

He'd been captivated the moment she stood and dared to risk the wrath of a duke, particularly one with a reputation that was the stuff of children's nightmares.

"Miss Synclaire." He executed a flawless bow.

"Duke." She dipped her head as she followed his movements with her eyes. Eyes that didn't hold a trace of fear, merely *interest*.

The effect on his body was most inconvenient. Eastly pulled out his chair, and out of habit, checked its structural integrity. At six foot five, he was not a small man, and the delicate furniture so fashionable today was ill-suited to his size. The specimen groaning beneath his grip was no exception and was an example of one of many reasons why he preferred the comfort of his own home.

But there was nothing for it; he couldn't very well stand. So, he hooked Harriett's *Umbrella* on the back of the chair and sat. With extreme caution.

Miss Synclaire leaned to her left and watched. Slowly, she straightened. "Five pounds says it doesn't last the hour."

The duke shifted in his seat, testing its strength, then returned her gaze and pulled a flask from his jacket. "Deal."

She narrowed her eyes. He tossed her a wink—*what in the hell had gotten into him?*—then, tucked away the whisky and opened the basket.

He felt her eyes upon him as she prodded, "I heard you never appear in public."

He paused for the briefest of moments, hoping it was imperceptible, and pulled out the roast. "And I heard you were a timid mouse of a woman."

He glanced over. She pasted on a false smile. "Perhaps, you shouldn't heed such Banbury stories. Mayhap, neither of us should involve ourselves in rumor."

He dipped his head and unwrapped the meat, then slipped a knife from his boot. As he made the first slice, he said, "You know, small children create tales of horror about me, and sensitive women faint at the sight."

She snorted. "It's probably more your beastly personality than the scars upon your face…"

He froze. She dared to speak of his scars? Most people avoided even mentioning them, even indirectly. Hell, most could barely look at his face. Miss Synclaire had no such qualms. On either count. Still—

He leaned forward; his knife gripped tightly in his paw of a hand. "Are you sure about that. Take a close, hard look. Miss Synclaire. Do you like what you see? Do you fear it? Have a taste for the macabre?"

She leaned forward, mirroring his posture and catalogued his face in earnest. He had to fight to keep from squirming, from blushing for goodness sakes. When her eyes reached his mouth, hers parted, the slightest bit, and her small, pink tongue darted out, moistening her lips.

He fell back in his seat and swallowed. And found himself rock hard beneath the table. Good God. Now more than ever he felt the need to wipe his hand down his face.

Or better still, jump in the icy Thames and cool his heated limbs.

He pulled on his best scowl and met her eyes across the table. Hers were wide. So, he wasn't the only one rocked by their obvious physical compatibility.

But then she narrowed hers. "I take no issue with your scars." Her voice was higher pitched than the soothing alto he'd already learned to crave; obviously not as calm as she'd like him to believe. She cleared her throat. "You'd probably have an ego the size of an elephant without them."

Had she just called him handsome?

"Besides," she twirled her hand in the air. "Children will be children. I have a nephew who thinks I'm so old, he's constantly checking my forehead for fever and questioning my constitution."

The duke imagined a precocious dark-headed nephew who resembled her. Wide curious eyes. Green, like emeralds. Like hers. And suddenly he was imagining *her* child. Theirs.

He cleared his throat. No. No talk of children. Especially theirs. He changed the subject as he arranged their plates. "Did you prepare all this yourself?"

"Naturally." He looked up in time to see her roll her eyes and dart a glance to his sister.

"How do you know Theo? From the Society for Wounded Stuff?"

"You mean, the *Ladies' Society for the Care of the Widows and Orphans of Fallen Heroes and the Children of Wounded Veterans*?"

Jesus. He was impressed when his sister said it but was ruthlessly turned on to hear the ridiculous words spoken in that sultry tone. She had a voice for the bedroom; it seemed to slide over his skin and into his trousers, coaxing his cock out to play.

The woman was *dangerous*.

He dipped his head in confirmation; he couldn't very well speak at the moment.

"Yes, of course." She answered.

He took the opportunity to think of swimming in the Thames, then started mentally reciting best practices of crop rotation. Eventually, he was able to settle himself enough to stand and deliver her plate; he'd assumed since she prepared the basket, she liked everything in it.

She looked up at him and smiled. "Thank you."

For some inexplicable reason, he had the irrational urge to fall to his knees before her, and...well, he didn't know what. Or why. Pledge his everlasting devotion? Dangerous, indeed.

He cleared his throat. "How do you take your coffee?"

"Black." Just like me.

He caught her dart a glance at his trousers as she said it, and he practically stumbled back to his seat.

And then he did run a hand down his face, audience or no.

Much more of this and he was going to expire on the spot.

Never mind that his brain screamed: *Imagine the possibilities.*

Oh, he was imagining them alright. All of them.

CHAPTER 5

For some reason, he seemed uncomfortable, so she asked, "Are you well?" And she nearly snorted, for she'd sounded suspiciously like her nephew just then.

He tugged at his cravat and cleared his throat. "Fine."

His voice was strained, which meant he didn't sound fine at all, but she wouldn't press.

She leaned back and took a bracing sip of coffee, then asked, "Why don't you go out in polite society? You don't seem the type to be afraid, less to care what anyone else should think."

If he was hoping for genteel conversation about the weather, he was bound to be disappointed. Somehow, she didn't think that would be a problem.

He took his own sip of coffee. "I don't care, and certainly don't fear them, you're correct. I've just found I don't have time for their nonsense. And the nonsense is practically universal. I'm sure you understand?"

She laughed. "Why, I quite believe there was an insult in there somewhere."

He smiled. "Definitely not an insult."

She nodded. "I suppose it's true to say that people aren't exactly lining up to befriend an outspoken young woman with strong opinions. I daresay," she chuckled, "you cause women to faint, and I give them megrims."

They shared a laugh at that. What a pair they'd make, cutting a swath of destruction through polite society. The mutual understanding was…nice.

Their conversation continued for what felt like a handful of minutes; they each had a surprising amount to say and argue over. They talked politics, religion, war—all the subjects normally taboo for mixed company, and the conversation was refreshing.

Eventually, Artie sat back on a sigh and chanced a look around the room. Then, leaped to her feet, for the room was practically empty. They'd clearly been talking for longer than a handful of minutes; the servers had started removing the tables and chairs and taking down the bunting…everyone else was gone, apart from Theo standing to the side, studiously avoiding making eye contact while trying to hide a smile, but thankfully, acting as chaperone.

They'd never even noticed everyone leave. She turned to face the duke, her eyes wide.

He cleared his throat. "Did you come alone, Miss Synclaire?"

She nodded. "I did." She let rooms in a women's boarding house, using the money from a small inheritance that was just enough to keep her fed and comfortable so long as she mildly economized. Fortunately, she was clever with needle and thread, and her clothes were far better quality than one on her income might imagine. Though tonight, she'd been invited to stay with the Duchess of Haverford, so that she might safely stay for the ball and late supper without worry, for her regular rooms had a curfew, one she would never be able to make.

She began, "Well, this has been—"

"Would you like to tour the fair?" He blurted. He followed with a bow. "Pardon, that is. I would be honored if you'd join myself and," he nodded towards his sister, "my sister as we tour the fair for an hour before we must return."

"I would love to." His request was clearly impulsive. As was her reply.

A servant appeared as if summoned. "Your Grace, I'd be happy to pack up the basket and see it returned, if you'd like."

The duke nodded. "That would be fine, thank you. Oh!" He turned and retrieved The Umbrella from the back of his chair. "See that this is returned to Lady Harriett Ross." He glanced at Artie as he added, "Tell her I have no need of it anymore."

Artie swallowed.

His eyes flared with passion.

Better still, he'd thanked a servant.

He walked around the table and held out both elbows, and Artie and Theo each captured one.

Lord knows, it felt *right*.

The sight of the River Thames frozen over was something spectacular to see. Tradesmen of all sorts had set up booths of every variety to sell their wares—from fancy wooden stalls, to haphazard tents; it all came together as a feast for the eyes. People from all walks of life gathered and roamed, taking in the sites, gesturing with excitement, and searching for items to purchase. Food was plentiful; Artie sampled hot apples, gingerbread, and hot chocolate. She also saw coffee, purl, roast mutton, and black tea and plenty of gin and ale. An elephant was reputed to be somewhere below Blackfriars Bridge, though she never saw it, but she did see a setup for nine-pin bowling. And throughout it all, peddlers wove through the crowds, calling out more wares to be had.

And then there was the dancing.

Artie spun around, her eyes likely alight with excitement, for she so loved dancing. She danced every single day, even if only by herself in her rooms; it was her one guilty pleasure for a woman as practical as herself.

The duke, who'd been remarkably congenial up until that point, suddenly broke into a fierce scowl. "No."

She hadn't even asked anything.

But clearly, he knew what she was about. Theo kicked him in the shin, but he remained firm. Artie crossed her arms and tilted her head left and right. Then, she looked at him and lifted her chin. "Why not? You appear to have two working legs."

She wasn't sure when she'd decided she could talk to him with so little deference, much less argue with him. But her tongue was more in concert with her temper, and both were a number of steps ahead of her brain.

Nevertheless, she crossed her arms and awaited a reasonable explanation.

He folded his own arms and glared back but remained mute. Lord deliver her from stubborn men.

The Good Lord knew life was bound to involve fireworks when two stubborn people entered into disagreement.

"Look, Duke. I'm going to dance. Even if I have to dance with the elephant. Or the one-armed man with a wooden leg selling hot buns."

His scowl cracked. Just the tiniest bit. And he raised a brow. "The leg selling buns?"

She was about to reply when a voice cut across their hearing, the sound loud with no pretense at being subtle and dripping with disdain. "Society barely bore her presence even before she took up with Beastly. They'll never tolerate her now. Might even lose the lease on her rooms."

Driscoll.

The duke spun around and before anyone could blink, wrapped his fingers around Driscoll's neck. One handed.

The foul man grabbed and pulled at the duke's wrist, but his efforts were utterly ineffectual.

The duke leaned in close, but Artie heard him all the same. "It seems someone has already damaged your face. But I'm warning you now. You wouldn't survive a single blow from *my* fist. Better still, I bite." Then, he tossed the man to the ground and turned his back.

"We're leaving." No discussion. No smile. No pretense of considering opposing arguments to stay. Just, no.

Beside her, Theo sighed, hooked her arm around Artie's, and murmured. "All that progress…"

"What do you mean?"

"You'll see." Theo glared at her brother's back. "Stubborn fool."

The duke turned and winged his arms. She slid her hand into place, but disappointment tugged at Artie's heart, and she chided herself for a dupe. But today had been quite unexpected and extraordinary.

Perhaps, it had all been one-sided after all.

CHAPTER 6

The carriage ride was arduous. The three of them sat there, Theo and Miss Synclaire on one side, he on the other, in absolute silence, the air fraught with tension. The only sound to be heard was the din of life outside the carriage doors, horses' hooves on cobbles and ice, drivers calling out to their cattle carefully navigating the treacherous roads. Despite the fog, he could see Miss Synclaire clenching her jaw, and he wanted nothing more in that moment than to toss his sister, Theo, out the door, something he would never do, and pull Miss Synclaire into his arms, something he was *desperate* to do.

He clenched his hands into fists. He wanted to kiss her, gently and passionately, fiercely, and tell her he would never leave her side. To *beg* her forgiveness while groveling at her feet.

For the first time ever, he hated his lot in life. For the first time, he wanted what he couldn't have with an intensity he'd never known before. It left him anguished.

Even after the attack that had left him so scarred, he'd never felt such hopelessness. Such loss. And he realized with absolute certainty, he'd take on a thousand more scars for a lifetime with her, a woman so graceful, so vivid, so intelligent, so beautiful, so perfect —for him. A woman who completely embodied every single thing he'd ever dreamed of wanting in a companion, a mate, a wife.

But Driscoll's filthy yet valid reminder had been timely and true. If he claimed her, he would have everything, but he'd rob her of so much more.

As the carriage slowed to a stop before Haverford House, Artemis finally glanced his way and the hopeful look that crossed her face in that moment made everything so much worse. She'd been confident and brave whilst standing up to the mighty Duke of Beastly, and throughout the day, her light was a bright beacon in a dim and foggy world.

Still, he said nothing, and they exited the carriage in utter silence. He saw her to the door, which the butler opened promptly.

And when she turned to face him to say good night, he couldn't help but reach out, unconsciously, and slide his hand across the edge of her hair, smoothing a loosened strand of her dark tresses between the tips of two fingers.

The light that sparked in her eyes as a result tore at his heart, damn his impulsive self.

Her eyes softened. "Will you attend tonight's ball?"

He wanted so badly to say yes. Aloud, he said, "No. It's for the best."

Her smile fell, and she stepped back. He clenched his fists to keep from reaching for her, immediately aware of the loss, the cold settling into his bones.

In a tone covered in frost, she said, "You don't get to decide what's best for me, so if you don't attend, it's purely what you think is best for *you*." She turned to leave. Then paused and tossed back. "If you do not come, send your secretary. I'm still owed a partner for at least one dance."

Then, she crossed the threshold, her head held high, and the butler slammed the door in his face.

As the carriage pulled to a stop in front of their house, his sister made quick work of exiting the vehicle, not even waiting for a footman to assist her with her descent. He couldn't blame her for her hasty retreat, but he in no way intended to let her off so easily.

Theo was halfway up the stairs when the duke crossed the threshold. He began removing his gloves. "Theodosia," he warned.

She paused mid-step, and he watched her shoulders slump. He winced, but it did not soften his stance. "My office. Now."

She was pacing before the hearth when he stepped into the room. She paused for only a moment, then continued her circular route.

"Mouse?" he queried as he crossed to the cabinet holding his whisky.

She snorted but didn't stop.

"*Painfully* shy," he added, as he poured himself two fingers full of liquid relief.

He glanced over; she had the good grace to look chastised, somewhat. She was not a doormat. But she quickly resumed her march.

He tossed back the contents of his tumbler, sighed, then, placed his glass on the table and turned, crossing his arms. "...concerned her basket will receive no bids...impossible to convince her to come... Miles away from anything resembling the truth." His voice raised on the last, till he practically growled the words. He raked his hand through his hair. "Theo—why?" He hadn't intended that bit to sound so like a plea. His anguish was all his own.

She turned to face him then, her hands twisted before her. She kept opening her mouth to begin but couldn't seem to find the right words. Then, "She doesn't have friends—"

He snorted. "And you are?"

She dipped her head in acknowledgment. "A friend...," She rushed forward, resting her hand upon his folded arms. "but you've heard her." Oh, he had, alright; he was never going to forget that voice.

Theo continued, "She'd probably have less trouble if she weren't so outspoken. Men don't like a woman who speaks her mind, who has opinions. Did you note the type of men vying for her basket? The singular man besides you, that is."

He hadn't at the time. He'd only had eyes for the spitfire. And then he'd had no other thought but to *win*.

Theo's reasons were all well and good, but he could sense she wasn't telling him everything. "And...," he prompted.

She blushed but remained stubbornly mute.

"You're not attending the ball until I have answers."

She lifted her chin in stubborn defiance. She was not wrong in disbelieving his threat, but he was not an imbecile either. "Aunt Harriett. You two were conspiring, playing matchmaker."

She marched away from him but tossed back, "Lot of good that did."

He was mildly offended to be right. "I'm perfectly capable of finding my own wife, Theo."

"Not if you never leave the house!"

He ground his teeth, biting back a scathing retort. Unwilling to own up to that truth.

And she wasn't finished, having worked herself up to a reasonable level of pique. "What could it have hurt to dance with her, Chess?"

He'd never admit to being downright afraid. Afraid of falling for a woman he'd only just met. Afraid if he took her in his arms, he'd never let her go. Having those feelings happen despite all that. And then—

As if reading his mind, Theo said, "And then Driscoll. You heeded the words of a man who is nothing but vile intent and hot air? You're better than that."

"So is she..." He hadn't meant to say it aloud.

Theo rushed back over to him, and he warned her against offering her pity. She stopped short. "What—"

"He was right." Chess admitted. "My presence would only make things worse for her. I can bear it for myself because I don't care. Society is all nonsense anyway. But I can't force it upon her."

"Dear brother, mine," She cupped his cheek with her hand, and he felts his jaw flex as he fought back emotion. "Did you learn nothing whilst dining with Miss Artemis Synclaire?"

And on that note, Theo turned to leave. Leaving him with his thoughts. His regrets.

But before she stepped out the door, she turned and added, "If you thought for one moment Miss Synclaire was the type of woman who would accept a man who thought to make that sort of choice *for* her...then, you don't deserve her after all."

And then, she left.

Theo raced to her writing desk, prepared to pen a missive:

Aunt Harriett,

The ship is floundering. Direct hit from enemy quarters. Both passengers bailed. Urgent. Help is needed.

Theo

She pulled the bell. When her maid answered the summons, Theo handed her the note. "See this is sent to Dansbury House post haste. And, Annie. Remember to talk to His Grace's valet. Make sure his best formal wear is ready for when His Grace prepares for the evening."

Annie curtseyed. "Yes, milady."

Poor Chess. We're not finished with you quite yet.

Poor Chess! Ha!

CHAPTER 7

Harriett Ross skirted around servants clamoring to and fro as they prepared for the Society ball that was to take place in a few hours and walked into the Unicorn Parlor of Haverford House, her arms open to embrace her friend, the duchess. "Eleanor," she said and kissed the air beside Her Grace's cheek.

"Harry," the duchess returned. "It's been far too long."

"Indeed."

"Please sit," The duchess gestured to two chairs beside the fire, while her ward, Miss Matilda Grenford, poured tea from a pot where it had been left to steep on a side table.

The duchess asked, "Harry, you know my ward, Miss Matilda Grenford."

"That I do. Miss Grenford, a pleasure. Have you brought that young man Charles up to scratch?"

The darling girl blushed and said, "Very nearly, Lady Ross."

Harriett chuckled. "Well, do let me know if you need my help. I am renowned for showing the less intelligent sex the error of their ways. I can be quite persuasive."

The women shared a hearty laugh.

"Harry, to what do I owe this unexpected pleasure."

About that. "I'm here to see your guest, Miss Artemis Synclaire."

"Of course," the duchess glanced to her niece, "My dear, can you see if Miss Synclaire is available to receive guests?"

Miss Matilda curtseyed, of course.

Harriett liked Eleanor and Matilda. And approved of Eleanor protecting her guests from all visitors, even friends.

A few minutes later, Eleanor left to see to preparations, and Miss Synclaire entered as Harriett was perusing yet another unicorn tapestry in the magical room.

Miss Synclaire crossed the room, confident and with bold strides. Harriett approved.

"You wanted to see me, Lady Ross?"

"Aunt Harriett, please." She looked the young woman up and down. "Tell me what happened after the breakfast? I would have stayed, but my gouty toe was paining me something awful."

Miss Synclaire folded her arms. "If I am to call you Aunt Harriett, I would appreciate it if you called me Artemis. As to after the breakfast, I went to the Frost Fair with the Duke of Eastly and his sister, Theo. Then, we left."

Harriett raised a brow. "Is that all?"

"Should there have been something else?" She countered.

Good. She liked Artemis, immensely. Theo had an excellent eye for matchmaking. Harriett grinned.

"I received this letter from Lady Theodosia." She handed the missive to Artemis, figuring the woman would respond best to absolute truth. No games. A woman of intelligence and conviction and strength. Much like herself.

Artemis returned the note and remained thoughtful for a moment. Then, "Everything was proceeding rather well, I must say. He is..." She blushed, a telling sign. "We are compatible, and I appreciated—" She shook her head, then lifted her chin. "Until I suggested we dance. He turned cross, but not for long. Then, Driscoll arrived."

Harriett nodded. "That man is vile. Surely, the duke stood up to him."

"Oh, splendidly. But then his entire demeanor changed; he withdrew, and we left." Artemis spread her arms as if to say, 'And there you have it.'

"I see." Harriett touched a finger to her lip and turned toward the fire, glancing over the carved unicorns making up the mantel and surround, lost in thought.

Then, she spun to Artemis, an idea forming. "We haven't a moment to lose—"

Artemis held up a hand. "But what if I don't want a moment. What if I don't want him at all."

Harry peered at her, seeking the veracity of her words. "Is that true?"

Artemis bit her lip, but then narrowed her eyes. "I don't want a man who has to be tricked or cajoled into seeing me. And I certainly don't want one too cowardly to stand up with me."

Harry smiled. "As you should, dear. As you should. Never you fear, Artemis. You hold faithful to that truth. Always. I'll take care of the rest."

Artemis looked skeptical, and Harriett could hardly blame her.

Eastly House

Chess had poured himself a second whisky an hour ago but had yet to take the first sip. He twirled the glass in his hand watching the fire light the crystal and the smooth amber liquid swirling within.

His sister and Artemis were not wrong. He'd been a fool, and the realization stung his pride.

And he'd have to eat crow, publicly, for he saw no other way but to go to the ball after all. If he wanted her, trusted her, respected her, he'd have to allow Artie to make her choice. She was worth it.

Almost immediately, his heart felt lighter. For the first time in over ten years, he was hopeful, looking forward to a future that didn't feel quite so bleak. Better still, a future that was full of promise.

Resolved that he knew what he needed to do, he was about to finally take that first sip, when someone burst through his door. He leapt to his feet. "It's *1814* for goodness sake, doesn't anybody knock anymore? Oh." It was Aunt Harriett.

He watched, hiding a grin, as she approached, *The Umbrella* once again resting on her shoulder like a soldier's musket. And she appeared fierce, ready for battle.

He suspected *he* was the enemy at large, and he once again had to hide the smile that threatened.

He watched her march across the room and come to stand at ease before him. With a warning in her eyes, she asked, "Why are all of you men—at least, the seemingly more intelligent examples of your sex—such imbeciles?"

He assumed the question was rhetorical. Or a trick. Either way, coward and imbecile that he was, he was not going to answer *that*.

After a moment, she snorted. "Perhaps not quite such a halfwit after all." She stood *The Umbrella* before her and rested both her hands atop it. "Look. You seem like a reasonable man. Have you ever met one such as Miss Synclaire?"

He could say honestly, "Never."

She nodded. "And how often do you think a gel like that comes around?"

He hesitated.

She glared.

He smiled. "Never."

She nodded. "Perhaps, you're not such a lost cause after all."

"Do you remember what this does?" She held *The Umbrella* aloft.

"I do."

"Do you need it?"

"I don't."

She looked at him in wary disbelief. "So, I don't need to bash you over the head with it?"

He laughed. "Definitely not."

She smiled then. "Good. Welcome to the club."

CHAPTER 8

Artie glanced into the grand ballroom at Haverford House and whistled a long, slow breath, her eyes wide with wonder. The flags and bunting from the marquee at the Frost Fair had been transported here, and with the addition of the crystal and candles and carved ice and diamonds and gilding and fancy gowns and tiaras, the effect was wondrously magical. Her eyes struggled to find a place to land, for as soon as she found something to admire, something else just as remarkable caught her eye.

A wave of disquiet seemed to hover over the ballroom as the majordomo announced her arrival, but perhaps she was being overly sensitive, for, as she scanned the crowd, no one appeared to be looking her way, all of them as indifferent as they'd always been to her arrival.

She skimmed the crowd for Theo or the duke, for after her talk with Aunt Harriett, she'd felt sure the woman could perform some sort of miracle. But after her failure to find them, her stomach churned as her hopes waned, and she chastised herself for a fool. Then, she pasted on a smile and lifted her chin, vowing never to allow a weak man to have such power over her emotional state again. She was at a glorious ball, and she would make the most of it.

Oh, but she was a fool to cultivate what was only a flicker of possibility. He'd made it perfectly clear he would never attend an event such as this, much less *dance*. As if dancing were such a horrible thing. What had he said? Oh, yes, "No. It's for the best," she thought, in her haughtiest, whiniest, *dukiest* voice.

"Miss Synclaire."

Startled, Miss Synclaire spun around and curtseyed rather deftly, if she did say so herself, at the Earl of Trehallow, who bowed before her. "Lord Trehallow."

"May I have the honor of a dance?"

She was reasonably surprised; it wasn't often she danced at an event such as this. She'd nearly left her dance card in her room. On a whim and a hope she would never admit aloud, she'd brought the fan deck with her. "I would be delighted," she said, as she handed over her card and watched, still somewhat surprised, as he signed his name by a cotillion.

No sooner had he stepped away, then the Earl of Hamner arrived and asked the same, settling his name beside an English country dance. Then, Viscount Osgood and Viscount Penrhyd also claimed dances. Unprecedented in her personal experience.

After the Marquis of Aldridge claimed a *waltz* of all things, Artie was convinced something was afoot. She'd barely finished that thought when she caught Aunt Harriett's eye, who offered her a grin and an obvious wink. Mystery solved.

Artie shook her head. Bless her. And she was thankful; it helped soothe away the sting of being stood up by a would-be beau, curse her optimistic nature.

When her waltz arrived, Aldridge was prompt as ever and escorted her to the center of the floor amid a flurry of whispers.

"Do you ever get used to it? The whispers and stares?"

Aldridge lifted one corner of his mouth. "Not precisely, you just get better at ignoring it."

She nodded. "Fair enough."

As the set began, he kept her the appropriate distance, no dame of the *ton* would ever find fault. He was charming and handsome and a wonderful brother to the Grenford sisters, Matilda and Jessica. The perfect brother in all the ways that mattered for two ladies who would be otherwise shunned by the *ton*. Artie was so happy for them.

She was about to ask him yet another question when, a hush fell over the crowd and a murmur of whispers floated about on the air. She started to turn, curious to see what was amiss, for she couldn't hear precisely what was being said over the sound of music, but Aldridge, strangely enough, pulled her closer, too close for propriety's sake. She narrowed her eyes. "What are you about, my lord?"

"Making a foolish man suffer. And gladly," he returned with a smile.

Artie tried to turn, and Aldridge tightened his grip. "Don't be quite so obvious. I'll turn you in good time."

She laughed and batted at his shoulder. "If you're not careful, we'll be married by ten." But then he turned, and her breath caught in her throat at the sight.

Eastly.

Her heart leapt, and she licked her lips. *He is here.*

And he looked…well, quite *livid* actually. He glared daggers at Aldridge, and she turned to find Aldridge grinning, mirth practically dancing in his eyes. By the look of things, he was courting certain death and enjoying every minute of it.

He leaned closer and whispered in her ear. "Bravo, Miss Synclaire. You've caught yourself a splendid man." He chuckled once again. "And if I'm not mistaken, my life hangs dangerously in the balance." He pulled back, his eyes twinkling, and he gave her a wink. "Shall we put him out of his misery?"

She thought for a moment. "Hmm…not yet."

Aldridge laughed and spun her with more enthusiasm.

When they stopped, Eastly was there, a furious glare on his face.

To his credit, he held his fists in check, which was something, considering they all knew Aldridge was deliberately goading the man. The couples around them took one look at Eastly's face and twirled to the edge of the dance floor, watching with eager eyes.

Aldridge turned to her, a question in his eyes. "Miss Synclaire?"

She nodded. "It's fine."

Aldridge bowed. "Miss Synclaire. Your Grace, she's all yours." But he stopped beside Chess, who didn't bother to look his way, and said, "You don't deserve her, and she's a particular friend of my mother's. I will hunt you down if you hurt one hair on her head."

Still staring at Artie, Chess growled. "Leave us."

After Aldridge left, Chess's gaze softened. He cleared his throat. "Walk with me?"

She tucked her hand in the crook of his arm. "Are you going to be a beast to every man who pays me any mind?"

The duke snorted. "Only those who deserve it."

She bit her lip to fight back a smile. This was more like the banter they'd shared when they met. "Duly noted."

He clasped his opposite hand over hers and squeezed, then released her to open a door leading out to the balcony.

The night air was bitterly cold, such that her breath billowed out visibly before her with every exhale, though after the heat of the ballroom, the cooler air offered blessed relief. She could feel the radiant warmth of the man by her side, like he was her own personal hearth, and she snuggled deeper into his heat, to hell with society and their sensibilities.

Against the balustrade, in a darkened corner away from prying eyes, Chess said, "Artemis. May I call you Artemis?"

"I rather hope you would."

"Artemis. I never dreamed I'd ever find a woman who so completely embodied every fantasy I ever had of the woman I would one day marry."

"You actually fantasized about that?"

He laughed. "This is hard enough as it is; don't interrupt." And he dropped a kiss on her nose. "But I found every single quality the day I met you."

She couldn't help herself. "You know that would be *this* morning."

His eyes skated over her face. "Unbelievable, isn't it?"

She felt his gaze everywhere and suddenly felt the earnestness behind his words. "Unbelievable," she agreed and touched her hand to his cheek.

For a moment, he closed his eyes. Then, "I cannot believe I almost gave it all up—"

"The chance to argue with me?"

He touched his forehead to hers. "And to make up."

"To shun society with me?"

"And to parade before them and show them how little we care."

She wrapped her arms around his neck. "Well, then there's nothing for it, get on with it then."

He pulled back as much as the length of her arms would allow. "It?"

She leaned in, and stood on her tip toes, closer, her lips a hairsbreadth from his. "Kiss me, my beast. Here, now."

He didn't hesitate, his arms wrapped around her, and he swooped in and kissed her. Finally.

He lifted her from the ground as he did, holding her fast to him, and there was nowhere else on earth she'd rather be. He pulled away, then dove in again, nibbling at her bottom lip, her top.

Eventually, they slowed, their kisses tender and heartfelt.

"Artie?" he asked.

"Yes?"

"May I have this next dance?"

"I thought you'd never ask. Besides, you owe me five pounds."

"I owe *you* five pounds. That chair lasted for far longer than an hour…"

And the door closed behind them.

CHAPTER 9

2nd February 1815
Eastly House, London

Chester Mansfield, 8th Duke of Eastly, groaned at the sound of knuckles rapping smartly against his study door. "Whoever it is can bugger off," he growled, though his warning held no real heat. He was a happier man now, satisfied.

And despite his bellow, Chess heard the door behind him open and a sultry, feminine voice answer, "Husband, mine, I'm in desperate need of your assistance."

Chess turned away from the window with a ferocious smile, in time to see his wife, Artemis Mansfield, Her Grace the Duchess of Eastly, march across his study without concern for his gruff pronouncement, which by now she was well aware he didn't mean.

She circled his desk and settled back upon it as was her usual habit when she wanted something of him, her hands resting on her belly, rounded with their child.

He came to a stop before her. "Oh?" he queried and settled his hands over hers and was rewarded with a soft kick from her belly. They briefly touched foreheads and shared a smile. Then, he pulled back and added, "In need of funds?"

She nodded. "Precisely." And added a bat of her lashes.

He snorted. "What do the *Ladies' Society*—"

She raised a brow, and he grinned all that harder.

He continued, impressively, "—for the Care of the Widows and Orphans of Fallen Heroes and the Children of Wounded Veterans want now?"

She gifted him with her largest smile and patted his cheek. "Well, done, my love."

Satisfied, she continued, "We're having another auction."

He groaned, but it was half-hearted at best.

"And a Venetian Breakfast, an auction, and a ball." Her eyes lit with excitement, "All at the Duchess of Haverford's home, naturally."

"Naturally. Last time I had this conversation, my impish sister was telling me a bunch of tarradiddles about this Mousey woman who feared she'd received no bids. What a bunch of Banbury tales they were."

She raised her brow again. "As I recall, you quite enjoyed the outcome of all those shenanigans."

He laughed. "Indeed, I did. But surely, you don't have another Mouse for me to rescue?"

"Rescue?"

"You know…"

"I do. No, this time, her name is Lady Theodesia Mansfield."

His sister? "Never heard of her."

Artie pursed her lips.

"What's Theo done now?"

"Oh, nothing so ruinous. It's just, well Aunt Harriett and I…"

He groaned and wrapped his arms around his adorable wife, then said, "No."

But she smiled because she knew his "No" really meant "Yes."

"It's a good thing I love you."

"It certainly is. And a good thing I love you."

THE END

OTHER BOOKS BY AMY QUINTON

What the Duke Wants

England 1814: Upstanding duke desperately seeks accident-prone wife from trade…

What the Marquess Sees

He is a marquess with a woman to protect & an assassin to thwart. She is… not nice.

What the Scot Hears

Reticent Scottish lord pursues mouthy American woman. What could possibly go wrong?

How to Take Revenge On a Disloyal Scot *A short story.

Love is… revenge? Because what else's a girl supposed to do when she learns the man she loves has found himself a bride?

The Umbrella Chronicles: George & Dorothea's Story *A short story, part of *Never Too Late*, A Bluestocking Belles Collection

St. Vincent's days as a bachelor in good standing are numbered.

The Umbrella Chronicles: James & Annie's Story *A short story, part of *Follow Your Star Home*, A Bluestocking Belles Holiday Collection

Prodigal duke seeks professional matchmaker for matrimonial assistance. Prefers foolproof plans in 10 parts. Magical solutions accepted. Missteps likely.

ABOUT AMY QUINTON

Purveyor of Humorous Historicals. Offering Indecent Aspirations and Ribald Indiscretions with a Blend of Suspenseful Angst. Part Magic—All Romance. Rated MA.

Amy Quinton is an author and full-time mom living in Summerville, SC. She enjoys writing (and reading!) sexy, historical romances. She lives with her husband, two boys, three cats, and one dog. In her spare time, she likes to go camping, hiking, and canoeing/kayaking... And did she mention reading? When she's not reading or traveling, she likes to make jewelry, sew, knit, and crochet (Yay for Ravelry!).

Sign Me Up!
Newsletter: https://app.mailerlite.com/webforms/landing/u4s4j6

Learn more about Amy at:
Website: amyquinton.net
Email: AmyQuintonAuthor@gmail.com

facebook.com/AmyElizabethQuinton
twitter.com/AmyQuinton

THE BELLES WOULD LIKE YOUR HELP!

Book reviews help readers to find books, and authors to find readers. Please consider writing a review for *Fire & Frost*, even a couple of sentences telling people what you liked (or didn't like) about the stories. Reviews can be posted on Goodreads and on most eRetailers websites. For links to this book on those sites, see the *Fire & Frost* page on the Belles' website: https://bluestockingbelles.net/belles-joint-projects/fire-frost/

Malala Fund

The Bluestocking Belles have chosen the Malala Fund as the charity they support, and to which they donate some of their royalties. Periodically, they take on projects intended to directly support this cause, which exemplifies their personal values and intentions: the right of girls and women to do whatever they choose with their lives.

How can you help?

Make a donation to our Team Page at https://www.classy.org/team/89502

Buy our holiday anthology when it releases each year.

OTHER BOOKS BY THE
BLUESTOCKING BELLES

Bluestocking Belles' box sets

Find buy links and story blurbs for all the following books on our website at https://bluestockingbelles.net/belles-joint-projects/

25% of proceeds on the following books benefit the Malala Fund.

Valentine's From Bath (2019)

The Master of Ceremonies announces a great ball to be held on Valentine's Day in the Upper Assembly Rooms of Bath.

Ladies of the highest rank—and some who wish they were—scheme, prepare, and compete to make best use of the opportunity.

Dukes, earls, tradesmen, and the occasional charlatan are alert to the possibilities as the event draws nigh.

But anything can happen in the magic of music and candlelight as couples dance, flirt, and open themselves to romantic possibilities. Problems and conflict may just fade away at a Valentine's Day Ball.

Follow Your Star Home (2018)

Forged for lovers, the Viking star ring is said to bring lovers together, no matter how far, no matter how hard.

In eight stories, covering more than half the world and a thousand years, our heroes and heroines put the legend to the test. Watch the star work its magic, as prodigals return home in the season of good will, uncertain of their welcome.

Never Too Late (2017)

Eight authors and eight different takes on four dramatic elements selected by our readers—an older heroine, a wise man, a Bible, and a compromising situation that isn't.

Set in a variety of locations around the world over eight centuries, welcome to the romance of the Bluestocking Belles' 2017 Holiday and More Anthology.

It's Never Too Late to find love.

Holly and Hopeful Hearts (2016)

When the Duchess of Haverford sends out invitations to a Yuletide house party and a New Year's Eve ball at her country estate, Hollystone Hall, those who respond know that Her Grace intends to raise money for her favorite cause and promote whatever love-matches she can. Seven assorted heroes and heroines set out with their pocketbooks firmly clutched and hearts in protective custody. Or are they?

Eight assorted heroes and heroines find more than they've bargained for when they set out for Hollystone Hall for a charity ball.

MEET THE BLUESTOCKING BELLES

The Bluestocking Belles (the "BellesInBlue") are eight very different writers united by a love of history and a history of writing about love. From sweet to steamy, from light-hearted fun to dark tortured tales full of angst, from London ballrooms to country cottages to the sultan's seraglio, one or more of us will have a tale to suit your tastes and mood.

Learn more about the Bluestocking Belles at:
Website: www.BluestockingBelles.net/
Newsletter: http://eepurl.com/dAJU_9
Teatime Tattler twice-weekly gossip magazine: https://bluestockingbelles.net/category/teatime-tattler/
Free books: https://bluestockingbelles.net/teatime-tattler-free-books/

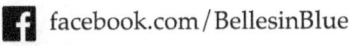 facebook.com/BellesinBlue
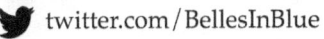 twitter.com/BellesInBlue
pinterest.com/bellesinblue
 instagram.com/bellesinblue

www.ingramcontent.com/pod-product-compliance
Lightning Source LLC
Chambersburg PA
CBHW020515260626
47156CB00006B/2008